"WHATEVER HAPPENED

to the

ZODIAC KILLER?"

An Unexpected Answer
From Angel Armies and Human Friends
In the Classic War between Good and Evil

BY KATHERIN B. FITZPATRICK

Based on a True Story

PRESS

"*Whatever Happened to the Zodiac Killer?*"
by Katherin B. FitzPatrick

Printed in the United States of America

ISBN 9781629525624

www.xulonpress.com

Dedicated to my three daughters, Yvonne, Karen Lee—and Jaina, (Lindy) who went along for the wild ride in my womb.

ACKNOWLEDGEMENTS

I would like to thank a number of friends, editors, writers and screenwriters who encouraged me to tell this story based on our true experiences, and shape it into a book and a screenplay.

Special thanks to my dear friend, Ann Ault, actress, author and screenwriter for her endless patience, prayers and personal support!

Thanks to Gayle Mercer, writer and author, who took the time to do last minute proofreading editing and critique.

To my longtime friend, Christine Fry of QOA Entertainment in LA, writer, screenwriter and film producer, for your undying faith and a dream that this tale based on our true story, would one day be a film.

Thanks to "Grandma Ruby" who was not only a character in this book, but my real life Mom as well. Her lips were always filled with faith and encouragement for this project.

Lots of thanks and hugs to my young nephew, the very creative and talented Isaiah Thomas who pushed me into doing a Facebook page for "Whatever Happened to the Zodiac Killer," screenplay and book project long before I was ready! It was "Sharon's" young adult daughter who saw it, and ultimately brought us together to be able to add the true story of her Mom's face to face encounter with the real Zodiac, the man, shortly after his attack on her friends and college mates at Lake Berryessa back in 1969. It gave all of us some rare insight his personal demeanor and character.

Thanks to Tony Smith, Private Investigator from Liverpool, England, who let me borrow his name to use for my real life detectives, both Junior and Senior!

And last of all, who should be first of all . . . the Lord God Almighty who sent warring angels to follow us, shield and protect us, and intervene in the most miraculous way the night of our clash with the Zodiac Killer. Those angel armies . . . they are real!

M ost names have been changed or only first names used. For historic purposes, I kept the name "Sergeant Tedesco," as he was the detective from the San Francisco Police Department whom we personally worked with, and he also had a long history of very good work on the "Zodiac Killer" case over the years. This experience is based on a true story, but some parts have been changed.

TABLE OF CONTENTS

CHAPTER ONE

THE FIRST TIME HEARING OF HIM

The pink and golden sunrise reflected magnificently across the San Francisco Bay as the waves gently lapped against the shoreline, etching wavy foam lines in the sand. The panoramic view of the city from the hills was truly one of the most beautiful sights on Earth. Soon the sound of the cable cars on California Street would signal the city's awakening. The business district was already coming alive to the rumbling cacophony of traffic noises rising from bustling cars, buses, and trolleys. Among the first merchants to greet the morning, the flower vendors trundled out their colorful carts arranged with a wide variety of seasonal blooms. The elegant lines of the Golden Gate Bridge stood out brightly against a slowly lightening blue sky, still edged in pink, as the early morning sun rose higher over the hills.

During the 1960s through the late 1970s, a dark nefarious character, a murderer known only as the "Zodiac Killer," terrorized the city of San Francisco, and beyond. Preying upon victims in the city and various parts of the Bay Area—including Vallejo and Benicia in the North Bay—he was truly a phantom-like killer. Little was known about the man except that he seemed to be a native of the San Francisco Bay Area. However, when he was overcome by the monster demon within him, he sometimes spoke of in his letters to the *San Francisco Chronicle*, he became another being. Although he was diligently pursued by the police, he was never captured.

The mystery revolving around the "Zodiac Killer" ultimately became one of the greatest unsolved mysteries of all time. In mid-October of 1978, after writing one last letter to the *San Francisco Chronicle* threatening to strike and kill again that weekend, he suddenly and inexplicably disappeared forever. This is a story that few people know, and has never before been publically revealed. These events actually begin to unfold further north of San Francisco.

In a quiet corner of Northern California, the delightful fragrance of orange blossoms filled the air from groves of orange trees clustered around the landscape, growing in neighbors' yards. Chico, California, was home to the quaint, yet lively campus of Chico State College. On the streets that lined the neighborhood just adjacent to the college, were clustered rows and courtyards of "granny houses," both large and small. These Victorian homes often served as both fraternity and sorority houses.

Emerging from a picturesque old home with a large porch on Chestnut Street, Tina Blackwood, an attractive 20-year-old woman, locked her door then walked briskly down the steps toward her workplace at the *Chico Enterprise Record*, the regional newspaper. She was obviously about seven months pregnant. It was 1969.

Two years earlier, she and her husband Billy had decided to move from the Bay area to Chico so they could be closer to Billy's extended family, including a brother named Pete. While newly married, and still living in the Bay area, Pete would call every weekend with plans Billy could not resist. The two brothers were avid hunters, all seasons. Billy wound up making the drive up to see Pete, and his family, almost every weekend. Often, that also involved hunting and fishing. After a full work week in San Francisco in the business district, Tina looked forward to spending time with Billy on the weekends. However, she found herself often alone and now having mixed feelings about their new environment. It was a beautiful community nestled in the Sierra Nevada foothills, offering outdoorsmen easy access to mountains, lakes, and rivers, but Billy was often away with Pete, and a new circle of rough-looking friends. The move also revolved around Billy going to school on the GI bill. It all seemed to be working out, kind of, she thought. But her husband's mind and affections seemed to be drifting. He was starting to look and act like, a very different person.

Tina drifted deep in thought as she walked the last few blocks to work. It seemed like everyone in the neighborhood had orange trees growing in their front and back yards. Reaching out, she picked a large orange off a tree near the sidewalk. Suddenly, a large German Shepherd rushed out, lunging toward Tina, barking, teeth flashing. Tina stepped back in fear as the dog's snapping jaws neared her. But then the charging dog stopped suddenly with a jerk. Relieved, Tina saw the dog had a short chain latched to his collar. She dropped the orange into her purse. The dog continued to bark at her, jaws snapping, as she made her way down the street to the newspaper building. The sign on the impressive large brick building read The Chico Enterprise Record.

As Tina entered the busy newspaper office, the clock on the wall read seven o'clock. It was the beginning of another very active day in the world of local and regional news. Busy reporters and writers of different genres typed busily on their old black typewriters with that familiar hum that filled their ears for hours at a time. Tina's co-worker, Libby, an attractive upbeat woman of about thirty, glanced up from a stack of papers with an inquisitive look, greeting Tina with a silly grin.

"Hi, Tina! Are you going to look over the new AP wire stories for me?"

"I guess. Did anything earth shaking come in over the night hours, or come in early from New York?"

"Oh, not really. Just more on the Manson killings, and the 'Zodiac Killer.' You'd think that guy would take a break." Libby frowned, shaking her head. "Hasn't it been over five years now? The Zodiac's been active again lately."

Tina put her purse and lunch bag down, and poured a cup of coffee for herself. Her name, Tina Blackwood, was clearly visible on a nameplate on her desk.

"You wonder how a guy like that can even live with himself," Tina commented dryly. "Okay, you scan the new business section, and I'll take Charles Manson and the Zodiac Killer stories. Chuck is handling the local stories. I'll do some typesetting on the regional news pages later this morning. I think all of us will make it looking at page one by one o'clock or so."

Sitting at her desk, Tina scanned the stories off the AP service and drank her morning coffee, taking a bite of a sugary donut as she worked.

"This Zodiac guy is such an ego-maniac. He writes his symbol— that circle with the cross through it, on everything he does, sometimes even on the *bodies!*" she said, holding up the paper with the haunting circle.

Tina looked over the open paper, and laid it down in disgust. "Can you believe this, some woman took a ride from him because he looked so mild and trustworthy and was viciously attacked but before that he made her throw her baby out the window!" Tina covered her face with her hand. She held up her donut with a few bites out of it, "Honestly, is this any way for a pregnant lady to start off her day, I ask you?"

Libby glanced up at Tina. "What?"

16

"Is this any way for a pregnant lady to start off her day?" Tina said again. Libby laughed.

"Well, Tina, you are stronger than most. I give you credit for that much!" Libby came closer to Tina, whispering. "I mean, that husband of yours . . . Has he even come home lately? I feel so sorry for you, and what you're going through with him."

"Billy . . . well, we've been married almost five years, but ever since we moved up here, he's fallen in with the wrong kinds of friends. I think maybe after the baby is born, things will be different." Libby rolled her eyes. "Well, just keep hoping for that, Hon."

As Tina returned to work, Libby walked away with a parting comment. "I'll be back. I have to check with Jeff on some of these editorial changes!"

A few hours later, Tina and another co-worker, Connie, were proofing stories at her desk when the typesetter from the back appeared. The machines hummed briefly as the doors opened and then shut again. He was carrying page one of the newspaper. It was about 1:00 p.m. All the editors and writers came over and clustered around the copy desk as four pairs of eyes studied the page for typos. Tina noticed the first flaw.

"Here's one . . . " she marked the spot with a pen.

"Here's another one . . . needs a capitol *P* here," remarked Ed, one of the senior editors. Fellow editors continued to examine the page.

"I think it looks pretty good today . . . Anything else?" Tina asked, looking up at Ed.

"Nope . . . I think we're good." Ed handed the copy for page one back to the typesetter from the back shop. The other editors returned to their work stations. Tina headed back to her desk to pick up some materials newspaper staff call *"time."*

"I'm going to go ahead and type 'TIME' material, and get it done before four o'clock, then this tired pregnant lady needs to go home and take a nap!" Tina yawned. "We'll have a good bank of informational stories that can run anytime to use as fillers," she said, talking softly to herself. Then Tina noticed something new coming over the AP wire machine in the corner of the room. She walked over to it and read the headline, "New Couple Attacked by the Zodiac at Lake Berryessa."

"Not again!" exclaimed Tina, feeling both shocked and saddened. She ripped the article off the machine and just stared at it. She read part of the article out loud to herself: 'College students Bryan Hartnell and Cecelia Shepard were attacked by a man thought to be the infamous 'Zodiac Killer,' in the late afternoon while sitting out on a picnic blanket at Lake Berryessa . . ."

***

Meanwhile in the quaint wine country town of Napa, California, in a rented house near the college, Sharon a petite blond, an 18 year old college student, was holding a newspaper in her hands bearing the exact headline. She sat in tears and overwhelmed by this news as Bryan and Cecelia, the victims, were her friends and college mates from the local Pacific Union College. Wiping her tears with her hands she gasped, "How could this have happened to my friends?"

Suddenly, there is a knock on the front door. Sharon put the newspaper aside. She opened the door to a familiar neighbor, a fifteen year old named Ricky.

"Sharon . . . I had to come by! I'm so sorry about the news!

"Yes, Ricky. Come in. I was just reading about it in the papers. I'm still in shock. How I wish I'd never helped Bryan get his car fixed. The Karmann Ghia was broken. They thought about not even driving up there at all," said Sharon sadly. "We were all over at the college that day, me and Brent, Cecelia and Bryan. Once the car was fixed we thought about all going up to Lake Berryessa together, but then just the two of them drove up there."

"It looks like Cecelia is in the most serious condition. They think Bryan may make it," Ricky said, breaking a little smile.

"Yes, I talked to Cecelia's mom from the hospital this morning but it's still not sinking in, not even after reading the account in the paper. Cecelia has lost a lot of blood. Come in and sit down for a minute. What's happening? Is there a reason you came by just now?"

"I just had to come by and see you and Jill . . . but there's something else. Sharon, I just got off the city bus, and I felt that I had to come by and tell you something."

Sharon stared at Ricky, looking perplexed. "What is it?"

"On the city bus there was this man . . . I can hardly describe him. He sat on the bus bragging to the people around him about his occultic powers and deep knowledge of Zodiac . . . the stars, you know. This man kept talking about the mystical connection to the human spirit, like he was king of it all. He just seemed really creepy and weird. He was probably in his mid to late forties, wearing large light rimmed glasses. Suddenly, he got up and left the bus and walked into the Aquarius Bar downtown. I just had a weird feeling about the guy."

Stunned, Sharon stared at Ricky. "Ricky, the police took a call from a man who claimed responsibility for the attack on Bryan and Cecelia. They traced it to a phone booth in downtown Napa. He described the unique encryptions left at the scene of the crime to verify it was him, *the Zodiac*. I have to go down there now!" Sharon walked over and grabbed her coat.

"But Sharon . . . you're not 21!

"I'll get Jill and Patricia to go with me!" Sharon looked around the room. "Where is Jill anyway? Jill!" she called out, looking up the stairs. Jill appeared at the top of the stairs holding an open textbook. She was studying her homework.

"Jill . . . get your coat and come with me! We need to check out something at the Aquarius Bar downtown!"

"What?" Jill replied with a questioning look.

"I'll explain on the way! Let's stop by and see if Patricia can come with us!"

As the late afternoon sun shone brightly on the multi-colored glass stones of the exterior door of the Aquarius Bar, Sharon and her two ponytailed sidekicks parked on the city street a block away from the entrance.

"Let's go!" said Sharon exiting and locking the car door. Jill and Patricia followed closely next to her. "We'll tell the Bartender we're waiting for our older brother." They cautiously entered the bar and noticed there was one long bar stretching across the room with five round tables and chairs to the right filling the open space of the room. There were a few people in the bar, patrons of mixed ages. Then Sharon spotted him. He was a strange looking auburn haired man with large light rimmed glasses who was sitting in the back of the room chatting with another male student.

"There he is, back there!" Sharon whispered to Jill and Patricia. The girls smiled weakly in an effort to conceal their fear. Sharon spoke to the Bartender on duty, an aging Italian gentleman. "We are just waiting for our older brother. We would like to order some sodas and sit back there," Sharon gestured to the table where the suspicious man was seated.

"I guess that's okay," the Bartender said, as he wiped off the bar with a long towel.

Sharon glanced to the back of the room where the suspicious man was seated. He was talking excitedly with a male college student as another college aged girl sat down at the table with them. The Bartender poured their sodas in tall clear fountain glasses, and soon Sharon, Jill and Patricia walked over with their drinks and took their seats at one of the round tables next to "him." Sharon noticed that the suspicious man was about 5'8" to 5'10" tall, medium build and had auburn hair with a receding hairline in the front, and perhaps a little longer in back, at least to his collar. He was a very plain looking man, wearing large light rimmed glasses. He matched Ricky's description, but he also matched the sketchy description of the *Zodiac* written about in the newspapers over the past year or so.

The suspicious looking man with the large glasses seemed to immediately notice the three young college girls, and had watched their every move as they walked toward him.

"Just talk and visit with me normally," Sharon instructed the two of them in a careful whisper. They felt as if his eyes burned through them like hot coals. Then he stood up and walked directly over to them, holding his drink in his hand.

"Hello girls . . . how are you? Are you waiting for someone?"

"Yes, we are waiting for our older brother," Sharon answered, trying to stay cool.

"Well now, isn't that nice?" he said, taking a sip of his beer. "I was just visiting with a couple of students here about some of the deep mystical things of the Zodiac. I have a very deep soul connection with the stars. I feel a special dark energy from them. They give me special powers," he said, wearing a sinister smile.

"Oh, really . . . such as? Sharon asked bravely.

21

"Such as . . . I will tell all three of you what sign of the Zodiac you are!" he bragged with a grin.

"But you don't know our birthdays," commented Jill, her eyes widening even larger.

"I don't need to know your birthdays!" he bragged. Let me stand here for just a moment. My Spirit Guide will instruct me." He closed his eyes for about eight seconds. Then he spoke. "What is your name?" he asked, motioning toward Jill.

"Jill . . ."

"Jill . . . you are a Capricorn . . . and over here," motioning toward Sharon, *"You* are a Sagittarius. And you are . . ."

"Patricia."

"Patricia, is a Leo . . . *Leo the lion*. You are a rather pretty lion, I would say. He laughed lightly. Patricia looked serious as she knew he was right about her sign. Sharon and Jill were also struck with both fascination and fear at these accurate predictions. Jill and Patricia's eyes were glued to Sharon's face. Sharon took a breath. She was still looking cool.

"That was uh . . . very interesting. I'm Sharon, and you are?"

"Bill . . . Bill Williams." Sharon wondered about his answer. Why should he tell her his real name? The "Zodiac man" removed his glasses, and put them in his shirt pocket. Sharon noticed he was wearing a dark plaid shirt, and dark Khaki colored pants with black dress shoes. He had thrown a light weight coat over the back of his chair.

"So, Bill . . . what do you do?" Sharon asked a little awkwardly.

"I am a rose gardener," he answered with a broad smile. Sharon noticed that he was a very conservative, plain looking man with a pale complexion, and an oblong shaped face with a slightly square

22

jawline. His receding hairline in front was a contrast to a little length slipping down to his back of his collar.

A wave of fear came over Sharon as she realized that this must have been the man Bryan and Cecelia met in their moment of terror that day at Lake Berryessa. She was only aware of sketchy details from the news article, but she read how Bryan and Cecelia had been sitting on a blanket on the grass. A hooded figure approached them dodging in and out of the pine trees using them for a cover . . . then the attack. This time it was with a knife. Sharon couldn't bear to think about it. She struggled to cover up her true feelings as she looked into the face of this monster of a man.

"Really . . . a rose gardener? What a delightful profession." Sharon wondered if the nervous sweat on her brow was becoming obvious by now.

"It gives me time to think and meditate on the deep, dark mysteries of the universe . . . and to do my planning."

"*Planning?*" Sharon asked in curious tones.

"Yes, I do some traveling. I work on cultivating my deep mystical powers. Someday I will have slaves in Paradise. I have created special personal encryptions concerning this mystery.

At this comment Jill and Patricia looked nervously at Sharon.

"You know, if you will excuse me, I need to see if I can call my brother, and find out why he is so late."

Sharon slipped out to the front of the room where the bartender was working behind the bar. She spotted the phone behind him on a table.

"I need to use the phone!" she said to the Bartender in a nervous whisper, looking into his eyes beseechingly.

"Do you want me to call the police?" he asked casually, chewing his gum.

Terrified, Sharon wondered if the "Zodiac man" heard that comment. She quickly glanced to the back of the room. "Bill" was still smiling and chatting with the male student and the young girl student who was there when they arrived. She gave a sigh of relief.

"Yes!" The Bartender dialed the number, and handed her the phone. Soon a voice came on the other line.

"Napa Police Department," a man from the station announced.

Sharon spoke in a slow deliberate whisper, "I need to talk to a detective or Captain, or someone in charge!"

"Is this an emergency?"

"Yes!"

"Hold on . . ." A few moments passed that to Sharon seemed like an eternity. Fear mounting, she glanced to the back of the room. "Bill" was still chatting. Then a new voice came on the line.

"Captain McGuire, here . . . what can I do for you?"

"My name is Sharon Townsend, and I am here at the Aquarius Bar in downtown Napa. My friends Bryan Hartnell and Cecelia Shepard were the ones who were attacked by the Zodiac Killer just a few days ago!"

"Yes, very sorry to hear that."

"Listen carefully . . . I have to whisper. I followed a lead that the man who was possibly the Zodiac was talking to people about his weird beliefs and occultic powers here at the Aquarius Bar. We came over here, me, my sister, and a girlfriend. We've been watching him and talking to him, and *I'm sure* it's *him!*"

"What makes you think it's him?" McGuire asked.

"He meets the description, for one thing . . . he's about 5'8" to 5'10," about forty five, medium build with auburn hair. He's a very plain looking man wearing large light colored rimmed glasses. He came over to us and told us our Zodiac signs without even knowing our birthdays!"

"Like mind reading?"

"Yes! He says he is 'going to have slaves in Paradise.' He says all kinds of weird stuff only the Zodiac says! Please come . . . come now! *He's here!*"

"That sounds like him for sure!" McGuire agreed. "But that's a job for plain clothes police, and we have none on duty at the moment, Miss. Can you call back later?"

"What?" she groaned. Sharon was on the verge of tears. "I can't believe this! I guess you are not coming! Yes, I'll call back later." Sharon looked up, getting ready to walk back and join the girls. To her horror and amazement, "Bill" was standing right there next to her. Her heart leapt up to her throat. "I guess my brother is not coming," she said to the bartender, attempting to recover. She handed the phone back to him, in front of "Bill."

"I just came back up here to get another beer." The bartender handed him a new bottle.

Sharon made her way back to their table. "Bill" was not far away as he returned and sat down.

Patricia leaned close to Sharon.

"Sharon, you're white as a sheet!"

In a whisper, mouthing almost silently, Sharon responds.

"The police can't come!" The girls' eyes grew wide with disappointment. "We'll think of something."

"Did you find your brother?" asked "Bill from the other table.

"No. His friend Gerry said he was on the way. But if he doesn't show soon, we may not stay much longer," Sharon lied. "Bill" smiled an evil grin. Sharon noticed that his eyes seemed lifeless, and were shaped much like shark eyes.

"Well, while you're waiting, let me tell you a few dark secrets of the universe, as I was just sharing with these two students here."

"Bill" pulled up a chair and started talking about his strange beliefs, and dark powers that gave him an advantage in everything he did, and saved him from every bad circumstance.

"I will live a long life, and die a natural death one day," he bragged. The girls continued to listen to his strange and vain philosophies. Then Sharon got an idea.

"Bill, could you meet us back here another time? We are interested . . . we really like what you are saying. But we really need to go right now. I forgot we are supposed to meet someone from our study group at 4:30. We're college students at Pacific Union College," Sharon explained, weaving a new story. "Bill" thought about it for a few moments. He smiled a wicked smile. "Tuesday. What about Tuesday, about 2 o'clock?"

"Okay, I think that will work." Sharon looked into the wide eyes of Jill and Patricia. *"Tuesday it is!"*

***

Back at the Chico Enterprise Record, The hours slipped by as stories were typed and entered by Tina. The clock on the wall finally read 4:00 p.m.

It was quitting time, and Tina couldn't be more ready to go home. She slipped by her work area with her purse and some newspapers under her arm, exiting out the front door of the newspaper building with a sigh. She walked home the same way she came, past the same house with the orange trees in the neighbor's yard. This time the barking dog was gone. She was relieved. A few moments later she was back in front of her small rented Victorian house, a few blocks from the college. She opened the door with her key, and went inside.

Tina immediately noticed that her husband, Billy, was already home. She noticed that he had lately taken on a rough look, wearing a beard, sloppy T-shirt, and casual jeans, like work clothes, and dirty boots. A few of his friends were there with him. They appeared to be rough-looking motorcycle types. Some were hippie-like in appearance.

Tina put down her purse. "Billy, aren't you home a little *early* today? I thought you still had classes this afternoon?" Tina looked closer. Billy and his friends appeared to be loading gel capsules with some type of material. "Billy...what is that?" Tina wondered.

"Mescaline . . . we are making *mescaline* capsules."

"What?"

Billy and his friends cast scornful looks at Tina, as if she was clueless.

"Mescaline capsules . . . " Billy grinned at his wife as he tapped more powder into the capsules. Tina felt terrified. She realized they must be doing some type of illegal drug manufacturing process in their home. Tina fumed.

"Billy, I am going to walk down to the grocery store, and pick up a few things. When I get back, I expect you and your friends to be all finished with this, do you understand?"

The men all glared at Tina. She closed the front door, and strode purposefully down the street toward the small corner grocery store a few blocks away. Upon entering the market, she immediately spotted the manager, an old gray-haired man wearing an apron. He was working on the produce section of the store.

"Ed, do you carry the dark green leafy lettuce, like Romaine? All I see here is the head lettuce."

"There is not much demand for it, Tina. I only carry what is in demand."

"Well, I'm demanding it. Can't I order it? I'm a starving pregnant lady, and I am tired of going to restaurants and paying such a high price for a crab salad or something with it already made up with dark green lettuce! I'm having these *cravings*, you know?" Ed just gave her a blank look, and sighed.

"Tina, I don't know right now. I'll see what I can do." Tina loaded a few items in the bag—some apples, peaches, and a couple of frozen dinners.

"It's hard to cook for only one. I do like buying these. My husband is hardly ever home these days." Within moments she checked out, and walked out the door.

She entered the house cautiously and looked around, wondering if Billy's friends had left. Billy was in the kitchen, putting a couple of dishes away. He looked annoyed.

"Well, they did what you said . . . They left."

"What is this, Billy . . . some kind of drug production going on in our very own living room? Maybe I should report all of you!"

"You wouldn't dare!"

"What has happened to us, Billy? We came from Christian backgrounds. I married you thinking that you and your family were wholesome people. Well, your parents are at least. We moved up here away from our former life in the Bay area so you could go to school on the GI Bill, and you turn into another person . . . a person I don't even know!"

Billy frowned. He looked down uncomfortably. Tina took a deep breath, but then continued her tirade.

"Even when we were first married, and living in California, your brother Pete called every Thursday or Friday trying to lure you up here on the weekend for hunting or fishing. You missed Sunday after Sunday of church services. You started forgetting what you stood for . . . what *we* stood for. Did it ever occur to you that you just took a new wife, that we needed to be together and cultivate our relationship . . . not be with your brother? Are you married to your brother? Now, *this*. These are his friends, aren't they?" Tina fumed. Billy's eyes met hers before he stormed out the door and drove off in his old truck. The raucous engine noise echoed off the houses as he roared down the street and disappeared. Tina was frustrated and angry but mostly, she felt abandoned.

***

Students walked briskly between classes talking and chatting on the campus of Pacific Union College in Napa, CA. Captain Jim O'Toole of the Napa Police Department walked resolutely across the grounds, and soon appeared in the Student Hub building. He was looking for a pert 18 year old blond student named Sharon Townsend whom he had only spoken to on the phone. She was convinced that she, her sister and her friend, had encountered the real Zodiac Killer at the Aquarius Bar only the day before. He was there to find out if it was really true. O'Toole spotted her standing by the cafeteria looking in his direction.

"Sharon?" he asked walking up to her. Sharon had already been looking for him.

"Yes . . . Captain O'Toole. Let's sit over here where it's a bit more private." They walked into a sitting room with a sofa and chairs and a door they could close. Jill and Patricia were already there.

"Where would you like for me to sit?" he asked. Sharon pulled up a chair for him so they could sit in a small circle. O'Toole pulled out his notebook.

"Tell me everything you remember about your encounter about this man and why you thought he was the Zodiac," O'Toole said.

"We acted on a lead from a teenage neighbor kid who said he saw a man riding on a city bus he was on acting very suspicious, talking about his 'Zodiac powers that he drew from the stars' and his 'deep knowledge of the secrets of the universe.' Ricky said that he got off the bus and walked into the Aquarius Bar that afternoon. He felt we needed to know. After hearing his description of this 'creepy man,' I felt compelled to go down there," Sharon explained. "I wasn't 21, but I took Jill and Patricia with me . . . He was still there when we arrived." Sharon told in great detail their experience, and their conversation with the man who called himself "Bill."

"A few times Patricia and I got pretty scared, but Sharon just kept leading us on . . . telling us to stay cool," Jill admitted.

"The more he spoke about his strange beliefs, the more we suspected he had to be the real *'Zodiac,"* Patricia added.

"When the police officer on the phone said the police couldn't come because there were no plain clothes police on duty . . . I almost lost it right there!" Sharon admitted.

"Sorry," O'Toole said apologizing. "It's just that that is the way we really do have to handle a case like this . . . it would have been for your safety, too."

"I just want to see him captured. He has hurt and killed so many people, and now Bryan and Cecelia ..." Sharon said, teary eyed.

"I understand Bryan is doing fine. They think he will recover," O'Toole said reassuringly.

"I know . . . but Cecelia lost a lot of blood from the attack. She passed away in ICU just the other day," Sharon reported with sadness in her eyes. O'Toole closed his notebook for a moment.

"I know . . . I'm very sorry."

"Well, girls . . . I came out here to talk to you this afternoon because I have done a lot of interfacing with the San Francisco and Vallejo police on the Zodiac case over the last year or so, and I know a lot of the most recent research."

"Do you?" Sharon asked with wide eyes.

"Yes. I don't want to scare you girls but that man had to be the real *Zodiac*. Some of the things he said to you he only said in letters he wrote to the police! It identifies him as surely as a fingerprint!" The girls' eyes widened with a new sense of conviction. What they sensed about "Bill" really was true, according to O'Toole.

"He said he would meet us again . . . to talk further, on *Tuesday*," Sharon said. At hearing this, O'Toole was gripped with a sudden sense of urgency.

"*Tuesday* . . . Oh my God, that's in just two days!"

"I want to help you capture him . . . so does Jill and Patricia. We'll be there, if you'll be there," Sharon said resolutely.

"Oh we'll be there . . . you can be sure of that!" he promised. I'll call out every plain clothes police car and officer I can find!"

Oh, Captain . . . one more thing. You mentioned codes and encryptions left at the scene of the Lake Berryessa crime . . . Bryan and Cecelia . . . if you show them to me, to us, I think we might be able to crack the codes. He said some things to us that may have given clues," said Sharon.

"Sure thing! Let's make an appointment to meet tomorrow at the Napa Police Station, and get a plan for Tuesday. Can you make it?"

"I think Jill has class, but Patricia and I can make it," Sharon said looking over at Patricia, who nodded "yes."

"Thank you girls for everything. You are very brave." Sharon showed O'Toole out of the room.

"Are we really brave?" asked Patricia with a little grin.

"Or maybe just a little crazy!" Jill added.

The next afternoon, O'Toole met with the girls at the police station as planned. He went over some safety tips and strategies for Tuesday's potential encounter with "Bill."

"There will be plain clothes police both outside and inside the bar. You sit near the entrance of the bar, in case you need to exit quickly. I can't guarantee what might happen in an ambush with him. He is often known to be armed," O'Toole instructed them.

"We'll be fine," Sharon assured him with a smile. Patricia looked confident. Then it was time to look over photos of the Zodiac codes and encryptions left at the crime scene. O'Toole pulled out some police files, and prepared to open them.

"Are you ready for this?" he asked. "I'll only show you the codes and writings themselves." said O'Toole.

"Okay . . . thanks," said Sharon, feeling relieved. Patricia moved a little closer as O'Toole spread the photos out on the table. Sharon and Patricia looked them over. Would they get new clues and revelations they wondered? About thirty minutes went by. Then Sharon got an idea. She opened her purse, and pulled out a compact with a mirror on it.

"Let's try this . . ." she suggested. Sharon held the mirror up to the writings as she and Patricia studied them more carefully. "Just as I thought. Give me that pen . . . Patricia write this down, here it is: First of all, these symbols . . . they are two Zodiac signs. He is saying here, 'I like killing couples the most. They will be able to procreate slaves for me in Paradise . . . Here are the Zodiac signs of these two people who will die and be my slaves: Pisces and Aquarius.'"

O'Toole was awestruck. "May be that's why he was attracted to the Aquarius bar."

"Maybe." Sharon and Patricia felt relieved to be able to bring some new light to the mystery."

"Are you ready for Tuesday?" asked O'Toole. Sharon and Patricia looked back at him with confidence.

"Yes . . . We are ready for Tuesday."

***

It was Tuesday. The multicolored glass stones on the door of the Aquarius Bar shone brightly in the afternoon sun. Sharon, her sister Jill and friend Patricia walked down the block toward the entrance to the foreboding location of the bar. This time, plain clothes police were everywhere in cars parked in front, some of them ready to go in and take their places inside the bar. They would be watching and waiting for any sign of the man suspected of being the Zodiac Killer to show up.

As Sharon and the girls approached the door, Sharon looked across the street to see a car pulling up in front driven by a man with their friend Bryan sitting on the passenger's side. Although he was only recently discharged from the hospital, he wanted to be present if there was even a slight chance that the man who attacked him and killed his girlfriend would be captured that afternoon. Their eyes met briefly. Sharon smiled at him. Bryan nodded, and smiled back. Sharon leading, she opened the door to the bar, as Jill and Patricia followed. Sharon noticed that the same Bartender was on duty.

"Back again, eh?" the Bartender winked. They ordered their sodas and took a seat at a table near the front of the room. Captain O'Toole also sat at a round table near the front of the room. He briefly opened his jacket to show Sharon his gun in a holster, then closed his coat once again. They had discussed with O'Toole that morning the maneuver of sitting near the front of the room in case the girls needed to exit quickly. It was planned that they all appear strangers to one another.

Sharon and the girls sipped their drinks quietly, glancing around the room, particularly watching the front door. Captain O'Toole was enjoying an iced Cherry Coke and periodically glanced over their way. Two more men, plain clothes police, entered and sat at O'Toole's table. He spoke quietly with his colleagues.

"Joe and Ted are out in front and Terry is across the street keeping an eye out. We'll see what happens." He and his men occasionally glanced over to the girls table. Sharon had been instructed to signal them with a nod if she saw "Bill" enter the room. The girls tried to make small talk. Thirty minutes went by. Sharon looked at her watch. Outside on the street in the parked car, Bryan and his friend who had driven him there, continuously watched the front door. More time passed.

Inside the bar, the three girls have waited patiently. They ordered more sodas and some snacks. O'Toole and his police colleagues also ordered some snacks and sodas. They waited. They glanced around, they watched.

"It's been over an hour, Sharon. Maybe he's not coming," Jill said.

"Yeah, maybe he senses trouble," Patricia chimed in.

"I know . . . let's wait a little longer," replied Sharon.

***

Meanwhile, some miles away in the country suburbs, outside a brick mansion surrounded by colorful rose gardens, "Bill" was leaving and walking toward an old white car. He threw a travel bag in the back seat. "Bill" looked up briefly as if sensing something on the wind, but then opened the door of the car and got in. He drove off down an old rough gravel road and soon was leaving the Napa city limits sign behind him and taking the freeway exit toward San Francisco.

Back inside the Aquarius Bar in downtown Napa, O'Toole looked over at Sharon and the girls.

"It's been over two hours. I doubt if he is coming," he said with a look of disappointment.

"You're probably right. If he knew our Zodiac signs without knowing our birthdays, perhaps he picked up on our plan for the ambush. He said often that 'he knew about things ahead of time,'" replied Sharon, as she recalled some of "Bill's bragging comments.

"Kind of like mind reading . . ." O'Toole said, repeating his earlier comment.

"Yes . . . kind of like mind reading," Sharon said, with a tone of sadness in her voice.

Outside the bar, two plain clothes police officers walked over to the car to talk to Bryan and the driver. They shook their heads as they broke the bad news that the man who was expected apparently would not be showing up. A wave of disappointment swept over Bryan's face. Then the driver of the car pulled out and left.

On the freeway headed north, the old white car driven by "Bill" continued to speed toward the city of San Francisco. On the busy streets downtown, a middle aged taxi cab driver wearing a red plaid shirt had driven off into the early evening looking for people who needed his services. The shade of night was about to fall on the city, and the Zodiac was about to move toward his next crime.

***

The baby was born December 25, 1970. She weighed seven pounds, two ounces. Tina named her Yvonne Suzanne. What a bizarre Christmas day it was. Billy showed up only briefly at the hospital to look at her, but then disappeared again. Tina was only allowed to have orange Jell-O during labor, but after the birth, the hospital staff nurses brought in a nice turkey dinner with all the trimmings. The next day it was time to go home. Tina's mother-in- law, Marian, drove her back to her little house on Chestnut Street. By now, Tina was staying at home on maternity leave.

"It's just you and me, honey," Tina said, as she picked her new baby up, tenderly. Turning to Marian with tears in her eyes, she added, "Marian, you've been a good mother-in-law, but I have to do this, you know that," Tina said sadly.

"Yes, honey, I know." Marian embraced her briefly. She then left Tina to drive back to the home where she lived with Billy's father up in the foothills of the mountains. For those few days, Tina felt unbearably lonely. The following week, the family pickup truck showed up at Tina's doorstep ready for the move back home to the Bay area.

"Mom, Dad, it's so great to see you! Come in and see baby Yvonne!" The new grandparents glowed as Tina's dad, Henry, picked up the first grandchild in their family. Tina was the oldest of four children: a brother and two sisters.

She is so pretty!" Grandpa Henry remarked, as he picked her up from her crib.

"Look at that smile!" Tina's Mom, Ruby remarked, tenderly.

"We'll be glad to have you back home, Tina. Don't worry about anything. Everything will be all right," her dad, Henry said, kindness shining in his eyes. Tina always remembered her dad being there for her. This time was no different.

It took three trips with the family pickup truck to get everything back to Tina's childhood home in Walnut Creek, California. On the last trip she and her dad loaded both the baby's crib and her bed mattress and frame onto the pickup. It barely fit, but with one last push, Henry got it perfectly in place then slammed the back tail gate of the truck firmly shut. They jumped into the front seat of the pickup and headed out toward their home in the Bay Area. Tina felt a new sense of unity with her family, and now she was returning home with baby Yvonne. On the last trip, the baby stayed back with Tina's mom, who was thoroughly enjoying being a grandma for the first time. Henry glanced over to Tina with his usual fatherly smile. Tina smiled back feeling like a little girl again safe in her father's care. As they drove closer, the familiar green signs on the freeway read, "San Francisco 125 miles." Tina breathed in the fresh air, relieved to be back home again.

Walnut Creek, the familiar East Bay city area where she grew up was a welcome sight, bringing back many pleasant memories from Tina's youth. Fortunately, the family home had as many as five bedrooms, depending on how the rooms were divided. There was even one off the garage which was the old music room/art studio where Tina used to paint on canvas and her brother Joe taught guitar lessons during high school and college days. Soon, Tina and baby Yvonne's room was comfortably arranged with her bed on one end and the baby crib on the other. It was good to be back home, but strange and sad at the same time. She knew her marriage to Billy, once the love of her life, was ending.

***

Elsewhere in the San Francisco Bay area, a mysterious man was gripping an automatic handgun in his right hand and an engraving tool in the left. He was etching a circle with a cross through it on the gun's metal frame. The symbol supposedly represented his view down the gun barrel as he drew a bead on his victims. It was a marking that came to be known as the "Zodiac Killer Symbol." He was left handed.

Not far away, at the San Francisco Police Department, one of several detectives reviewing the evidence of the Zodiac murders was handing his colleague a stack of documents detailing the latest developments in the case. "Here you go, Tony," said the detective.

Tony Smith Sr. was a middle-aged man with a furrowed brow. On his hand, he wore an heirloom gold ring inset with a large tiger-eye stone. One of the veteran detectives on the case, Tony looked a bit worn from stress and lack of sleep. He scanned through the new paperwork on the phantom killer.

"Look at that!" Tony exclaimed. "He got away again! One of these days, we are going to catch that SOB, and I want to be there so I can look him straight in the eye!"

CHAPTER TWO

THE BEGINNING OF A NEW LIFE— NEW FAMILY

The morning light filtered in as Tina awoke in her bedroom at her family home. Baby Yvonne was still resting peacefully in her crib. Pleasant breezes wafted in through a partially open window above her head as she listened to the familiar and friendly sounds of parents dropping off their children at the elementary school across the street, the same sounds she heard day after day growing up there in her youth. It just felt right.

Tina rose and lifted the fussy baby out of her crib and took her into the kitchen where her mom, Ruby, was already making coffee. Its sweet aroma filled the air.

"Good morning, Tina! The coffee will be ready soon . . . and here's the morning newspaper!"

Tina glanced at the headlines and flipped through the body of the Contra Costa Times. She marveled that there were actually happy headlines and wonderful stories inside of people doing all kinds of productive and positive things with their lives. As she looked through the paper, she noticed an advice column written by a young woman columnist still finishing college, a psychology major. Her column was called "Ask Sharon."

"Mom . . . look at this? Here's a column written by a woman named "Sharon, out of Napa, California. A reader asks, 'How do you re-build your life after a divorce and a new baby?'"

"Sounds like a good article for you!" winked Ruby.

"Not everybody is as lucky as me to have great parents and a great home to move back *to,*" Tina smiled warmly. She glanced over the article by Sharon, then got up and handed the baby to her mom. "I'd better make the baby formula."

Ruby enjoyed holding the baby while Tina got the bottle ready. Soon her dad, Henry, joined them for coffee and breakfast before he left for the Real Estate office in downtown Walnut Creek, where he was the Broker. Tina already saw how being back home with her loving, supportive parents would give her the foundation to rebuild her life and create exciting and fresh new directions.

Over the next few years, Tina considered what she wanted to do with her life. Through special training programs at the local Contra Costa County and some Christian ministry sources, Tina began to work with a team of leaders and other individuals who put together a facility called "Teen Hope." She worked there as a part-time counselor to both teen boys and girls who had been runaways, or who were coming off addictions. The facility was founded and supported by Tina's church and other local non-profit organizations. Sometimes though, the hours grew long, and the problems complex, making it hard trying to care for a little one too.

Tina made a decision to go back to school in San Francisco for medical assisting. After her studies were complete, she landed a job with a family practice office in Doctor's Park, near her parent's home. It was ideal. She was able to come home at lunch and be with Yvonne during their two-hour lunch break. Tina liked the primary Doctor, Dr. Lang, and the other medical staff there. She saw a good future for herself there. The heartache over her split up with Billy sometimes weighed heavily on her heart, but she tried to look ahead and see the bright spots.

A divorce was inevitable. Billy had never acted interested in getting back together and she knew it was best that he stayed away. Over the next couple of years of single life, Tina dated a few very nice men, but then Russell George came along. She met him in a Christian single's group that met twice a month in her city. Tina was intrigued from the first moment she laid eyes on him. He was tall, six feet four, dark, and handsome. She found herself wondering, "I wonder what it would be like to be married to someone like that?"

Less than a year later, Russell lifted up a bridal veil to kiss the new bride . . . *Mrs. Tina George.* It was June 26, 1976. A new blended family had begun.

Life was an adjustment at first. Tina was still working in the medical office, and Russell was a busy plant manager for a building materials company in Martinez, California, where he had been transferred by his company from the East Coast. Grandma Ruby stayed with Yvonne part of that first year, but before long, it was decided that Tina would be a stay-at-home mom. Russell and Tina also decided they would plan to have at least two more children.

By the spring of 1977, they had moved into a brand new home in the Southampton area of Benicia, California, a quaint, picturesque town by the bay on the Carquinez Straits. Benicia by the Bay, in Northern California, was a lovely seaside town with restaurants and shops near the water, and views of windsurfers and sailboats from the sidewalks and decks. It was the town where famous author Jack London had lived and worked during his youth.

The mailbox in front of a beautiful, two-story high-end home with a view of the bay now read: Russell and Tina George. The setting was definitely a high contrast to her near poverty lifestyle with Billy in the mid-sixties. By early summer of 1978, Tina was pregnant with her second child.

***

New Life . . . New Family . . .October 1978

On this October morning, Tina was busily working in the kitchen making breakfast. The kitchen there was always sunny and pleasant, with a stunning view of the Carquinez Bay through the picture windows. On Saturday and Sundays, Tina loved cooking a hot breakfast for the family, including bacon, eggs, freshly baked apple popovers, fruit, coffee, and orange juice. Weekend breakfasts were always very special. Once again, Tina was wearing a maternity top, and was obviously pregnant, about five months. The "baby" daughter, Yvonne, from the former first-marriage days was now seven years old. Tina walked over, and put some scrambled eggs on Yvonne's plate, then on her husband's plate. She filled her plate from the stove and sat down with them. Meanwhile, her husband, Russell, was very absorbed in the Sunday newspaper. Tina kindly called his attention to the food in front of him.

"Russell, are you going to eat your breakfast, Hon?" Russell lowered the newspaper, and looked over at Tina.

"Oh . . . yeah, sure."

"Honey, this is going to be a different sort of Sunday for us. We're going to the birthday party for David at Lydia's house in San Bruno, then we are going over to visit the church in San Francisco tonight. It's far overdue for us to visit that Evangel Temple on 14th Street and see what really goes on there. I really need to see it for myself."

"Yes, so do I," Russell agreed, sipping his coffee.

"I mean, they say during the services that clear, fragrant oil is appearing on people's heads, and on their Bibles out of *thin air*," Tina remarked expressively. "The pastor says that he sees *angels* anointing the people's heads and Bibles! I've heard our friends talk about it long enough. I want to see it for myself. If they are faking it, I'll know," she said, as she poured cream into her coffee. "I mean, even the newspapers call it a 'supernatural phenomena.'"

Russell was not hearing her. He still had his head buried in the Sunday news article about the Zodiac.

"The Zodiac . . . They say he is threatening to strike this weekend, like today, *Sunday!* He wrote a letter to the San Francisco paper. He states his intentions very absolutely... Look, right here, Tina." By now Tina was beginning to feel a bit frustrated.

"Russell . . . can we talk about something that is really important, here?" she jokingly pleads with him.

Russell looked up briefly from the open newspaper.

"We are going to that church service after the birthday party at Lydia's. We need to get a feeling for what is really going on over there, you know? It could be a hoax, or something."

"Well, when people like the Freeman's, Doug and Gina, come back from there saying it really happened . . . and their son Tommy, the kid is a real teenage dynamo with a Bible . . . it gives it a lot of credibility in my mind. But you're right. We need to see it for ourselves."

"After the birthday party at Lydia's, we'll leave Yvonne with my folks, and go over. The service downtown is at 7 o'clock." Russell was still completely absorbed by the Sunday newspaper.

"Russell . . . what are you reading now?"

"I'm still on this editorial story about the Zodiac Killer. He is threatening to come back. He says he is going to strike this weekend . . . Sunday. That's *today,*" Russell reemphasized.

"Oh brother . . . does that guy ever rest?" I had to read about him all the time as a proofreader at the Record. It made me sick the way his mind worked."

"Honey, he has been on something like a two-year break. He states his intentions very clearly. He's going to strike this weekend. Look right here." Tina walked over and took her dishes to the sink.

"Like I said, I had to read about him and his escapades way too much, up in Chico. I mean, every morning for who knows how long . . . It was the Zodiac and Charles Manson."

"What a way to spend your day, eh!"

"Yeah, that's what I used to say!"

"He must be some kind of a Satanist . . . or maybe he is just possessed by the devil. I guess he gets some kind of thrill out of killing people on a Sunday," remarked Russell.

"Honey, he gets a thrill over killing people on *any* day. Sunday is no different . . . or maybe there are just less police on duty that day."

"There's actually a little sketch of him here with the story made from a witness who actually survived a Zodiac attack a few years ago."

Shrugging it off, Tina took his plate and headed to the sink.

"I need to get the dishes in the dishwasher, and get us ready to head out of here in a little while." She poured her daughter another glass of orange juice. "Are you looking forward to spending time with Grandma and Grandpa tonight?" she asked Yvonne and winked.

"Yeah, Mommy!" Yvonne grinned.

"Let's get dressed, now." Tina scooted Yvonne off toward her bedroom to get her ready.

That afternoon, their family group of about twenty people, were assembled at Lydia's house in San Bruno to celebrate her son, David's 24th birthday. David, Tina's brother-in-law, was a handsome young man, a Latino mix with expressive eyes and a big smile. Her married sister, Sandy, was there with her daughter, about the same age as Yvonne. Tina's mom and dad and a few other assorted friends were also present. They all gathered around David to watch him blow out the brightly lit candles on the birthday cake.

"Make a wish, David!" Lydia beamed, wearing a big smile. He hesitated briefly to think about it—then David blew out all the candles. Lydia was a lively Latino woman with expressive eyes and a hearty laugh.

"Great! You get your wish!" Everybody laughed. Lydia reached for the ice cream, and a scooper. "Sandy, do you have the plates?"

"Yes, right here!" She started passing them out to everyone.

"Did you make coffee, Lydia?"

"Yes . . . Russell. I knew you would ask!"

"Decaf, I hope?" Tina asked.

"No, sorry. I was under the impression you were in for a rather long evening. You're going out to see what happens at that church on 14th Street, aren't you . . . Evangel Temple?" Lydia carefully poured the coffee into their cups as she spoke to them.

"Yes, we are. I have to see it for myself."

"For a very long time . . . fourteen or fifteen years . . . this phenomenon has been going on out there, 'Heavenly oil' just appearing on people's heads, and on their Bibles," Lydia explained.

"Have you ever gone out there to see it for yourself?" Russell wondered. Lydia sat down with her piece of cake.

"No, but my friend Frances from my church, and Father Drake, went out there. They say it's the real deal. I believe them."

"Well, we will see soon, won't we?" answered Russell, with a curious grin.

"Let me know how you feel about it after you sit in the service and see it for yourselves. I'm curious what your opinion will be. Speaking of watching the time . . . it's about six o'clock now. You'd better start heading out in the next fifteen minutes. Traffic into the city is always busy, even on Sunday!"

"Okay, I'll get my coat. Russell, are you coming? Yvonne, honey, you are going home with Grandma and Grandpa tonight." Tina organized herself and Yvonne as she and Russell prepared to leave. Shortly, the two of them walked out the front door toward their car, a late model Subaru four-door sedan, which was parked in front of the house. They got in, and soon drove off, heading out into the night. It was only the beginning of their great adventure.

CHAPTER THREE

PREPARING FOR THE CHASE

The Sunday evening traffic was just as busy as any weekday commuter traffic. Tina and Russell drove patiently through San Francisco, watching their directions, being very careful to take the correct exit. Soon they were within a few blocks of the church.

"I think we're close . . . There's 12th street. You know what? We're in the 'Mission district.' That's just great!" said Russell, thinking about the area having a reputation for being unsafe. "I hope we don't get mugged just trying to get to church!" They drove up to 14th Street and parked their car about four blocks from the church. Tina and Russell carried their Bibles as they walked briskly in the dark with only low street lights burning along the block. It was early evening, but in mid-October, it was already getting very dark by then.

They stepped spritely up the stairs and walked directly inside the church. As they glanced around, they noticed that in the foyer there were many framed newspaper articles posted. "Russell, look at this." Russell came over and peered at the dozens of newspaper articles posted on a wall dedicated to press coverage on the appearance of the "heavenly oil."

"Wow! They definitely have gotten some press coverage on this over the years!" Tina continued to scan over the articles. As a former proofreader, Tina read quickly through a few of the articles.

"Russell, do you notice? None of the news agencies seem to criticize what happens here. They just seem to report that it really *does* happen here. Tina quoted . . . "'Heavenly Oil Authentic Phenomena' . . . Here's another one, 'Oil Appears as Angels Appear' . . . Hmmm."

Russell looked over at Tina with a curious grin.

"Well, are you ready for church?" He winked.

Russell and Tina went inside the old church. It was filled with people sitting on old-fashioned wooden pews. The church perhaps would ordinarily seat 150, but it was a quiet Sunday night with about 75 people in attendance. They recognized a few familiar faces, and then slid into the second row. Tina leaned over and whispered to Russell.

"The Freemans are here, Doug and Gina, and there's Tommy right in front of me in the very first row." Tommy, a friendly teenager, turned around and smiled. The church organist, who had been playing softly, suddenly launched into the lively old hymn "Victory in Jesus." Russell and Tina each grabbed a hymnal, and joined in the singing. People were clapping and singing joyfully. Tina found herself studying the ceiling above her, while the lively music played. It was a solid off-white finished wallboard . . . no cracks, no contraptions of any kind . . . a perfect ceiling; her eyes scanned back and forth across it. Russell also looked up above, wondering if there was anything unusual.

"Well, there is certainly nothing on the ceiling . . ." he whispered to Tina, leaning close.

"It is a perfect ceiling," Tina agreed.

"Perfect."

Pastor Gino, a fifty-something man of Latin origin, got up from the front row, and walked up to the front platform to address the quiet Sunday-evening congregation.

"Good evening! It's so nice to see all of you here, and I see we have a few visitors with us. Thank you for joining us. He opened a well-worn black leather Bible. "I would like to compare a few scriptures from the Bible tonight. But first, let's open in prayer. Heavenly Father, how we long to come into your presence. Thank you for your son, Jesus, who died on the cross for us to make that possible. Let us have spiritual ears and spiritual eyes, which the Lord Jesus spoke of in your Word, that we may fully receive what you would have for us this evening. Amen!"

The congregation, softly echoed, an "Amen!" Pastor Gino began his message.

"I would like to start by turning to Zechariah, chapter four, verse six. Then keep your finger in the Gospel of Matthew, where we will go next. Zechariah four, six: 'Not by might, not by power, but by my Spirit says the Lord!' Here God is reminding us that we can do anything with God's blessing and power behind us! This verse is often quoted by itself, but do you notice how the verses one to three leading up to it mention the oil? In the Bible, the oil is always the symbol of the Holy Spirit. This is how God dwells in us, and empowers us to do mighty things!"

"Now, let's turn to Matthew, chapter twenty-one, verse twenty-one." The soft sounds of pages rustling filled the air. "Jesus has just cursed the fig tree for not bearing fruit, and it withered up." Pastor Gino read, "And Jesus answered them, 'Truly I say unto you, if you have faith (a firm relying trust) and do not doubt, you will not only do what has been done to the fig tree, but even if you say to this mountain, be taken up and cast into the sea, it will be done; and whatever you ask in prayer, having faith, and really believing, you will receive.'"

"Now, in the Bible when it says 'mountain' it's referring to a problem much bigger than you that you cannot solve. 'Be cast into the sea, and it will be done.' Do you believe it? If God said it, then it will be so. It is a matter of whether you have small faith or large faith. And in Hebrews, chapter eleven, it tells us that without faith, it is impossible to please God. Let's turn now to John, chapter fourteen, verses twelve to fourteen." He continued to read to the congregation: "'I assure you, most solemnly tell you, if anyone steadfastly believes in Me, he will be able to do the things that I do, and he will do even greater things than these, because I go to the Father.'"

Pastor Gino looked up, and said this part by memory: "'And I will do (Myself whatever you ask in Jesus' name) representing all that *I am*, so that the Father will be glorified…yes I will grant, I myself will do whatever you ask in *my* name.'" The pastor began to share his thoughts. He was a very expressive speaker and liked to use his hands as he talked.

"So you have just heard two of the most powerful scripture passages that promise God will act on your behalf if you ask in Jesus' name . . . and have strong faith, and do not budge!" He stepped down from the platform closer to the people as he spoke.

"Do not fear to walk through the open doors God has for you! Walk in His strength, and his power, and it will come to pass. Even if it seems like you might be in danger...do not fear! In Psalm 91, the Bible declares that He shall give the angels charge over your safety! How many times can we think of those incidents where God has sent his angels to preserve us in times of danger? There are so many times!" Pastor Gino paced the aisles while holding his open Bible, talking "up close and personal" with the crowd.

"In Hebrews 1:4, the Word says, 'Are not the angels all ministering spirits, or servants—sent out in the service of those who are to inherit salvation?' If God is sending angels to watch over you . . . rejoice! It means that one day you are destined to inherit salvation and inherit heaven. If they saved you from a calamity . . . then it's not yet your appointed time. God knows you have very important work to do here!"

Suddenly, Pastor Gino's attention was caught by something he saw on the platform. He ventured down closer to the congregation as he spoke.

"I see angels standing on the platform. They appear to be from ten to thirteen feet tall, and are dressed like soldiers, standing to attention, holding shining shields and swords . . ."

Turning to Russell, Tina whispered, "*Warring angels* . . . !"

Pastor Gino looked directly at Tommy in the front row of the church. "Tommy, I see an angel about to anoint your head with oil!" Tina looked straight ahead at the back of Tommy's head about fourteen inches away. She was in the second row, directly behind him. Tommy had dry blondish-brown hair, a little curly, slightly long to the back collar. At first it appeared dry but then as Tina studied his hair more closely, it was becoming wet with fragrant oil. Tina put her hand on the hair on the back of his head. As she touched his hair, her hand quickly became covered with clear fragrant oil. The oil began to drip down the back of his head to his neck. Tina had the same clear fragrant oil on her hand, and forearm now.

"Russell, look!" Russell looked on with amazement.

Pastor Gino gestured to the woman sitting to the left of Tina. "I see an angel about to anoint your Bible with oil!" Tina looked at the woman. She had a black leather zipper Bible on her lap, which was zipped shut. She suddenly unzipped it and opened the book. Tina looked over at the open Bible, which was completely dry at first. Then she saw what looked like a water droplet on the right side of the open page. Within seconds the drop of oil grew, as the fragrant oil spread all over the open Bible until it was saturated. The woman was amazed. Tina touched it reverently.

"It's the same fragrance!" Tina remarked. Tina realized that the angel must have been standing right over her. "Well, they must be right here!" she said, whispering to Russell, who gave her a silly grin

Pastor Gino looked over at a man on the other side of the church, "Sir, an angel is about to anoint your head with oil!" Soon, his head too was wet with fragrant oil. The man raised his hands, praising God, speaking softly. Pastor Gino began to explain the history of these supernatural happenings.

"Some of you here tonight are new. This phenomenon has been going on here in the services for some years . . . fourteen years now. It would seem that God would just want to show his presence in this dark corner of the city!" Pastor Gino pulled out an envelope and a piece of paper. "This is a lab slip from the science and technology division of a prestigious college here in our region . . . UC Berkeley. Our staff decided to submit a lab request to be done on this oil. We didn't tell them anything about it. I just brought it in and requested to Have the test done on the oil . . . a complete analysis. I felt this would be important to certain people who consider themselves scientific thinkers . . ."

Russell was on the edge of his chair with suspense. Tina smiled, as she waited for the pastor to complete his story.

"About one week later," Pastor Gino continued, "I received a call that the lab work was completed, and that I should come and pick up the paperwork on it, so I drove out to the university campus in Berkeley to hear their opinion. The supervisor of the lab met me with this piece of paper. Pastor Gino held up the lab report. He said to me, 'So what planet did this oil come from?' I wondered where he was going. 'What do you mean?' I asked him. He said, 'Oil is always derived from something such as corn oil, olive oil, peanut oil, cottonseed oil . . . but this oil has *no earthly origin!'*"

The congregation erupted with applause. Tina glanced over at Russell. He just shook his head in amazement. Pastor Gino wrapped up his message for the evening.

"I leave you with that thought. Praise God! Go in peace, and I hope to see you back here again next Sunday!"

The service was over. People were smiling and milling around, visiting with both friends and newcomers. Tina was greeting some of their friends. Russell walked over to Pastor Gino.

"Do you mind if I see the lab slip?" He handed the slip over to Russell.

"Not at all . . . certainly. Have a look for yourself." Russell looked it over. He read the lab results, smiling with fascination.

"'No earthly origin.' It has the UC Berkeley logo on it.'"

"Of course," answered Pastor Gino.

"I consider myself a God-fearing man . . . It's just that I have never seen anything like this!"

"Neither had I until it just started happening all of a sudden about fourteen years ago," Pastor Gino smiled. "One evening I was just giving an ordinary sermon from Matthew, chapter six . . . the sermon on the Mount, and the Lord's Prayer. . . when I saw them appear for the first time. The angels seem to appear first on the platform up here, then move down into the congregation."

"And the oil?" Russell asked.

"That too . . . it puzzled me at first. I had a hard time finding a Bible reference for it, except that there is one passage that refers to 'oil running down Aaron's beard.' It was an Old Testament episode."

Pastor Gino stepped up to an alcove by the altar with small bottles on tables. "These bottles fill up with the tops on them." Meanwhile, Tina stepped over to join the conversation. "People used to bring larger vessels, but the angels stopped filling the big ones . . . just the smaller ones. Here." He handed a small bottle of the oil to Tina. "You may take this one."

"Thank you!" She opened the small bottle about three inches tall. "Mmm! It's the same fragrance!" Tina screwed the small black top back on. She observed a few golden drops on the bottom of the bottle, then tipped it up a little to look at it more closely. Pastor Gino continued his explanation.

"Most of the oil seemed to have that characteristic . . . clear with a few golden yellow drops."

"Interesting," Russell smiled. "Well, thank you, pastor. It's been a very enlightening and amazing evening. Your sermon was very good too!"

"Thank you, and come back again." Russell and Pastor Gino clasped hands in a friendly departing handshake. Russell walked Tina out toward the exit of the church.

"Let's go, Tina. I want to take you to that Mexican restaurant on Geary Street before it gets much later. It's the same place I go to when I come to the city with the staff from work when we see our company's attorney . . . It's the guy's favorite!"

"What? Isn't it about nine o'clock . . . or later?"

"Aww! Come on, honey. It's not that late!"

"Well . . . okay, Russell." They walked toward the side exit, and left the church.

Once outside, Tina walked down five steps to the street lit only by a little light from the church porch. She looked back, as something tugged at her mind and spirit. Russell walked ahead of her toward their car. Tina looked into darkness toward the exit and the steps in the dimly lit twilight. Russell kept walking toward the car. Tina stared into the darkness with a keen awareness she couldn't explain—that the whole battalion of angels who were active in the church service had just followed them right out the side door exit and onto the street.

"What?" she spoke softly out loud to herself. Tina stood in the darkness, and looked around. As if a window from the supernatural had opened up just a little crack, she sensed a subtle light, and a transparency of wings had just clustered around her.

"Are you . . . there?" She took a step down the street, looking back inquisitively. The angelic beings followed. Russell called out to Tina, wondering why she was holding back.

"Honey, where are you? Are you coming?" Tina finally began to walk slowly in his direction down the dimly lit street. She looked back over her shoulder, sensing a subtle light and the presence of angelic figures. She didn't know how to express what she was really thinking—about the angels following them out the back door of the church. Tina looked over her shoulder again, with a questioning look. The angels continued to follow her.

"Coming!" She walked up next to Russell. "You know, you almost have to go to a church meeting like that and pick up a few angels just to walk back to your car safely!" she blurted out awkwardly.

They slipped into their car. The angelic beings swirled around their vehicle. Unaware, Tina and Russell drove off toward Geary Street. Russell and Tina were still marveling over what they just witnessed in the church.

"Tonight we saw matter appear out of *thin air!*" Russell said, becoming a little emotional.

"Yes, we did!" Tina smiled back. Tina couldn't help thinking about the book of Genesis and the creation of the earth. "'Let there be light . . . let there be land, separated by the sea . . .' Let there be, and it was," Tina smiled, as she spoke. "This night we saw God transport oil from the unseen realm to the physical realm. This will be a special night to remember always!"

Soon, the two of them were inside Russell's favorite Mexican restaurant on Geary Street, enjoying their meal. It was time for smiles, good food, and to reflect on the happenings of the day . . . and the evening in a little church they would never forget.

A few miles away, unknown to them, in the semi-darkness, a man's hand was loading bullets into an automatic weapon. He was left handed.

At the restaurant, the waitress came over to Russell with the ticket.

"Okay . . . now wasn't it worth it?" Russell asked Tina, with a little laugh.

Across town, this same mysterious man put the loaded gun into his left pocket. He was a "leftie." This was an unusual gun, in more than one way. It had an engraving on it: A circle with a cross through it like the cross hairs of a scope on a rifle or gun.

Back at the cozy Mexican restaurant, Tina and Russell were finishing up their romantic late night dinner together.

"Now, wasn't that worth the extra time?" Russell asked one more time. Tina popped a chocolate mint into her mouth.

"Yes, it was!" replied Tina. Russell looked at his watch. "Let's get going . . . can we?" Tina yawned.

"Yeah . . . it's about ten-thirty or so," Russell agreed. They collected their coats, and started back outside toward their car.

At that same moment, a few miles away in the Melrose district, another couple, Todd and Jeanne, were having a serious talk at her house.

"Todd, I'm glad you came by to pick me up. We needed to get away from the house for a while, and just go out and talk."

"Okay, Jeanne . . . where do you want to go?"

"I know it's late, but let's just take a drive." Todd and Jeanne drove off into the night in his late model blue Chevy.

Not far away, in yet another part of the city, a debonair young man dressed in a dark tux was carefully placing an engagement ring into a black velvet ring box. He put it in his pocket. Within a few minutes he picked up his twenties-something girlfriend, dressed in a beautiful long gown, and black high heels. They drove off in his black Mercedes Benz.

As Tina and Russell drove away, Russell announced, "It's not that late. Let's stop by a few of those ocean lookout spots before we hit the Golden Gate Bridge on the way back home."

"Yes, it *is* late. What are you thinking? I am just a tired pregnant lady here. I don't care about looking at those places this late!" Russell was not listening. He drove off, as if he was like a puppet on a string or hearing the beat of a different drummer.

Meanwhile, a mysterious man who was alone in an old white car, was driving down a dark, lonely dirt road toward the ocean shore, not far from the Presidio. The car looked like a mix of makes. It looked like an old white Fairlaine Ford in the front, yet like a Chevy Impala with the red stripes on the side, encased in silver like chrome. The car was driven by a Caucasian male. He appeared to be in his late forties or fifties, plain looks, thinning light hair, receding hairline, wearing large, light rimmed glasses. His oblong shaped face had almost an angular looking chin and jawline. He was wearing a white turtleneck sweater and a gray blazer.

The ocean shore was lit only by the moonlight. Four couples were walking on the sand, talking. Some were holding hands. He pulled up near the shoreline, turned his car engine off, and waited. He watched. Would any of them leave? Would one be left *alone*? A period of time passed. He finally started up his car and turned back toward the road, and the Presidio. Upon leaving, he passed Russell and Tina going the opposite direction to the shoreline. Tina couldn't help but notice. She turned her head watching as he passed by. He was obviously a single man alone in a lover's lane area at about 11 p.m.

Tina looked over at Russell. "That's odd." They passed the "mystery" car, and drove up to the sandy shore. There they saw couples walking on the sand in the moonlight, as ocean waves gently rushed to and fro with the tide. It was about 11:15 p.m. Tina looked around uncomfortably.

"Russell, where are we? This is too dark and too cold to want to walk out there. I mean, it's mid-October, and it must be after eleven o'clock." They watched the scene for a few moments. "These people must be into something weird," she commented dryly.

"Okay . . . you're right." Russell pulled around, and headed back toward the main road.

Meanwhile, back up on Lincoln Boulevard near the Presidio, a couple was in their car talking sitting in a late model blue Chevy. It was Todd and Jeanne. They kissed a time or two, then continued their conversation. The mystery man in the old white car pulled up behind them. He turned his lights off. He waited alone, like a predator . . . silent, watching, waiting for his chosen moment. Todd and Jeanne were oblivious to his presence. The man fondled a gun in his left pocket. He started to pull it out and look at it, but would rather watch the couple in the car ahead of him. Would he act?

Suddenly, Russell and Tina's car appeared, as Russell was looking for a spot to park they immediately saw the "mystery man" whom they had just seen not ten minutes prior, sitting in the same old white Fairlane, with red with chrome stripes on the side. He had pulled up behind a couple in a blue Chevy. His headlights were turned off and he appeared to be waiting there. Tina and Russell pulled in behind him.

"There's that same guy! What kind of pervert is he, anyway? Scoping out the lover's lane spots, or what?" remarked Tina, sounding annoyed. Once the couple in the car ahead of him was no longer alone, as Tina and Russell had now appeared, the "mystery man" turned on his engine and headlights and proceeded to pull out and turn around in the middle of Lincoln Boulevard to drive off in the opposite direction.

While he slowly maneuvered his full turn around in the middle of the road, clearly visible in both sets of headlights, Tina studied the man's face carefully. She confirmed that he was mid to late fifties, wearing large, light rimmed glasses. He seemed cautious and uncomfortable about his position between the two couples. They had about fifteen seconds to observe him close up, and fully lit . . . his appearance, his car, his objective.

"What do you make of him?" Russell asked Tina.

"Hmm . . . This guy could work for IBM. He looks conservative. But he must be a 'perv' of some kind." Within thirty seconds, the mystery man had turned around in the middle of the road, and had briskly driven off in the opposite direction.

Tina glanced around. "Russell, I cannot see anything here. If the ocean is out there, I can't see it. Can't you do a tired pregnant lady a favor, and take me home?"

"Okay . . . but one last stop. We're going to drive over the Golden Gate Bridge, then see the view of the city from Vista Point before we get on the freeway to go home!"

Tina rolled her eyes and groaned a little. "Okay Russell. Let's go."

From high above, where angels perch, Tina and Russell's car was seen driving east over the Golden Gate Bridge. The shining angelic beings armed with fiery swords from heaven, filtered and drifted down toward the parking lot below by the famous lookout area. Within moments, Russell took the familiar Vista Point exit. Their car entered the parking lot and began to head forward past some of the empty parking spaces where the public stood to view the spectacular sight of the San Francisco Bay. Russell looped around to look for parking. There was a black Mercedes Benz parked in the parking lot. To their left, a short distance away, the mysterious man got out of his car and was reaching into his left pocket, heading toward a young couple on the ocean front lookout. The couple was formally dressed, facing each other, clasping hands. It looked like a proposal about ready to happen. Then the young man pulled a ring box from his pocket and opened it. Tina observed the entire scene clearly from their car, as they approached.

"Russell . . . there is that same guy, in the gray blazer, driving the old white car!" Tina exclaimed.

The young couple standing there were *alone*. The young man lifted up the open ring box before his girlfriend's eyes.

Meanwhile, the "mystery man" appeared to be reaching for something in his left pocket. He headed resolutely toward the couple standing at the ocean lookout. One more quick look over his shoulder revealed Russell and Tina in their car, looking squarely at him. Upon spotting them, he became extremely agitated. The pain of discovery filled every part of his being. He was now faced with a dilemma. If he open fired on Russell and Tina, the couple in front would see it. If he shot the couple in front viewing the bay, Russell and Tina would have witnessed it. His white car and back license plate were facing Russell and Tina's vehicle in plain view. In a few moments of hysterical madness, the mystery man decided to run, dashing frantically back to his car.

The powers of hell seemed to rumble like thunder. From the unseen realm, the angels lowered their fiery swords creating a protective barrier.

In a flash, Russell remembered the newspaper article, and the sketch of the Zodiac's face by an eye witness. Suddenly, reality kicked in with lightning bolt conviction.

"That's the Zodiac . . . let's get him!" Russell exclaimed excitedly to Tina. She looked back at him with a look of a thousand question marks.

Frantic, the Zodiac opened his car door and jumped inside. With engine roaring and tires squealing, he sped back out across the parking lot toward the freeway. Russell followed, accelerating to match his speed. The Zodiac driver nervously looked both ways, then proceeded to force himself through an entrance, opening back onto the freeway . . . anything to get away from the two witnesses. The Zodiac—spotting them in the third place in the space of 25 minutes, observing him stalk a number of unsuspecting couples—must have figured that they were undercover police, and panicked. There was no natural explanation for it. He had always mocked the police for being stupid, and vowed, *"You will never capture me!"*

In a split-second moment, the onset of a sudden, tense high-speed race after the "mystery man" began. They knew by now, without a shadow of a doubt, that he must be the infamous "Zodiac Killer." Russell's adrenaline flowed as he accelerated and sped toward the white mystery car as it came to the entrance to the park. No one was coming. "Zodiac" got by with it, and sped off, making a sharp right. Russell and Tina continued to race frantically, determined to catch the Zodiac escape car.

Maneuvering toward him through the wrong-way entrance, at high speed was an illegal move, but Russell continued, racing onward after the white mystery car.

"I hope no cops saw me!"

"In this case, it might not be a bad idea?" Tina replied in a terse whisper. Their intention was just to get his license plate number and back off. But the great speed by which they had to travel in an attempt to get close to his car, was something they hadn't counted on. But there was something inside both Tina and Russell, a like trait: they were not the types to give up easily once this close to an important breakthrough.

As they sped off, taking that sudden right, racing toward the old white car, which was moving at incredible speed in supernatural fashion, a mysterious light began to break into the darkness. Moving in from the unseen realm, large bright soldier-like angels followed, descending and surrounding them in the atmosphere above the car, swords and shields up. They were the same angels who followed Russell and Tina from the church. They successfully overtook the large demonic creatures in their path, emanating from the Zodiac car, engaging them in tense warfare. The fiery creatures from the dark realm that controlled the Zodiac were forced to back away from Russell and Tina, as strong and fearsome-looking angel armies from the unseen realm protectively surrounded them.

Russell and Tina were now well into a high-speed chase on the Novato freeway after the mysterious old white car, obviously designed and disguised as a high-speed escape car. They accelerated well up over 110 miles per hour. The other cars on the freeway seemed oblivious to their chase.

"Tina, you're the one with 15/20 vision, 'Ms. Hawk eyes!' Can you see the license plate number yet?" Russell gasped.

"*Almost*! Get closer!"

"The old white car . . . it must have a really big engine. He is way out in front!"

Transparent, fiery-looking demonic creatures flared up off the Zodiac car as it madly and frantically sped down the Novato freeway. Russell pushed the late model Subaru sedan to the limit, but it was obviously no match for the Zodiac escape car, but he did make some headway. The speedometer of the Subaru sport sedan read 120 MPH.

"Tina . . .Tina . . .you've got to see it! Can't you see it?" Tina was straining to try to see the license plate in the dim light.

"Almost . . . *almost*!" Russell was madly racing, straining, trying to make headway. Tina couldn't help wondering, what if Russell followed him down an exit and had him cornered? He was armed and they were not. They really just wanted the license plate number. Tina fumbled a pen from her purse.

At that moment, a car on their right moved in between Tina and Russell, and the white Zodiac car. It was apparently changing lanes to prepare to take an exit on the far left of the six-lane freeway.

"*Oh my God, no!* That car . . . it's blocking my view!" Tina winced with disappointment. The car directly in front of them was cutting in close, and forcing them to suddenly slow up to avoid hitting the car. The white Zodiac escape car surged ahead at great unexplainable speed. A large transparent demon creature which seemed to magically peel off the side of the car in a flame, laughed, and mocked at them. Russell successfully navigated to avoid the accident. The shining angelic creatures moved into protective mode toward Tina and Russell's car. "Russell, watch out!" Tina cried out frantically.

"No problem!" Russell gasped, slowing down and gaining his composure.

"Russell . . . where is the car . . . can you *see* the car?" Russell was straining further . . . looking ahead, now growing distraught.

"Where did he go . . . did you see it? I don't see the car!" moaned Tina.

"Oh, no! He must have taken an exit up ahead!" There were four exits up ahead of them in the far distance. Inside the car, Russell and Tina looked stunned. They had him, but then he seemed to disappear, evaporating into thin air.

"He practically disappeared into thin air! It's like he dropped into a sink hole from hell," said Russell.

"Yeah . . . how well I remember. At the last minute, he always had the 'phantom advantage,' and escaped," Tina remembered. Russell then slowed their car to about 45 miles per hour.

"Now, what?" Russell continued to drive forward, slowly, looking around.

"Look! There's an exit for the California Highway Patrol." Russell immediately took the CHP exit on their right. "What a stroke of luck. Let's go!"

Russell drove the car slowly down the exit, and pulled in front of a regional outpost for the California Highway Patrol. They pulled up right in front of the building, noticing that the lights were still on. They got out, and rushed anxiously inside. A lone officer was still on duty.

"Can I help you?" he asked.

"Yes!" Tina was breathless. "We have been in a chase with a man we think is the 'Zodiac Killer!'" The officer appeared ready to hear their story.

"What made you think he was the 'Zodiac?'" the officer asked

"We read in the paper that he was threatening to strike again, this weekend . . . *tonight!*" Russell continued. "After a church service and a late dinner in the city, we were taking the long way home, stopping at some lover's lane ocean lookout sites. We saw this mysterious guy alone in a white car, who later appeared to be stalking couples in two other locations, but nobody was alone once we came along, so he would move on. When we drove into Vista Point lookout a few minutes ago, and we saw him for the third time in the space of twenty-five minutes . . . stalking again, we knew it must be him. He was getting out of his car heading right toward a couple looking out at the bay. He seemed to be reaching for a gun in his left pocket when he saw us. He panicked . . . and ran back to his car, and forced himself through the entrance, not an exit, to get back on the freeway. I picked up on who he was right away." Russell explained.

"We wound up in a high-speed chase on the freeway. Honestly, we were pushing well up over 100 miles per hour, but the old white car must have been really souped up. It must have had a big engine in it like the Batmobile. It was a disguise, just like him, an old white car with a big engine."

"Did he appear armed?"

"Yes. . . he was reaching into his pocket as he left his car, headed for the couple. He appeared to be reaching for a gun."

"When he saw us for the third time in the space of about twenty-five to thirty minutes, he must have thought we were plain-clothes police! He panicked big time, and scrambled to escape the scene as fast as he could, but we were right on his tail."

"He was armed, and you were not . . . but you were chasing this guy . . ." He looked at Tina who was obviously pregnant. "Okay . . ."

"We were just after the license plate number, and I almost had it! We were within seconds of seeing it, when a car cut in front of me and slowed us way down. He shot way ahead of us, then seemed to just . . . disappear!" Russell said, talking with his hands.

"With what we saw, and an identity, I think the police could have picked him up," commented Tina. The officer continued taking notes as they spoke.

"What did the suspect look like?"

"About five feet ten, medium build . . ." Russell began, as Tina followed up.

"Late middle-aged, mid-fifties, I think; thinning light hair; receding hairline; gray wool suit; white turtle-neck sweater; wearing large, round, light framed glasses. A very mild-looking guy, actually," said Tina. The officer looked up as he wrote out his report.

"Can you describe this high-speed escape car?"

"Yes. It looked like an old white car, like a '69 Ford Fairlane, but it had the stripes on the sides like a Chevy Impala . . . red stripes with silver chrome," Tina stressed.

"Okay, have a seat, please. Let me get on the radio and put out an 'All Points Bulletin.'

It sounds like this could be the real deal. In the meantime, please fill this out."

Miles down the freeway, back inside the Zodiac escape car, the driver was sweating bullets, and was obviously very nervous. His expression was that of total exposure, discovery, and fear. He continued to speed south along the coastal route taking highway one toward Southern California.

At the CHP outpost, the officer immediately got on the radio to all the Highway Patrol cars in the region. He told them to look for a suspicious man who was driving an older model white car, with red stripes on the side.

"Attention, this is an APB to all cars in the Golden Gate, Sausalito, and Novato freeway region. A stalking suspect . . . could be the 'Zodiac Killer,' has been reported. He was chased down by civilians just east of Vista Point, but escaped. He is thought to be armed, late middle fifties, thinning hair, gray suit and white turtleneck sweater wearing large, light framed glasses. Approach with caution. I repeat, *approach with caution.* He is thought to be armed and dangerous. Report back here if the suspect is spotted by your car." The officer finished the announcement, then came back to talk to them again.

"Okay, that's all we can do for now. We'll have to see if any of our patrol cars spot him. You'll get a call tomorrow from the San Francisco Police Department, probably from a man named Sergeant Tedesco. He's been a veteran investigator working on the Zodiac case probably well over ten years by now. Will one of you be available to talk to him?" Russell looked over at Tina.

"Yes, I will be. My husband will be at work. He's a busy plant manager. Just have him call the house. This is our number." Tina scribbled their number down. The clock on the wall read 1 a.m.

"Okay, go home and get some rest." The officer showed them back out to their car.

Russell and Tina soon drove back onto the freeway, and headed further east toward their home in Benicia.

Meanwhile, the Zodiac-mystery man was nervously driving in the dark, sweating profusely, though it was a cool October night. He sped his car further south as he listened to voices that whispered into his ear suggestions from hell.

Tina and Russell were not yet home. In the dark of night, on their family room floor, a strange light came over the Sunday newspaper Russell had been reading that morning. The headline of the news article, "Will the Zodiac Strike this Weekend?" began to glow as a transparent red flame. The newspaper quickly ignited, and went up into mysterious flames. Suddenly it turned to dust, like wispy ashes, as the newspaper disappeared into nothing more than light gray ashes on the family room floor, never to be found again.

CHAPTER FOUR

TIME TO TELL THE STORY TO THE SAN FRANCISCO POLICE

The next morning, Russell finished a quick breakfast, while Tina leisurely drank her coffee and looked over her notes for the day ahead. Suddenly, she spotted some tiny gray ashes on the family room floor. She walked over and picked up a broom and dustpan from the closet.

"Honestly now, where did this come from? What did the kids track in here?"

"So, Tina, what time are we supposed to get this call?" Russell asked her.

"I don't know . . . he just said 'tomorrow morning.'"

"Okay, you handle it. I've got to get going! The plant does not run by itself." He gave Tina a quick peck on the lips as he prepared to leave.

"Let me know how it goes." Russell grabbed his briefcase and was soon out the door.

Meanwhile, further south, it was early morning in Southern California, at an unknown beach. The Zodiac was sitting in his car by the ocean. The waves were lapping up softly onto the shore. He was looking out at the waves, emotionally tortured. It was morning, but it seemed black as night to him.

Back in Benicia by the Bay, Tina was in her short, satin robe, sipping coffee, and finishing her breakfast. As she took the dishes over to the sink, the phone rang. It was shortly before 9 a.m.

"Hello, this is Tina . . ."

The voice on the phone answered: "Is this Mrs. Tina George?"

"Yes . . ."

"This is Sergeant Tedesco, San Francisco Police Department."

"Oh yes. We were told to expect your call this morning."

"So, you saw a man in a white Volkswagen?"

"No! That was the 'Son of Sam!' Did your men spend all night looking for the wrong car?" Tina said, slightly horrified.

Hundreds of miles away on a beach in southern California, the legs of the Zodiac, wearing gray pants, and lace-up black dress shoes, walked alone on the sand.

"Can you describe the car to me again?" Tedesco asked Tina.

"It looked like an old white Ford Fairlaine, like a '69 . . . but it had stripes on the side with chrome like a Chevy Impala . . . red stripes! I think this escape car was designed to look like a mix of makes, to make it hard to describe."

In the bright morning sun, some 800 miles away, the white escape car of the "mystery man" was parked on the sand. Now there was no driver.

From his office in San Francisco, Tedesco continued his interview with Tina.

"I see," he remarked. "Unusual."

"Don't you see? The car was a disguise, just like him. It had a big engine, designed for the escape," Tina emphasized. Tedesco was becoming increasingly intrigued.

"Let's go over what happened again. I have some information here from the Highway Patrol officer who took the report from you and your husband last night."

"Okay." She braced herself for the long story. "We had decided to go over to the city after a family birthday party last night. My husband and I wanted to go the church on 14th out there at Evangel Temple with Pastor Gino. We had heard so much about it."

"The church with the 'angel thing' going on . . ."

"Yes . . ."

"Right . . . right, I know the one. That church has been in the news for years. They say there is an amazing phenomenon that happens there. Most people here in the city know about it."

"Yes. It does happen! It was a very amazing service to say the least!" Tina replied, It was the first time we'd ever been there. After that, it was about nine, but my husband wanted to go out to dinner at that Mexican Restaurant on Geary Street, so we did. By then it was about ten-thirty, or something like that. Then he wanted to stop by a couple of lookout view stops before hitting the Golden Gate Bridge to go home. So we started driving out there. As we drove on a dirt road toward the ocean on the first stop off Lincoln Boulevard, a man drove slowly toward us in a white car. He was late middle-aged, fifties, big glasses. This man was leaving the scene, alone. It just seemed weird to me."

"I see . . . no suspicion yet."

"Not really . . . just a weird vibe, like 'what is he doing out here alone at almost 11 p.m. at night?'"

"Yes . . ."

"We drove up to the ocean shore where there was bright moonlight, and couples who actually were walking around out there. I realize now that he was leaving because no one there was alone."

As Tina continued her story to Sergeant Tedesco, hundreds of miles away, on the ocean shore, the black shoes of the Zodiac made prints in the sand and small waves washed them away.

"Makes sense," Tedesco reasoned.

"I felt strange just being out there, and I told my husband, 'It's too dark and cold here, let's just leave.' So we did, and drove out to Lincoln Boulevard by the Presidio. As Russell was looking for a place to park we noticed the same guy in the white car with the red stripes and chrome on the side. He had just pulled up behind a couple sitting alone alongside the road with their lights off. His lights were off too. As soon as we came upon the scene, he started his car, his lights went on, and he turned around to leave. I asked Russ, 'Who is this guy . . . some kind of a pervert?' I realize now, he was leaving because those people were no longer alone. He slowly turned his car around in plain view of me and Russell. Both of us had our headlights on, we could have seen the license plate, but I wasn't thinking about who he really was yet."

"What did you notice about him?"

"He just seemed strange . . . fifties, thinning hair, big glasses, white turtleneck sweater, gray blazer, pale, conservative looking, like a nerd-sort-of-guy who might be the type to work for IBM, or something."

"Are you really sure you didn't see his license plate?"

Tina hesitated. "Yes, and no. I had every chance to in our bright headlights . . . maybe I even *did* see it, but I didn't think to take it down. He drove off. I told Russell once again, 'It's really too dark to appreciate the view. Let's just go home.' I mean by now, I was a tired pregnant lady, you know?"

Tedesco chuckled.

"Russell said, 'One more stop, just after the Golden Gate Bridge—Vista Point!' By now it's about going on midnight. I really was not entertained, but off he drove to Vista Point. It was on the way home anyway!"

"Now this is where the chase began . . . if I remember correctly from the officer's report."

"Yes! We took the exit after crossing the Golden Gate Bridge. Russell drove south across the parking lot, to look for a place to pull in, when we saw the same man in the weird, old white car. He was parked right next to a black Mercedes Benz. He was the only one around, except for a couple standing out by the shore looking at the view of the water and the Golden Gate. They were standing facing each other, clasping their hands, as if he was going to propose or something."

"What happened then?" Tedesco asked.

"He was leaving his car, and reaching into his left pocket for what seemed to be a gun, when he saw us. He was suddenly terrified. He must have thought we were plain-clothes police or something. He immediately turned on his heel, jumped quickly back into his car, and started it up. Russell looped around for a closer look. We were right in front of him, maybe twenty feet away. Then Russell said, 'That's the Zodiac . . . let's get him!'

The Zodiac guy dashed back to his car, started it, and rushed through the entrance, not an exit, forcing himself through it to get back on the freeway as fast as he could. Russell and I followed. The chase began there. We chased him up over 100 miles per hour, but he stayed way out in front. The old car was a disguise, just like him. Apparently it was souped up with a big engine designed for the escape."

"Interesting! What happened next?"

"We pursued him. I was straining to see the license plate. Usually, I can see small print even at night . . . but he was driving so fast. Just when I thought I could see it, a car changed lanes and got right in front of us blocking my view. Russell immediately slowed to avert a crash. The Zodiac guy then took the advantage, accelerated and shot way ahead. All of a sudden, we realized we could no longer see him, and figured he took one of the four exits up ahead. That's when we got off the freeway, and took the Highway Patrol exit on the right. Was that ever a welcome sight!" Tina exclaimed.

Tedesco paused. "Most people who think they've seen the Zodiac . . . Well, we feel they have *not* seen him. But we definitely think that was who you saw last night," Tedesco said to her in a serious tone of voice.

"It seemed to be for sure! I am an artist of sorts. I could draw a sketch of the face of the man, and send it to you?"

"That would be most helpful!"

"I should send it to . . ." She wrote down the address.

"I should mention all the police cars and Highway Patrol combed the area last night looking for him, but no luck. It sounds like he must have been traveling at high speed and was just about ten minutes ahead of any surveillance net we dropped at about 12:30 a.m."

"Sounds like it. You were looking for the right car, weren't you? It was a white car with a red stripe down each side?"

"Yes. I was only testing you!"

Tina laughed. "Okay! One important thing, though: I think you should talk the police department into keeping this out of the papers. I think he believed we saw his license plate, and everything he was doing. If we keep letting him think that . . . he will lay low."

"Good point. I'll see what I can do. And one more thing . . ." Tedesco paused.

"Yes?"

"I'm not a particularly religious man, but I think it was a very good idea you spent two hours in that 'angel church' before you went chasing the Zodiac Killer around the city!"

Tina laughed, "I think you're right. It was kind of like divine providence, though. We'd never been there before. Amazing, huh? I'll send you the artwork on the face of the 'mystery man' within a couple of days, okay?"

"Great! I'll be in touch on a few more details soon. Thanks for your help."

"Okay . . . Good-bye for now." Tina hung up. "What time is it? I've got to get started on my day! It's a good thing Yvonne is already over at Mom's." Tina trailed upstairs in her nighty toward the shower.

Later, Tina spent the day at home away from the studio. Evening had come, and dinner was already on the stove. Tina heard Russell drive up, and soon he appeared, putting his briefcase down. He immediately noticed Tina sketching.

"Hi, honey . . . what are you doing?" Russell wondered.

"I am sketching the face of the mystery man . . . the Zodiac." Russell came over to look.

"Hey, you're good!" he smiled approvingly. "That does look like him."

"Does it? I don't think I could ever get the ears just right . . . " mumbled Tina, struggling with accuracy. "Sergeant Tedesco from the San Francisco Police Department called today. I went through the whole story with him."

"Great, honey!" Russell continued to watch her sketch the face.

"It also looks a lot like the 1969 sketch I saw in the paper that Sunday morning. He's a little older in your sketch," Russell commented.

"Well, he would be . . . about nine years. Where *is* that paper? I want to see that sketch," said Tina. Russell glanced around.

"Oh, I don't know, Tina."

"It's got to be around here somewhere" Tina frowned, feeling a little agitated. Russell walked over and looked through some newspapers.

"It should be here, but I don't see it," said Russell.

"*Honey!*"

"Don't sweat it, Tina. Maybe it's better if you don't see it."

"I'm just curious."

Russell walked over to the stove. "Is this dinner? I'm starved." He served himself up some dinner as they talked. Tina brought her sketch pad and came over to sit with him at the table.

"By the way, is that Lamaze class this week?

"Thursday night . . ."

"Okay . . . good, because I have an important meeting with the men at the church Wednesday night."

"Just think, our baby girl will be here in mid-February! Maybe even on Valentine's Day!" Tina beamed.

"Are you sure it's a girl?"

"Yep. That test at the doctor's office never fails!"

"If you say so, Tina! Just don't buy too many pink things until after the baby is actually born."

"Okay, Russell," Tina sighed. She continued sketching. The drawing of the face was finished that evening.

A few days later, the kitchen phone rang. Tina answered.

"Hello, Tina . . . Sergeant Tedesco here. I wanted to call and let you know that we got your sketch of the man you think was the Zodiac, the man you and your husband saw last Sunday night."

"Yes . . . ?"

"It looks just like other drawings we have, done by people who say they saw him leaving the scene of the crime."

"Great . . ." Tina beamed. "It looks like we are on to something!"

"Yes, but until he surfaces again, we're frozen."

"Like I said—this story needs to stay quiet. I noticed there was nothing in the papers."

"Yes, I convinced them to keep the police report out of the papers for the sake of public safety," Tedesco replied. "You know that Zodiac . . . He watches daily what the papers say about him."

"Thank you! But I'll tell you what I did see—an article in the *San Francisco Chronicle*. I saw it at the grocery store. Some reporter said the threats for the Zodiac Killer to return and kill last weekend must have been from an imposter, because nobody turned up dead!"

Tedesco laughed, "I see."

Tina continued, "Well, we know *why* nobody turned up dead. Once he saw he wasn't alone around those couples, he moved on. Those last two couples—they escaped being blown away by sheer milliseconds."

"Sounds like it. Listen, I'll keep you posted if there are any new developments or anyone we need to have you take a look at, and you will do the same for me?"

"Of course I will!"

"Good-bye, and thanks. You and your husband are very courageous people."

February 12, 1979

It was a sunny February day at the Martinez Community Hospital. The Alternative Birth Center in the local hospital was the choice for the birth of their new daughter. Tina and Russell were in the hospital bed, queen size, with their new baby girl, Linda Suzanne. The stained glass lamp and the antique rocking chair added extra warmth to the room. Tina held her new baby tenderly as Russell looked on, smiling.

"She's a *ten* for sure! Nine pounds, two ounces . . . and look at all that hair!" Russell said proudly.

"It's definitely better if they gain weight after they are born. That was hard work!" Tina grinned.

"You were great, honey!"

"Linda Suzanne . . . I like that name. The sisters have the same middle names now."

"Look at you in the maternity ward, running around in your pajamas." Tina laughed.

"It's kind of fun to visit with all these new moms." Russell grinned happily.

"Mom is going to be staying at the house for a few days, helping with housework and with Yvonne."

"Speaking of Yvonne, isn't your Mom due in here with her any minute?" Russell wondered.

They heard a "knock, knock" . . . at their door. It was Grandma Ruby, with eight-year-old Yvonne, who just had a birthday that December.

"*Ruby!*" Russell remarked, greeting her as Yvonne entered carrying a large stuffed bear with a big green bow around its neck for the new baby. Tina glowed when she saw them.

"Mom . . . Hi, Yvonne. Look at that bear!" Tina said reaching out to hug her little girl.

"It's for the baby . . ." Yvonne smiled. "I named him 'Greg, the bear.'" She sat it on the bed by Tina and the infant, her new little sister, wrapped in a blanket.

"Thanks, honey. Did you pick that out?" Yvonne nodded proudly.

Ruby laughed. "Russell looks so funny in the maternity ward here, running around in his pajamas!"

"He's been pretty good at ordering the nurses around too!" A nurse entered with two iced drinks, fruit punch, for Tina and Russell.

"For the parents," the nurse smiled. They visited as a happy family group for a while longer. It seemed like time stood still that afternoon in a special sort of bliss. For that moment, any thoughts of the man called "The Zodiac" were far, far away.

CHAPTER FIVE

TIME MOVES ON

Tina and Russell's House—1985

It was a beautiful day with blue skies smiling over beautiful Benicia by the Bay. The fog had long since burned off and the friendly blue skies appeared. The sun shone brightly on the water in the distance, as the sailboats shared the straits with the oil tanker ships travelling to ports all over the USA and beyond. Tina walked up to the front door with "Lindy," whose sixth birthday was that day.

They walked inside, already expecting a small crowd. Tina's Mom, and some family friends and cousins were there for Lindy's party. New to the group was Lindy's three year old sister, Kerry Lee, born in 1982. Yvonne was now 13 years old and already acting like a teenager.

The partygoers, led by Grandma Ruby, joyously sang, "Happy Birthday" to Lindy.

Lindy's face lit up with smiles, much like the candles on the cake. The birthday group of about twelve friends and family came over and gathered around Tina and Lindy, as Tina sat with her daughter by the birthday cake. Tina had a bevy of girl cousins near Lindy's age, and a little older, who were about eight and ten years old.

"Kerry Lee, come sit with Grandma. You just had a birthday the end of December. Do you remember how old you are?" Little Kerry Lee held up three fingers.

"Look Lindy, six big candles . . ." Tina smiled at Lindy, as Grandma Ruby carefully lit them.

"Get ready to blow them out . . . but first make a wish! Do you have a special wish?" Tina asked her. Lindy grinned, closed her eyes for a moment to think it over, then nodded, "Yes."

"*Big breath!*" Lindy blew out all the candles. The happy group applauded.

"Very good, honey! You get your wish. Are you going to tell your wish?"

Lindy hesitated to say it, then laughed a little. "I wished for lots of presents!" Tina laughed.

"Oh well! Terry, can you bring them in from the bedroom? Sherry and Yvonne will help!" The girls returned with twelve wrapped boxes with bows.

"Oooooh!" Lindy squealed.

"Which one do you want to start with? She reached for one, as her mom helped using scissors. It was a Candy Land game.

"Candy Land . . . your favorite! Oh Lindy, look—now you don't have to go over to Elizabeth's house when you want to play Candy Land!"

The TV was on in another room. Russell was on the phone, but was just getting off.

Tina entered with Lindy, as a few older kids followed. "I wondered where you were . . ."

"Sorry, honey. It was the new Station Manager, Rob Moore. It looks like I'll have to go in later on and direct the *California Tonight* program, and then stay late and do some editing. There are some programs that have to get on the air by next Monday."

"Well at least my segments are done!" Tina said, happily. "How did you like my story with the Panda bears at the San Francisco Zoo?"

"It was golden! It seemed that we were the only station that got that kind of footage with the Panda bears. You feeding them their bamboo at the end of the story was very cute, too . . . *Primo!* Great ending!"

"They didn't come out of their cave for any other of the Bay Area TV stations . . . only for me," Tina beamed proudly.

"What? How did you pull that off . . . Just luck, or what?"

"Not luck. I prayed before we got there. I said, 'God, you brought those animals two by two into the ark for Noah, so please talk to those bears before I get there, and bring them out!'"

"*What?* That's amazing!"

"When I got in front of the Panda bear habitat with the crew, the bears poked their heads out as if they were expecting me, and came right down. They were rolling around on the ground holding their paws, and acting like clowns. The zookeeper was amazed. He told me that nobody else got really great footage like that." Tina grinned proudly.

"Wow . . . '*Tina power!*'"

"No, it was a '*God thing*.' No doubt in my mind."

"Thanks Tina. Who would have ever thought to ask God to bring the Panda bears down? You brought in the best footage of all for our station!"

"My pleasure. Are you coming in to the party now?"

"Sure . . ." Russell suddenly caught the comments on the TV news, and stopped. The TV news commentator spoke.

"Reviewing the new 'Zodiac story:' Someone painted graffiti-like symbols on a building in Vallejo after a new book on the 'Zodiac Killer' had just come out earlier this month. Hear more on this story in just a moment." Shortly, after a commercial break, the newscast continued as they all listened further.

"A building in industrial park in Vallejo has been painted with the Zodiac and other cryptic like symbols of witchcraft, after a new book was just released chronicling the various stories and cases surrounding the phantom killer. The book about the Zodiac, just released earlier this month, leaves the question open, 'Is he still out there?' Apparently someone wants you believe he is . . . or maybe he *really is?* This is Ted Smith reporting from Channel 10 news." Tina looked inquisitively over at Russell.

"Russell, he wouldn't risk reappearing over something like that, now would he?"

"I doubt it . . . probably just some kids playing pranks. Maybe you should call the Vallejo Police and set them straight sometime soon." Russell winked.

"Well, maybe I will. Come on everybody, back into the dining room where the party is!"

Tina and Russell walked back into the dining room. Some of the older kids had already heard part of the news story.

"Grandma, we just heard the news on TV . . . the Zodiac . . . he's back!" Sherry said, looking suddenly scared.

"Now, Sherry, that's not what the newsman said," Tina remarked dryly.

"I don't think that's what he meant," Grandma Ruby agreed.

"Tina always notices the new stories about the Zodiac . . . because of the past connection," Russell smiled.

"And *you* don't have a past connection? You were the maniac driver that night chasing him. I was just the pregnant lady in the driver's seat!"

"I just thought we could get his license plate number," he reminded her.

"Well, God knows we tried. I mean, I shudder to think how different the story might have turned out, with just a few moments one way or another. We could have been one of the couples he was stalking!"

"You were being protected by a band of angels, remember?" Grandma Ruby said.

"Yes . . . we were." Tina was suddenly overcome with a solemn reverence.

"Never in my life was I so glad we didn't skip church!" Russell chuckled. "So what do you make of this latest report of his 'appearing'?"

"*Kid's pranks*. It has to be. He would never risk reappearing over something so petty. The stakes are too high," Tina answered. Russell cut more birthday cake, as he listened.

"I tend to agree with that."

"I want to tell my teacher and my class that you chased the Zodiac killer," said Terry, the other little cousin. Tina knew she needed to successfully impress the children not to talk about the Zodiac secret. It could potentially be a danger to both them and others.

"Kids . . . listen to me. Come over here, all of you." About eight school-aged children from about eight to twelve years old gathered around "Aunt Tina." Tina held Kerry Lee on her lap.

"You have to promise me . . . do not talk about this with your friends at school, or friends anywhere. Do not ever tell your class or your friends or your teacher that Mommy and Daddy, or Aunt and Uncle, chased the Zodiac."

"But *why*, Aunt Tina?" Sherry asked with an imploring look.

"*Because, he might still be out there*! The last thing he needs to hear is that we, who chased him that night, never did actually see the license plate. Got that?" The children gathered around Tina, bug-eyed.

"I think it's time to tackle the kitchen!" Russell said to break the tension. "I'll help," Grandma Ruby said as she brought over some of the plates, and party decorations.

***

In a home located somewhere in the East Bay area, a young boy about twelve, was carefully walking up some stairs to an attic. It was dark, and he acted as if he did not see clearly at first. He slowly and cautiously opened the attic door and walked in. His young hands paged through newspaper clippings about the death of his grand-father. He was wearing a family tiger eye ring that belonged to his Grandpa, Tony Smith. How many cases did his grandfather solve while wearing the ring? He wondered picking up an obituary notice listed in the newspaper, and a picture of his Grandpa in an old frame. He gazed at it fondly.

Then he picked up an old brief case, and blew off the dust and opened it. His fingers paged through folders and papers. The boy stopped. He suddenly saw a folder, which read: "The Zodiac—Latest Evidence." Another read: "Latest sightings." And then a red folder with a tab that read, "Death by drowning . . . Santa Barbara, CA."

The boy stopped. His hands were paging anxiously through the papers. His young face, lit only by one dim light bulb in the attic, shone with excitement, he had discovered something big. He closed the door and studied the material for hours. In the dark, only a light from the attic shone from the boy's house. It was very late, way past his bedtime. He would return to the "secret place" another time.

***

A few weeks passed. Russell and Tina were very active in the Young Marrieds group in their church. Tina decided they should go to the potluck dinner they had on the schedule at Jenny and Bob's there in the neighborhood. Tina prepared her favorite casserole for the event.

"Russell, are you almost ready?" She called out up the stairs. "I've got this casserole out of the oven, and we need to get going pretty soon!" Shortly, Russell appeared from upstairs, walking into the kitchen.

"Are you sure you want to go to this 'Young Marrieds' potluck tonight? We could have gone out just the two of us to La Verage. It's your favorite French restaurant."

"Russell, I'm surprised at you. Sometimes we just need to go out and be with some of the other couples from our church. You like Jenny and Bob, don't you?"

"Yes, I like Jenny and Bob . . ."

"Well, it's at their house. Let's go." Tina loaded her casserole dish into a box, and walked toward the door with Russell.

Russell and Tina arrived at Jenny and Bob's home. About thirty other people were already there from the 'Young Marrieds' group. Jenny greeted them.

"Tina and Russell—it's so great to see you! Oh, just put the casserole right here. Does it need to be warmed up?"

"It's still pretty warm, I think." Bob spotted Russell and walked over.

"Hey, Russell . . . how's it going? You know, I have been thinking about volunteering for the media department at the church."

"Sure, Bob . . . We can always use a few new people." Another acquaintance, Ralph, walked over to talk to Russell. He was about 35, and worked for the police department.

"Hey, Russell, it's good to see you!"

"Hey, Ralph, how is it going with the new job? Is it the Richmond Police Department?"

"Yes, but we've been doing a lot of interfacing with the Oakland Police lately. *Busy.*"

Their group of friends were moving around, talking and visiting as they were dishing up the various potluck foods, main dishes and desserts, getting situated to sit down and eat.

"Okay, who wants to say the blessing over the food? Russell, what about you?"

"Sure." Russell smiled, then bowed his head, and began a short prayer: "Dear Lord, thank you for this food, and the many people who brought and prepared it. Thank you that we had a blessed and safe day, and can sit down and enjoy this meal all together tonight. Amen."

"Amen! You don't know how much I appreciated that prayer. I had a very close call out on patrol today!"

"Did you? Like what?"

"A big dude about four hundred pounds tried to pull a knife on me, but luckily my patrol partners, Rob and Joe were prepared. We brought him under control pretty fast, and threw some handcuffs on him. But it was pretty tense there for a while."

"I don't envy what you guys go through on the job."

"You guys never know from day to day who or what you will run into."

"Who knows? Maybe one day you'll run smack dab into the Zodiac Killer or something!"

Tina froze at the comment.

"You know for years there has been a rumor out there among police circles that the Zodiac was found dead somewhere . . . that he possibly even *killed himself.*"

Tina's eyes got big as she listened, chewing her food. She glanced over at Russell.

"You mean they think he committed suicide?" he asked Ralph.

"Yeah. I don't know any more than that. It's probably just a rumor."

"Yeah, probably just a rumor," Russell agreed.

At the end of the evening about ten o'clock, Tina and Russell were back in their car driving home.

"So, what do you think about what Ralph said about the Zodiac killing himself?"

"Who knows? It doesn't sound like there is any evidence to support it. If it was a real story, it would have been plastered all over the news."

"Really? Our story was real, and it wasn't plastered all over the news."

"Now, honey, you worked really hard to prevent that, remember?"

"Yes, I did, didn't I?" Tina sighed, as they continued the drive home.

The TV Production Years

It was a normal bustling morning in the George household. The clock on the kitchen wall read 7:30 a.m. Tina was busily packing lunches for her husband and their two school-aged girls. She carefully checked the hot cereal on the stove. Tina wore high heels and a dress and was ready for another work day at the TV station.

"Russell, are you going to come down here and eat this hot cereal or are you going to embarrass me and try to eat from a bowl with a spoon while driving?" Russell appeared, wearing a short-sleeved dress shirt, with a tie and dress pants.

"Honey, give me just a minute. Let me peek at those segments in the office here really quick! I have two shows to direct this morning, and I'm not sure which video segment we're using in the programs."

"Am I in it?"

"Not this time. I think we'll use the story about the family from Sacramento . . . the re-enactment we filmed about two weeks ago," Russell decided.

"Oh yeah, great story! What a day that was. We lost a camera battery, and almost couldn't finish filming." Tina winced, remembering back to the day.

The local Sacramento station, what a lifesaver they were, giving us one! Tina, is the coffee ready? I'm going to take it with us when we go."

"You know when you went from plant engineering to TV engineering, did you notice how much crazier our lives got?"

"Since our building materials company got taken over by Gen Star IV, and the new company fired all the current management and put in their management, a sudden career change had to happen, honey. I think we are handling it very well, actually."

"Well, all those years we gave on Sunday to the morning broadcast at church in the production studio is paying off now. At least we had something to transition to."

"Listen, you're having fun being sort of a TV personality on the *California Tonight* show. Don't tell me you're not. So where are you and Greg, the video shooter, off to this week?"

"Today I'm just doing some 'man on the street' interviews. I still have to finish making up my questions. What time is it? Maybe I can work on them while you're driving over. Before the week is out, we're getting over to the San Francisco Hilton to do a segment on the arrival home of the Bay area Olympic Gold medal winners.

They'll be receiving them home with a local parade, then after that I'll do the interviews with them at the hotel. You'll love that one!"

Lindy and Kerry Lee rushed in, sat at the table, and poured cereal into their bowls. Yvonne, their big sister, followed.

"Where are those protein flakes, Mom?" Yvonne asked.

"Right here! Hey girls, let's get some milk for you." She then went back to Russell's comment. "Yes, I'm sure you will enjoy that 'Olympic Athletes Returning Home Story'! I understand from the hotel staff that they're setting up a very nice interview area for me in one of the grand ballrooms with a view of the bay over our shoulder."

"Very good! Let me know when you get that story done. I want to air it right at the top of the show."

"Okay! How is everybody doing here? Lunches are packed. We need to be leaving here by 8:15 everybody!"

"I'm okay, Mom. I have my lunch," Yvonne said. "I'm leaving for school now. See you later."

"Remember to go over to Mrs. Palmer's house after school. I won't be home until about 5:30 tonight."

"Okay, Mom. Love you!"

The family loaded into the car parked in the driveway. Their family car, a late model light silver Buick Skylark, gleamed in the sunlight. It was purchased brand new the week Lindy was born. Everybody was busily putting their stuff in the car. Tina had notebooks and her briefcase. The kids had their backpacks for Grandma's house after school.

"Russell, give me a minute." Tina said as she tried to negotiate her seatbelt. Russell pulled out quickly, and darted off down a steep hill toward the freeway entrance. Tina struggled to get belted.

"I don't know what's the matter with this seatbelt! Russell, could you wait just a minute?"

"I don't want to be late! We have to gather in the studio at 8:30 a.m. for a meeting . . . *8:30 sharp!*"

"Well, at least this morning you are not driving while trying to eat a bowl of hot cereal at the same time," Tina said, looking relieved.

"I do okay. Have I ever had a wreck doing that?"

"Well, let's not find out!"

Soon Russell, Tina, and the family had rolled safely into the parking lot of KYTN–Channel 10–Central Christian Broadcasting Network. The family emerged from the car, and soon went inside.

They all walked into the entry of the TV studio reception area. The kid's Grandpa Henry was waiting for them. Lindy and Kerry Lee were happy to see him.

"Grandpa!"

"Hey, are you ready to go?"

"See you later! Have a good day at Grandma's and Grandpa's," Tina said waving good-bye. Lindy and Kerry Lee went off with their Grandpa Henry, just like so many other mornings.

Tina and Russell walked into the administration area, then the production building. The technical staff busily rushed here and there getting ready to begin a new taping in the main studio.

"I need to go meet the crew."

"Let me stop by my desk, and I'll get out to the studio in a few minutes, and see how they're doing," said Tina.

Tina walked to her cubicle and desk near the production area, then put her purse and briefcase down. She had a thought, grabbed the phone book, opened it, and paged through it.

"Vallejo Police Department," she sighed. "Oh, maybe later."

Russell was in the master control and technical directing area. The sign above read:

California Tonight, Technical Dir. Russell George. Russell was on the headphones, talking to the crew.

"Les, I need a sound level out there. Is everybody 'miked up'?" Russell asked. Tina walked through the dark room toward the door. Everybody was at their posts, looking at the monitors revealing the set, the talent, three studio cameras, and staff in an adjacent production building. She exited toward the other neighboring production building, and walked across the parking lot, entering the studio where the program was about to begin. Bea, an older Hispanic woman about 60, who was one of the set coordinators, and sometimes, floor director, approached. She wore her floor-director headset.

"Hello Bea!" Tina smiled.

"Tina, how are you? Good morning!" Bea smiled politely. The host and talent were seated on the set, and the program was soon to begin taping.

"Is everything going okay over here? Is everybody on the set miked up? Russell was trying to get a sound check. How is the lighting?" She looked up, and glanced around the set. "Are the techs all finished? We want to roll in about five minutes," Tina said insistently.

"I think we're close," Bea said, looking at her watch.

"Well, we're not live like tonight at 8:00, but it's a good dry run for tonight. Some of the talent who came in early this morning have planes to catch later, about mid-day," Tina reminded her.

Jenny, another young floor director and producer, talked with the talent on the set. "Hi, Tina! I think we are about ready to go." She was on her headset, communicating with the technical staff. Russell, how are we looking on your side?" Jenny asked, waiting for his instructions.

Russell's voice came across on the headset to the crew. "We are still balancing the lighting. Where's that white card?" A young set tech put up the white card for Russell and the camera crew to set the "white balance."

"Okay, Jenny, you and Bea have it all very well under control over here. I'm going back over," remarked Tina, walking toward the administration building.

Tina entered back through the door to her production desk area. "Okay . . . they will be well on the way into the show in a few minutes!" she said, talking to herself as she sat down at her desk. "Let's see, we have ten shows of *Your Health Today*, set to roll next week." she sighed, as she looked over the files. The phone book on her desk was still open. "You know, let me make this call while it's on my mind." She dialed the number.

"Vallejo Police Department."

"Can I talk to your chief investigator?" Tina asked.

"That would be Sergeant Harmon. What is this regarding?" a voice on the phone asked.

"The latest Zodiac activity . . . the writings on the buildings."

"Do you have new evidence?" the woman asked.

"Maybe," mused Tina. "Can you just let me talk to him?"

"Hold on, please." Soon a man's voice came on the line.

"Sergeant Harmon, here. Can I help you?"

"Hello, this is Tina George. I live in Benicia."

"How can I help you, Tina?"

"I have noticed in the news that there has been some new Zodiac activity in the form of writings on some buildings in Vallejo as a result of the new book that's out about him," Tina explained.

"Yes, that's under investigation, ma'am. What do you know?" the officer asked.

"That for sure he would not come out and risk making any sort of appearance over anything that small."

"Oh, really? Now why would you say that?" Sergeant Harmon asked. Tina took a deep breath.

"Well, I have not yet talked to you on this Zodiac case yet. I haven't talked too much to anyone since our big chase situation back in October in 1978 . . . I mean it is now 1986."

"Big chase?"

"I don't know if you were aware that the man who was the Zodiac announced to the *San Francisco* in mid-October of '78 that he would strike and kill over the weekend . . . that Sunday."

"I remember something like that," Officer Harmon replied.

"As it turned out, my husband and I were over there and wound up in a late-night chase with him as he left the scene of the crime, like the third time."

"Left the scene of the crime?"

"I mean, it was *almost* the scene of the crime. We saw him stalking couples in three locations. After he was about to gun down a couple at the third location, we broke into a chase leaving Vista Point on the other side of the Golden Gate Bridge. Really, the San Francisco Police know all about this. It's on record."

"Really? Who was chasing *whom,* if I might ask?"

"We were chasing *him*, actually."

"Really? Now that's a switch."

"Initially, we were just trying to see his license plate number," Tina explained.

"Well, *did* you?" Officer Harmon asked.

"Yes, and no. A car got right in front of us just when I could have seen it! I saw it earlier when he was turning around at the second stop, but wasn't watching for it, as far as writing it down."

"Oh, too bad . . ." The officer responded in disappointed tones. "Would you agree to hypnosis?"

"Oh, stop it!" Tina laughed.

"That's really too bad! You were so close!" he said. Tina heard him tap his pen.

"Yeah, I know! Listen, I went all through this with the San Francisco Police. They have had the story on record since the first night it happened. I drew them a new drawing of the face too. They agreed to keep it out of the papers that we never got the license plate number as a matter of public safety. The Zodiac has laid low all these years. I know he would not re-appear over something this petty. The stakes are too high."

"I see . . . Well, you may be right. We have a handwriting expert working on it right now. We'll know something in a few days. You can call back if you like."

"I will . . . I think I will. Just remember what I said. He has been laying low since that night . . . no more murders. It would be nice to keep it that way?"

"Yes, it would. And, ma'am, for the record, if you could leave some contact details with my assistant, I would appreciate it."

"Sure thing," Tina agreed.

A TV production tech walked in while Tina was on the phone giving her information. Chet called out, and motioned to her to return to the studio.

"Tina, Russell says he needs you on the set. Bea needs to take a break."

"OK Chet . . . I'll be right there.

After a long production day, Russell and Tina drove back home with the kids after work. They enjoyed the view of the Bay as they drove home over the Benicia Bridge. The view of the sun setting on the water, and the white and rainbow-colored sails of dozens of sailboats which dotted the bay, was breathtaking.

The commute was only about twenty minutes when they finally arrived in the driveway of their home in Southampton. Tina and the kids got out, and Russell followed. Dinner was soon in the making.

Tina whipped together a quick meal, and before long the family settled in around the table, enjoying some of her slow-cooked chicken.

"Thank goodness for Crock-Pots!" She grinned, tossing the bones onto another plate.

"Good dinner, honey. I like those green beans and parsley red potatoes too."

"I'm going to pack the leftovers in those little microwaveable containers, and stack them in the fridge, and we'll be set for a few days!"

"Aren't you *clever!*"

"I've been listening to Joan—that news anchorwoman out of New York—give tips on *Good Morning USA*—- about how to manage family life, cooking, etc., while trying to do a job like this. Sometimes she has really great ideas!"

"Yes, it's sometimes challenging. It's not always dinner at six with the family," Russell admitted.

"Well, tonight it is." Tina smiled.

"Tina, I may still have to go back tonight. I have editing to get done."

"Oh, is this going to be another 3 a.m. thing?"

"I don't know. You know how it is. They put shows in the *TV Guide,* and we don't even have them edited yet." Russell said, shaking his head.

"I am beginning to dread that magazine being delivered to my desk each week. I'm afraid to look in it. Joe called from the *TV*

Guide Today magazine last week. He said to me, 'Tina, I need a three-line description for *Your Health Today* shows.' I said, 'You know, I'm editing it, so I'll give it to you right now.'" Then he asked about the Valentine show we did with the couples that we just made into a special feature. He asked me, 'What is the title of the show?' I said, 'I will finish editing it after lunch. I'm still deciding. I'll tell you what . . . I'll give you three choices. Call me back in an hour.'"

"So what did we call that program?"

"That's the *Love Speaks* program, darling. You'll have to give it a listen sometime!"

The girls finished their meal as Lindy looked up from her dinner plate.

"May I be excused?"

"Us too. We want to play with our Barbie townhouse upstairs," Kerry Lee said.

"Correction, you and Lindy want to play with the Barbie Townhouse. I have homework to do," said Yvonne, taking her plate over to the dishwasher.

"Okay, girls." They scurried off. Tina stood up and picked up the plates and glasses.

"You know, I talked to a Sergeant Harmon at the Vallejo Police Department about this latest episode with the Zodiac writings all over the buildings with the cryptic Satanist lingo, you know."

"What did he say?" asked Russell, cocking an eyebrow in curiosity.

"He listened. He wanted our contact info. But I sense they're getting really distant to feeling that we're still being considered as any sort of expert on the case, at least not like before. You know it's been a few years now. I don't think these new people take me seriously . . . take *our* story seriously. Not like they used to, anyway. I mean, we do know exactly what the guy *looks* like."

"Yes, that should be worth something. But don't get too wrapped up in it," Russell warned. "This story has been out there for years, and who knows if it will ever be solved?"

"You're telling me." Tina laughed.

CHAPTER SIX

SECRET EVIDENCE GATHERED

Back in the home in the East Bay area, the boy wearing the tiger ring, now a teen, returned to his "secret place" often, spending hours discovering new and hidden facts known only by his grandfather. He was especially curious about the file about the death by drowning and found himself wondering why the things he had discovered there never had been brought out to solve the Zodiac case.

***

The next morning in the North Bay, it was the beginning of a busy day at KYTN–Channel 10–Central Christian Broadcasting. Inside the main production building everybody was on the set about to begin. The floor director talked to the host and talent on the set, while Tina walked through the studio with her folder. One of the producers, Gary, gave her a nod and a smile.

"'Morning, Tina. How are you?" Gary asked with a friendly nod.

"Good. Are we about ready to roll?" asked Tina brightly, looking at her production paperwork.

"Yes. Bea is into the studio countdown right now."

The opening music came on, and the show's introduction played on the monitors. The camera crew was on the studio floor getting ready, as they lined up their shots. Tina could hear Russell distantly on the headset.

"Camera one, frame up that opening shot on Larry. We're coming into the studio in five seconds!"

The monitors picked up the opening scene, as the host, Larry Bingham, opened the program.

"Hello, and welcome to our latest edition of *Open Forum*. Tina checked over her list on a clipboard. "Today our special guests are coming to us from the San Francisco City Council." Tina nodded to the tech staff.

"I'm going back over to the other building." Tina exited the main production building, and headed across the parking lot.

Tina soon emerged on the other side, walking through the editing area. She spotted Russell on the headset in the master control area, but walked by and sat at her desk for a few moments. The phone rang. It was the receptionist.

"Tina I have a call for you from the Vallejo Police . . . a Sergeant Harmon. Can you take it now?"

"Sure. Put him through." A man's voice on phone answered. "Hello, is this Tina George?"

"Yes, hello," Tina answered.

"Sergeant Harmon here."

"Did you find out anything new?" Tina wondered.

"I'm calling you back because I thought you would want to know that the handwriting expert discovered the new writings on the buildings to be that of an imposter," he admitted.

"I knew that!" Tina responded pertly.

"Well, I thought you would want to now it's now official. You'll be hearing it announced on the six o'clock news tonight."

"Thank you so much for calling…"

"Sure thing. Good-bye," the officer said.

Tina put the phone down. She smiled, and rose up from her desk, walking toward the production area, while talking to herself.

"I knew it!"

Driving home after work, Tina and Russell talked alone in the car. The colorful pink and golden sunset reflected on the water of the bay as they drove home over the bridge.

"It's kind of nice the kids are staying over at Mom's for a couple days. It kind of gives us a nice little break."

"It sure does!"

"Just like my news anchor friend in New York. She couldn't do it without her folks stepping in either!"

"I'm sure her husband appreciates it too," Russell responded, warmly. "Listen, I got a callback from the Vallejo Police Department today."

"Yeah?"

"The so-called returning Zodiac . . . He was an *imposter.*"

"Oh yeah? Tina strikes again!" Russell laughed.

"Sergeant Harmon said the handwriting expert determined the so-called Zodiac writings were not authentic. The police and the *San Francisco Chronicle* have quite a few handwriting samples from him, you know."

"Yes, by now, I'm sure they do. What do you think happened to him? Where do you think he disappeared to?"

"I don't know. He could be laying low in South America, or he could be the check-out guy in the supermarket downtown. He could be the postman. It's hard to say. One thing is for sure: He believes we got his license plate number, and he has disappeared since that night . . . *Not a trace.*"

They finally pulled up into the driveway of their home. Russell looked at Tina, a romantic twinkle in his eye.

"Well, since we have a break from the kids, what do you say to a little candlelight dinner, my dear?"

"That sounds lovely! Who's doing the cooking?"

"I will fire up the grill, and cook the steaks if you make the other stuff."

"It's a deal!" She gave Russell a lingering kiss.

***

Meanwhile, in a house far away in another part of the Bay area, the hands of a high school aged youth anxiously looked through papers in the dim lighting of his attic. He was wearing the same gold heirloom ring with the tiger-eye stone that his grandfather wore. Suddenly, he found something new and important. He pulled a chain string that lit up a light bulb nearby, bringing greater illumination. The youth held the paper up to the light to study it in more detail. It appeared to be a photograph of some kind. Hope filled his face. Had he finally found the answer to the mystery he was searching for?

Benicia, California, 1988

The sun shone brightly on the water in the North Bay as Tina and Russell drove swiftly over the bridge on the way to work at the KTYN broadcast center in Concord. The white seagulls soared high in the sky over the sailboats in the Bay, once again making a beautiful view over the blue waters of the Carquinez Straits.

The day started off like normal with a group meeting inside the main studio. Studio cameras were parked in the background, as they sat in a circle of about twenty members of staff and technicians.

There was always a devotional before the business meeting. This time it was led by Jenny, one of the young production assistants who attended the same church as Tina and Russell. She greeted the group, opened her Bible, and read a passage from Luke. "These are the words of Jesus: 'No one lights a lamp and hides it! Instead, he puts it on a lampstand to give light to all who enter the room. Your eyes light up your inward being. A pure eye lets sunshine into your soul. A lustful eye shuts out the light and plunges you into darkness. So watch out that the sunshine is not blotted out. If you are filled with light from within, with no dark corners, then your face will be radiant too, as if a floodlight is beamed upon you.' This passage is from Luke 11:33-36. I like that Living Bible translation, don't you? We are putting a great light on a hill to the world with the programming from this station! We are broadcasting that 'light' out not only locally and regionally, but around the world! The same goes for our personal lives, including the way we work together here among ourselves. Let's not forget what we stand for and continue to be patient with one another, especially when things get stressful during production!" The crowd laughed a little, relating to what she said. She shared a few more thoughts and then it was time to start the business meeting.

Rob Moore, the General Manager, stood up to open the meeting. He was a professional-looking man about 45, wearing a dark suit. "Thank you, Jenny! Good morning! I just wanted to touch base on a few things this morning. We'll be changing the combinations to enter the building, so be sure to pick up your new cards from Rochelle at the reception desk by this afternoon. The new studio jackets are in, so be sure and get one in your correct size. The boxes are over in wardrobe in the main studio," he explained, holding up a box. "I also have a bunch of magnets and deflectors here, be sure to pick up yours and wear them in your pockets when you work around the screens, monitors and editing machines in the 'techy' areas."

"Hey, they actually care that we might be getting too much radiation working around the equipment. That's cool!" Tina whispered to Russell. Rob, the General Manager continued his presentation.

"And production staff: You know it's the policy to have at least 22 shows in the 'can' before we start a new series. Some of you will have to work extra hours to be sure those programs get edited and reserved like they are supposed to be. I don't foresee us giving out any bonuses this year the way things stand. If we can raise more money through our marketing, and increase the number of commercials we are doing for some of local merchants . . . particularly the local car dealerships, maybe we'll see things pick up for bonuses by Christmas. We'll just have to pull in the belt. Meanwhile, on the reserve programs, just be as creative as you can in how you schedule your reruns with master control, and Ray at *TV Guide*, and we'll be fine, at least for a while. Anything else? Okay, let's go make TV programs!"

Everyone got up and scattered toward their work stations. Tina was troubled by Rob's comments about the tight budget.

"Rob and his wife sure find the money for those expensive clothes, and 'work trip vacations,' as he calls them!" Tina said to Russell, sounding a bit disgruntled.

"Yes, I know," Russell frowned. Both Tina and Russell were educated in television broadcasting and had given up higher paying opportunities with other major networks. They had longed to create and produce inspirational and family programming. But at times they wondered if their work and efforts were adequately appreciated. It certainly did not reflect in their paychecks. Russell reported to Studio "A" to begin directing the crew in a morning television taping.

An associate, Carol, from the upper administration management, approached Tina. She was a tall, thin, fashionable looking of woman about 35. She was a 'show horse,' as they say, and looked like a model or actress herself.

"Tina, may I have a word with you . . . over here?" Carol motioned for her to step aside.

"Sure . . . What's going on?"

"Listen, ABCN just aired nationally a documentary last night, *'The Zodiac . . . Ten Years Later'* At the end, they re-enacted the scene in which you and Russell chased him. They re-dramatized the scene, and made a strong point that you two were the last ones to see him alive." At the mention of this, Tina became very nervous.

"What? They didn't use our names, I hope!"

"I don't know. I only just heard about it. Of course, Jack works at ABCN."

"Oh yeah . . . your husband, Jack, he's been working there for years now. Well, I hope they didn't reveal our identity. I didn't just twist the arm of the police off all these years to keep this quiet for nothing!" They walked down the hall together, talking.

"How would I find out? I'm not sure I want to see the video . . . Just find out a few simple answers about how they handled it," Tina asked.

"I'm not sure. Maybe Jack knows," Carol replied coolly. They said good-bye, and parted.

Tina rushed nervously over to the master control area where she knew Russell was working.

Russell was currently on the headset with Les in audio, the camera crew, floor director, and lighting staff, getting ready to roll within minutes of a live broadcast. Tina walked over, and bent down close to him, cheek to cheek. She whispered tersely to Russell.

"Russell, can you turn your headset off for just a few seconds? I need to talk to you!"

Russell switched his headset off.

"We're about ten minutes to air!"

"Russell, I just heard from Carol that there was a nationally broadcast documentary on last night produced by ABCN out of San Francisco, *'The Zodiac . . . Ten Years Later.'* They re-enacted us doing the high-speed chase after him leaving Vista Point, like we were the last ones to see him alive." Russell was instantly alarmed. He ripped off his headset.

"What! How would they even know about it?"

Old police records maybe . . . *Carol and Jack maybe?"*

"*That's right!* They are one of the few close friends we talked to about it. Jack works high up on the ladder now at ABCN." Russell frowned. He wiped his face nervously.

"That did occur to me, but I didn't confront her about it."

"That's just great! They didn't reveal our names, or anything, did they?"

"I don't know. I'll try to find out. You know I just don't like collecting things about the Zodiac. I don't really want the video around our home, even if I could get one. There's too much negative demonic energy that comes off anything to do with him."

"That's fine. See what you can find out. I've got to get the show rolling here."

"Okay, honey. I'll look into it."

Tina went back into her office, sat down at her desk, and grabbed the phone.

"ABCN, San Francisco, please. The admin office number," she said nervously. The operator answered.

"ABCN, San Francisco . . . how can I help you?

"Hello. You aired a documentary titled '*The Zodiac . . . Ten Years Later.*' Do you know who the producer of that was? I'm Tina George, a Producer out here for Channel 10 in Concord, in the North Bay," replied Tina, straining to be polite.

"Let me transfer you." Tina nervously waited as she heard the line ringing. Finally she heard a voice.

"Gary Swift, Production."

"Hello, Gary . . . I'm a producer out here in the North Bay for Channel 10, Tina George. Can you tell me who produced '*The Zodiac . . . Ten Years Later*' documentary?" There was a brief pause.

"I'm not sure I know, exactly. It was a joint venture with our local station and our New York station."

"Did you see it?"

"No. Why do you ask?"

"I have a special reason for wanting to know if certain information was revealed."

"Well, I might be able to get someone from our New York station to call you back."

"Can you answer one question? Was a local ABCN staff member involved, Jack Hansen, a Producer from the San Francisco station?"

"I don't know, ma'am. Perhaps our affiliate in New York could answer that for you."

"Who do I ask for out there?"

"Whoever is the Director of Special Productions," Gary answered dryly.

"What? You don't have a name for me?" replied Tina, getting a little upset. "Listen, Gary, I know this may seem a little strange to you, but my husband and I were the ones who chased the Zodiac back in 1978, and I need to find out if our identity was revealed in this documentary!"

"*You* chased the Zodiac?" he laughed. "Maybe it should be *you* who should be producing a documentary. Listen, I am due in a production meeting in about two minutes, if you don't mind."

"Fine, I just thought maybe you could help me." She heard a sudden "click" on the other end of the line. "Hello? Hello?" She looked back at the phone receiver. "Fine!" Tina hung up, feeling a little disgusted. She finished out the day by five, looking forward to going home.

Later that evening, Tina was back at home having dinner with the family. Mealtimes were always a warm time to gather and just talk about what was going on in their lives. As a mom, Tina couldn't help but take a fresh look at her girls.

"You girls are growing up so fast!" Tina said proudly.

"Yes, they are!" their dad agreed. Russell cut the roast beef, and Yvonne politely passed around the green peas and salad.

"So, did you find out anything?" Russell asked, serving himself some salad.

"I'm not so sure we should talk about it right now," Tina replied winking, and nodding toward their kids.

"Oh, I see. Just tell me, was *Jack* involved?" Russell asked, as he lifted a curious eyebrow. He then realized Tina wanted to talk in "code."

"I'm not sure. I was told to call New York, Special Productions. The local guy did not have an answer for me," Tina replied.

"I see. I wonder if we should just confront Carol and Jack about it?" Russell asked her.

"Do you want to? I mean we have to work with her every day, you know what I mean?" "You're right. I already feel like sometimes she doubles for the Wicked Witch of the West, as it is."

"Russell!" Tina laughed, putting her hand over her mouth.

"Is that the *Carol* we know, Mom?" Yvonne laughed. Lindy giggled.

"Girls, eat your peas now. Your father and I need to talk." Tina and Russell got up and walked into the next room.

"Well, you know what I mean, "Russell groaned. "She comes down on us with the hammer at the most inopportune times. How are we supposed to produce good TV programming? Sometimes things are a bit controversial, like those Dr. Blaine programs about the true origin of aids—HIV. She was so afraid of the controversy surrounding his theory she held all three programs back from airing. How are we ever supposed to do interesting programming? I mean, hasn't she ever heard of using a disclaimer after the program? All the big networks do it."

"Let's not go there tonight." Tina started back to the kitchen. "Lindy, Girls . . . if you're finished, why don't you watch TV in the next room, okay?"

"Okay, Mom." Yvonne and the younger girls immediately headed for the family room. Tina and Russell continued their discussion.

"Well, her insisting on holding back those shows really chapped my hide. I mean what a huge news break that was!" Russell leaned back with a sigh. He changed the subject back to the original. "So, do you think we really have anything to worry about on this Zodiac thing? It's been ten years now."

"I don't know. If our identity was revealed, and he ever heard about it, he could not only feel confident about coming back, but may be even trying to look for *us*."

"Are you going to try to follow up with the production manager in New York, whatever his name was?"

"I'll try . . . but I get the distinct impression I'm getting the run around."

"Do you think they're afraid of a lawsuit, maybe?"

"Perhaps . . . which leads me to think they were most likely *not* to have used our names. In that case, we have nothing to worry about."

San Francisco Earthquake—October 17, 1989

Tina left the TV Station late afternoon. The clock on wall read 4 p.m. Soon, she drove over the Carquinez Bay Bridge. It appeared to be a completely normal late afternoon. By the time she reached home, Russell was already there, working on their family van in the driveway. She briefly greeted him and went inside. She heard the girls playing upstairs. Tina put her purse and notebook down, and then walked over to the library table in the living room where she had a pile of health product orders from the *Your Health Today* TV show to fill. She briefly picked up a few of them to look over.

"I wonder if I have this product already in stock to ship out?" she said, talking to herself.

Suddenly the table, the room and the walls shook. The walls seemed to move like Jell-O, swaying up and down and from side to side.

"*Oh! Earthquake!*" Tina looked around in amazement.

The girls' book shelves in their rooms upstairs rattled loudly. Yvonne, Lindy, and Kerry Lee ran downstairs in a wild frenzy. Tina instinctively stood in the doorway going into the kitchen. She looked outside.

"Oh God . . . look at that! The lawn out there . . . it looks like the humps on the back of a giant dragon moving under my lawn!" Tina marveled at the sight of the rare phenomena, as green humps moved up and down under the lawn, literally like the back of a giant proverbial dragon. Tina stared out the window at the strange sight.

"Mom! Earthquake!" Yvonne called out frantically.

"Earthquake!" Kerry Lee squeaked.

"The walls are shaking!" Lindy screamed.

***

Across the miles, the Oakland Bay Bridge, swayed. The roadway on the bridge broke, and opened up as a red car fell sharply into the bay. On the Oakland freeway, the upper freeway ramp collapsed onto the lower freeway, crushing rows of cars down below.

***

Back at the house in Benicia, Tina called out, "Where's your father?"

"He's still in the driveway with the van!" Yvonne yelled, over the noise of the rumbling earthquake.

Russell dashed inside, nervously.

"Tina, where are you? *Kids?*" The earthquake rumbled through for about 90 seconds and then stopped.

"Oh my God . . . I wonder if the city of San Francisco is still standing?" Tina blurted out. They all looked at each other in shock.

They discovered later that sections of the San Francisco residential and business areas had collapsed, along with the Marina district. Sections of the overhead freeways in Oakland had collapsed and fallen on the freeway below crushing and trapping cars.

Russell looked around. Angels, unseen, smiled gently among themselves, then drifted back up to the skies to the heavenly realm.

"Look, there is not one crack in the wall, or a broken window!"

Yvonne looked around their house. "The builders of these homes came to talk in our school and said they designed them to rock and roll with a quake, but not to break."

Tina was relieved. "Well, they certainly knew their stuff, didn't they?"

As she inspected further, Tina was amazed. "No, this was more than just good construction, this was a *miracle*. There is not one crack in the wall, and not one broken window!" They looked at each other puzzled but happy.

"Turn on the news. The radio will be quicker than the TV," said Russell.

Yvonne turned on the radio next to the CD player.

"We interrupt this broadcast to announce that there has just been an 8.9 earthquake to hit San Francisco and Oakland. It seemed to have an epicenter in Watsonville, near Santa Cruz. Stay tuned for more news in the upcoming hour."

"Wow. I can see we're going to have our hands full at the station—reprogramming, and doing new stories. I wonder how bad the damage really is? I hope our station in Concord is okay." Tina remembered the transmitter.

"What about the RCA Tower on top of Mt. Diablo? It was already dropped once by the helicopter the day they tried to mount it. It can't take much more," Tina winced.

"I'd better call master control at the station, and see what's going on!" Russell grabbed the phone. "I hope we still have a TV station!" He dialed. Tina waited in suspense. "Les . . . Les, is everything all right over there? What? It is? We're still on the air? How is that even possible?" Tina and Russell stared at each other. "Thanks Les, I'll be in touch. We'll have to go up tomorrow and check the transmitter on the mountain!"

CHAPTER SEVEN

NEW REVELATIONS

Spring 1989

The sign outside in front of the high school in the upscale East Bay city of Walnut Creek read Northgate High School. Due to the long hours her mom and Russell were working in the TV world, Yvonne started attending high school near her grandparent's home, sometimes going back forth.

It was around noontime at the high school cafeteria. Yvonne was talking to a new friend, a young man about 17 years old, over lunch. They were deep in conversation nodding and smiling at each other as they sat across the table. He was the same youth who had been going up into his attic over the years, discovering and studying records about the Zodiac Killer. It was apparent he was the grandson of the former veteran detective on the case, Tony Smith Sr. On his hand he wore the familiar heirloom, the gold tiger-eye ring which had belonged to his grandfather.

On the cafeteria table, students had dumped out a variety of games and puzzles. There was a big jigsaw puzzle lying in pieces on the table in front of them. As they closed their conversation, Yvonne pushed a puzzle piece toward Tony. Tony smiled, and nodded. He pushed the matching piece to Yvonne's piece to make one large piece. The two teenagers looked at each other with a smile of discovery. Now the picture of the Zodiac Killer was complete.

It was late afternoon. Tina's Dad, Henry, had dropped Yvonne by the family house in Benicia. Yvonne entered the kitchen, and put her books and purse down, looking for Tina.

"Hi, Mom!"

"How was your day, honey? I just got home from the studio myself. We had to do a morning edition of *Open Forum*."

"It was a good day . . . a pretty amazing day, really," answered Yvonne.

"Oh, why do you say that, honey?"

"I talked to my friend Tony at school about you and Russell chasing the Zodiac Killer back in 1978."

Tina looked shocked. "Yvonne, you *didn't!* Remember all these years we told you kids not to talk about it to your friends and teachers! It was very important that you take that seriously!"

"This is different, Mom. Tony's grandfather was a key detective on the case for over fifteen years, but then he died. Tony followed the details of the case for years, even as a kid, up until now. He knows what happened that night after the Zodiac escaped you and Russell after the chase on the freeway. He's going to call you."

"*He does*? *He will*?" Tina looked shocked.

"Yeah . . . he may call even as soon as tonight!"

Later that evening, Yvonne was already upstairs in bed. It was a Friday night sleep-over for Lindy, her little sister, Kerry Lee, and her cousins, Terry and Sherry Lynn, around eight to ten years old. In the living room, Tina talked to them about their toys.

"Girls, if you are going to make all that noise hauling the Barbie Townhouse downstairs to play, please try not to wake your older sister who's sleeping!"

"Okay, Mom," Lindy sighed. Suddenly the house phone rang. It was a light-colored, old-fashioned Victorian-looking phone, matching their antique look décor in the living room. Tina answered.

"Hello, is this Tina?" A young man's voice answered on the other line.

"Mrs. George, this is Yvonne's friend, Tony." Tina was already feeling a swell of anticipation.

"You may call me Tina."

"Tina, Yvone talked with me at great length about you and your husband and the chase with the Zodiac on the Novato freeway leaving Vista Point, back in 1978."

"Yes, I royally chewed her out about it, too. But then she told me why she talked to you."

"Yes. My grandfather was a key detective on the case for over fifteen years, but then he died. Ever since I was quite young, I followed the story and the evidence he gathered, with great interest. I think part of the problem was that after his death, certain pieces of the puzzle just slipped through the cracks."

Tina listened intently, burning with curiosity.

"I believe most people who think they saw the Zodiac, really didn't see him. But I feel quite sure that was who you saw that night."

"Wow, you sound just like Sergeant Tedesco. He said the same thing." Tina felt excited, yet controlled.

"Yes, he was also a very key person working on the case."

"So, my daughter says you know something . . . like what happened, after he left us and disappeared off the freeway."

"Yes, I think I do."

"Yes . . .?"

"Around the same time frame this happened with you and your husband, a few days after, or possibly as soon as the next morning after the chase, the guy the police always thought it was, turned up dead, washed up on the shore in Santa Barbara. Apparently, he parked his car, then either jumped from up above, or walked into the waves at ground level, and drowned himself."

"Oh, my!" Tina replied, trying to control her shock.

***

Stepping back in time, a man fully dressed in gray wool pants and a jacket, wearing black dress shoes, walked into the ocean on a lonely beach. As he ventured further and further out over his head, he was swallowed up by the waves. As his spirit passed into death, the hideous face of a demonic spirit leapt from the waves and was released high into the atmosphere.

***

Tina and Tony continued talking on the phone, as the drama unfolded.

"So, reconstructing the situation the night of the chase, it was just as you thought: You could have seen the license plate of his car, but that other car cut in front of you. Yvonne said he took the advantage, and shot way out in front on the freeway, then disappeared."

"Yes, there are four exits right there, maybe. We couldn't see which exit he took. It was his classic 'Phantom Escape,'" explained Tina, feeling the vibe from the past.

"I'll tell you which exit he took. Highway 1 South, along the California coast. He probably drove all night until he got there and decided he would walk into the waves and end his life," Tony stated adamantly. "He just walked into the waves, and let the ocean swallow him up. It could have been as early as the next morning."

"Wow, *amazing*." Tina was stunned. In her mind's eye she was reliving the scene. She could see him so clearly. "I got the distinct impression that he believed we had everything we needed to identify him. I mean, we saw everything on that second stop in full-beam headlights from our car, their car, and his car, as he slowly turned around in the road. By the third stop at Vista Point, he ran scared." Tony listened on, nodding his head.

"I agree. There was a man whom the police had already suspected was the Zodiac serial killer, but they could not link him to the crimes strongly enough to pick him up. But along with what you saw that night, it would have potentially have linked him to the crimes, especially if you had gotten the license plate number. The police could have at least picked him up as a suspect for questioning, for sure!" Tina and Tony were amazed as they put the two pieces of the puzzle together with words and memories and descriptions. Then Tina remembered the drawing.

"I did a drawing of his face which the police said matched other drawings they had from other witnesses."

"That would have been another strong piece of evidence," Tony commented.

Meanwhile, the girls played in the living room at the far end. They did not pick up on the entire conversation, just bits and pieces. They giggled and became noisy. Tina stopped a moment to correct them.

"Girls, can you play a little more quietly? Mom is on the phone!" She went back to the conversation with Tony. "Sorry, I've got a little girl sleepover going on here with my daughters and their cousins. Where were we?"

Outside in the darkness, the spirit realm was not unaware of this conversation. Large reptilian, hideous-looking creatures—demons— actively gathered around the house, and on the roof of the home. One very tall, ugly one was near the front window. He was the spirit of the Zodiac that escaped and was released into the atmosphere when the man who was his host died the night he walked into the ocean waves.

Inside, Tina sat in the light of the living-room lamps, still deep in conversation with Tony.

"The drawing you did of the face for the police . . ." Tony inquired. "Did you get a really good look at him?"

"Yes! When he decided not to stay parked next to the second couple he tried to stalk, he turned around very slowly in the road with his headlights and our headlights on. I found myself studying his face very carefully. He just seemed weird to me. If I had been looking for a license plate, I certainly could have gotten it then."

"Would you agree to hypnosis?"

"Oh, stop it!" She laughed. "I've been asked that before." Tina paused. You said the man the police always thought it was turned up dead, shortly after the chase. Why was he suspected?"

"The police broke into his old broken-down mobile home. Somehow, they did it without a search warrant, based on another suspicion of some kind. They found his Satanist stuff, pentagrams, dead animals in the freezer, other things mentioned in Zodiac let- ters . . . even an identity on some mail and bills. However, they never had what they needed to warrant them being able to pick him up or make an arrest. He was never seen escaping from any of the Zodiac murders."

"Interesting . . ." Tina mused.

"I mean, here was a late middle-aged guy who was not particu- larly strong, medium size and weight," began Tony.

"He was wearing a gray blazer, matching wool pants, black dress shoes and a white turtleneck sweater. He looked very ordinary," Tina added.

"Right . . . may be just under six feet tall, thinning hair, big light rimmed glasses . . ." Tony added.

Tina shook her head, frustrated. "I can't believe the irony of this! Here we are describing one of the most wanted criminals of all time like we are looking right at him! Why couldn't the police get a handle on his identity?"

"In 1978, when the guy they always thought it was turned up dead, washed up on the shore—somehow it was just left at that," said Tony, bluntly.

"This is what I don't understand. The San Francisco Police had our story on record since that night in mid-October. Sergeant Tedesco believed that was who we saw—*the Zodiac*. I did a drawing of the face. They said it matched other drawings they already had. So, why was I not contacted to at least look at a picture of this guy who washed up on the shore, dead?"

"That is the million-dollar question."

"So much for all that high-tech forensic police stuff you see on TV! I mean, I don't get it," Tina said, disappointed.

"It was also around the time frame in which my grandfather passed away. Apparently, some key evidence never did make an official connection."

"I guess not!" Tina whined.

"Well, thank you for calling and filling me in. Don't you think San Francisco Homicide should hear about this?"

"You might try. You may find they are not as receptive to new evidence as you would hope."

"What? *Why not?*"

"It's just the way it is."

"Okay, well, I'll give it a try sometime this week. I mean, you'd think they would care. I mean, between you and me, we've practically solved the case!"

"Still no license plate . . . still no name." Tony sighed.

"Well now, whose fault is that? I mean when a funky-looking old white car with silver chrome and bright red stripes on the sides turns up abandoned on the beach somewhere—and a dead guy washes up on the beach nearby who is probably the driver, somebody should put two and two together!"

"Yep . . . like I said, the last details slipped through the cracks. He escaped again, so to speak."

"The Phantom Advantage, even in death," Tina said, remembering.

"Yes, exactly. Well, you can try talking to the police—even give them my name if you want, and my grandfather's name. It was the same as mine—Tony Smith, and Tony Smith Sr."

"Thank you, I will."

"Goodnight . . . and good luck."

"Goodnight . . . and *thanks*."

Tina moved forward to hang up the phone. The very moment the receiver hit the phone cradle, a wild, hideous, demonic, hyena-like scream pierced the air! It sounded unearthly, like a combination of a human cry and a wildcat scream. It seemed to be coming from just outside the front living room window. All the little sleepover girls suddenly froze in terror, then screamed in fear, and in a mad dash, as a streak of pink flannel and bunny slippers, they all scrambled up the stairs into the master bedroom, and slammed the door shut with a loud "Wham!"

The strange unearthly cry even awakened Yvonne upstairs, who was asleep.

"Mom . . . what was that?" There was a sudden sound of a door locking on Yvonne's bedroom door. The very shocked Tina looked around, feeling a strange tingle of her nerves.

"Hold on, honey." She walked, and looked around again, surveying the situation. Now . . . what was *that*? A voice out of hell? So we struck a nerve there, did we? It's the *truth*, isn't it? Of course Russell is at work, video editing until 3 a.m. tonight." She walked briskly upstairs to the bedroom door.

"Okay girls . . . Mommy, Auntie is going to need to go to bed soon." Tina tried the door. It was locked. "Girls . . . open the door. This is not funny!" Tina heard Lindy's voice from behind the door.

"Mommy, we're scared! It's the *Zodiac*!"

"Girls, I need to go to bed soon. I will be back in a few minutes, and expect for you to open the door." Terry spoke out from behind the closed door.

"But the Zodiac is out there . . ."

"Zodiac . . ." echoed Kerry Lee and Sherry, softly and fearfully.

"The Zodiac is *not* out here." Tina looked meekly over her shoulder. "That's silly."

She heard Lindy's voice from behind the locked door, "Mommy, what was that noise? It was a *monster*."

"It was *not* a monster. We'll find out more about it in the morning. I'll be back. Girls, I need to sleep in my own bed tonight, do you hear me . . . Lindy . . . Kerry Lee . . . Terry . . . Sherry Lynn?"

Tina walked carefully back downstairs. She peeked cautiously through the separation in the curtain in the front living room window. She saw nothing. Tina sighed. She opened the door and looked out. See saw nothing, and came back inside.

"Why is it always like this?" As if speaking to a spirit in the room, she threw her arms up in the air and shouted, "Touché!" It was a "war," and now the spirit of the Zodiac had "one up" on Tina.

Outside, transparent angelic figures surrounded the house. Up on the roof, some large angels appeared with heavenly swords. At their appearance, the large ugly demonic creatures had to shrink away and leave. One of them was recognizable as the spirit of the Zodiac. In the spirit realm, two tall shining angels with swords appeared at the front double-door entry. They crossed their swords across the entry to block out the evil ones. The Zodiac spirit had to now shrink away. He unhappily disappeared into a black mist, and was soon gone.

It was now the wee hours of the morning. Tina was sleeping in her clothes with a pillow and a blanket on the family-room couch. While asleep, Tina relieved the scenes from the Zodiac's suicide as he walked closer and closer to the ocean shore . . . then into the small waves . . . then into the ocean, and then the waves billowed over his head. Once the man was dead, a large hideous monster demon with sharp teeth and horns on is reptilian head shot up put of the water, and was released into the atmosphere. Tina winced painfully at this ugly and scary scene.

The room was dimly lit from a light in another room. A rattling noise at the front door was heard as Russell unlocked the door. It was 3:30 a.m. The noise from Russell entering caused Tina to wake. She was troubled by the strange dream, and by the releasing of what seemed to be the demon spirit of the Zodiac into the atmosphere. She stayed lying down on the couch for a few moments, pondering the mysterious dream. Russell went upstairs expecting the door to the master bedroom to be unlocked.

"Why is this door locked? Tina?" The daughters and cousins began to wake, making noises. "Girls . . . why are you in there? Open this door right now!" Russell knocked loudly on the door a couple of times. "Come out of there!" The sleepy little girls opened the door, as they then hurriedly ran into Lindy's bedroom, quickly locking the door behind them.

A tired Tina, in her jeans and T-shirt with bed-head hair appeared, as she came up the stairs.

"Sorry Russell. They got scared and ran up here about nine o'clock, and there was no getting them to open the door."

"So . . . what were they scared of?"

"The Zodiac," Tina answered sleepily.

"What?" Russell laughed weakly. Tina gave him a blank look. "Tell me you're kidding."

"Russell . . . really, this is a story you are going to have to hear about in the morning." Tina walked inside their bedroom with Russell, and closed the door with a click of the lock.

At breakfast the next morning, Russell finally heard more about the strange horrific episode.

"So, let me get this straight. Last night, you get through talking with Tony, the grandson of the deceased detective on the Zodiac case. The moment the phone receiver hits the cradle, a wild, demonic, blood-curdling cry came out from out of nowhere?" Tina was in her fuzzy bathrobe, and poured herself some coffee.

"Not exactly from out of *nowhere*. From in front of the living-room window, outside."

"From out of nowhere, in front of the living-room window, outside. Go figure." Russell said, shaking his head.

Yvonne appeared, and sat down at the table with a notepad and pen in hand.

"While you've been guessing what that could have been going on last night, I called the Vallejo Police Department just now. Russell looked over at her. He was curious now.

"And?"

"Last night some druggies from Vallejo were wandering around out here in our neighborhood, yelling and acting all weird. The police arrested them and brought them in," Yvonne explained.

"Well, that sounds like a pretty good explanation," Tina reasoned. "A demonic spirit could have moved even through the crazed druggie guy, and screamed out. We're people who know the Bible. Those things happen."

"You worked with teens addicted and coming off drugs and witchcraft at the Teen Hope Center here in the Bay Area, and you know those things happen," Russell agreed.

"Yeah, that was a real 'light breaking into darkness' situation," said Tina, remembering those days. "The devil was not one bit happy to lose his little trophies steeped in drug addiction and crime—but the kids sure were happy to be free. Great memories! But let's be logical here. What are the odds the 'wild scream' would happen right at that very moment I learned the truth, and hung up the phone with Tony? I think we hit a nerve out of hell."

"Well, it sounds like the culprit is currently residing at the city jail so you can stop worrying about it, okay?" Russell reasoned. The girls looked relieved. Terry, the girls' eight-year-old cousin, was in the group sitting around the table.

"I'm so glad. That really scared me!"

"Me too," echoed Kerry Lee. Tina was relieved the girls felt better, and began to change the subject.

"So Russell, are you really off today and tonight? They didn't talk you into directing any new programs today or tonight did they?"

"Nope . . . I am really off. I have a date with the lawn mower, and some yard work, and maybe later tonight we could all watch a movie at home and make some caramel popcorn." This brought a happy reaction from the kids.

"Yay!" all the girls cheered. Tina smiled. Everyone's fears seemed to be put aside, for the time being.

"In the meantime, you girls might want to play outside on the trampoline. I just got the new spring fixed and it's all ready to go," Tina said, happily. The little girls cheered again.

"Yay! Cool. Thanks, Mom. Let's go!" They all made a mad dash out to the backyard.

"Our girls and Terry . . . the cousins, are all growing up so fast! It almost scares me," Russell grinned.

"Yeah, sometimes it makes me feel kind of old." Tina pouted. Russell laughed a little at this comment.

"No, honey. You've definitely still got *it*."

"Still got '*it*?' Thanks, honey!" Tina beamed. Russell pulled her into a warm embrace.

Later on, that evening, the TV was on as the girls prepared to pick out a video to watch.

"Okay, girls, have you picked out which video you want to see yet?" Tina asked.

"Lindy wants one of those *Cinderella*, *Bambi*, *Snow White* type of videos. We want something more modern," said Terry. Kerry Lee chimed in.

"I like Bambi."

"Well, Lindy also likes *Gone with the Wind*," said Yvonne, offering a suggestion. Lindy put her arm over her forehead, play-acting.

"*Oh, Brett . . . Oh Scarlet . . .*" Yvonne watched, then commented dryly.

"On the other hand, I don't know if I can stomach that one even one more time, really."

Meanwhile, the evening news broadcast continued. Suddenly, the news commentator from the regional news came on with an announcement.

"Police have just brought into custody a man who has been dubbed 'The Hillside Killer.'" The story caught Tina's attention for a moment.

"Characteristics of these homicides in the Bay area over the last few months have led police to suspect that he might be the original Zodiac Killer, who has come back after a sudden disappearance in 1978."

Tina watched the TV screen with the picture of a middle-aged man with dark hair and a beard. She reacted when she saw the man's picture.

"What? That's not him!" Tina said, talking out loud to the TV screen. Yvonne sighed, and rolled her eyes.

"Here we go again."

"Russell, look! That man is not the Zodiac." Russell squinted, looking at the TV.

"He doesn't seem to be," he agreed.

"It looks like the San Francisco Police are going to get another call tomorrow . . ." Yvonne said, with a little laugh.

"Now, honey, should I let them pin that on an innocent man?"

"It doesn't sound like he is exactly *innocent!*" said Yvonne.

"Well, he is not exactly the Zodiac Killer. Russell and I both know the face. Besides, according to Tony, the Zodiac is *dead.*"

"Well, now you have *two* reasons to call the San Francisco Police," remarked Yvonne.

"Yes, I do . . . and I will . . . on Monday morning. Now, do we know yet which video we are going to watch yet?"

"I know, let's watch the new *Robin Hood* movie!" voted Yvonne.

"No . . . The beginning of that movie is a little scary, even for me." Russell shuddered.

Tina looked at the TV listings in the newspaper.

"Here we go. There's a special National Geographic documentary on baby animals in the wild!"

"I vote for that one!" Lindy cheered.

"Baby animals!" echoed Kerry Lee.

"I guess it will be okay," said Yvonne, sounding like a teenager.

"It's all settled then," said Tina. "Baby Animals in the Wild. Now, where is that popcorn?"

Chapter Eight

Dark Forces Press In

If the veil could be pulled back, and we could peer into the unseen spirit realm, we would see them—those dark fallen angels who had escaped from the pit of hell to now walk the earth daily and oppress humans, if they can. Some of them are supreme princes of darkness. The spirit of the Zodiac was not about to rest once he knew that Tina and Russell were aware of him, and knew the truth about his evil human host, the Zodiac serial killer. The man, the Zodiac, who spoke of him as "the monster within me," was rolling and writhing in fiery pain in the depths of hell, but the spirit who drove him ultimately there, was loose.

Tina sat at the kitchen table wearing her satin bathrobe, sipping tea and munching on a breakfast bagel. Over her shoulder, unseen to her, a hideous demon face on a tall reptilian body appeared out of nowhere. He was the same spirit that inhabited Zodiac which screamed and escaped out into the atmosphere from the ocean waves. He had also lurked outside the living-room window the night of the mysterious, unearthly scream. It was he who cried out a painful cry of discovery that night. His eyes turned glowing red. He gave off a smoky, foul presence.

Tina flipped through the phone book looking for a number. Back in the shadows, he watched from over her shoulder.

"Okay . . . husband's at work, kids are at school. Let me make this call." Tina stopped and sniffed the air. "Is something burning in here? "She looked over at the stove. "No, I don't see anything. Hmm . . . Did the dog or the cat have an accident in here?" She looked under the table. "No. I don't see anything. It must be just my imagination." She continued to flip through the phone book. "I ought to know this number by heart by now. Here we go!" The phone rang on the other end, then Tina heard a voice speaking.

"San Francisco Police Department," a woman's voice answered.

"Yes, hello," Tina replied. "Can I talk to Sergeant Tedesco, please?" Invisible to Tina, the Zodiac demon spirit moved and swirled around her, as if both curious, and angry. He continued to watch and listen. She does not sense his presence. Tina waited to hear if Sergeant Tedesco was available.

"Sergeant Tedesco? I'm afraid that's impossible."

"But, why?" Tina wondered.

He is retired, ma'am," she answered. Tina looked disappointed.

"Oh. When did that happen?"

"A few years ago, I think."

"Well, let me talk to Homicide, then," Tina asked.

"Very well, let me see who is in." She paused to connect the call.

"Sergeant Pierce here. How can I help you?"

"This is Tina George. I am used to talking to Sergeant Tedesco on the Zodiac case . . . "

"Yes, well, he is retired now. What do you know about him . . . the Zodiac?" asked Sergeant Pierce. Tina gave a deep sigh as she sank deeply into a big chair.

"Well, we are starting all over at the beginning, aren't we?" She paused, then launched into her story. "It's on official record that my husband and I got into a high-speed chase with him on the Novato freeway in mid-October 1978, after seeing him stalk couples in three locations. The chase broke out as we were leaving Vista Point on the other side of the Golden Gate Bridge. After about ten minutes, he dashed way ahead, and we lost him." The police officer listened politely and patiently.

"I see. Isn't that when he disappeared like *completely?* I think I remember this old report."

"Yes. I talked Sergeant Tedesco into convincing the press to keep it out of the papers for public-safety reasons. We were after his license plate number, but a driver got in front of us just when I was about to see it, and I missed the chance. That report could have wound up in the papers." Tina moaned. "But the police agreed that it was important to keep it out of the press."

"Yes, I think I *do* remember this story. There was a surveillance net dropped, and APB. Our patrol cars looked for him all night, but had no luck," Sergeant Pierce remembered.

"Yes. I spent years telling and warning my kids not to talk to their friends at school that their Mommy and Daddy chased the Zodiac. If it ever got out on the street or in the press that we never really got his license plate number, he could have come back. We just figured he laid low all these years, fearing he could be too easily picked up if he chanced making any more appearances."

"That he did . . . lay low. There has not been a trace, except possibly for a new guy, 'The Hillside Killer.' We have been wondering if it was him, the Zodiac, just back under a new name," Sergeant Pierce replied.

"That's one of the reasons I called. I know the face, body, and build of the man who is the Zodiac. I did a drawing for police the week after the chase. That man you're holding in jail is *not* the Zodiac. I'll swear by that. My husband and I both know his face. Look up the drawing on file by Tina George, 1978. What the police are seeing is a pattern of men possessed by the *spirit of violence*. The spirit of violence is no respecter of persons. It will come in to anyone who opens the door to it. That's the only pattern! Listen, this is the other reason I called: I told my kids for years not to talk about the episode to their friends in school. My daughter Yvonne came home from school last week, and told me she talked to a kid named Tony . . . Anthony Smith. I was upset with her at first, until she clarified that he was the grandson of one of the key detectives on the case, Tony Smith Sr. He said he followed the case with great interest over the years since he was just a small kid. But his grandfather died, and some of the important facts seem to have slipped through the cracks. This Tony kid said, 'I'm going to tell you what happened after the Zodiac got away from you during the chase that night.'"

"Yes? What was his theory?"

"After more than ten years . . . this piece of the puzzle came together. Wouldn't you know a high-school kid was the one to put it all together?"

"Yes? And?"

"It seemed that after he shot ahead and escaped from us, he took the exit for the coastal route south, running along the ocean, driving all night until he got there—the Santa Barbara area somewhere. The Zodiac then parked his car, and either dropped in from up above, or walked straight into the waves from ground level, and drowned himself. He was found washed up on the shore the next day, dead. The kid said the dead body was the man the police always thought it was, but they had no evidence to directly connect him to the crimes, so they couldn't pick him up. What we witnessed that night—him stalking couples in three locations, then running recklessly from the last location leaving Vista Point—would have given the police what they needed to pick him up, at least for questioning. He must have been convinced we were plain-clothes police, looking for him." Sergeant Pierce patiently listened to Tina's story.

"Are you sure you didn't see the license-plate number, perhaps when he was moving slowly?"

"Yes, and no. That's the flaw in this whole thing. At first, when I did see it, he was pulling around slowly in all of our headlights, but we didn't suspect him. Later, he was traveling too fast, and a car got in between us, blocking my vision. We had to slam on our brakes to keep from hitting the car in front of us. But I feel sure he thought we saw his license plate. He mocked the police, calling them 'The Keystone Cops.' He was terrified of being picked up."

The demon spirit, with red glowing eyes, was hidden in a black mist over Tina's shoulder. He was listening in, and seemed both curious and angry.

"Hmmm . . . very interesting. I will have to have somebody check on this. Santa Barbara County Records," Sergeant Pierce repeated to himself.

"I am very disappointed I was not called to view at least a picture of the body," Tina said. "Sergeant Tedesco and other investigative staff told me they felt sure that's who we saw. Then this guy washed up on the shore dead, and they don't call me to look at him? I don't get it. And that would have been classified as a 'John Doe,' not a 'homicide.'"

"I'll do some checking, and call you back," Pierce responded abruptly. "Good-bye, Mrs. George."

"Thanks, Sergeant Pierce. Good-bye." Tina stared at the phone receiver. "Good-bye." She hung up and sighed. "I think I need a little inspiration from the Psalms before driving over to the station." Tina picked up a black leather-covered Bible, and opened it up on the kitchen table. "Ah, here we go, Psalms 138. 'In the day that I called, you answered me, and you strengthened me with strength in my inner self.'" A soft light seemed to glow around her as she breathed and drank in strength from on high.

The Zodiac demon could not bear to be in the presence of such strength and light. He grimaced in pain, and disappeared with a groan and a shrill cry.

Tina got up from her seat and looked around. "What was that?" Tina glanced around. She walked over to the front door, and opened it, looking around further. Children played outside in a neighbor's yard on the lawn, laughing, playing, and making shrill sounds while they waited for the school bus. "I guess it was just those kids," she reasoned. Tina then went upstairs to get dressed, and prepare for another afternoon at the family Christian broadcasting station.

As Tina came down the stairs she noticed an open newspaper on their entryway table. An article suddenly caught her eye from a column entitled "Ask Sharon."

"Hmmm, where have I seen this before? That columnist out of Napa . . . the newspaper at my Mom's house . . ." Tina picked it up and looked it over more carefully. "I met the Zodiac Killer face to face. . . . me, my sister Jill and another girlfriend from the college where I was attending in Napa. No words can describe his dark evil countenance and bragging mouth. We followed a tip that he was at the Aquarius Bar in downtown Napa only days after the attack of my two college mates, Cecelia Shepard and Bryan Hartnell. . . . "

Tina was shocked. She read further. Sharon described him in great detail. "It was 1969, and he was about 45 at the time. He was a plain looking man with auburn hair and had a receding hairline. He wore glasses with large light colored rims . . ." Tina's mouth fell open in wonderment. This woman she had never met was describing the same man she and Russell had seen stalking the couples in San Francisco that mid-October night back in 1978. There was no doubt about it. Tina realized that she and Russell were certainly not the only eyewitnesses. She put the paper aside to think about it later.

That evening their family was all gathered together at the dinner table. Tina served the girls, while Russell cut the meat.

"Russell, did you get those three programs edited today?" Tina asked.

"Yep!"

"Great! I won't have to worry about the guy from TV Guide Today calling I'll actually have an answer for him." Tina smiled, looking relieved.

"So, Mom, did you make the call today?" Yvonne asked, wondering.

"Oh you mean to the San Francisco Police? Yes. Sergeant Tedesco has retired, so I had to start all over again with somebody new, a Sergeant Pierce. You know, I just don't think they take this all very seriously. I mean, he listened politely, but I could tell it wasn't like before. Maybe they just don't care about this story anymore."

"Oh, I think they care. It's just that, put yourself in their place, there are a lot of new cases to solve—new murders, new homicide puzzles. They're under pressure, just like us, in a way. We start on projects that have a lot of production elements, then here comes something new that just has to get on the air, so our focus changes."

"I guess so," Tina replied, pushing around the broccoli on her plate.

"Was I in the car when you chased the Zodiac?"

"You were in Mommy's tummy . . . so you don't remember, of course."

"Lindy, don't tell me you didn't remember that part!" Yvonne laughed. Lindy looked embarrassed.

"I wasn't too sure," she blushed.

"We are all very lucky to be here. The story could have turned out a lot differently." Yvonne suddenly looked serious.

"The Lord looked down from heaven, and just decided to hold us in his loving hands that night. He sent his angels to protect us every step of the way. He knew your Daddy and I had a lot more to do yet in this life, and that Linda Suzanne here needed to be born safe and sound. He is a very wise and loving God." Tina looked at Russell tenderly.

"Yes, He is," Russell smiled back, in soft agreement.

The phone rang. Russell picked it up.

"Hello? Yes, let me have you talk to Tina since she's the one who made the report." He handed the phone over to Tina. It's San Francisco Homicide." Tina took the phone receiver.

"Hello? Yes, this is Tina George." She listened to the reply from the voice on the phone.

"This is Thomas Jensen, San Francisco Homicide. I did some checking on your story about a body washing up on the shore in Santa Barbara in mid-October of 1978." Tina was breathless.

"Yes?"

"I find no record of any homicides in Santa Barbara County around that time."

"But how can that be? A veteran detective on the Zodiac case, Tony Smith, knew all about the body washing up on the shore."

"I don't know, ma'am. I didn't know him. It must have been before my time here. Okay? Thanks for calling in. Good-bye." The officer hung up abruptly.

"Wait—come back!" Tina looked at phone. "Too late . . . He hung up."

"What's the matter, honey?" Russell asked.

"He said there were no *homicides* around that time frame. But when an unidentified body just washes up on the shore, it's not a homicide . . . It's a John Doe. That would have been classified and handled differently—if it ever was recorded at all. I mentioned that to Sergeant Pierce. Why do I seem to keep having to tell the police how to do their jobs?"

"Sorry, honey. Maybe you can give them a call back sometime."

"I will . . . you know there was one more thing I meant to bring up before he so abruptly hung up." Tina went and got the newspaper from the entry way table. "Look at this, Russell . . . We are not the *only* eye witnesses around who know what the real Zodiac looks like! "Look at this story from a woman in Napa who came face to face with the Zodiac after he attacked her two college friends at Lake Berryessa."

"I think I remember that story," Russell commented, looking over the article.

"I *definitely* remember the story! I saw it when I worked up at the Chico Enterprise Record back in 1969," Tina recalled. 'The point is . . . why do they keep trying to pin the Zodiac murders and identity on other men when there is you and I who know what he looks like, and this Sharon Townsend who knows what he looks like? The police even verified it."

"Good point, Tina. Pretty crazy, huh?"

"I guess so. This whole thing is wearing me out, really. I don't want to think about it anymore right now." Tina put the newspaper aside. She decided to change modes.

"You know, it's long summer days right now. Before it gets dark, I need to do a few errands. I'm going to take the girls with me. I need to pick out some new play pants and swim suits for them before the sale is over. Come on, girls!" Tina gathered Lindy and Kerry Lee, and they walked out to the car.

Suddenly, a dark mist from the unseen realm appeared. It followed them, and swirled around the car. In contrast, a bright light appeared, and the transparent forms of tall angel figures and wings appeared. The angels intervened with the dark mist from hell, and dispelled it with great energy and a burst of light. Tina reacted quickly, shielding her eyes.

"Wow, what was that? The sun seems unusually bright today." She put on her sunglasses, as she pulled out of the driveway with the girls to start her errands. As she emerged from the department store with Lindy and Kerry Lee carrying bags from their shopping trip. They walked out to their car together and drove off toward home.

"You know, this car is on empty. I'd better get some gas," Tina reminded herself. She pulled into a gas station on Old Benicia Road, near a big oil refinery. She pumped the gas, as the girls waited patiently in the car. In the unseen realm, the dark demonic mist returned, and swirled in a mystical fashion around the car. By now the girls were playing inside the car, teasing each other. As Tina drove off, she paused at the driveway, ready to pull out onto the road. Due to a bend in the road ahead, and some bushes, the view ahead was blind. The girls bounced around and giggled in the backseat of the car.

"Girls . . . *be quiet now!*" Tina glanced into her rearview mirror and stopped the car. The rearview mirror became like a video screen which revealed a large 18-wheeler gasoline tanker which had left the oil refinery, and was barreling down the road directly toward her. Tina waited instead of pulling out. Bright powerful angels from the unseen realm blocked the road with their shining swords.

"Wow, look at that! Better wait. The huge tanker truck filled with newly loaded gas, barreled by in front of her. Then reality suddenly hit. "Wait just a minute!" Tina realized that the only view she would have had in her rearview mirror was that of the gas station parking lot. Her rearview mirror seemed to glow mysteriously then it slowly faded back to normal. "Oh my God, we could have all been killed! That truck was never *behind* me. "God gave me a prophetic warning in my rearview mirror! The girls looked back her, awestruck.

Relieved, Tina pulled up in the driveway of their home, and went inside with Lindy, Kerry Lee, and their shopping bags. Russell was reading the newspaper.

"Listen to me!" Tina lowered the paper with her hand to get his attention.

"What is it, honey?" Russell asked.

"Some angels just saved us all from a fiery wreck just now. It was *amazing!*" Tina exclaimed.

That's nice."

"No . . . Russell, listen to me! I was getting gas at the gas station near the oil refinery out on Old Benicia Road. Afterwards, I was about to pull out on the road to drive back here. As I was leaving the driveway of the gas station, my view of oncoming traffic was not good. It was blind, not a good view of the cars coming toward me at all. I heard the sound of the rumbling of a large truck, but I couldn't see it. I was about to pull out, when I stopped. I saw a blinding light, then in my rearview mirror I saw a huge 18-wheeler gas tanker barreling along, coming in my direction. I stopped cold."

"Good, honey. That was very good of you. You always were a very careful driver," said Russell matter of factly.

"No, honey . . . Don't you see? The only thing that would have reflected in my rearview mirror would have been the gas-station parking lot. God let me see the speeding truck ahead on my far left, way ahead of time, like a video in my rearview mirror. If I would have pulled out, the kids and I would have been killed in a fiery wreck!" Russell finally understood. He quickly put down the newspaper.

"Tina! Thank God, I'm so glad you and the kids are safe! They hugged, and time seemed to stand still for a moment as they were grateful to be alive and well, and back home with each other. That night was a special evening, treasuring life and being together.

Later, in bed alone, Tina was dreaming about the close call with the gas tanker truck that could have instantly killed her and the children. She saw the dark spirit of the Zodiac at different places around the home, and around the family, waiting . . . watching silently in the shadows, as if waiting for the right moment to pounce. Frightened, she woke to hear Russell enter downstairs. The clock on the nightstand read 3:10 a.m. It had been another late-night video-editing session at the station. He didn't come upstairs right away. Tina heard him in the kitchen, so she went downstairs where she saw him making a sandwich.

"Hi, Sweetie. Did I wake you?" asked Russell, as he bit into the sandwich.

"Kind of," Tina said, brushing the sleep from her eyes. "I was having some really strange dreams."

"About what?"

"We'll talk about it later."

"Well, since you're up, I was going to talk to you about a project I think we need to do. I was given this song, "The Letter." The Assistant Station Manager, our new one, Don Walter, really wants us to produce this idea as a music video for the new telethon coming up. The theme of the telethon will center around the state of the American family. Can you listen to it?"

"You mean right *now*?" Tina yawned. "I'm not really up, and I was having those strange dreams. Honey, do you ever notice this mysterious black thing that sometimes creeps around the house?" Russell was not fully listening, and gave her a strange questioning look.

"Let me put the tape on," Russell insisted.

He went over to the stereo unit in the next room and played "The Letter," by Tim Waddington. The song told the story of a little girl, around eight years old, who saw the conflict and fighting between her parents, and was torn up by it. She wished that they could read "The Letter" from God, the Bible, and realize their lives and their love could be healed by it, if they would let it happen, and say "yes" to God. Ultimately, within the short story of the song, this does happen. It had a happy ending of the family being healed by God's love. The song closed tenderly. Tina was obviously moved by the lyrics and the story of the song.

"I think we just got talked into another project," Tina said, a bit teary eyed.

"Rob was hoping you would see it that way!" Russell said with a broad grin.

"What's the timeline on this music video, Russell?" Tina asked.

"If we can do it, they want it filmed, edited, finished, and Fed-Exed out to the New York station for *New York Tonight*, on Thursday for the big Friday-night show, featuring the theme, 'The current state of the American family.'"

"It is 3:30 Tuesday morning, Russell," Tina said, suddenly looking very serious. Russell looked back at her squarely in the face.

"We can do it, honey," Russell insisted.

"The only way we can do it is if *we* play the couple, *Lindy* plays the little girl, and we begin shooting here at our own house . . . like *tomorrow!*" Tina said, looking annoyed.

"Lindy is a very good actress. Everybody loved her in the new commercial we shot last month." Tina just stared him in the face with a blank look, with her mouth open.

"I'll call Doug first thing in the morning, and we'll organize a camera crew to come out here."

"I'll have to keep Lindy out of school for a day."

"She gets out of school at 2:15. We could do all the pre-shots with us, and work with her later. Yvonne could meet her, and walk her straight home."

"Russell, let's get some sleep. We have got to be crazy to live like this all the time!" She headed for their upstairs room, Russell followed. It was just another ordinary night in Tina and Russell's crazy life in the broadcasting world.

The next morning, Tina heard the production van pull up in front of the house. She was still tired from lack of sleep.

"Dear God, I just can't handle this anymore . . . help me with this today!" Tina quickly put on a robe and went downstairs. She opened the door to let in Doug and Tom, the video shooters with all their cables, microphones, video cameras, tripods, and other equipment. Russell followed behind her to greet their work mates from the station.

"Doug . . . Good morning, my man! And Tom . . . come on in, and don't forget those two monitors out in the van," said Russell, already directing.

"Mornin'!" Doug grinned. He looked around. "Hey, Russ, once I get everything in, let me know where to set up, for starters." Tina went upstairs and put on the clothes she knew she would need for the scenes in the video. She brought her robe with her, knowing it would be used in one of the scenes at the end where the husband and wife are having morning coffee, looking happy and reunited. Tina came down the stairs to get ready for the video shoot. She determined to adjust her attitude and get through it. She was ready with a smile as Russell walked over. .

"Okay." Russell walked over to talk to Tina. "Since we're going to wait for Lindy, we're going to shoot around the scenes we'll do with her later. We'll start off with the 'husband storming out the front door with suitcase scene.'"

"That's you," Tina said playfully.

"That's me."

"While Doug sets up, I'd better alert the neighbors that there could be some yelling around here, and you storming outside with a suitcase, but that it's only play-acting."

"Okay, honey. If you want to," Russell laughed.

"Yes, I want to," Tina replied, coolly.

Tina walked outside, and spotted their elderly retired neighbors, Tom and Bernice, trimming bushes across the street in their front yard, while Tina's friend Judy walked her dog.

"Hey, Judy! How are you?" Tina asked.

"Great! Good morning. Isn't that the TV production van parked outside your house?"

"Yes. I'm glad you asked." Tina called out to her neighbors across the street.

"Tom and Bernice!" They looked up, in Tina's direction. "I need to tell you something! We are filming a re-dramatization of a couple and a family story to illustrate a music video we are producing for our station. This couple is yelling, and screaming, and the husband storms out the front door with a suitcase. Russ and I are playing the couple. Later this afternoon we'll film both indoor and outdoor scenes with Lindy. It's going to get pretty hair-raising around here! I just wanted to let you know . . . and anybody else who is home right now, or today. It may be getting pretty loud around here. Don't call the cops. It's only us play-acting!"

"Well, I'm glad you warned us!" Bernice chuckled and winked.

Tom laughed, and kept on clipping the bushes.

"And no lawn-mower noise today! Can you wait on the lawns?" pleaded Tina.

"Sure thing, Tina," Tom promised.

"How *interesting*! You and Russ live such interesting lives!" Bernice gushed.

"Sometimes," Tina responded dryly.

Shortly, Tina re-entered through the front door to the living room.

"Okay, I've got that covered."

"Since we're in our street clothes, let's shoot the argument in the kitchen first. We'll seem to be arguing over the checkbook. Tina, go get your checkbook," says Russell, directing.

"Well, now this is just like real life!" She laughed. Russell mentioned to Doug about starting in the kitchen.

"Doug, let's shoot in the kitchen. There's enough natural light that we may not need to throw up any more lights." Doug followed with his video camera; Tom followed with cables and microphones.

"Okay, Doug . . . Tina . . . there will be no audio on this video. This scene is just to illustrate the couple in the story fighting. Tina, start doing something in the kitchen, then I will intervene, acting upset over the money spent in the checkbook."

"Okay." Tina pulled some celery out of the refrigerator and chopped it on the board with a kitchen knife.

"Doug, frame up the shot. Let's roll!" Doug aimed the video camera, framing up Tina in the shot. "Rolling . . . 5, 4, 3, 2, 1, We're in!"

As Tina worked in the kitchen, Russell came in holding an open checkbook, and appeared to be angry. She turned around. Russell pointed at the checkbook, and threw his arms around in a rage. Tina interacted in defense, yelling back. She ad-libbed the dialog which would not be heard on the music video track.

"You don't understand . . . the kids need school clothes. And I had to take the car in for repairs last week. I had no choice!" Tina wailed.

"Oh, you sound so innocent. All I know is we have overdrawn the account this month about $600. So how did that happen?" Tina looked distraught, and shook her head.

"I don't know. It must be because your check deposited late, or something!"

"There is something called a phone. You could have called me. I don't want to talk about this anymore." He stormed out of the room. Doug signaled Russell and Tina.

"I'm pausing the video right here. Great stuff, you guys." Doug remarked. "Great fight."

"Phew! That's a lot of negative energy!" Tina said, sweating just a little. "Fighting is hard work."

"It's time for the 'storming out of the house with the suitcase scene now,'" said Russell.

"Yep, that was on the shot sheet I scratched out this morning. I think this is called 'flying by the seat of our pants,'" Tina laughed, shaking her head.

Doug followed Russell upstairs to their bedroom with the video camera, while Tom followed with the cables. Russell put on a coat, and looked for a suitcase.

"Okay, let me put the suitcase on the bed. Start close up on it, then pull back to bring me into the shot. Ready?"

"Rolling . . ."

Russell opened the suitcase, and threw in socks, T-shirts, pants, and a shaving kit, and then zipped it shut. Russell took the suitcase by the handle and went over to the open door of the bedroom.

"Cut! Doug, get down to the bottom of the stairs with the camera!"

Doug moved down to the landing at the base of the stairs, as he filmed Russell angrily rushing down, opening the front door, and then slamming it behind him. Russell waited at the exterior of their home at the door.

Bernice and Tom continued working in their front yard. Tom clipped the tall junipers by the driveway.

"Well, here it goes. Tina warned us." Tom winked at Bernice.

"A little fireworks for the TV screen!" Bernice chuckled, and snipped the rosebushes.

Russell walked back inside. "Doug, do we need a take two on that?"

"Only because I want to try throwing up a light in the stairwell. That shot could turn out to be a little too dark." Time passed, with the shooting and reshooting of scenes. But for the most part, things moved rather quickly.

Doug and Tom positioned Tina and Russell at the kitchen at the breakfast table. This was a very key scene in the music video, as the couple seemed to move toward reconciliation. Tina was in a bathrobe and Russell was wearing flannel pajamas. There was an open Bible in front of them. They talked and smiled as if there had been a happy new resolution reached in their relationship.

"Okay . . . This is the happy ending to the story—this four-minute movie! Cut! I think we have enough of that one. Will Lindy be home from school soon? We are ready for her to do her scenes."

"It's 2:45 . . . any minute," said Tina. "Yvonne is walking her home. We'll give her a break, a sandwich and some juice, and she should be ready before too long."

Soon there were noises on the sidewalk out in front of the house. The front door opened. Lindy and Yvonne had arrived.

"Right on cue! Hi, girls," Tina greeted, and then walked toward them.

"I got Lindy a cold drink in the cafeteria. She's feeling pretty good," said Yvonne.

"Are you, honey?" asked Tina.

Lindy nodded, and continued to suck her cold drink through a straw.

Well, we're ready for your scenes, and Doug is here ready to go. We'll have to get you into the right clothes. Do you want to do the dancing, twirling scenes first . . . and the trampoline? Or the pretending-to-cry scenes?" Tina asked.

"Let's save the heavy acting until last." Russell suggested.

Soon, Russell and Tina were on the front lawn with Lindy. Doug was in front of her ready to shoot the scene.

"Okay, Lindy, this is at the end of the song, 'The Letter,' do you remember? We played the song, and this is where the little girl is really happy that her parents read 'The Letter from God,' the Bible, and they are now acting loving toward each other, and everything between them is healed. So you are feeling very happy, and you are going to do ballet twirling scenes, just like in dance class . . ." Tina instructed her. Doug artistically framed the shot.

"Rolling . . ."

Lindy, who was about eight years old during the filming of this video, with long flowing blond hair, launched into her scene. She wore bright pink, and the outfit had long sashes that flowed in the wind with her celebrative dance moves. A rose garden was in the background. Tom and Bernice strained their necks to see what was going on.

"Look at that . . . Is that sweet or what?" Bernice gasped.

"That Lindy, she's got talent!" Tom beamed.

The graceful Lindy danced a skillful ballet on the lawn for about ten minutes. Doug was taking the video from different angles, even laying on the ground shooting upward at the dancing Lindy. Tina smiled. She already knew this video was going to turn out exceptionally well.

"Okay, I think we've got some really good stuff there! Thanks Lindy!" Lindy stopped the dance, then hugged her mom. Russell walked over to them.

"It looks like we are ready for the scenes in bed at night, where Lindy will be 'crying.'"

"Remember, honey, we talked about doing scenes where you pretend to cry. The little girl in the story is very sad about hearing her parents fighting, and she begins to cry. Did you practice this in your acting classes last month?"

"Yes, Mom, I can do it," Lindy assured Tina.

"We can use eye drops to make tear trails on your face . . . to make it easier."

"Okay, if you want too."

"Let's roll . . . Tina, let's get Lindy into her pajamas upstairs. Let's go!" Russell said, directing them. "Doug and Tom, are you coming?"

Soon, Lindy was in position on her bed. Tina, nearby, coached her. Doug entered with the video camera on his shoulder.

"Low lights . . . shades down," Doug said to Tina. "We're going to simulate a moonlit room. Are you ready, Lindy? Let's see you looking sad. Take one!"

Following direction, Lindy tossed and turned, looking like she was grief stricken. She feigned crying as Tina looked on.

"Cut! Okay we need the eye drops. Let me check the medicine cabinet," Tina said.

Soon she returned with a bottle of soothing "get red eye out" type drops. She knelt by Lindy's bedside.

"Okay, honey. Let's do the 'tear trails'." Lindy laid back for the eye drops.

"Mom, that stings!"

"What? It's soothing eye drops," Tina said, looking at the label. "I use them in my own eyes." Lindy was really crying now. Doug got the camera ready, and into position.

"Let's get the shot . . ." said Doug, rolling the video. Lindy was crying now, the real tears were flowing. He got a few seconds of the real tears, but then Tina stopped him.

"Cut! Stop! Lindy, baby, I don't understand! Let's splash water in your eyes right away!" Tina said, becoming alarmed. Russell walked into the room.

"What's going on? She is crying a little hard here."

"I don't get it. I just used regular drugstore eye drops that I use to relax my eyes, and get the red out. She said it hurt." Lindy splashed water in her face. Tina handed her a big soft towel.

"Aw, honey, I'm so sorry. I was just trying to make tear trails. Those drops are made for eyes."

"I'm okay, Mom. I *really* cried that time!" she laughed, blotting her wet face.

"Yes, you did! Spoken like a true actress." Tina hugged her. "I had no idea, baby!"

"Are you okay? Take a break. In a few minutes when you are ready, let's get Lindy on the trampoline. Are you okay, honey? Let me see those eyes."

"I'm okay, Dad," Lindy grinned.

"Good, honey. What did you do, beat her or something?" Russell laughed.

"Oh Russell, stop it! No, it was the eye drops. Who would have ever thought?" Russell looked at the bottle. "It should have been fine." Tina shrugged.

"It's a mystery. What can I say? I use them." Russell worked to get them back on track.

"When she's ready, put her in a cute play outfit. Use the sweatshirt with the rainbow on the front. That will work."

"Great idea! Lindy, let's get you a snack. It's time for a little break here!" Tina said, taking her downstairs.

After a brief rest, and a snack, Lindy was ready to resume acting. They went outdoors into the backyard. Lindy immediately headed toward their in-ground trampoline. She was back in good spirits by then. Doug prepared to frame up the shot, while Tom stood by to watch the action on the monitor.

"Okay. . . Do we have a white balance?" asked Russell.

"Here, use the back of my T-shirt," volunteered Tom. Tina rolled her eyes.

"So, where is the white card?" Tina asked.

"This will work . . . Really, I'm fine," Russell insisted. "How is it looking on the monitor, Tom . . . Doug?"

"Good. Is our star actress ready to roll?" Doug asked. Lindy walked over to the scene.

"That's me," Lindy grinned. "Do I talk or just jump?"

"Just jump. The video will go with the closing part of the song, and will freeze-frame on you and your rainbow shirt for the close. It's all in the editing, later," her dad explained.

"It's nice to see you visualizing ahead, dear," Tina commented.

"Lindy . . . *go!*" Lindy stepped onto the trampoline and immediately went into her moves.

Tina stood off to the side with Tom, as they watched Lindy on the monitor.

Lindy bounced and whirled on the trampoline with precision. Tina continued to remember the history.

"The girls rolled and tumbled on this trampoline before they could even walk!" she spoke softly to Tom as they watched her on the monitor.

"It shows." Tom smiled.

"Wow . . . great stuff, Lindy. Give me a big smile! Good girl! Jump directly in front of the lens," said Russell, directing her in the closing scenes. A freeze-frame of Lindy, her long blond hair flying, arms out, rainbow on her shirt front and center, showed dramatically up on the screen.

"Wonderful! I'll work on that a little more when I get into editing. Great acting, Lindy!" Tina praised Lindy who by now was sporting a big smile.

"You were great, honey! Your acting coach would be proud—and I'm very proud of you!"

They all went inside, as Doug and Tom unhooked the equipment, and got ready to take it back to the TV Station. Tom and Bernice still trimmed the hedges outside in the front yard across the street.

"Do you suppose there's any more," Bernice asked, looking over at Tom.

"Nope. I think they are all done. You will just have to see this one on TV, Bernice."

Inside the editing suite at the studio at work, it was now late evening. Russ was on the headset, listening to the song, and viewing the opening scenes of the music video, *The Letter*—the opening scenes of Lindy outside on the lawn and in the rose garden, daydreaming, and wishing her parents would stop fighting, and just love each other. Russell glanced over at Tina.

"This is going to be great once it's finished. The video will be the centerpiece of the program this Friday evening for *New York Tonight*."

"You've been here all day!" Tina frowned.

"And I'll be here all night until it's finished. You did a great shot sheet. It'll come out just like we expected. It's going to be late. Why don't you just go on home, Tina. You can see the finished product in the morning before we ship it out by FED EX to New York." Tina gave him a hug and a little peck

"Okay. I brought a bunch of great leftovers for you that you can warm up in the break room. Be sure you catch a few winks on the couch here!"

"Thanks honey. I'll see you in the morning when you come in to work."

"I can hardly wait . . . Bye!" Tina said, departing to drive back home.

***

While Tina drove home, her thoughts tumbled as she listened to the soft music on her CD player. "Oh Lord, how do we live like this? Who would have ever thought? We live with this TV work day and night . . . and night and day."

Tina drove up into the driveway, and went inside the house. She turned the lights out, and started upstairs to bed. Lindy's room was next door. Tina heard her wake, and rustle about.

"Mom, is that you?" Tina went in and sat on Lindy's bed.

"Hi, honey . . . Did your big sister get you to bed on time?"

"Yes, but I was hoping to see Daddy."

Kerry Lee appeared in her pajamas, and climbed up onto her Mommy's lap.

"Daddy is working lots of late nights these days, trying to get production ready on time, like the music video you were just the 'star' in!"

"It seems like he works late more and more," Lindy said in a complaining little girl voice.

"I know, honey. It's been like this for such a long time. We hope we can change that soon.

"I hope so."

"Goodnight, honey . . . Mommy's got to get her sleep too! Grandpa's going to come be with you again tomorrow. Come on, Kerry . . . Let's get you back in bed. Let's all try to get to get some sleep now."

"Okay . . ." Lindy rolled over and soon went back to sleep. Tina shut the door, and got ready to go to bed herself. Sleep always makes things better by the next day, Tina reasoned.

The next morning, Tina anxiously drove over the bridge to the TV Station in Concord. After the kids got settled with their Grandpa Henry, she walked into the editing suite where Russell worked on the video. Tina noticed that he was still seated at the controls, viewing the results on the screen.

"Good morning . . . How's it going? You look tired," Tina said, giving him a little hug.

"I should look tired. It's been a long night! But we're almost finished, just a few more finishing touches. Les, up in the sound booth, has worked his magic to sweeten the audio on the song."

"Russ . . . I think we have it. Do you want to roll it for Tina?" Les called out.

"Sure . . ."

The music video rolled, with the opening music, as the story was told through the song lyrics, and the visuals, as Lindy, Russell, and Tina artistically and sensitively illustrated the story of the broken family healed by loving principles from God's Word, the Bible. Tina watched. She got a little emotional as the song ended on the last note, and the freeze frame of Lindy with the big smile wearing the rainbow T-shirt appeared.

"There you have it . . . a four-minute movie, starring the George family . . . Well, part of the George family!" Russell announced, with a happy grin.

"Great job, you guys!" Les remarked, sporting a big smile.

"It's beautiful, Russ!" Tina said, wiping a tear from one eye.

"Well, you and Lindy were great actresses, too. I'm going to have them run a few copies. We'll get one off to channel 55 in New York, by FED EX this morning. It has to be there by tomorrow afternoon."

"Sometimes I just don't know how we do it, Russ . . . month after month, year after year," Tina said in an imploring tone of voice.

"We always come through with the great shows and programs, and we get them out on time, too." Russell smiled, looking over at Tina.

"I mean *us*, Russell. How do we live like this? Lindy asked for you last night when I came in, Kerry Lee, too. She's only six. Are you and I going to be strangers to them growing up?" Tina got up and shut the door to the room. "Are your headsets off?" Russell turned the 'off' switch.

"Yeah."

"Something's got to change here . . . *Will* it ever change?"

"Tina, you know how it's been going. We're a new TV station. From the beginning, you, me — all of us who pioneered the station figured the first few years would be tough, then later after some good telethons, the salaries would get stronger, and there would be more personal time off."

"But's it's not happening that way is it?" Tina said, looking upset.

"No, it's not. Just when we think we have raised good financial support in a telethon, the money just stays at the top. You and I who create all the programs that bring in the money . . . we're living like paupers in comparison," Russell admitted.

"You've got that right! Russ, what are we going to do about it?" Tina begged him.

"Pray? Pray about it . . . Isn't that what we always do?" asked Russell.

"Yes, we will pray about it," Tina agreed. "Oh Lord, you see our dilemma . . . please help us!"

Russell agreed with her, as they paused briefly at the thought.

"I'm with ya, Tina!" Then Russell remembered something yet to be done. He went through some papers, then handed Tina a production sheet from his pile.

"In the meantime, here is the shot sheet and the script for the new PSA about parents teaching their kids how to brush their teeth right . . . good dental hygiene! I'll send Doug and Tom out there to our house to shoot it tomorrow afternoon. Be sure the kids are ready to do some acting." Tina sighed, and took the shot sheet from Russell.

"Okay, Russ."

"I'll see you at home tonight."

"*Promise?*" asked Tina with a little smile. "I was just saying that it was the only room of our home that has not been on TV."

"Well, now, it's one hundred percent!" Russell laughed.

The next afternoon at the George house, Doug and Tom, his assistant video shooter, were on the scene at the family residence, shooting scenes for the PSA Russell requested. Doug sat on the closed toilet seat pointing the camera toward Kerry Lee, receiving a toothbrush that Tina handed to her as the Mom in the shot. On went the toothpaste, in went the brush into Kerry Lee's mouth. Tina instructed her about brushing her teeth, per the script.

"Let's get one more take with Lindy brushing her teeth." Lindy moved forward into position in front of the sink, with Tina when they hear the front door opening.

Yvonne came in from school. She took a look at the scene.

"Am I in this one?" she asked.

"No, you're good. We're just using the little kids for this one."

"Good. I have lots of homework to get done!" She spread her work out on the table.

"When we're finished here, get some B-roll shots of the water running, me talking to Lindy and giving her the brush, putting toothpaste on the brush, things like that."

The phone on the table next to Tina rang. "Tom, can you get that for me?" Tina called out.

Tom picked up the call. "Yeah, Russell, I think we'll have it all wrapped up here at least within the half hour," Tom said.

"Great!" Tina had a thought: "Tom, will you ask Russell if he's going to be home this evening for dinner?"

"Tina wants to know if 'you'll be home for dinner tonight?'" Tom asked, repeating her question.

"Not likely . . . Too much editing to get done."

Tina took the phone receiver away from Tom.

"Russell, you've hardly been home since Friday. What's up?"

"Babe, like I said, I have so much editing to get done, and Gary wants me to direct two shows this afternoon, and one tonight."

"Russ, you're fifteen minutes away. You could at least come home for dinner."

"We'll see. Oh, by the way. Gary would like us to put up the singer of 'The Letter,'" Tim Waddington, for a couple days while he appears on the *Coast to Coast* program. He doesn't mind staying in a home. We can do that can't we?"

Tina felt like screaming, would this never end? She took a deep breath, "I guess. It means I have to go into high-speed prep mode though," she said.

"You can do it, hon . . . I know you can!"

"Yeah, I can do it. I can always do it." Tina sounded a little stressed.

"Okay. . . I'll see you later. Love you." Tina looked at Yvonne.

"Okay, we're in high-speed company-is-coming mode now. We've got a guest artist staying with us."

"Who is it this time?" Yvonne asked.

"Tim, the singer/songwriter of 'The Letter.'"

"Oh, that one. Well, that should be interesting. I suppose this means I have to clean my room." Yvonne frowned.

"Well, you should be cleaning your room anyway. But it *does* mean you're going to help me with a little house cleaning today and tomorrow."

"I guess. I do have homework, you know." Yvonne sighed.

"I know. When you want something, it's a good thing I don't say, 'I work,' you know!"

"Okay . . . okay," said Yvonne, getting into work mode.

Doug had been reviewing the video he just shot in the bathroom with Kerry Lee and Lindy.

"I think we have everything we need to edit the PSA for Russell. I'm gonna pack everything up, and get out of your way!"

"Okay, thanks, Doug." His assistant rolled the camera cables to pack up the equipment. "Give Russell my regards. I guess I'll run into him sometime, someday!"

"You two definitely have an interesting life. I have never seen anything like it."

"Yeah . . . We live like movie stars without the big money!" She laughed, painfully.

The video shooter guys headed out the door with their equipment. "Yeah, without the money, or the time," said Tina, a little upset. She shook her head, and crossed her arms, wondering at that moment if things would ever really change.

CHAPTER NINE

A NEW BREAKTHROUGH BEGINS

It was a usual day at the broadcasting center. Tina worked in the viewing room in master control with all the many screens turned on with live broadcasts. As Tina viewed the screens with the normal network news playing, a production colleague, Tanya, stood next to her as she watched an interview on the monitor by a celebrity host out of New York.

"That Rav Zepeda guy has been around forever, at least twenty years. He must have one of the top jobs in broadcasting out of New York," remarked Tina.

"I think he's actually known more for being an investigative reporter. He's helped crack some big cases. Rav is considered pretty controversial, but the public still loves him," Tanya remarked.

"What network is he with again?" Tina asked with an inquisitive look.

"ABCN . . . I think," Tanya replied.

"Thanks! You've just given me an idea." She winked.

Tina slipped into her production office and closed the door. She flipped through her Rolodex.

"Oh, where is that number?" she said, talking to herself. Tina had trouble finding it. "Just let me get it through directory assistance. I don't have a lot of time." Tina dialed the number. "ABCN-New York, please . . . Yes, it's a broadcasting center. Yes, thank you." She scribbled down the number. A voice came on the phone which said, "Connecting now."

"ABCN. How may I direct your call?"

"The news director, please."

"I will connect you now." Tina waited, while tapping her pencil on the desk.

"News Director . . . Zak Williams speaking."

"Yes, Mr. Williams, my name is Tina George. I'm a producer with KTYN out here in Northern California. Listen, I have what I think is an important story for Rav Zedpeda. It's a big story with room for more investigation to really bring it around. I know he loves stuff like that. If he's in, do you suppose I could connect with him for a few minutes?"

"Well, I'm not sure he's back . . . He was out on location this morning. . . What is this regarding?"

"I know what happened to the Zodiac Killer . . . the phantom serial killer out of the San Francisco area who disappeared in 1978." Zak was silent at first, and then sounded shocked.

"You *know* what happened to the Zodiac Killer?"

"Yes, I do."

"Hold on . . . Don't go away... I will find him! Stay right there! I'm going to put you on hold. Don't go away. What was your name again?"

"Tina . . . Just Tina."

"Okay . . . Stay right there. I will find him!" Zak sounded a little frantic.

Tina was on hold . . . five minutes . . . eight minutes. She looked at the phone.

"I think it's been about ten minutes . . . ." She sighed.

Tina looked down, as she felt doubtful about making the call. She reasoned further during the long hold time and talked to herself quietly. "It could still be too soon . . . The public should know . . . especially the Bay area...but it could be too soon." Tina paced. Still no Rav Zepeda on the phone. Meanwhile, her doubts grew. "What if someone sick impersonates him, and kills somebody and puts 'Zodiac' all over it?" she reasoned. Tina paced back and forth in her office. She made a decision. Tina slowly put the phone receiver back down on the cradle. The line disconnected. At that very moment, Rav got to the phone.

"Hello . . . hello . . . ?" No one was there now. Tina had made her decision. "Zak, who was that woman?"

"I don't know . . . Tina . . . somebody."

"Tina . . . *somebody*? That does not help me!"

Tina sat in her office with her hands over her face in frustration. "It's still too soon." There was a knock on door. It was a studio tech.

Tina, Russell needs you in the studio. Can you come?"

"Yes . . . yes. I'll be right there," Tina said, heading over to the studio. Her open willingness to talk about the Zodiac story to a major news network would have to wait until far into the future.

Late the next afternoon, Russell was at the front door with the singer, Tim Waddington, helping him with his suitcase. As they entered, they saw that Tina had the table set for dinner. She greeted Russell and their new house guest with a kind smile.

"Hello, Tim . . . I'm Tina! We're so glad to meet you! She shook his hand, cheerfully.

"Yes, I recognize you from the music video..."

"And here's Lindy . . ." Tina beamed.

"Yes, I recognize you too! *Very good acting job, young lady!*"

"Thanks," Lindy blushed.

"And this is our youngest child, Kerry Lee. She wasn't in the story."

"Yes, I heard you were at Grandma's house during the filming," Tim said. Yvonne came down the stairs, and walked over.

"And this is Yvonne, our oldest daughter."

"Hi…glad to meet you. Great song, by the way!" smiled Yvonne.

"No words can express how I felt when I saw the finished product, with the great acting of your family to illustrate the story! I guess you might say I got pretty choked up."

"Well, it helped during our telethon for the New York station. A good support level was raised," Russell said with a smile.

"Well, I'm glad to hear that!" Tim said, with a soft country drawl.

"Do want to put your suitcase over there, and sit down for dinner? Everything's ready," Russell said. They all walked over, and gathered around the table. "Tim, perhaps you could say grace."

"I'd be honored." Everybody bowed their heads. "Lord, thank you for this wonderful family. I pray a blessing over their lives for all the great service they do. Bless this food to our bodies, I pray … and bless the hands that prepared it, Lord. In your name we pray. Amen."

"Amen. Thanks, Tim!" Russell grinned.

They enjoyed eating together and conversing about their lives, and Tim's life out on the ranch on the Indian reservation in the lower Yakima Valley in Washington State.

After a while, the kids left and went into the other room to play and watch TV. Tina and Russell continued to talk with Tim.

"So you lead a pretty interesting life. How did all this TV work begin?"

"Our church was a broadcast center for eleven years, then we branched over to the big station with the license for the San Francisco

Bay area. It took seven years to complete all the work to get it finally done. Then the big tower was placed up here on Mt. Diablo."

"Devil Mountain, they call it around here," Tina added. Russell nodded.

"Yeah, the day the helicopter flew up with it to put it in place, it was dropped. I'll never forget the sight of it sliding down the side of the mountain."

"Ouch!" Tim remarked, sipping his coffee.

"Yeah, no kidding." Russell smiled. "Fortunately, the insurance replaced it, and before long we were up and on the air, all over the San Francisco Bay area and the South Bay. Recently, we opened in Fresno, then even in New York. It turned out we produce a lot of programs that are nationally and internationally syndicated and up on satellites. It's been an interesting last few years."

"But lately Russ and I have been having more discussions about how it is just too heavy handed on our family life being the parents of small children. Haven't we, honey?" Tina added. She looked over at Russell, knowing he wasn't quite sure about the decision yet.

"Yes, we've been talking about that more lately. It's just that when you've worked as a television producer for about a decade, it's hard to transition to something else . . . Same thing with Tina."

"Well, what did you do before?"

"I was a plant manager for a building materials company, with over about one hundred employees."

"I see. What about Tina?"

"I worked as a medical assistant for a family-practice doctor before the TV work. I don't know if I would go back to that, particularly," Tina remarked.

"Russ . . . I possibly have an idea for you. There's somebody I want you to meet in Yakima, Washington. He has a big plant that employs about 400 people, and they do international business out of Yakima. If you really want to make a change, I think he would hire you in a heartbeat," Tim smiled.

"I'm a civil engineer originally, but I've been away from the plant management job for a few years now," said Russell.

"The rest of the story is that the owner is a church-going man who supports the local Christian TV station. They plan to expand and break ground for a new station in the very near future. He's going to love meeting you and Tina. You could do both." Russell and Tina smiled at each other. They wondered if this was the breakthrough they'd been waiting for.

***

The next day, they walked into the Concord airport in Northern California. They met a smiling Jere who helped them load their luggage into his private plane. He was a happy-looking man in his late forties, dressed casually and ready to get the trip underway. Soon, he was seated skillfully at the controls of a handsome looking private plane. Tina and Russell were on board and seated, feeling a swell of excitement and anticipation. Jere was the corporation owner in Yakima. He was at the controls of his plane, waiting for instructions from the control tower.

"Are you ready for a great adventure?" Jere asked with a broad grin.

"Sure. It was nice of you to fly down here, and pick us up in your private plane!"

"No problem." Jere's plane soon took off, and flew high into the sky north toward Yakima International Airport in Washington State.

They arrived at their destination late that same afternoon. After an overnight rest in a local hotel, Russell and Tina were shown around a television studio that appeared to be in an industrial park next to other sub locations for the other company Jere owned. One of Jere's staff met them, and showed them around the television-studio complex.

"Hi . . . I'm Randy! I'm the station manager. Jere's told me a lot about you. We actually see your programming from KYTN in Concord, here in Yakima."

"Really?" Tina asked. She knew the programming went out regionally and nationally, but didn't always know just where.

"Yes . . . we love that *Your Health Today* program! And my kids love *Superbook.*"

"How many shows are you producing here right now?" Russell asked Randy.

"Only one flagship program. We act as an affiliate and a relay station for the big international Christian station out of Southern California. We hope to do more locally produced programming. That's where you two come in." Tina and Russell were led through more large rooms and studios as they finished touring around the station.

"One of our staff will run you back to the main office up at J-1 to meet further with Jere." They stepped into a van and were driven up to the executive office at the J-1 building.

Russell and Tina entered and sat down in front of Jere's desk. They felt encouraged by the possibilities. Jere spoke to them, smiling.

"I'd like to have you two come to work for me. I'd have no problem paying you considerably more than you make now." His hand reached out and gave Russell a piece paper with a figure on it. Russell and Tina smiled at each other.

"That's very good." Tina nodded in agreement. "We would have to go back, and sell our house," Russell said, waiting for Jere's reaction.

"No problem. I'll wait for you!" Tina and Russell felt a sigh of relief, and a sense of rescue all at the same time. They knew this was the opportunity they had been waiting and praying for!

Two days later, Russell and Tina were back at home, sitting up in bed late at night, talking about the potential move. It was a tender moment in their relationship as they talked about their future.

"Russell, you know it's the best thing for us . . . don't you?" said Tina, pleadingly.

"Yes. It's just that we're moving out of state, away from family, the kid's grandparents . . . pioneering something new . . . again."

"Yvonne has been planning for a while to attend college here. I guess she could stay behind and live with my folks. I'll miss her!" Tina seemed to ache as she spoke. "God will help us, if we put him first, Russell. You know that."

"Yeah . . . I know that."

Tina hugged him, and gave him a kiss. They fell asleep peacefully. It was the beginning of a whole new life.

CHAPTER TEN

PLANNING THE MOVE— SELLING THE HOUSE

The next day, Tina was on the phone with a local real estate company. She and Russell decided to use a husband wife realtor team named Dom and Sylvie. They seemed aggressive, dynamic, and the right people for the job.

"Yes . . . We will notice the sign go up today? That's fine . . . And possibly a hot-air balloon? I guess that's okay too. It's all part of the marketing, I suppose." Tina nodded, as she listened to Sylvie on the phone. Tina looked at her watch. She knew she needed to drive to work and join Russell soon.

Meanwhile, back at the KYTN studio in Concord, Russell talked to Rob, the station manager, in his large executive office.

"I suppose I can understand your desire to make this move," said Rob, with obvious tones of disappointment.

"Tina and I have given it our heartfelt consideration. It's really the best thing to do for our family," explained Russell.

"I understand the timing is contingent on you selling your house."

"Yes, sir."

"Well, keep me posted, and we'll work on making the transition as seamless as possible."

Russell stood up and shook hands with his boss, Rob.

166

"Thank you, sir!" It seemed to Russell that Rob was being more understanding than usual. Was it because they were short-handed, and few qualified people would work for the low wages offered there?

"In the meantime, we have a show to do! I believe they're waiting for you in Studio One," said Rob.

After Tina arrived at the station, she and Russell walked down the hall together toward the main production studio, talking.

"So, how did he take it?" Tina asked, raising a curious eyebrow.

"Okay . . . I guess. He said he would work with us to make the transition as seamless as possible. We're just here until the house sells, whenever *that* is!" Russell said.

"You know, since the earthquake not long ago, things in Real Estate are moving more slowly than usual. It might be a while."

"Well, then . . . it might be a while!" Russell ducked into master control toward his spot as technical director. Tina walked back toward her desk in production as they started another day in the TV production world.

***

Winter seemed to arrive slowly. It was December, and Christmastime-decorating mode at the George's house was in full gear. Tina adorned a Christmas tree with bright red, shiny, shellacked apple ornaments, and sprigs of white baby's breath with silver ribbons.

"That looks cool, Mom! Look at all those apples!" Lindy remarked delightedly.

Yvonne walked over and looked the tree up and down. "What's up with the apples, Mom?"

"This year, we're celebrating moving to Yakima, Washington. It's like the apple capitol of the world, or something like that," Tina answered.

"Yeah, I noticed those souvenir mugs you and Dad brought back from Yakima had apples on them."

"Yep! There are apple orchards everywhere! It's going to be our new home." Tina smiled warmly.

"It would be really hard to leave my friends, Mom." Yvonne frowned.

"I know, honey . . . but you would make new friends," Tina reminded her.

"I'm going to be a senior next year . . . I was going to attend college here."

"We'll talk about it more, later. I mean, you could stay here with Grandma and Grandpa if it had to be. We'll think about it a little more, okay?"

"Okay, Mom . . . I know we can work something out."

"Yes, we will, honey! Now, it's Saturday . . . and you are pretty good at making dinner when Mom is busy. How about we work on some of that sweet and sour chicken you're so good at making?" Tina suggested to Yvonne.

"Sure! I think we have everything here." Yvonne opened the refrigerator door for a look.

"I'll tell you what. I need to go be involved in a late-afternoon broadcast of that Center Stage Christmas show. So you look after Lindy and Kerry Lee, and you're the Chef for the day!

"Okay, Mom . . . I can handle it! Do you know that Lindy and Kerry Lee have been sneaking into the Christmas goodies you baked that are in the big freezer out in the garage?" Yvonne snitched.

"*Girls?*" Lindy and Kerry Lee looked sheepish and guilty.

"Those chocolate fudge balls rolled in coconut are *so good*, Mom!" Lindy confessed.

"I like those round cookies that look like a wreath with all the candy balls on them!" Kerry Lee grinned.

"Oh girls . . . the decorated cookies! Listen, I make those in batches so your father can give them as gifts in tins. Girls, there are some chocolate-chip cookies in the kitchen freezer. Can we stick to those when you need a treat?" Tina scolded them.

"Okay, Mom." Lindy sighed. Kerry Lee looked disappointed.

"Yvonne, you watch them now! I've got to get ready to go to the studio. 'Ladies,' I leave you in charge." Tina took off her apron and gave it to Yvonne.

At the broadcasting center, the master control area was humming with activity. Russell was on the headset. Out on the set there were three studio cameras with operators, a floor director, and one overhead camera on a crane called a "sky-cam." The Christmas program was in its last forty-five minutes or so, and Tina was at her desk on the phone

"I need to get back in there pretty soon. This has been quite a big Christmas show! We have half a dozen of some of the top Christian music artists in the country headlining this program. It's been really fun to meet them! They've been arriving in on our shuttles from the airport and the hotels at different times. Rochelle, Joan, and I did a very nice buffet table for them so they would have something to eat when they first arrived here," Tina reported to a work friend at another location.

"Oh Tina, you are always quite the hostess!" her colleague on the phone replied. A floor tech from the studio suddenly poked his head around the corner.

"Tina . . . Russell's asking for you. He needs you in the studio, right away!"

"Okay . . . gotta go, Ramona. Talk to you later. Just send all those music CDs we've been talking about. I'll have to make editing decisions on them by next week. Bye." She hung up suddenly. *"Coming!"*

Tina walked into the master-control area. Russell was on the headset as the technical director with a live show in progress behind the glass in the studio. It was the big Christmas music show they had been planning for over the last month or two. The main music presentation from the artists was over now. The hosts sat around a warm living-room type set with a large brightly lit Christmas tree, fireplace, and all the appearance of a cozy home decorated for the holidays. The five featured artists talked about their Christmas memories from the past. Russell had turned off his headset for a moment to talk to Tina.

"Tina, we're in the last 45 minutes of the show. I need you to do something for me."

"Like what, Russell?" Tina wondered.

"I need for you to drive home, and bring a couple large trays of those decorated Christmas cookies from the freezer that you've been making over the past few weeks. Then I want you to sneak them on the set, and put them on the end table on each side. We're going to close the show and roll credits over the guests eating the goodies."

"Wow, honey. . . I don't know if I have time to do that! I would have to drive all the way home over the bridge . . ."

"One more thing . . . I want the gifts wrapped in paper, bows... everything. Choose some items that would suit the guests out there. They will unwrap them too, while the credits roll at the end." As he talked, Tina was going into a mild shock.

"Russell . . . if we had talked about this a few days ago, maybe?" Tina suggested. Russell was not hearing her.

"Go! I know you can do it! Be back here in 35 minutes . . . no later!" Tina got up and headed toward the door.

"So this is what I get for walking on water more than once around here?" said Tina, continuing to look shocked.

Tina got in her car, and pulled out onto the road. On the way to the freeway, she spotted a haggard looking old man in worn out clothes wearing a hat and winter scarf. He was standing near the freeway entrance carrying a large sign on a roughly made post that read, "Jesus Saves!" Tears welled up in Tina's eyes. "Jesus saves . . . Oh Jesus, save *us!*" she prayed. "How did we ever get into such a stress-mess . . . and how do we get out of it Lord? We've tried so hard. We came to this TV network with such high hopes. We wanted to use our talents for you, Lord. But no matter what we do it's never good enough . . . we get little credit. I'm sorry Lord, I know that's my pride, but it hurts. Russell is killing himself . . . and our family. And Rob doesn't seem to care. He just takes more of the money and more of the glory for himself! We don't know what to do . . . *rescue us!*"

As Tina drove onward, she didn't notice that far behind her the figure of the old man with the sign transformed and reconfigured into the form of a thirteen foot tall glowing angel, then disappeared.

Tina maneuvered around cars and big trucks to get home as fast as she could. It was about a fifteen-minute commute that needed to be done in about eight. She got caught behind three big trucks at the Benicia bridge toll plaza, and fumbled for a dollar in change.

"Here you go!" she said, practically throwing the change at the toll-plaza attendant. Tina drove up into the driveway then dashed quickly for the front door of the house. She rushed excitedly into the kitchen.

"Girls . . . I have to load those Christmas cookies from the freezer onto two large trays, and take them to the station. Help me. Run . . . get them!"

"What?!" exclaimed Yvonne.

"Not the chocolate coconut balls!" Lindy frowned.

"Yes, *everything!* Where is the Christmas wrapping paper? Tina yanked open a drawer of the dining room sideboard. "Here we go!" She then ran upstairs to their master bedroom. Tina looked around the bedroom. She grabbed a beautiful African necklace off her jewelry tree.

"This is perfect for CiCi!" She then grabbed one of Russell's new sweaters. "Here we go . . . for Jim." She opened a new shirt still in the wrapping. "Sorry Russell, this was one of your presents!" Tina dove quickly into their closet. She banged around, throwing out some ties, high heels, and other objects, including a red Valentine bra. Tina soon emerged with some new ties, cufflinks, and a cowboy hat. "This is perfect for the country singer! Where's the box? Here we go!"

In a few minutes, Tina was shoving the gifts in gift bags and boxes, wrapping and taping in fast motion, sticking bows on everything. She had wrapped six gifts in holiday wrapping paper or inserted them into holiday bags.

"Girls, here I come . . . Where are those cookies?" The girls emerged into the kitchen with boxes and Tupperware containers filled with cookies. "Here we go . . . Careful now! We don't want to break them! Where are those cookie trays?" They loaded the cookies onto two large trays. "Help me get out to the car girls . . . Come *quickly!*"

"It's Mrs. Claus going to her sleigh!" Yvonne laughed. Lindy and Kerry Lee watched, giggling.

"Are you going to bake more cookies, Mom?" Lindy asked, as Kerry Lee looked a little sad.

"Of course! Let's go!" Tina quickly loaded the goodies into the car.

Breathless, she quickly sped back over the bridge in her car. She drove up to the station, and emerged with the first tray of cookies. She quickly went in to get a few hands to help her unload.

"Russell, I'm back!" A few techs followed her in with the other trays of cookies, and the large bags of presents. Russell turned off his headset when he saw her coming in.

"Good job, Tina! This is what I need you to do. Take the two trays of cookies out to the studio. Lawrence, follow with the bags of presents. I'm going to have the cameras on the guests as they speak. Quietly go in and put the cookies on the end tables on both sides of the set. Put on a headset, and follow my direction. I'll keep the camera off you. Then go put the presents under the tree. *GO!*" Tina looked a little scared and unsure of herself, but she started out to the studio where the live program was going on. She stopped and kicked off her shoes, and was in her stocking feet. A few production assistants with soft soles quietly followed her to assist.

The host, Jim, was leading a discussion among the singers regarding their past Christmas memories. Russell was on the headset directing the crew.

"Camera 2, close in on Chuck as he talks. Camera 1, prepare a shot of the top of the tree where the angel is . . . Camera 3, stay close on Jim as he listens to Chuck's story. Tina...slip the presents under the bottom of the tree . . . Very good, honey." The assistants carefully handed them over, as she laid them down by the lower branches.

"Now, Tina . . . the camera is not on you, so slip the tray of cookies on the table by Michelle. Good . . . now, the camera is on Jim talking, so go to the far right and get that other table, put the tray of cookies there."

Tina responded quickly to the direction, then quietly slipped off the set. She returned through the door to master control behind the glass. She took a huge breath of relief.

"Okay . . . Jim is getting ready to close. We're going to roll credits over the talent eating the cookies and opening the presents. Tina designated the gifts for the talent . . . their names are on them . . . Bea, on floor . . . can you hand the tray of cookies to the first one closest to the table? Get that going . . . Stay off camera, now. Watch out for her camera 2 . . . Very good!"

The studio cameras captured the warmhearted scene of the talent eating the Christmas cookies and passing the tray around. Close up shots revealed scenes of the Christmas tree and wreath cookies, beautifully decorated. One of the singers opened her gift, an African necklace. The other male singers opened their gifts of sweaters and shirts.

"Hey, some of those gifts look familiar!" Russell laughed.

"They ought to! Some of it's your stuff and my stuff, and even some of the presents I was going to *wrap*." Tina announced.

"Okay . . . go to black. Good job, everybody!" said Russell. The Executive Producer/General Manager, Rob, beamed.

"Great job, Russell! How did you ever think of that? What a great way to end the show! That was very creative, Russell!"

Tina frowned. She looked worn out.

"It was sort of a . . . last-minute inspiration," Russell smiled, looking over at Tina.

"This could mean a nice Christmas bonus for you. You make us look good. I don't know what we'll do after you two move away. Anyway . . . very good work!" Rob gave a rare happy nod of approval, then left the room. Tina looked over at Russell with a dark cloud over her face. She was definitely unhappy.

"Russell, I would have really appreciated at least a one-day notice on that idea."

"I'm sorry, honey. But hey, you were great!" Russell replied, looking happy as a clam.

Tina sighed, looking tired.

"I'm going home right now. I have a lot to do. The house is on *Realtor Tour* tomorrow.

"In *December?*"

"Yes, in December. We will have the Christmas look in full swing . . . fire in the fireplace, decorations, cookies and all!"

"Okay, honey. See you later tonight."

"Yeah, see you later tonight," a tired Tina replied.

The next day, Russell and Tina's home looked very clean and decorated for the event. The For Sale sign was prominent in the front yard. Realtors, and mortgage brokers dressed in business attire, arrived at the home. A Realtor couple, Dom and Sylvie, who were working with the listing, hosted the realtor tour. The woman, Sylvie was in the kitchen serving hot apple cider. Christmas cookies were on the counter, along with pictorial real estate fliers displaying the home. The phone rang. Sylvie answered. It was Tina on the other line at the restaurant. Tina was with Kerry Lee and Lindy at a fast-food burger restaurant. It was about noon, and they were eating burgers and fries.

"Sylvie . . . how's it going?" Tina asked, using a pay phone nearby as the girls ate their lunch.

"Great . . . Dom and I counted about sixty-five to sixty-seven Realtors who've come by—and it's not even one o'clock yet." Their Realtor beamed happily. Tina, back at the burger place with the kids, juggled the phone and watched the girls squish out their ketchup onto their trays.

"Great . . . does that mean any of them have a buyer for our house?"

"It might mean someone has a buyer for your house. Three Realtors already want to know if they can show your house tomorrow afternoon to their clients."

"Oh, that's great!" Lindy and Kerry Lee squirted ketchup at each other. "Girls . . . stop that! "They giggled, dipping their fries on each other. "So, how much longer do I have to stay out here before I come home?"

"Can you give me until 4 PM?" Sylvie asked. Tina was in pain.

"Three more hours? The kids are actually off from school today. It was some teacher's project day, or something."

"Can't you do a little shopping?" Sylvie suggested.

"A little shopping? Okay. I'll see you around 4:15 p.m."

Late that afternoon, Tina finally returned home, coming in the door with the girls, tired and bedraggled. The house looked like it definitely had a party. Dishes were in the sink, and kitchen garbage cans were full with plates and party food. Tina picked up a note from Dom and Sylvie, "Great time . . . Very good realtor tour . . . about seventy attendees!"

"It looks like they had a great time . . . Nice fliers too!" She looked over the pictorial fliers of their home. "Okay, girls, it's a good thing that we ate at the mall!" The home was decorated for Christmas, and colored lights lined the windows, including the living-room window. It was about 5:30 p.m., and it was already getting dark outside.

"Girls, can you go upstairs and get your jammies on? We'll find a movie to watch or something. Lindy, help your little sister get changed," Tina said, in motherly tones.

"Okay, Mom!" Lindy replied. Tina removed her coat, and kicked off her shoes.

"Ah . . . it feels so good!"

As Tina relaxed, a man's face appeared at the window, somewhat distorted by the darkness and Christmas lights. He was a middle-aged man with glasses, and appeared to be peering into the living room. When Tina saw him, she recoiled in surprise, and she screamed nervously.

"Who was that?" The girls heard her from upstairs. They quickly rushed down to investigate.

"Mommy . . . what's wrong?" Lindy got a brief look at the man's face standing on the stairs, but then he slipped away.

"Who was that?" Lindy asked, wide-eyed.

"I don't know." Lindy and Kerry Lee came down the stairs and into the living room, and then stood by their mom.

"A man's face . . . Did you see it?" Tina gasped.

"Just for a quick second . . . Who was that?" Lindy wondered.

"I don't know." She went to the front door, and looked outside.

"Is your sister still upstairs doing her homework?" Tina asked. Yvonne was already coming downstairs.

"Okay, now what's going on?" Yvonne wondered.

"A man was looking in from outside . . . right there!" Tina pointed to the living-room window. Yvonne opened the door, and looked out.

"I don't see anybody. What did he look like?"

"Oh, middle-aged . . . big glasses . . ." Tina said.

"Oh really . . . kind of like . . ."

"Kind of like the man we saw over ten years ago, the Zodiac?"

"But Mom, we know he's dead!" Yvonne said to her Mom, passionately.

"Correction . . . we *think* we know he's dead!" Tina said, suddenly doubting.

"He *is* dead . . . according to Tony, and the facts."

"I really wish that I had gotten a call from the police, and the Santa Barbara Coroner to look at that dead guy who washed up on the shore. I mean, we're always going to wonder, you know?" Tina frowned.

"I wouldn't worry about it, Mom. If you see him again, call the police," Yvonne replied. The little sisters were holding on to her.

While they walked into the next room, the mysterious man returned to the window to peer in. On his face appeared an evil grin, as he laughed a sinister laugh. He then quietly slipped away into the night.

The next morning, Russell and Tina got out of their car to walk into the TV Production building. As they walked together, Tina talked to Russell about the weird episode.

"I'm telling you Russell, the man was staring right through our living room window!"

"You know, I heard you talking about this in your sleep last night!" He laughed.

"It's not funny, Russell!"

They went inside the building toward their respective work areas. Russell continued to talk to Tina about the episode.

"Is it because he resembled the man we saw stalking couples so many years ago? Is that why you're so rattled?" Russell asked her.

"Yes . . . that might have something to do with it."

"We'll talk about this later. Right now we'd better go into the morning staff meeting. Rob's waiting." The group of TV staff members assembled inside the main studio.

"Good morning, everyone!" Rob said, greeting the employees. Russell and Tina sat down together. There were about seventy-five production staff people present.

"Let's open in a word of prayer. Let's always remember whose TV station this really is, and that we hope God's name is glorified in all we do here," said Rob, bowing his head. "Lord, let us keep mindful of you as we go about our days here. Help the staff in their creative process. Let it be the highest standard possible. Help us in keeping our many deadlines, let us avoid the times we are tempted to be short with one another. Instead, let us exercise patience and kindness. In your name we pray, Lord. Amen!"

"'Highest possible standard . . .' " Tina couldn't help but think that it was more like the slaves of Pharaoh making bricks without straw. But they made it happen month after month, year after year.

"Russell, I want to commend you and the crew for a job well done on the *Center Stage Christmas* music spectacular that was produced earlier this month! Very outstanding job!" The group clapped. Tina looked over at Russell. It had been a lot of pressure on both of them, but it did turn out well. Rob continued. "We still have a few more live Christmas shows to complete. Gary, how is the *It Came Upon a Midnight Clear*, drama coming along?"

"The drama troupe will come in here Thursday afternoon about 3 p.m. We'll be ready to film that Thursday night by seven o'clock. We can run it over the weekend, Saturday and Sunday nights, then rerun the *Center Stage Christmas* show Sunday night and Monday night,' Gary answered.

"Good! And how about the Christmas dance festival program?" Rob asked Gary.

"We're set to film that Friday at 4:30 p.m. We can do reruns on that all next week, plus canned videos of Christmas Bible stories and the *Nutcracker*. I've got the slots filled. Here's the schedule." He handed the papers to Rob.

"Good," Rob responded. "It looks like things are under control. How about the 'flagship program? Are the hosts and guests all lined up? We have more music than usual this coming week."

"We're good!" Jenny replied.

"Where is Steve in set design?" Rob asked, looking around. Steve raised his hand.

"You and the crew need to have the main set decorated by tomorrow night's show." Steve nodded.

"Okay . . . I have three on the crew for sure," Steve reassured him.

"Anything else?" asked Rob. No one responded. "Okay . . . let's go make TV programs!" Russell looked at the list written down on his notebook. How did Rob manage to keep such a straight face while loading on the huge list of demands, Russell wondered. Rob would complement him on one hand, and then pile on an unrealistic work load on the other. It was seriously beginning to grate on him. He knew more every day that Tina and he had made the right decision about a change.

In master control, behind the glass, Russell took a seat, and put the headset on. He was the TD for the show about to happen in the main studio. As Russell looked over his list of available crew, he noticed a couple people were out sick. He looked over at Tina.

"Tina . . . I need to you to sit by me and help do the countdowns, and give signals to the crew. Ted is out today." Tina took a headset and put it on.

"Okay. I guess I can spare the time. If Ray from *TV Guide Today* calls about what the new program listings are, he'll just have to wait," she winked.

After a day of work at the TV studio, Tina and Russell drove home.

"I can't believe I got to sit next to you all day, sort of like the assistant TD director." Tina grinned.

"Did you have fun?"

"Yeah . . . kind of. You've been working so many hours, it was kind of a neat way to be together for the day."

"Well, I think we work together more than most couples do," Russell replied warmly.

"Only when we shoot out on location directing the crew," Tina objected. "We've been doing hundreds of studio shows over the last two months, Russell."

"Well, you could create more on-location material for *California Tonight*. People love your work on CT," Russell, suggested.

"Thanks . . . Their producers have been going more toward a talk-show format. It's a big mistake if you ask me."

"Yeah, the show has been a lot more boring lately," Russell commented. Tina became more serious. She was feeling emotional and frustrated about their lives at the TV Station.

"It's a lot more than that. Let's admit it Russell, the last couple of years this career has turned into the 'job from hell.' The station manager and leadership talk a good game . . . they put on shiny godly faces, but then they treat us unfairly, and fill our lives with unattainable expectations and pressures. Rob may have been an okay Pastor, but he was never meant to be a television station manager. He's turning into a real tyrant . . . and Carol. She's a young woman with far too much power, if you ask me! I don't know how Jack even lives with her."

"You're absolutely right. We've both known about it, and felt it for a long time now," agreed Russell. "This is why trusting God for this move is the right thing. There are a lot of unknowns, but we know it's the right decision."

"Yes, it is the right decision," said Tina looking into her husband's eyes with conviction.

"I know we've both been feeling the pressure from just . . . everything. My dad dropped the kids by late this afternoon after Yvonne got home. Let's put some worries aside, and have a real dinner together tonight, okay?"

"Okay!" Russell replied warmly, as he pulled into the driveway.

Within an hour, Tina had made a nice meatloaf dinner with mashed potatoes and the trimmings. The family table was set, and the girls were seated around with Russell. Tina served everyone.

"Mom, that looks so good! Mmmm . . . I love mashed potatoes," Lindy said, looking hungry.

"Yum! I love those little baby carrots with cinnamon on them," Kerry smiled, getting out her fork.

"This is the first dinner we've had all together like this for a while," commented Yvonne.

"Very good, honey!" Russell beamed, happy as a clam. The family was eating at the table, talking about their day, including the kid's school issues and the latest happenings at Grandma and Grandpa's house.

"Lindy, can you go get that family Bible devotional book from the coffee table in the living room? We can read a few of the verses after dinner," Tina suggested.

"Okay, Mom!" She got up and walked into the next room. Lindy had the book in her hands when she looked up and saw the mystery man at the living room window. His face was distorted by the darkness and the glow of the strings of Christmas lights on the window inside, and outside. She shrieked in terror when she saw him.

"Eeek! Mommy . . . Daddy . . . It's that man again!"

"That guy by the window . . . let's find out what's going on!" Russell rushed out the front door. He saw a man just under six feet tall, with balding hair and glasses, late 50s or so, standing and peering in the window. Russell tackled him. The whole family rushed outside to look at the crazy scene. Russell and the mystery man were soon rolling around on the ground. The strings of Christmas lights had snagged the man around the head, and he was all tangled up with lit lights. Russell was kind of disheveled, with his hair all messed up.

"Who are you . . . and why are you stalking my family? You . . . you . . ." The mystery man looked a little shocked. He had strings of lights around his head and shoulders, blinking. At first, he said nothing. Soon, they heard a neighbor lady calling out from down the block. She walked up to the rather comical-looking scene.

"Uncle Reynaldo . . . Where are you? There you are! What happened to you?"

"He attacked me," he answered, pointing to Russell.

"You've been stalking my family!" Russell responded back sharply.

"Uncle Reynaldo, have you been looking into windows again? We told you not to do that anymore! The neighbors will think you're a peeping Tom!" She scolded him.

"Or worse." Tina frowned.

"We thought it might be the Zodiac!" Lindy chirped.

"I'm sorry. Uncle Reynaldo came to live with us last month after my brother passed away. He suffers from a bit of dementia. I think he was a little curious about your family because he has seen some of you on television," apologized the neighbor lady.

Lindy had her arms around Tina's waist and Kerry Lee around her knees. Yvonne just stood nearby glaring at him.

"I'm very sorry. We have to go home now." She took her brother by the arm, and walked back down to the sidewalk with him. Russell brushed himself off, and straightened his hair.

"Well, I'm glad that got straightened out! How could we have ever known?" asked Tina.

"I'm sorry, Tina . . . it kind of threw all of us!" replied Russell.

"Wow . . . will I ever be glad when we move away to Washington!" They all went back inside the house, and tried to get back to a normal evening. However, Tina's thoughts more than ever were shifting to their move, and on their new life coming up in Yakima, Washington.

Spring 1990

The front yard of the George home revealed a very prominent For Sale sign. The family had to make the special effort to keep the home and yard neat, tidy, and impressive. It was early spring now, and the daffodils were just peeking up in the flower box in front of the house by the lawn.

Back at the TV station, Tina and Russell packed up to return home after a day's work. They walked out to their car, and drove toward home. Russell drove along, worry creasing his forehead.

"I don't know, Tina. The house has been on the market for *months* now. What's wrong? Homes used to sell in Benicia by the Bay in a few days . . . maybe a week. There are a lot of 'For Sale by Owners' on the market, even right now."

"Like they say, the market seems to be frozen over right now," Tina reminded him.

"*Just our luck!*" groaned Russell.

"Dom and Sylvie said they were going to try something new. Sylvie said we might even see the new 'marketing thing' when we get home tonight," Tina winked.

They soon drove past the Benicia Bridge toll, toward home. They took the familiar Columbus Parkway exit, and were almost there.

As Russell and Tina drove up to their house, they suddenly saw that there was a giant 100-foot tall red-white-and-blue hot-air balloon in the front yard, bearing the familiar real estate logo, tethered down. Tina rolled down the window.

"Russell, do you see what I see?"

"Yeah . . . It's huge!"

Once inside the house, Tina immediately got on the phone with their real estate agents.

"Sylvie, you didn't tell me you were going to put a 100-foot tall hot-air balloon in the front yard!"

"I did say *balloon*. Pretty nice, huh? That should bring attention to your home for sale!"

"Is it even legal? What ever happened to ads . . .and open house?"

"We'll do that too!"

"I mean . . . you forgot the flashing beacon on top for low-flying planes!" Tina exclaimed.

Russell looked on. He laughed out loud, in spite of himself.

"How long will it be up there?" Tina wondered.

"I was thinking two weeks?" Sylvie replied.

"Two weeks?" Tina looked at Russell. Russell shrugged his shoulders when he heard the news.

"We'll have a brown spot on the lawn where the base is, but I guess we can survive it," Russell said.

"Okay . . . only two weeks. Russell said it could hurt the lawn. We don't want that."

"Two weeks, then I'll send somebody to take it down."

"Okay." Tina hung up.

The months wore on as the "For Sale" sign remained in front of their house.

"Honestly, Russell, what does it take to sell a nice house like ours? It's been five months already!" Russell sipped a cold drink as he listened.

"You already know, Tina. Something happened after the last San Francisco earthquake. The market just froze over for a while."

"But we're not damaged out here. Benicia sits on a solid rock shelf. We did not have one broken window or crack on our wall," Tina reminded him.

"It doesn't seem to matter. The public emotionally froze over. We have a nice four-bedroom house, but I think it's going to take a while."

"Do you think Jere up in Yakima is going to wait for us?" worried Tina.

"He says he will. I just talked to him a few days ago. He's fine with waiting for us."

"Okay, then." Tina sighed. Russell sat by Tina on a big love seat in their living room.

"It will be worth the wait. We'll have more time together as a family. We'll get a place in the country. The kids can get a horse . . .go fishing in the creek. It will be different," Russell promised.

"Do you think so? I hope so." Tina gave Russell a peck on the lips, then a silly grin. The thought of a slower life with more family time was playing delightfully in her imagination!

The next day, Tina was at home watching TV in the kitchen, doing the dishes. The music video *The Letter* unexpectedly came on, in which she, Russell, and Lindy were the actors that past year. In her kitchen apron, she paused and looked on fondly. She shed a tear as she remembered the story. It was because of that short production, and meeting the singer from Yakima, that circumstances came about to change their lives. Tina remembered Tim coming over for dinner, Russell helping him in with his suitcases, and all of them talking and smiling over dinner. She took off her rubber gloves, and put them down, as she sat on the chair next to the screen, and watched the ending to the video.

"Now our lives are going to change forever, because of a song. But that was how God spoke to us, wasn't it," she said softly to herself. At that moment, Tina heard noises at the front door. The girls were arriving home from school.

"Hi, Mom! Lindy and Kerry Lee are right behind me!" said Yvonne, walking into the kitchen.

"Hi, girls . . . That was some timing!"

"The bus just left us off at the corner. Mom, were you crying?" Yvonne asked.

"Oh . . . just a little. Sometimes I cry when I'm happy . . . or just moved. The music video that we did last year just aired on the TV about ten minutes ago. It brought back special memories, that's all!"

"Yakima . . . Yakima! I can hardly wait. Can we get a ranch with a pony?" asked Kerry Lee.

Tina put her up on her lap.

"Maybe . . . We'll have to see what we find when we get up there." The phone rang. Tina picked it up in the kitchen. It was Russell on the line.

"Tina, we just reran *The Letter*. Did you see it?"

"Yes . . . I cried."

"Why, honey?" Russell asked with a little laugh.

"Because God is so good to begin to heal our lives, just like that story . . . and because that song changed our lives. Now we're moving away from the Bay Area to a small country valley named Yakima."

"No regrets, now."

"No regrets," agreed Tina.

"Actually, the real reason I'm calling is that Dom and Sylvie called me about doing an open house this Saturday. They're doing a Mexican theme for Cinco De Mayo."

"Oh really?" wondered Tina. "Sounds nice."

"Sylvie says they're bringing over the big sombrero, and other festive clothing and food. They're giving away a trip for two to Acapulco in the drawing," announced Russell.

"How's that for promotion?" Tina chuckled. "I can hardly believe it!"

"They want us to take off somewhere with the kids for about four hours. Why don't we see about leaving the kids at your mom and dad's, and we'll take a drive up to the ocean?"

"Sounds great to me. You don't have to direct any studio shows on Saturday?"

"No. This will be a day for just you and me," Russell replied. It was another chapter in the house-sale saga.

***

Finally the day of the special, festive open house came. Dom and Sylvie arrived, and put an open-house sign out on the front lawn. They went inside the front door with their costumes and decorations.

"Are you ready? Ole!" exclaimed Sylvie, happily. She wore a Mexican dress, and put a long-stemmed red rose in her teeth. Dom wore a big sombrero. He put it on his head for a proud moment.

"How do you like this, eh?"

"We'll be bringing in some Mexican food. It's out in the car. We should get some really great traffic today!"

"I would say! Giving away a trip to Acapulco in the drawing! Wow, you two better sell the house soon. You're racking up *some* expenses!" Tina laughed.

"We're counting on it, so you two and the family can be on your way to Yakima, Washington," Dom winked.

"Well, Okay . . . We'll be out for a few hours! Good luck with all this. We'll be anxious to hear how it goes!" Russell and Tina stepped outside to their car, and drove off to enjoy their afternoon. As Russell drove, he looked over at Tina.

"I really think we needed this."

"Yeah, it's kind of a forced day off, or at least a big change in our normal schedule!" Tina agreed. They drove out on the freeway toward the coast to enjoy a pleasant afternoon at the ocean. In a about an hour, Tina and Russell pulled up to the ocean shore, farther up north by "Goat Rock."

"This is a pretty spot. Let's take a walk. Do you have the camera?" Russell asked.

"Yes, right here!" Tina replied, pulling out her small camera case.

The two of them walked along the shore, as they felt gentle breezes in their hair.

"This feels so good. No deadlines . . . no Ray from *TV Guide Today* calling." Tina laughed.

"Yeah . . . it's great just to unwind."

"You know, they'll want us to produce more new TV shows once we get to the new station in Yakima," Tina reminded him.

"I'm trying not to think too much about it right now."

"Think about how great it will be to live so close to work—no big commute, no congestion, no toll bridges, no smog . . . more family time," Tina imagined out loud.

"I'm looking forward to it," Russell smiled. He gave her a hug as they continued to walk on the beach. The relaxing time on the beach passed quickly, and soon it was time to drive back home, and check up on their open house.

Tina and Russell walked inside to find Dom and Sylvie looking ecstatic.

"Tina . . . Russell, we had almost one hundred people through here today!" Dom exclaimed happily.

"Did we sell the house?" wondered Russell.

"We have four very interested people," Dom replied.

"That sounds promising," Tina responded. Sylvie was packed up and ready to go.

"We'll let you know more after we talk to them further. One party wants to come back tomorrow with their parents."

"When . . . what time?" Tina asked.

"Let us call you back tonight." Soon Dom and Sylvie were out the door packing their car to leave. It was a successful and productive day!

"Well, the house doesn't look too bad for having almost one hundred people through!" commented Tina, looking around.

"Check around," said Russell. "I always wonder if something might be missing. I get nervous with that many people coming through. You can't watch everybody."

"That's true. Well, my dad will be dropping the kids by tonight."

"Oh, that's great! It will save a trip."

"I've been looking over these ads from the Realtors," said Tina. I'm sure we'll find something just right when the time comes. Many of these houses also have one or two acres, a place for a horse, a barn, but still close to town."

"Only ten minutes away from downtown and the skyscrapers, eh? Only in Yakima! *Are* there any skyscrapers?" Russell asked.

"There are a few . . . look right here." Tina showed him a promo page of Yakima and the downtown area.

"Oh, yeah. I see them." Russell said looking more closely at the photos.

"I'm concerned about Yvonne. She wants to stay here, and go to college. She also loves the sunshine and the beach! She's such a California girl!"

"I'm sure we can work that out with your parents, can't we?"

"I think so. It's just kind of a mom thing. I'll miss her." Russell gave her a warm little hug.

He knew how she was feeling, but it was a time of transition in which they were both learning to grow, embrace, and accept change.

Summer 1990

Tina was on the phone in the living room at home. "Russell... Dom and Sylvie say they have a couple who's looked at every four-bedroom, two-bath home in Benicia, and they want to make an offer on our home! They're already into a 30 day escrow. If we take the offer, we'll have to move fast!"

Russell was listening to Tina on the phone. He sounded a little worried.

"Wow, are we ready to move that quick? I mean we've been ready for months . . . but I thought we could at least have more closing time than that . . . Sixty days, maybe?"

"I think we can do it," Tina said confidently.

"I just called Floyd and arranged for his home at North Tahoe for our family vacation. We'll have to cancel it."

"It's okay. We have to keep our priorities straight. Didn't we always say that God knew the best timing?"

"Yeah, we did," Russell agreed.

"Well, okay, then."

That evening, their Realtors arrived with the offer on their home. Dom and Sylvie sat with Tina and Russell at their dining room table and looked over the offer together, nodding in agreement. Tina and

Russell finally signed the papers. Dom and Sylvie left. Russell and Tina looked at each other, knowing it was time to take their plan of action for the big move into high gear.

"Well, tomorrow it'll be time to call the moving company, and Jere wanted to pick us up in his private plane when it's time to go look at houses up there."

"Yes, there's lots to do," Tina agreed, as she picked up a Realtor Home's Guide magazine. I've looked at all these listings the Realtors sent. She showed Russell a particular listing with pictures. "This home is very unique, Russell. It's a six-bedroom, three-bath, three-floor home with four fireplaces, on one half acre with a pool and a view of the Valley! It's almost 4,000 square feet."

"Wow . . . look at that price," Russell agreed. "We don't see reasonable prices like that on property around here!"

"The style and the colors already fit our taste and our furniture. I think we need to get up there right away and make an offer on it!"

"It does look nice. The soonest we could possibly get up there is this Friday . . . maybe."

"Do you think? I hope it's not already gone. It's a buyer's market up there right now. The good homes are really moving fast! Dixie, one of the realtors, said that if you even take time to go out and have a quick lunch, the house you just looked at could be gone!" Tina said, shaking her head.

"We'll just have to see what happens. They're training a couple of new guys to take my place. We just can't leave before Friday." Russell looked at the magazine again. That house *does* look nice . . . a spiral staircase up three stories, and old stained-glass windows from a cathedral in France jutting up the front and in the interior of the home . . . very unusual!"

"I hope it's still there when we get into town," Tina pined, as she studied the photos. Lindy suddenly appeared in her pajamas.

"Mom, are we moving to Yakima, now?" Tina put her arm around her. Kerry Lee is close behind.

"Yes, girls, we are." Tina nodded.

"Does this mean I get a pony?" Kerry Lee asked.

"This *may* mean you get a pony," Tina replied, in motherly tones.

"Girls, it depends on the type of house we ultimately wind up with. It may be in the country, it may not be," their dad emphasized.

"Aww, Dad, it has to be in the country. We want a horse," Lindy insisted.

"We'll remember that when we look around up there. Okay, girls, back to bed now!" Tina headed them back upstairs, as their ponytails bobbed all the way back up to their bedrooms.

The next day it was time to start getting a whole variety of business ready, such as talking to the schools about the transfer. It was already August, but the kids would not be going to school in Benicia any longer. She needed the girls' records for the move. Tina walked into the elementary school with the girls, and then down the hall to the office.

"Girls, we have to get your school records for the new school up there in Yakima," Tina explained. A school office staff member, Mrs. Jenkins stepped up to greet Tina.

"Can I help you?"

"Yes, I called earlier. Our house has just sold, and we'll be moving soon to Yakima, Washington. I need scholastic records for Lindy George and Kerry Lee George."

"Oh yes, I remember now. Hold on, I'll be right back," she replied. While waiting, Tina overheard one of the secretaries talking to another office staff about a documentary she saw on TV about the Zodiac Killer."

"Honestly, Suzanne . . . it's hard to imagine what a lunatic that man was. This one couple was just at the park having a picnic, and he came out of the bushes with an executioner's mask on, and attacked both of them with a knife!" Monica exclaimed.

"Did you know one his first murders was just right out here on Lake Herman Road in Vallejo, or was that Benicia?" Suzanne asked, straining to remember the facts.

"Yes, it was Benicia . . . and another teenage couple was murdered in a park just off Columbus Parkway right over here in 1969. It's amazing to me that they have never caught the man," Monica stated, flatly.

"He just mysteriously disappeared in mid-October 1978 after writing one last letter to the *San Francisco Chronicle*. He said he was going to strike that weekend. But he never did . . . He just *disappeared.*"

"The newspaper thought the letter must have been written by an imposter, because nobody turned up dead," Monica said, as she picked up some papers from her desk.

Meanwhile, Tina and her daughters were listening while Mrs. Jenkins was looking for their files.

"The only one who is dead is that mean ol' Zodiac. My Mommy and Daddy killed him . . . That's why he didn't ever come back after that night," Lindy stated flatly, with childlike authority.

"Lindy . . . I told you girls not to talk about it," Tina scolded, blushing with embarrassment.

"But *Yvonne* talked about it!" Lindy reminded her mom.

"That was different," Tina replied sternly. "You did not see it, Lindy." Tina told the ladies, "I was pregnant with her at the time." The female office staff looked over at them, with shocked expressions. Meanwhile, Mrs. Jenkins returned with the school records.

"We did not kill the Zodiac . . . We only . . . *chased* him," Tina explained gently.

"He died later," Lindy explained. Mrs. Jenkins, who was coming in late into the conversation, had a sudden look of bewilderment.

"Girls, I told you not to talk about this at school," Tina frowned.

Here are your records for the girls, Mrs. George," said Mrs. Jenkins handing her some folders.

"Thank you . . . We'd better get going. Thank you, ladies." They watched Tina and the girls leave the school office. "Did we really just hear that . . . or what?" Monica whispered to Suzanne as they gazed at each other in amazement.

"Girls . . . and I told you, Lindy . . . not to talk about it! What must those ladies be thinking back there?"

"Aw, *Mom!*"

Tina drove off spritely to the next point of business. Now that the move from California to Washington was really in motion, there was much to do!

CHAPTER ELEVEN

THE REAL MOVE COMES CLOSER

That coming week, Tina had lists of things to work on every day concerning their move. One morning Russell and Tina were having their breakfast before leaving for work at the TV station. Their lunches were all packed. Soon the kids came down the stairs and were ready to ride with them to the workplace. Russell and Tina were still looking over the details of the real estate offer from the folder.

"You know, honey. I always thought if a family bought this house, they would really *want* the in-ground trampoline for their kids to play on," commented Russell.

"I did too . . . Every kid in the neighborhood has wanted to come over here and play on it with our kids, all these years."

"But *this* family wants it filled in! They're afraid their kids will get hurt on it. This is going to be no small matter filling it in. It's like the size of a small swimming pool under there!" groaned Russell.

"I know . . . huh? What are we going to do?"

"I'll have to order some dirt and gravel delivered, I guess. We have several shovels in the garage. I think I can get some of the men from the church to help me fill it in."

"Good plan, honey!" Tina smiled.

"Are we ready for Friday? Jere is flying all of us up there . . . kids and all! He says they can stay at his folk's house and enjoy using the pool why we look at properties."

"That's great! Oops! Look at the time. Let's get going to the station. Dad's picking the kids up today right after we get there!" Tina walked the kids out as the family started toward the driveway for their familiar commute over the bridge. Another workday began making new TV programs.

The next morning, as Tina looked over her notepad, they heard noises in front by the street. It was the neighborhood garbage company dropping off a large steel dumpster to the Georges' driveway.

"Honey, what is *that?*" Russell said, looking out the window at a massive steel dumpster

"It's a dumpster," replied Tina.

"A *dumpster?*"

"I know you're a pack rat, honey, but in our plan to move, we're going to have a four-way plan," Tina explained.

"*A four-way plan?*" wondered Russell.

"Yes. It either is going into the dumpster, going to the Goodwill, going into the garage sale, or it's going onto the moving truck when moving day comes. We absolutely have to thin out and clean out!" Tina said sternly.

"Well, I didn't think we needed a *dumpster.*"

"Believe me, honey, we do, and by the time we get finished we'll wish we had *two.*"

Tina disappeared into the next room, and then soon reappeared with piles of clothes on hangers. "I'm taking these down to the Goodwill drop off by the grocery store. You go through your stuff and let me know what you're giving away. Honestly, Russell. Some of your pants and jackets you've had since your college days. It's time to get rid of them! Sometimes it's embarrassing." Russell was looking a bit disgruntled. He held open the door for her as she carried the clothes out.

"I'll look through my stuff and see what I can do. Remember, we're going to meet Jere over at the Contra Costa Airport in Concord Friday to fly up there. Be sure you and the kids are packed. We won't need much. It will only be for a week at the most."

"Yes, I've got it under control," Tina reassured him.

Finally Friday arrived. They walked into the county airport in Concord, California. Inside a small private plane, Jere turned the key and the engine started up. Russell and Jere were in the front seat, and Tina, Lindy and Kerry Lee were in the roomy back seat. Soon the plane took off smoothly up into the air, headed north.

"This is a sweet little machine. I had a pilot's license at one time, you know," Russell grinned. "Then you can be the co-pilot. Here's the instruction manual. You can read the instructions on how to land this thing," Jere laughed. The private plane climbed higher into the sky toward the cumulous clouds, flying due north.

Inside the plane a couple hours later, the kids and Tina were viewing the mountains and scenery below with awe.

"I always stop off in Bend, Oregon, to refuel and take a break. There's a great runway at the resort out there," Jere explained. "Russell, are you reviewing the instructions about how to land this machine?" He laughed. Russell looked a little pale green, but he managed to nod.

Jere was only kidding, and he soon landed the plane skillfully on the runway of a Bend, Oregon, resort and golf course. Tina, Russell, and the kids disembarked from the plane and looked around at the resort grounds while Jere headed toward the control tower.

"I have to talk to the air-traffic control people, kids. Meet me in the restaurant in a little while!"

"Sure, thing!" Russell walked over to the resort restaurant with the family.

Once inside the restaurant, he talked to Tina about the flight. "I don't mind telling you, I was getting a little airsick . . . up and down . . . air pockets. Do I still look green in the face?"

"Oh, maybe pale green instead of dark green." She laughed. "I don't think the kids are too hungry either . . . maybe just some soup. They'll probably have a little food and some ice water while we wait for Jere. He doesn't seem very interested in eating lunch." After about a half hour, Jere appeared at their table at the restaurant.

"It's time to get back in the air. Is everybody ready?" Jere grinned, bearing his big toothy smile.

"Sure. Kids, let's go!" replied Russell.

They soon took off again in the Cessna, back up into the Oregon skies, headed north to Washington state and Yakima airport.

In about two hours, Jere and Russell, the "co-pilot," had landed the Cessna on the sunny runway of Yakima airport. Jere helped Tina, Russell, and the kids get off the plane, and then load into the company van. They drove off toward the exclusive Englewood Hill area, where Jere lived in a quaint A-frame home that looked like a European Hansel and Gretel house.

On the way, Jere talked to Tina and Russell about the plan.

"We'll get you all settled in tonight. Tomorrow, you connect with your Realtor. I'll call my folks, Rolf and Mary, and work it out for the kids to stay there and enjoy the pool while you go out and look at houses. It's going to be a warm one tomorrow."

"Oh yeah?" wondered Russell.

"Yeah, about 107 degrees." Jere drove up to the hills toward his house on Scenic Drive. Soon they were all settled in for the night, even Lindy and Kerry Lee.

The next morning, the family enjoyed having breakfast at Jere's house. Tina looked through the realtor materials and listings. Russell finished his coffee and orange juice.

"I need to call Dixie . . . I think we need to see that house with the six bedrooms, the stained glass windows, on half an acre with a view and the pool," Tina insisted.

"Okay, set it up. I'd like to see that house too."

"There are a few others, but that one is high on the list!" Tina said to Russell.

In a couple hours, Tina and Russell drove up with their Realtor, Dixie, to the tall, three-story stately cedar home with the large 12-foot stained glass windows jutting up the front.

"Russell, will you look at this place?" she said, gazing in awe at what resembled a church.

"I've never seen anything like it!" Russell admitted.

"Wait until you see it inside." Dixie smiled.

They walked inside, looked around, and immediately started up the three-floor spiral staircase to the next level.

"This is the kitchen. Wow . . . What a view—and look at that fireplace in the kitchen! There seems to be three living rooms. Let's see, there is one downstairs too. The tile is beautiful, sort of brick colored, with oak strips. I've never seen anything like it!" Tina looked on in wonderment.

"The master bedroom is the whole top floor. Are you ready?" asked Dixie. They took the spiral staircase up one more floor.

"Whoa, honey. Am I seeing things?" Russell asked, trying to get his bearings.

"The old stained-glass windows from the cathedral . . . they jut up two floors. It's sort of like a loft up here! Look at those tall ceilings and skylights!" Tina said, looking around, amazed.

"The bathroom has a jetted Jacuzzi-type hot tub, and a sauna," Dixie pointed out.

"Wait 'til the kids see this!" Tina laughed.

"But Tina . . . Russell, it's like I said this morning . . . There's an offer on it. If only you could have been up here a few days ago." Tina looked downcast, hearing this news.

"But the house is perfect . . . Even the colors are right," observed Tina. Dixie explained further.

"A businessman made an offer on the house just three days ago. But they still have to do the inspection, and hear back for sure on the financing. That's the only reason I'm showing it to you. You could make a backup offer," Dixie explained. Russell and Tina looked at each other, wondering what to do.

"Let's keep viewing homes. If there is any change on this one, let us know right away," Russell said to Dixie. Tina looked disappointed, but they decided to continue viewing homes.

Over the next five days, every morning and afternoon was filled with viewings of various kinds of homes, some in the suburbs and some in the country. Finally, they were back at Jere's house, taking a rest from the heat.

"Oh . . . honey, you know, it's the same old story. I wish we could take this house, and put it over here on these two acres . . . or that location, but another type of home," bemoaned Tina.

"I know what you mean. I feel that way too," admitted Russell.

"We are spending so many hours at it, I've called Ted to see some of these. Dixie doesn't have time to show that many. When we do look at homes, she shows up in tennis shoes like she's going to run a race. We've seen over thirty houses so far."

"I know . . . They don't like it, looking with more than one Realtor, but what else can we do?" Russell moaned.

"We're driving many miles, and looking at dozens of homes. But we *have* to find a home this week. The Nelsons are moving into our house in about three weeks!" Tina said, looking alarmed. Russell sighed.

"I know. When we do find the right house . . .part of what we need to tell people is, 'We love your house . . . we can pay cash . . . can you be out in about two weeks?"

"Right. It's a tall order. I have an idea, Russell. Ted had an amazing home listed when we were first looking at listings a couple months ago. The big-view home up on Meadowcrest Road, 5,200 square feet? I loved that one! The listing has expired, but he says the people still want to sell. They had a plan to move to Oregon. Here it is." She showed Russell the ad with the picture.

"Wow, look at that! Nice deck with balcony . . . right on the front, too—on one acre."

"It's in our price range also," Tina added excitedly.

"Well, why don't you ask Ted to get a hold of the owners and see if we can still take a look at it?" Russell asked. Tina immediately reached for the phone.

"I will!"

The next afternoon, Ted drove up Meadowcrest Road with Russell and Tina to the spacious view home up on the hill. He rang the doorbell, and the owners came to the door, and greeted them. They walked in, and gazed around at the living room and cathedral ceilings.

"This is Gary and Alona . . . Russell and Tina, George," their Realtor announced.

"Well, have a look around . . . Let us know if you have any questions. We do have well water here . . . Try some." The owner poured a glass for them.

202

"Wow, that's great. Very nice water!" commented Russell, looking refreshed. Ted showed them around further inside the impressive home. Soon they emerged out on the view deck in the front of the house.

"Look at this view!" Russell exclaimed.

"You can see the whole valley and the part of Mount Rainier from here," Ted pointed out.

Tina and Russell looked at each other, smiling. Obviously, they were liking what they saw. They seemed to agree they should pursue buying it.

"Gary custom built much of this home with very nice materials, as they really didn't think they would ever move from here," Ted explained. Russell glanced over at Tina. She smiled and nodded in agreement.

"I think we want to make an offer on this home."

"Great! Let's go back to the office and write the offer!" They said good-bye to the owners, and soon drove off with Ted back toward the Real Estate office.

Back at the Real Estate office, they worked on the offer with Ted. After about one hour, they finished the sale papers.

"I think they should like this offer, and it's all cash!" smiled Ted.

"We hope so! We're supposed to fly back on Saturday!" Russell reminded him.

Tina smiled back in agreement. She was really excited about the home on Meadowcrest. If they couldn't get the other home on Apple View Way, it was a close second choice, she decided.

The next day, back at back at Jere's house, Tina talked to herself. She and Russell thought they would have heard back on the offer right away.

"I wonder what's taking *so long?"* She looked at her watch. "It was an all-cash offer, set to close in three weeks. Suddenly, the house phone rang. Jere walked into the living room with the telephone receiver looking for Tina.

"It's for you . . . It's Dixie . . . something about the other house," Jere said. Tina got on the phone.

"Tina! I'm so glad I got a hold of you!" exclaimed Dixie, sounding relieved.

"You sound pretty tense. What's up?" asked Tina.

"The house you and Russell love, on Apple View Way . . . it's *available!"*

"What? But you said somebody had already made an offer on it?" Tina replied, puzzled.

"The potential buyer was a businessman . . . self-employed. But he had not yet done his taxes for the year. It didn't look good to the bank, so he didn't get his financing."

"That's bad . . ."

No it's good . . . for you and Russell. You can make an offer on it now," Dixie explained.

"But we just made an offer on another house," said Tina. Suddenly, Russell walked in with Jere and heard the conversation.

You *did?"* replied Dixie, sounding disappointed. "What stage is it in?"

"We made the offer, but they have not yet responded," answered Tina. Russell walked over and got in on the conversation. "Psst . . . Russell." She put her hand over the phone. "The three-story house on Apple View Way . . . It's available."

"What? Tina, really?" Russell asked in curious tones.

"The other buyer could not get financing."

"What should we do?" All ears were directed to Tina's phone. Dixie continued.

"You *could* withdraw the offer on the house on Meadowcrest Road."

"Withdraw the offer?" Tina asked.

"Yes. Call your other Realtor. I feel bad you called Ted on that other house."

"But you said you were going out of town that day. With us . . . every day counts!" The doorbell rang. It was Ted with the offer on Meadowcrest, papers in hand. Tina and Russell were looking out into the living room. Jere answered the door, and let Ted inside.

"Ted is here with a counter offer. Can you two come out to the living room," Jere called out.

"Ted just got here with the offer . . . It's a counter offer," Tina explained to Dixie.

"Perfect. Whatever the extra terms are, if you don't like them, just say you don't agree, and that will nullify the counter offer. Call me back after you talk," Dixie instructed them.

"Okay, bye!" Tina and Russell came out to see Ted in the living room. Ted held the new papers in his company folder.

"I have their counter offer right here. They countered back $5,000, higher on the sale price, plus they want you to pay extra and buy all the firewood stacked up around the house, and the heating oil in the storage tank," explained Ted. Russell and Tina looked at each other with a puzzled look.

"Honey!" replied Tina, feeling surprised.

"Leave the papers here and we'll talk it over," replied Russell, sounding disgruntled.

"I need to know for sure by tonight or tomorrow," Ted explained.

205

"We do too. Tomorrow is Saturday, and we have to fly back to California."

"Okay . . . Call me after you talk it over." Ted abruptly left. Russell and Tina looked at each other with a little smile now. They knew what they wanted to do. They rushed immediately to the phone and called Dixie back.

"Dixie, he was just here. We don't like the counter offer. The owners went up $5,000 on the price, and the want us to buy all the firewood stacked up around the property, and pay for the heating oil in the storage tank," whined Tina.

"That oil would normally come with the house," Dixie explained.

"So what can we do?"

"It's getting dark now, but in the morning let's meet at the house on Apple View Way, and if you are sure you want to buy it, you can turn down the counter offer on Meadowcrest, and write a new offer on Apple View Way," Dixie explained. Tina and Russell were happy and excited over hearing this information

"Fantastic!" Russell beamed.

"I am actually going out of town for a horse show in Spokane, but I'll stop on the way and show you the house! Let's say 9:30 a.m.," suggested Dixie.

"It's a deal!" Tina exclaimed.

"Let's be sure we're all packed. This will have us running short on time. Tomorrow is Saturday," Russell reminded her.

"I have to fly you back in the daylight hours. The headlights on my plane are broken!" Jere apologized weakly.

"Okay. We'll have to race for time then!"

The next day, Tina and Russell drove up to the house on Apple View Way in a borrowed car from Jere. Dixie was close behind in a fifth-wheel pickup hauling two horses in a horse trailer. She pulled in front of the house, and jumped out wearing riding boots, her jeans, and horsemanship gear. It appeared that another couple and a Realtor had just finished viewing the home, and was leaving.

"Those people look really interested in the house. How did they even find out, I wonder?" Tina said to Russell, looking puzzled. Dixie followed Tina and Russell up to the door on the second landing, and opened it up for them. They walked around the second floor spellbound. They inspected the tile floors with oak strips, fireplace in the kitchen, huge view windows, huge living room with high ceilings and skylights. Tina winked at Dixie. "You remembered what I said about liking houses with large rooms, eh?"

"This house has a few . . . You saw it the first time through. The whole top floor is the master bedroom."

"We would have to buy a little extra furniture. We were not quite set up for *three* living rooms," Russell laughed, weakly.

"The one downstairs is actually a family room . . . and the one over there is called a 'conversation pit,'" said Tina. "It has a sunken middle with a tile floor, and the furniture actually goes . . . up there," pointed Tina, to the upper ledge.

"I like it, though." commented Russell. They continued to look around the house. The tall stained glass windows seemed to tower above all, and smaller ones graced other parts of the house.

"What a view . . . 360 degrees, and look at that snow-covered mountain over there!" Soon they all met back in the kitchen on the second floor.

"I think this is the house don't you, Tina?" asked Russell, feeling excited.

"Yes, I do!" Tina agreed.

"I am scheduled to appear and compete in the horse show in Spokane in a few hours," Dixie reminded them.

"Just FED EX us the papers. We'll take it!" Tina said, excitedly.

"Can you do me a big favor and go by my office, and tell my broker, Jim West, you are going to buy this house? I'll take it as a verbal acceptance," requested Dixie.

"Sure. We'll drive back there on the way back to Jere's house. We have a plane to catch before it gets much later!" Russell explained.

Russell and Tina busily worked on organizing themselves and the children to return on Jere's plane. Then they took their borrowed car, and drove downtown toward Dixie's real estate office. They felt a little tense, and stretched, but they wanted that house on Apple View Way, and it was time to make their bid. They pulled up in front and rushed inside. The broker, a gray-haired gentleman named Jim West, was standing in the front office.

"Mr. West, we will take the house on Apple View Way, Dixie's listing!" Tina exclaimed.

"We'll pay cash . . . Just Fed Ex us the papers. Here's our address." Dixie had made a call to her broker, and he had been watching for their arrival.

"Dixie called me with all the information. It looks like you just bought yourself a house!" Mr. West smiled.

"I'm sorry we are in such a hurry! Here's our address and other information . . .just Fed-Ex us the sale papers! We have a plane to catch while it's still daylight!" Tina explained excitedly.

"Still daylight?" the broker wondered.

"The headlights are out," Russell explained.

"The headlights . . . *are out?*"

Russell and Tina politely excused themselves, and dashed back to Jere's house in their borrowed car. Tina and the girls gathered their bags while Russell was on the phone with the other Realtor, Ted.

"Ted we cannot possibly agree to all that extra stuff the seller on Meadowcrest wants us to buy, and they want us to pay to move them into storage too? I'm sorry, but we're going to make an offer on another house . . . Good-bye."

"Come on everybody . . . Let's get to the airport while I still have daylight to fly back with!" wailed Jere.

Soon, everyone piled into the car, and put their bags in the trunk. Jere pulled out of the driveway, as they raced off toward the airport.

Within minutes, Jere's Cessna was out on the air strip. He helped everyone board the plane. Unseen by them, Ted was in the distance trying to catch up to them, waving the sale papers on Meadowcrest high above his head.

"It's okay . . . The seller says you don't have to do *any* of those things! You can have the house... The first offer was okay! Can you hear me?" Ted called out frantically.

Within moments, the plane took off into the clear blue sky headed south toward California. Sadly, Ted just watched their plane climb higher into the sky, then it disappeared into the far distance, heading south.

The next day, Tina and Russell were back at home watching for the parcel from their Realtor, Dixie. Suddenly, there was a ring of the doorbell at the front door. The FED EX carrier handed her a flat package. "It's the sale papers!" exclaimed Tina, happily.

Soon Russell and Tina were sitting at the kitchen table at home in California, with coffee cups, happily signing the sale papers and writing out an earnest money check for the house on Apple View Way. Tina briskly put it in the envelope. "I'll get this over to the FED-EX station right away!" Russell smiled, and seemed very happy over their decision.

The girls had their little radio out front on the lawn, playing happy, upbeat music. Lindy ran with long pink and silver streamers past the For Sale sign in front of their house. It now had a *SOLD* sign pasted over it. Tina walked out the door, taking clothes and other items in bags to the car to drop off at the Goodwill stop. Russell put cardboard boxes and other junk from the garage into the dumpster. Although he fought Tina on getting it at first, he was actually growing fond of having the dumpster there. The guys working in the backyard put shovels of dirt into the hole where in the in-ground trampoline used to be.

The next day, a sign marked 'Garage Sale' was posted in front of their house. Russell and Tina directed a garage sale from their front driveway with every imaginable item, including lamps, tables, toys, bikes, and clothes on racks everywhere! Kerry Lee held a Teddy bear up to a little girl, with a price tag of .25 cents. She took it, and handed her a quarter.

At the end of the day, a very tired Tina sat on folded chair with the cash tray from the garage sale.

"Over nine hundred bucks . . . Wow . . . Just from used clothing, bikes, teddy bears, and extra stuff from around here," Tina said, amazed.

"Our bronze wear set from Thailand brought $200 bucks. We had a few high-ticket items!" Russell, reminded her.

"To think you almost talked me out of doing it!" Tina said, with a little smirk on her face.

"Honey, it just seemed too late to consider it!" Russell reminded her.

"It was just a matter of getting an ad in the paper, and a sign in the front yard...and bam, there you go! That was it! I had a system. Everything in this house was either going to Goodwill, the consignment shop, into the dumpster, or onto the moving truck on moving day," Tina reminded him.

"Good job, honey. I would have never believed that we needed a dumpster."

"We almost needed *two*. All that extra junk in the garage was *not* going on the moving truck!" Lindy and Kerry Lee came rushing in. Lindy had some cash in her hand, and Kerry with a new Teddy Bear.

"I think almost all our old toys wound up at Kristin's or at Mrs. Powell's day-care center," said Lindy. Kerry Lee was down to *one* new teddy bear . . . and 'Greg the bear' that I gave her the day when she was born."

"Very good, Lindy. The moving truck is due here on Wednesday. Everything needs to be packed. I have all your girls' school records in this metal box here that will stay right with my purse in the car," said Tina.

"You are so organized, honey!" Russell said.

"You still have more to do in the garage. We need to pare down to just your best tools, work bench, and some of my cases of books. I already gave some of them to the local Christian school for their students," Tina reported.

"I'll get there, Tina . . . it's just that . . ." began Russell, sheepishly.

"Just that . . . *what?*"

"Back at the station . . . Gary is really stuck to have someone direct two programs this afternoon and tonight. I said I would do it," Russell admitted. Tina was shocked.

"No! Russell! Tell me you *didn't?*" Russell looked embarrassed.

"I did. They're still struggling to replace me over there." Tina was steaming.

"We are moving in part . . . because they, as a station, have never been fair to us as far as time, demands, or salary. You don't owe

211

anything to them, Russell! When are you going to stop trying to be a hero? Right now, it's *us* who needs you . . . not *them!"*

"There should be time for both . . ." Russell reasoned.

"*No!* All those hours you're giving away will have us running late! The new buyers are moving in this weekend! We'll get charged one hundred dollars a day for any late days moving out!" Tina pleaded.

"I'll do my best, honey. I promise . . ." Tina frowned, and pouted, as she left the room.

The next day, Russell directed a studio show at KYTN. Delays caused the time to go later and later. Russell continued to look at his watch.

"Gary, these delays are really running me extra late. I told Tina I'd be home by now. We're preparing to meet the moving truck in two days," said Russell.

"I had no way of knowing we would run into these technical problems. I should have you out of here by 10 p.m.," apologized Gary.

"Tina is not going to be happy. I'm already in the dog house. You should've already been breaking in the new guy you've been telling me about," Russell pointed out.

"Dale? He won't even be arriving into town until tomorrow," explained Gary.

"Oh. Nice coordination, Gary. I guess it means I'll be up practically all night back at my house working on my packing for the move. Thanks," moaned Russell.

Late that night, Russell finally arrived home. It was very dark, no lights on. The wall clock in twilight read 11:30 p.m. Tina was still up. Packed moving boxes were everywhere, in every room.

"Russell, is that you? I thought you'd be home long before now," a tired Tina called out.

She switched on lights. "I was trying to catch a little nap. The girls are fast asleep."

"I wish *I* was fast asleep. Gary kept me a lot longer than I expected directing the programs tonight. We had technical problems on top of that."

"That's just great. We're supposed to be ready for the movers by Wednesday. That gives us less than two days. We are so far behind," cried Tina, with big tears welling up in her eyes.

"I know . . . I'm so sorry, honey . . . I'll work on my part. I know the garage has a long way to go."

"The part that really bothers me, Russell, is why do you feel so loyal to them? It's because the station has not been fair with us that we had to consider this move in the first place," Tina sniffed.

"I've been friends with Gary for a long time. It was sort of a favor. He seemed to really be stuck with his back up against the wall. I thought there would be time for both," Russell explained tenderly.

"Well, now you know there wasn't."

"I'll stay up a few hours and work . . . we'll be all right. You'll see."

"Thanks, honey." She gave him a little kiss.

The next morning Tina was in her robe having her breakfast coffee. The kitchen table was still unpacked, but moving boxes were stacked up everywhere on the lower floor. Russell entered the kitchen from the garage door by the laundry room. He looked tired and disheveled.

"Good morning, Russell . . . Do you want some coffee or some breakfast?" asked Tina.

"I've been up most the night . . . Just some coffee for now." A very tired Russell plopped down in the chair next to her. Tina poured him some fresh coffee.

"I hate to see you going through this."

"Well, I suppose it's my own fault," Russell admitted.

"We're supposed to be out of here, Friday night, or Saturday morning by the latest, so the new owners can start moving in. They wanted to start by putting boxes in the garage," warned Tina.

"Oh . . . That's just great. That is the hardest to pack, and the last to be packed. That's where I'm working now."

"Tonight we'll have to put a couple mattresses down in the living room. Our bed frames are ready to go." Russell rested his head in his hands, looking zombie-like. "I'm sorry, honey . . ." said Russell, with sad in the doghouse eyes.

Is your sister going to take the girls while we finish packing?"

"Yeah, Sandy will let them stay at her house while everything is torn up around here. I already took Yvonne, and her stuff, to Mom and Dad's. I'll miss her! This is really one of the hard parts of this move." Tina pouted a little over the loss. She then saw the walkie-talkies on the top of one of the boxes. "Did you get those walkie-talkies working?"

"Yep! That way we can keep in touch between you driving the Buick Skylark, with you and Lindy and me driving the Ford van with Kerry Lee, the plants, and the pets. If we get separated on the freeway, we can find each other and regroup," explained Russell, as he felt quite proud of himself.

"Great idea! Russell, you really need a nap," suggested Tina.

"You're right. I should lie down before I fall down. This move has been much harder on me than I ever dreamed," he said as he ran his hand through his hair.

The next morning was a sunny August day. Boxes were stacked everywhere in the front yard. While Tina packed the family car, their newer Buick Skylark, she kept looking at her watch. "The moving van should have been here by now," she said, worriedly. Russell came outside to look for her. He had more questions.

"Tina, did you call all the utility companies . . . the phone . . ."

"Yes. The phone company is the last one to call. You just never know."

"Shouldn't the moving van have been here by now?" Russell asked her.

"Yes, it's almost 10 a.m. They are an hour late. Let me try making some calls," answered Tina.

Russell was packing the van, including the large house plants and pet cages. He listened to Tina on the phone with the moving company. As Tina talked on the phone, she became increasingly frustrated.

"What? The moving van that was going to be picking us up broke down in *Oregon?*" Russell overheard. He was shocked and angry.

"What was that, Tina?" Tina was listening and taking down information.

"Why didn't someone call us? When can we get another moving van out here?" There was an uncomfortable pause. "Not until Friday? Oh no! You don't understand. We're camping out in our own home. The utilities are turned off . . . and I almost turned the phone off, too. Is that the soonest you can get a van out here? That's another two days!" Russell took the phone from Tina.

"What's the problem?" Russell listened. "The moving van broke down in Oregon? I see. It has to be Friday morning." Russell rolled his eyes. "I guess we'll just have to live with it. Call us if there is any change. Good-bye." Tina looked discouraged. "I can't believe it . . ."

"Tina, just call the utility and phone companies back . . . and extend everything through the weekend, just to be safe. It's going to be okay. Hey, at least it's August . . . warm summer nights, no problem," Russell smiled back weakly.

"Okay . . . it just seems like lately life is filled with a few too many curve balls!" Tina moaned.

"It'll be okay, Tina. It's a blessing in disguise. It gives us more time to pack and get ready for the movers," said Russell, pointing out the bright side.

"I guess . . . but it makes us late to get out of here for the new owners. I don't look forward to making *this* call," Tina moaned, as she looked up their number in her little book.

Late that night, in the dark twilight hours, Russell and Tina were laying on the mattress in the living room with a few loose blankets. Tina had a flashlight nearby.

"Are the kids okay?" Russell asked softly.

"Of course. The kids don't feel things like this the way we adults do."

"Did Tessa, our Mommy kitty, come back?" Russell wondered.

"I saw her this morning. When we gave away the last kitten, she actually went looking for it," replied Tina.

"It's just that when the mover's arrive, I don't want to be wondering and worrying where the cat is! The kids would never forgive me for leaving Tessa behind!" Russell reminded her.

"Did we ever dream so many details would have to come together, from filling in the hole under the trampoline, to thinning out the house of fourteen years of accumulated extra junk, to managing and feeding the kids while the house is all ripped apart, mapping the best route up there . . ."

"To finding the family cat by Friday morning," laughed Russell.

"Yeah, that too. I didn't know when I married you it would turn out to be such an adventure!" Tina giggled. Russell turned over, trying to get comfortable.

"Goodnight . . . Let's try to get some sleep.

"Okay," sighed Tina.

Friday morning finally arrived. The huge new moving truck pulled up in front of the house. It was their largest size, a big eighteen-wheeler, but there was a new problem. Tina briefly chatted with the driver, then glanced over at Russell.

"Russell . . . The movers somehow had the idea they could put us on with another load that's going in that direction."

"Oh no . . . What *else* can happen?" Russell looked around, then walked over to the driver, and the movers who were approaching. "Who can we talk to? We need a full truck this size to make this move!"

"I'll radio the main office and see what we can do," the moving guy replied.

"Any sign of the cat, by the way?" Tina asked Russell.

"No...she must still be out there looking for her last baby kitten."

"In the future when the new owners come to pick up the kittens, I'm going to have to show the babies to her as they are leaving," explained Tina. "Who said animals don't have feelings? I'm not sure what to do." Tina sighed.

"Well, we have a little more time now due to the latest mistake."

The driver left the moving van, and walked over to Russell and Tina.

"We're going to pack as much as we can here, then they're going to load a second truck."

"That's great."

"You'll pack out with as much you can on the first truck, but then a second truck will arrive. We' help you pack it, but it won't arrive up in Yakima until about one week later." Tina looked both shocked and disappointed.

"That's bad."

"It doesn't look like we have much choice," Russell replied. The driver with two male helpers came over to start the work.

217

"This will be an all-day load, so we'd better get started," he said briskly.

Just as they were told, loading did take all day. Tina and Russell helped bring out and organize what they could.

"Well, we have everything for this load. The drivers for the second rig will meet you in the morning for the rest of your boxes," the mover explained.

"You don't understand. We're supposed to be *out of here!*" Tina pointed out.

"It's the best we can do," the driver responded.

"Well, we have a mattress and a few items in our suitcases," said Russell.

"I'm exhausted, and I still need to vacuum and clean the house!" groaned Tina.

"We still have our phone. Let me make a call," Russell said, as he got a new idea. Russell dialed a number on the portable phone.

As the moving van drove off, Tina stood in front the house, then collapsed wearily on the porch swing in front.

"There are times when life can bring you lower than low . . . and, boy, do I feel low," Tina said to herself. Bernice, who had been watching through the window, came out with tall glasses of iced tea.

You two look really tired . . . Here you go."

"Thanks, Bernice. The sun's going down, but its still 85 degrees. I'm really tired," said Tina, wilting. Russell walked out of the house grinning.

"Tina . . . good news! The ladies from the church are going to come over and clean the house for us!" Bernice handed him a tall glass of iced tea. "Thanks Bernice!"

"Oh, honey . . . that is so wonderful!" Tina responded, coming back alive.

"Rhonda said she would organize about three or four women from the ladies ministry group and they will be over within the hour!"

Tina hugged Russell. "That is such good news! I don't have any more energy left for that extreme house cleaning. Every room needs to be vacuumed or swept!"

"Let's get some dinner, then we're going to hit the hay early. I told Rhonda I'd leave the back door open for them," Russell explained.

"You two have a restful night . . . Tom and I will miss you!" said Bernice, waving good-bye, a bit tearfully. She watched them drive off toward town and the restaurants.

Meanwhile, Tessa the mother cat was still searching for her last lost kitten.

The next morning, Russell swept the garage floor. Everything was out, packed, or in the dumpster. Tina was packing the Skylark, while Lindy and Kerry Lee played on the front lawn with a bright pink ball.

"Russell, the *cat* . . . Tessa has not returned. Honestly. She has lived here five years! She must still be out looking for her baby, Tina said coming into the garage out of earshot of the girls. If we have to leave without her, I don't know how to tell the kids."

"I just had a talk with your sister this morning. She's going to leave dry cat food and water out by her doorstep, and we'll do the same here. When she shows up, Sandy is going to keep her for us," Russell explained.

"Oh Russell . . . . that's perfect! That's a great idea!" said Tina, feeling relieved.

"I knew we had to think of something. I didn't want two little girls bawling their eyes out all the way up to Washington!" said Russell, shaking his head.

"Russell, do you have your bags packed for the van? I have the kids clothes and stuff ready to go!" Russell pointed to his packed suitcase by the garage door.

"Remember, we will only be staying up at Jere's house about one week until the second load arrives. Then we can move in all the way.

"That was really something thinking they could move us with somebody else!"

"The manager of the moving company here in town said they are going to cut us a check for one hundred dollars per day, two hundred dollars . . . for the inconvenience of the first van breaking down in Oregon," Russell explained, on a happy note.

"Well, at least that's something! Along with the garage sale money . . . over $900, we've got a little buffer to cover since you're not going to work right away."

"Do you have the walkie-talkies?" asked Russell, looking around.

"They're in my Skylark." She went out to the car, and pulled them out. Russell took one.

"Let's try them out. You sit in your car, and let me get into my van, just like we are on the road." Tina looked at the walkie-talkie, then turned it on.

"Bird to base . . . bird to base . . . Come in, Russell," Tina said, checking the reception. Russell was already seated in the van.

"I hear you, Skylark . . ."

"*Bird* . . . Bird to base . . . That's our code." Tina winked.

"Okay, Tina." Russell laughed.

CHAPTER TWELVE

GOOD-BYE, BENICIA . . . HELLO, YAKIMA!

The vehicles were finally loaded . . . kids, plants, and pets in cages. "Say good-bye to the house . . . here we go! " Russell said triumphantly from the front seat of the van.

"Bird to base . . . Here we go!" said Tina happily, settling in behind the wheel of the Skylark, Lindy at her side. Within seconds, a large moving van, obviously from the new people, pulled up in front of the home. It was a little too close for comfort, but they maneuvered around it safely and were on their way, Tina following Russell in the van.

The miles on the freeway seemed to sail by as they drove swiftly down the freeway headed north. The sign, HWY 5-North, seemed to follow overhead for many miles.

Kerry Lee sat by her dad in the van, sporting a big smile.

"Kerry Lee, how are the pets doing back there?" Russell asked. Kerry Lee turned around to check on their fluffy black and white cat, "Yogi," and their small Pom-terrier mix dog, Puppins."

"Yogi . . . Puppins . . . how are you doing?" Kerry Lee asked. They looked a little nervous because of the vibrations of the vehicle, but were surviving okay.

As Tina followed, she couldn't help but smile. Russell's van with the plants and pets made her think of a small Noah's Ark speeding down the freeway. Lindy, chuckled, "Look at that van! It looks like a little Noah's ark going down the freeway!" The plants in the back seem to sway, the cats meowed, the dog barked, and gave out a little moan.

As the two vehicles pressed farther and farther north on the freeway, the brown hills of California began to transform into the tall majestic evergreens on the side of the road, and the snow-covered mountains of the Northwest.

Tina and Russell in their prospective vehicles attempted to follow each other the best they could on the roads and freeways, but sometimes it was a challenge, especially for Tina. Suddenly, they were passing a small town, Fern Place, where they had to slow down to 35 miles per hour as they passed through the city limits. Russell had made headway about ten car lengths in front of Tina, and she was having trouble keeping him in view. To complicate things, he sped up. With turns and forks in the road that had come up ahead, she was about to lose him. In desperation, Tina sped up to try to gain visibility of Russell in the gray Ford van. About that time, a police car on a side street spotted her. The police officer sped out from a hiding place on the side of the road, and nabbed her. Tina watched the dreaded flashing red police light in her rearview mirror. She sadly pulled over.

"You were going 50 in a 35 zone, ma'am," the officer said, walking up to Tina's window.

"I'm sorry, officer. My husband and I are travelling in two cars trying to do an out-of-state move from California to Washington. He's travelled so far ahead of me, I've lost him now. We were trying to stay together. He's got one of the children, and I've got the other." The officer looked over the situation.

"I see . . . I'm sorry the two of you got separated, ma'am. I won't give you a ticket this time. Please watch the speed limit more carefully in the future. Is there anything I can do?"

"Thank you. No, I think that I'll have to just wait here until he comes and finds me.

I'll never catch up to him now."

"Okay, ma'am. The Highway Patrol station is right over there if you need further help."

"Thanks."

"What we will we do now, Mom?" asked Lindy, looking at her mom with those big blue eyes.

"I hope this stupid little walkie-talkie is still within reach of your father's van . . . wherever he is." Tina sighed. She picked up the walkie-talkie, and turned it on.

"Bird to base . . . bird to base, come in Russell." Tina heard some static, then a response.

"Tina . . . where *are* you?" asked Russell on the walkie-talkie.

"Russell, thank goodness. I'm pulled over on a side road, White River Avenue, just off the main road. You got too far ahead of me!"

"Okay let me turn around. Kerry Lee and I got to listening to music, and I guess I wasn't paying attention," Russell apologized. Tina waited in her car about fifteen minutes. Shortly Russell showed up alongside in his van.

"I almost got a ticket trying to keep up with you!" said Tina, sounding a little angry.

"Sorry, honey."

"You know, I'm not very good at reading maps and navigating these long trips like you are. I need you to watch for me so we don't get separated."

"I can see you are a little upset . . . sorry. Let's stop over here for some lunch."

Russell and Tina followed each other to a family pizza restaurant, and pulled in. Once inside they found a nice comfortable table. It was fairly noisy and busy with families and friends conversing happily. The TV was playing the regional station with commercials in between a talk show. They got seated, and started to order.

"Mom, let's get the deluxe special with everything on it!" Lindy chirped.

"That looks good," Russell agreed. Kerry Lee wrinkled up her nose.

"Eeeuuw! I don't like all that stuff . . . onions and green peppers and mushrooms on it."

"We'll get the cheese one for you. Then we'll all get the salad bar, and lemonade to drink. They make fresh-squeezed here, look," Tina pointed out.

While they waited, the TV program which was playing in the restaurant went to a commercial break.

"Coming this weekend to *The Century's Greatest Unsolved Mysteries...* This Friday on KTLB, *The Zodiac Killer*. From the 1960s through the 1970s, this Satanist serial killer stalked couples in lover's lanes, picked up stranded motorists, and also stalked and killed many individuals in both the San Francisco Bay area, and Vallejo, California. The Zodiac always mysteriously eluded the police, and was never captured," the television announcer read from the script. Russell perked up his ears.

"Honey, listen . . . ." Tina nodded toward the TV. The announcer continued.

"This man, the *Zodiac*, represents one of the greatest unsolved mysteries of all time. The question is . . . is he still out there?" Mysterious music followed his dialog. Tina reacted.

"Listen to that . . . the public is still fascinated with whatever happened to the Zodiac killer." A young waiter came up to their table with pizzas. "Well, we know, don't we?" The waiter, a young teen, overheard. He seemed a little shocked at her comment.

"Excuse me?"

"My husband and I chased him around midnight one evening, leaving Vista Point in San Francisco . . . and now he's dead." Tina was feeling a little cocky, as they were far away from the Bay Area. "We know . . . because we were there."

The girls chimed in. "Yeah . . . they were there." By now, the young waiter's eyes were bugging out.

He suddenly lost grip of the pizzas as he tilted the pan. The hot gooey pizza toppings slid right off onto Tina's lap, and the kids' laps, and on part of the table.

"Eeek!" Tina squealed.

"Mom . . . oh no!" Lindy gasped.

"Yuck!" Kerry Lee squeaked.

"I'm so sorry . . . I'll get more pizza! Here's a warm, wet cloth for you," the waiter offered kindly, apologizing. Russell was chuckling in spite of himself.

"That's what you get for talking about our secret, Tina. Remember, we are not supposed to talk about it?" Tina rubbed the pizza sauce from her blouse, and helping Lindy and Kerry Lee. "We are far from the Bay area, Russell. Besides, we know he's dead."

"We *think* we know he's dead," said Russell, reminding her.

Tina leaned over the table, and whispered, "Russell, he is dead."

"Why don't you help the kids change into some fresh clothes while they bring out more pizza?" Russell suggested.

"Good idea," Tina agreed. She took the girls by the hand, as they walked toward the van. Later that night, after the meal, Russell drove as far as Morrow, Oregon, where they got a motel for the night. The nice motel owner even let them bring their pets inside, and let them sleep on their beds. "Thank the Lord for small miracles!" said Tina.

The next morning, Russell drove that last stretch of freeway up Highway 97, across the Yakima Indian reservation, then right into the east side of downtown Yakima.

"Let's drive by our new house on Apple View Way. I have the keys right here," suggested Russell. Tina agreed. She was anxious to see the house again.

"Here we are . . ." Russell smiled.

"Yes, and the first load of furniture will not even be here for another four days. It's a good thing we're staying at Jere's house," sighed Tina.

"It was nice of him to offer."

"Well, at least I have all the books and stuff I need to study for my Washington State real estate test. Once things settle down, I'm going to get my license."

"What happened to doing TV work up here?" asked Russell.

"We'll see. I may be ready for a change," explained Tina.

"I think you'll be good at real estate, Tina!" Russell said. "Whatever you decide is fine with me." Soon, they walked inside the new house with the kids.

"Wow . . . What a view . . . and look at that pool!" Lindy said, getting even more excited.

"Look at that driveway. You and Dad always buy view homes, then I have to walk up the hill after school," frowned Lindy.

Kerry Lee was already playing on the winding spiral staircase.

"Mom . . . dad . . . look at me!" She said, peering down from the top of the stairs.

"If the kids were any younger, we couldn't risk them around this house. Look at all the loft, staircase, and high-low drops around here. This would be suicide for a toddler!" Tina pointed out.

"I need to check the pool, and call the pool service to bring it up to snuff. I don't think the pool-service people have been out here for a couple weeks." They went outside to look at the yard. After another half hour or so, they decided it was time to get up to Jere's house. He was expecting them.

Russell drove the van up to Jere's A-frame house up on the hill of prestigious Scenic Drive. He pulled up in front where Jere stood waiting for them by the front door.

"Hey, you're finally here!" Lindy and Kerry Lee ran to him for a hug. "Aww, girls! Come on in! Let me help you with your stuff!"

Once inside, they noticed stairs going up to a loft.

"Wow, what a cute home. This looks like a Hansel and Gretel house," exclaimed Lindy.

"Kerry, do you like this staircase?" asked Jere, watching in amazement as she climbed up the side frame like a little monkey.

Tina blushed. "She's our athletic one! Kerry Lee you *walk* up the stairs, not climb. It's not a jungle gym, honey."

"Let's take the bags upstairs." Tina and the girls followed. Jere came along behind them.

"This is the bathroom . . ." said Jere.

"Look, Mom! It has little shutters and rose buds painted on them. We're going to feel like princesses," Lindy beamed happily.

"You are princesses!" said Jere.

"We are going to miss Yvonne, though." Lindy frowned.

227

"Your dad and I will, too. She is growing up, and wanted to stay behind in the Bay area. We'll still be in touch. You'll see," Tina promised.

"That's good," said Lindy, feeling better.

"Let's put the pets in the backyard. At least it's summertime. Jere said the yard is fenced. It should be fine. As long as we put pet food out there, they will stay around."

Soon, everything was tended to and it was time to settle in for the night. In a few days, it would be time to move into their new house.

"Moving Day Yakima"

The big moving van was parked outside in front of the new home on Apple View Way. Movers brought boxes inside, and walked up the steep gravel driveway, as Tina, Russell, and kids were inside, busily unpacking.

"It took a week for both trucks to make it up here . . . but we are moving in now!" Russell said, carrying in a few more boxes. Tina was in the master bedroom, putting away clothes from the cardboard wardrobe box as Kerry Lee sat on the bed and watched. Lindy was in her room, busily organizing her toys and clothes. As the movers set up her queen bed, Lindy put away her things in her dresser.

"We will get to your room soon, Kerry Lee," Tina promised.

Daytime soon passed into evening. The family was at the kitchen table eating takeout Chinese food on paper plates. The familiar kitchen table and chairs were already up.

"Well, we made very good progress! The beds are up, and many things are already put away," Russell said proudly.

"Yes, we made very good progress. Didn't we, girls?" Tina winked. The girls nodded with their mouths full, smiling.

"Yeah . . ."

"Listen, I should go meet with Jere for a while tonight. You and the girls make yourselves comfortable, and I will be back later tonight," Russell promised.

"Okay, hon." Tina looked over at the girls. "I know two tired puppies who are going to bed early tonight."

Later that night, Tina was alone in the living room. The TV was set up and running. There were a few items set up in the living room and dining room, but many boxes were still stacked around everywhere. The TV announcer came on, reading a familiar script.

"Coming up next: Greatest Unsolved Mysteries: The Zodiac Killer. This Satanist serial killer, went on an extended rampage through the 1960s and the 1970s in San Francisco and Vallejo, but was never captured. This man represents one of the greatest unsolved mysteries of our century." Tina stopped and listened. She found herself talking out loud.

"There's that TV special we saw the ad for last week." Tina opened a folding chair and sat in front of the TV. "Let's see if they know about our chase . . . or how he really died." Tina watched in deep fascination. What do they know, she wondered? The voice of the announcer continued.

"In the mid -1960s, the first murder accounted to a man later called the 'Zodiac Killer,' was that of a couple who was parked out on the isolated Lake Herman Road in Vallejo, California. In later years, even more deaths occurred at his hand in Vallejo. He often wrote the *San Francisco Chronicle* describing his murder plans, and taunted Vallejo and San Francisco Police, mocking them, calling them the 'Keystone Cops.' One night, in the spring of 1968, the Vallejo police got a call from a man who called himself 'the Zodiac.'"

"This is the Zodiac speaking. I would like to report a double homicide. I just killed a couple of teenagers. You will find the bodies

229

in a car in a park just off Columbus Parkway." From Napa to San Francisco to Vallejo, a string of murders began to occur . . . usually young people parked in lover's lane areas. However, they were not the only targets." Tina had her hands on her face, looking nervous, wanting to cover her eyes at times.

"I just *hate* watching this stuff! Oh God, he was evil!" Tina winced. The actor depicting the voice of the Zodiac continued.

"This is the Zodiac speaking. I am the murderer of the taxi driver over by Washington Street and Maple Street last night. To prove this, here is the blood-stained piece of the shirt. I am the same man who did in the people in the North Bay area. The San Francisco Police could have caught me if they had searched the park properly instead of holding road races with their motorcycles seeing who could make the most noise! The car drivers should have just parked their cars and sat there quietly waiting for me to come out of cover. School children are nice targets. I think I shall wipe out a school bus some morning. Just shoot out the front tire and then pick off the kiddies as they come bouncing out." Tina was shocked. She ran her hand through hair, as she listened.

"How evil!"

"Experts, ballistic authorities...examined the spent slug and casing found in the Yellow Cab and determined that the weapon used to kill Paul Stine was a 9 mm automatic. But in their opinion, it was a different 9 mm from the one used three months earlier at the Blue Rocks Springs shooting of Darlene Ferrin and Michael Mageau.

"Based on the Zodiac's letters to the *Chronicle*, and his macabre inclusion of a small cut out section of the victim's bloody shirt, SFPD homicide detectives Bill Armstrong and Dave Toschi concluded that they were dealing with a psychotic egomaniac who thrived on publicity."

Tina fidgeted and finally stretched out on the floor on the living-room rug, with a pillow behind her head, feeling a little frustrated with the whole documentary. She took note that there was no mention of anything to do with their chase or how he actually ended his life. The documentary announcer continued.

"Evidence assembled from various and multiple crime scenes now included fingerprints, the suspects probable shoe size, a pair of men's size 7 leather gloves left in Stine's cab, extensive handwriting samples, spent slugs and casings from three separate guns for ballistic comparisons, and several police composite drawings of the suspect's physical description."

Tina suddenly sat up. She looked closer at the screen for the view of the sketches.

"In the hope that people who knew or had seen the suspect would possibly come forward, the San Francisco Police Department released a composite sketch, based on both the teenager's and Officer Donald Fouke's description. It was published in the *San Francisco Chronicle* October 15, 1969, and amended slightly, the sketch done by police artists three days later."

Tina was sitting up close to the TV as she studied the composite police sketches carefully.

"Hmm . . . The one on the right has some resemblance to the man we saw out there, but that sketch was done almost nine years prior . . . and he was *older.* The glasses are right . . . large light-colored glasses . . . hair line is right, but was thinning by the time we saw him nine years later. The chin and jawline are more like what we saw, but a little more broad with age by 1978."

"White male, thirty-five to forty-five years, five feet, ten inches, 180 to 190 pounds, medium build, light complexion . . ." Tina repeated what the announcer read off. "That part is right. That confirms my

231

suspicion: he really *was* closer to mid to late fifties when we saw him in 1978!"

"Light colored hair, possibly graying in the back; may have been lighting that caused this effect," the announcer continued.

Tina seemed to talk to the TV as if having a conversation.

"No, it was not the lighting. He *did* have light hair . . . thinning reddish or gray hair, receding hairline."

As time passed, Tina could not break herself away from this documentary. Tina was looking more and more tired. She was still sitting on the chair, listening to the entire broadcast.

"Although the police attributed some five homicide episodes to the Zodiac, the man himself claimed in a letter to the police, that he had killed more than 37 people.

As hundreds of leads poured in, SFPD detectives and the homicide department had every reason to feel confident that they would soon arrest the killer who called himself 'the Zodiac.' No one at the time ever imagined that four decades later the case would remain unsolved."

Tina finally turned off the TV. She collected her thoughts after seeing this latest documentary. Tina continued to sort out her thoughts, as she talked out loud to herself.

"One of those police sketches looks like the man . . . potentially nine years prior to when we saw him. The chin and the jawline are the key to the correct look of the Zodiac." She closed her eyes, remembering his face.

"I can still see him, turning around in the road that night, with all our headlights on . . ."

Suddenly, there was a noise at the front door. Russell had returned home, unlocking the door.

"Tina . . . I'm surprised you're still up this late."

"Russell, you'll never guess what just happened to be playing when I turned on the TV this evening."

"What was that, honey?" asked Russell.

"That *Greatest Unsolved Mysteries of the Century* documentary program . . . about the Zodiac."

"Really? You mean that one we saw advertised in the restaurant during the move up here?"

"The same."

"Did you save me any dinner?" asked Russell looking in the refrigerator. He brought out some of the Chinese takeout food which was still in the cartons. "What did you find out . . . anything new?"

"One of the police composite sketches they showed done in 1969, really looks a lot like the man we saw, but nine years later . . . older. Light glasses . . . not black ones, same looks, hair and build. Not exact. My sketch was better. I had to use my imagination. He was nine years younger in that sketch. When we saw him he must have been around 55, even 60, maybe."

"That seems right to me. He was definitely middle to late fifties. It's hard to peg men's ages," admitted Russell.

"He was so . . . possessed! *Demon possessed*, obviously. The way he talked about how he could not control the evil thing inside him. He also had this thing about killing people so they would be his slaves in Paradise. *Some Paradise*. Who would believe *that?*"

"Some Eastern religions . . . some Satanist cults."

"Yeah . . . take your pick. It all comes down to the same thing, doesn't it? He was controlled by an evil force out of hell," Tina moaned.

"It's all the same root, isn't it?" Russell agreed. "Any mention of the things we know from our own experience?" Tina shook her head.

"No, not at all. The chase we did from Vista Point in mid-October of 1978 was not mentioned at all. Nothing about his old white car with the red stripes on the side, with the big engine designed for the escape . . . nothing about him walking into the waves and killing himself. It was not mentioned at all. You know when I talked that police supervisor into keeping the report out of the papers way back then, it seems like the truth has gotten *completely* buried after all these years."

"It would seem so, Tina. But we have our own lives to live now. I wouldn't get too caught up in it."

"There is something in me that still wants to call San Francisco Police Homicide, and give them a piece of my mind . . . "

"Tina . . . ?"

"Nicely, of course." Russell saw Tina pick up the phone.

"Tina, it's late."

"What? They have people on duty at all hours. I wonder if any of the original staff still works there now? *They* took us seriously."

"Well, I'm going to bed. We'll talk about it later." Russell went upstairs to the bedroom. Once he'd gone from the room, Tina picked the phone, and dialed information.

"San Francisco Police Department, please . . . non-emergency number."

"Here you go!" said the operator.

"San Francisco Police Department. Can I help you?"

"Yes. Are any of your detectives in? I have some important information on a 'cold case.'"

"Everybody's gone home . . . It's late. There might be one person on duty back there. Hold on."

Tina heard the sound of the phone ringing. A male voice on the phone answered.

"Administration. Detective services."

"Yes, hello, my name is Tina George. I'm from the San Francisco Bay area, but I'm calling from Washington State. We just moved up here . . ."

"How can I help you, ma'am?" asked the officer on the phone, sounding very tired.

"I just watched an episode of *The World's Greatest Unsolved Mysteries . . .*"

The policeman at the police station, a mid-thirties male, drank coffee and ate a donut, with his legs up on the desk. "Great show. I liked it too. Did you see the one on the Black Dahlia Avenger?"

"No . . . I did not. I'm calling because I just saw the new one about the Zodiac Killer," began Tina. "My husband and I were key witnesses back in the late 1970s. We saw him stalking couples in three locations in the space of twenty-five minutes, and then we got into a high-speed chase with him. He eluded us, then disappeared forever. I originally worked with Sergeant Tedesco on the case. I think he's retired now . . ."

The police assistant continued to drink his coffee. He had two donuts on his desk on a napkin. He took another bite.

"The name does not sound familiar. He probably either retired or died by now."

"Oh, dear! Well, it has been quite a few years. Important clues and information surfaced about ten years later, after our encounter with him, but I noticed none of it was in the documentary," Tina said.

"It's probably because they still don't know what happened . . . or what happened to *him*."

Tina was annoyed.

"Well . . . *I* know what happened to him! Can you get me someone to talk to who will take me seriously?" asked Tina.

"Lady, just hold on for a moment, will ya?" He put Tina on hold, and then went to a back room where an officer was watching a late night football program.

"Joe, I've got a lady on the phone who says she knows what happened to the Zodiac killer. Can you take the call?" His police officer friend, Joe, was quite taken in by the game on TV.

"Tell her to leave me a message."

"Okay." He walked back over to the phone at his desk. "The detective on duty says he would like for you to leave him a message."

"Okay. I would be glad to."

Later that evening, Joe played back his voice mail message. He heard Tina's voice play back on the tape.

"Hello, sir. I understand you're the detective on duty but cannot take my call. My name is Tina George, and I am a lifetime resident of the San Francisco Bay area, but we just moved to Washington State. I wanted to call because I just saw a new episode of *The World's Greatest Unsolved Mysteries*, about the Zodiac killer. My husband and I were involved in the case back in 1978, but I noticed that none of the new information about the Zodiac was in the documentary. Can you call me back? I *do know* what happened to the Zodiac. Call my husband Russell George's new number at Basely Research in Yakima, WA., . . . I'm serious . . . I repeat, we *do know* what happened to the Zodiac."

The officer listened. He just shook his head, and made a face, looking annoyed.

"Some crackpot caller . . ." He hit the delete button, and then put on his coat, and left the station for the evening.

***

It was the first part of September, and Tina was up early in the morning helping the girls get ready for school. All of a sudden out of nowhere, there was a loud roll of thunder, and a ripping cloudburst. The rain came down like a great torrent.

"Wow . . . Look at that! It's September. They say it doesn't rain here very much, but today . . . look at that! Lindy . . . Kerry Lee . . . Listen, girls. I'm not going to expect you to go down there to the bus stop, and wait for the bus in that downpour. Let me get my keys. I'll take you to school this morning."

"Thanks, Mom!" beamed Lindy. Kerry Lee was now eight years old.

"Yeah, thanks, Mom!" They drove off to the school right behind the big yellow school bus.

They drove up to the front of their new elementary school, Apple Valley Elementary.

"Girls, I'm going to park and go in with you. I want to talk to the ladies in the office after you get to class."

They went in, using umbrellas, as the wind and rain beat at the back of their bodies as the girls walked toward their respective classrooms. Tina walked into the administrative office. Denise, one of the administrative assistants, greeted her.

"Hello Tina! I did find out more about the Yakima Youth Soccer Association for Kerry Lee. We don't have the forms here, but you can go downtown to this address this Saturday and they will be taking signups there." Tina smiled, and put the papers in her purse.

"Oh thanks! We'll do that."

Mrs. Elgin, the principal, walked out to greet Tina. She was a silver-haired woman with a kind smile.

"Hello again, Mrs. George . . ."

"You may call me Tina . . ."

"Tina . . . I wanted to let you know that in the beginning of each school year, the sixth graders go away for five days to something we call 'Camp Cispus.'"

"Oh, really?"

"Yes. There, they learn all about nature, conservation, plants, varieties of trees, and all different aspects of science relating to the earth. You'll want to get Lindy ready for that. There's a nominal cost for food, lodging, and transportation. They will take notes, journal and write about everything they learned there. When they return, they'll have assignments and write papers about what they learned there," Mrs. Elgin explained.

"I see. Well, that sounds like it will be a very good experience for them," Tina replied.

They conversed briefly as Tina gathered more information about Camp Cispus, and then she broke out her umbrella and returned to her car.

That evening in Lindy's bedroom, Tina took her temperature.

"Hmmm . . . 103 degrees. That is not good. I am going to have to get you to the doctor in the morning, Lindy," said Tina, feeling concerned.

The next day, Tina went back to the elementary school office to talk to Denise and Mrs. Elgin about the situation with Lindy.

"The doctor says that Lindy has strep throat. She'll need to stay in for a few days and rest . . . maybe even a week, he said. It's also highly contagious. No Camp Cispus for Lindy, I'm afraid. I can take a few of her other assignments to her. I think she could keep at least up with *some* school work."

"Okay . . . I'll alert her teacher, Mrs. Galbreath," answered Mrs. Elgin. "She'll get together some light homework for her so she doesn't fall too far behind."

Thanks," Tina replied with a smile.

The next day, Lindy was in her pajamas in the kitchen looking over the homework Tina brought home.

"Lindy . . . how are you, honey?"

"I'm a little better, Mom. My throat still hurts though."

"Your temperature was much better this morning. I know you don't feel too well. Just work on it a little when you feel up to it. I don't think they're going to expect too much from you this week."

"Well, everybody else in my class is away at Camp Cispus. I heard it was really fun."

"Only if you're well. Your dad took Kerry Lee out to the park to meet some of her new soccer friends. She'll start Yakima Youth Soccer pretty soon," Tina replied.

"She'll be really good at that. She runs really fast."

"I know. It wasn't too easy for me if I had to run after her when she chased the ball into the middle of the street! Do you remember what her kindergarten class did for her?"

"Yeah . . . I remember . . . the big, long banner."

"It must have been fifteen feet long! It read, 'Kerry Lee George: the fastest woman in the world: Olympics 2010,'" said Tina, remembering fondly.

"Yeah, that was funny."

"We're beginning to think that Kerry Lee has natural athletic abilities. I'm going to take you, and her, down to the Gymnastics Plus Kid's Gym here soon when you are both well, and get you enrolled. They will be able to tell your athletic levels."

"I'm more into dance, Mom...tap and ballet," said Lindy.

"Okay, my little ballerina. Are you ready for some chicken soup?"

"Yeah, I like the way you make it!" Lindy smiled. Tina served her soup, and helped her get comfortable.

It took almost a week for Lindy's recovery before she was finally well enough to go back to school. After her first day back, she came in with her school bag, and handed Tina an envelope.

"Mom, I think I'm really in trouble for missing Camp Cispus," said Lindy sadly.

"How could you be? You were out with strep throat?" She opened the paperwork revealing Lindy's grades. Tina's jaw dropped. "An *F* in English and writing, *F* in math and social studies and science, *F* in turning in homework! What is this? I turned your work in at the school every day while you were out sick!" Tina cried.

"I know, Mom."

Tina grabbed her coat. "I'm going right down there before they leave, and have a talk with them!"

Tina drove up to the school and walked briskly into the office. She spotted Denise. "Denise, is Linda Galbreath my daughter's sixth-grade teacher?" asked Tina.

"I believe she is," answered Denise.

"I need to talk to her about that week that Lindy was out sick."

"I think she's still in," Denise replied. "You can go on over if you want to talk to her."

"I definitely will."

Tina walked into the classroom. The teacher got up from her desk and walked over to Tina.

Tina pulled out the paper Lindy brought home.

"So, what is the meaning of this?"

"Lindy did not turn in any school work that was done out at Camp Cispus," Mrs. Galbreath replied.

"Of course not. She was too ill to attend *Camp Cispus.*"

"The entire sixth-grade class was out there, except for Lindy."

"Yes?"

"So she failed to turn in the work about what she learned at Camp Cispus."

"But I brought in the homework assignments she completed every day," answered Tina.

"But she was not at Camp Cispus to write about nature and what they learned about preserving the environment," Mrs. Galbreath answered.

"So how can she make it up?"

"She has to write about what she learned at Camp Cispus."

"But she wasn't at Camp Cispus," Tina cried.

"Well, I'm sorry then."

"You mean we cannot fix these grades because she was not at Camp Cispus?"

"That's right. She has to write about what she learned at Camp Cispus."

"You are not making any sense! How can she write about an experience she did not have?" Tina wailed, about to lose her composure.

"Perhaps Lindy could talk to one of the other students who went to the Camp," Mrs. Galbreath suggested.

"Listen here, Mrs. Galbreath, I'm not sure what kind of teacher you are, but back in California my daughter was thought to be an exceptional student. You saw her grade records. Her teachers told her she was a leader. Miss Taylor told her, 'Lindy, you are a leader. Be careful where you lead because the others will follow.' We move up here and the first week in, you give her all *F*s because she was out with strep throat? She did work, in spite of the fact she did not feel well, and was even running a fever sometimes."

"I'll arrange for her to sit in with some of the other students who went to the camp, and get some ideas on what to write about," offered Mrs. Galbreath.

"I cannot believe my ears!" Tina rolled her eyes.

Soon Tina was back at home, and it was now dinnertime. She complained to Russell, and explained the entire story to him.

"That's pretty strange, I'll admit."

"Well, Mom . . . Last May and June in my old class in California, we did a whole lot of work on nature, science, and preventing waste in the environment. I think I could fake it."

"Do you think?"

"Sure, Mom. And I'll talk to Jenna. She's my new best friend. She went to Camp Cispus. She let me copy off her."

"I can't believe this," said Tina. Lindy pulled out a piece of paper.

"Here we go . . . 'What I learned at Camp Cispus,' by Lindy George. I might even get an *A*. Tina and Russell glanced over at each other with a puzzled look, and just shook their heads. Life in Yakima was sometimes more of an adjustment than they ever dreamed it would be.

***

It was Sunday. Tina, Russell, and the girls were visiting their new church, Christian Life Fellowship. They listened to the inspiring message. Russell's boss, Jere, sat with them.

The pastor paced up front as he delivered his message. Pastor Matthews prepared to read from his open Bible.

"Do you know that it is a universal law of God that powers in the unseen realm, govern, shape, and mold what is in the 'seen realm,' or physical realm? You can read about it everywhere in the Bible. An example is from Daniel Chapter 11, with what was going on with all the unseen turmoil in the stratosphere above Daniel, in the land of

Persia . . . to verses in Hebrews that talk about all that was made, was made from that which was first unseen. Hebrews 11:3."

"If you've ever read about the story of King Jehoshaphat in II Chronicles Chapter 20, you are remembering an impossible situation of an evil army, dark forces surrounding the people of God. They were greatly outnumbered, and the situation looked impossible. But King Jehoshaphat did a very wise thing. He removed himself from the weight of responsibility of the situation, and announced to God, 'The Battle is the Lord's.' Well you know the end of this story. He and the people of Israel experienced a supernatural deliverance from the violence that was about to overtake them!"

"Zechariah 4:6 reminds us that it is 'not by might, nor by power, but by my Spirit.' You will succeed because of my Spirit, says the Lord God Almighty. You will succeed because of my Spirit, though you are few and weak."

Tina glanced over and smiled warmly at Russell and their daughters. She was grateful for their spiritual unity as a family, and all that God had done for them. The pastor continued his sermon.

"Today, right now in this life, you will seem to face many 'evil giants.' They take on many forms: financial difficulties, trouble in your home or marriage, addictions, a person or situation that has come into your life that seems so big that you just cannot handle or dissolve it without God's help. In Matthew 21:21-22, the insurmountable issue is referred to as a 'mountain.' He then read the passage. "But even if you say to this mountain be taken up and cast into the sea, it will be done. And whatever you ask for in My Name, having faith, and really believing, you will receive. And in helping others, God uses his righteousness to channel through us like a river...to help dissolve the evil in the situation." Pastor Matthews concluded his message.

Tina, Russell, Jere, and the girls visited briefly in the foyer of the church. Russell shook the pastor's hand. "That was a very good message, Pastor!"

"So how are you girls doing in the new school?" Russell asked as they drove home.

"I still don't feel very good. I get butterflies in my tummy. Everything is so new," said Kerry Lee.

"It will take some time. You will feel fine, soon. I promise. How about you, Lindy? How is writing about your experience at Camp Cispus coming along?"

"Fine, Dad. I think I'm getting an *A*. It's been a different sort of way to do a homework assignment. It has helped me know how to be an expert liar." Lindy chuckled.

The family car sped down the road, as Russell neared their house. "I'm not sure I like the sound of that!"

Next week came, and the family was getting more into a regular routine.

Russell returned home from work and Jere's world, involving a manufacturing plant, a TV production studio, and a regional broadcast center.

"Hi Tina! How is everything?" asked Russell, putting down his briefcase.

"Oh, pretty good, honey!" he gave Tina a little kiss.

"Jere unloaded some news on me today which was a little disappointing."

"Oh?"

"We lost a huge account that had to do with our machines that manufacture Styrofoam clam shells. One of our huge accounts caved in to environmental pressure, and canceled all of the product, and the

244

machines that make the product! It was a multi-million dollar loss," moaned Russell.

"Oh honey. . . I'm so sorry!" Tina sympathized.

"Yeah . . . It means shutting down a whole wing of the company. Jere's not sure yet what to do. But what it does mean . . . is that there will be no breaking ground for the new TV studio. All those plans will have to be cancelled."

"Oh . . . that's disappointing!"

"The whole idea of developing a new regional station . . . is not going to happen now. They may need you to do a few celebrity interviews for the current flagship program, but it's not going to be like we were hoping, honey." Tina looked a little disappointed, but recovered her feelings. "Well," she said, as she reached for the *Washington Real Estate Fundamentals* text book. "I figured I'd better have a backup. With all the Californians moving up here, real estate definitely is going to be busy!"

"That's what I like about you, Tina. You always bounce back okay." Russell grinned.

The next day, the home phone rang. Tina picked it up. The clock in the kitchen read 11:00 a.m.

"Tina, this is Mrs. Elgin. Kerry Lee's teacher just told me that all she does is put her head on her desk and cry. I think you need to come pick her up." Tina winced.

"Okay . . . I'll be right down." She immediately grabbed her keys and drove over to the elementary school. The move, new surroundings, and new people, had undoubtedly been the hardest on her youngest at only eight.

When Tina entered the school, Kerry Lee ran into her arms. Tina wiped her eyes and hugged her tight. As they walked to the car she asked, "Kerry, what's making you so sad? Has someone hurt you?

"Oh, Mom, things here are just so different. The school is bigger and everyone else already has friends. No one wants to play with me or include me at lunch and the teacher has no patience with me if I have a question. I just feel so dumb and left out."

"Y'know, honey, when I was twelve, my parents bought a new house in Walnut Creek, and we moved from the Bay area. It was two weeks before I would have finished the sixth grade. Everything was so new at the Walnut Acres School, I thought I was going to die. But I didn't. In time, and with God's help, everything worked out, and I made new friends too," said Tina remembering her own childhood. She was relieved to see a smile shine through the tears as they parked at the Fun Center and went in for ice cream.

"Mmm . . . This is good. I'm glad you talked me into the bubble-gum flavor, Kerry Lee! I know it seems really scary and different right now, honey. But soon you'll feel at home at your new school," Tina assured her.

"Promise?"

"*Promise.*

Tina gave her a comforting hug. As they watched the bumper cars zip around the arena.

"Wow, look at those little cars, eh? This Saturday we can come back with Lindy and ride them. You have one more Saturday before soccer practice starts. Would you like that?"

"Yeah, Mom!" Kerry Lee beamed.

"Do you think you can try a little harder to relax in school? We'll pray that God will bring you some new friends . . . and you can look forward to the bumper cars on Saturday!" Tina winked.

"Okay, Mom!" Tina took Kerry's hand and they headed to the car.

"Thank you, Lord, for giving me the words to say and please help Kerry Lee through this rough transition time like You helped me all those years ago, " Tina prayed as they headed home.

After dinner that evening, Tina washed dishes with Russell.

"Are the girls downstairs watching a kid's video?" She glanced around. "Good, you wouldn't believe what happened today. I got a call from Mrs. Elgin at the school. She said, 'Kerry Lee's fourth grade teacher said that all Kerry would do is put her head down on her desk and cry. She said, 'You'd better just come pick her up.'"

"Oh honey. How is she now?" Russell asked, concerned.

"Doing better. I took her to the Fun Center and got her an ice-cream cone. I told her about my struggles when I had to change schools about her age and it seemed to help. You know I thought this move might take a little adjustment, but I didn't know that it would be like *this!*"

***

The next day at school, Lindy was sitting at the lunch table outside with her new friend, Jenna. Suddenly Misty a known bully, and her side-kick, Sue, walked over to Jenna and started chiding her. They were always giving her trouble because she was shy and brainy. When they grabbed Jenna's lunch and dumped it on the ground, Lindy had enough. "Hey, leave her alone!"

"So, what do we have here . . . a California girl?" Misty chided. "Look at that poofy hair . . . and makeup."

"Pink lip gloss, no less." Sue chimed in.

"So why did you move up here, California girl?" Misty sneered.

"Because my parents changed their professions," Lindy answered politely.

"You look pretty fine, California girl . . . but what happens if that hair and face ever get messed up? We're not used to girls our age looking like you around here," Misty retorted.

"Back off, Misty," Jenna, said nervously, not wanting a fight.

"We 'farm girls' know how to fight."

"So do we *California girls!*" Lindy said, rising to face her opponent.

Misty took a swing at her. Lindy ducked, then grabbed her. They wrestled to the ground on the lawn. Sue cheered Misty on. Jenna looked on, frightened. Lindy got up, and took a swing at Misty, cuffing her on the eye. Misty fought back. Lindy swung again.

"Here you go, farm girl!" Lindy swung twice at the girl bully.

"Hey, now girls . . . Break it up!" A teacher said stepping between them.

"Misty started the fight, Mrs. Brown!" Jenna said, coming to Lindy's rescue.

"Why does that not surprise me?" Mrs. Brown sighed.

Lindy had grass all over her, and her hair was messed up. Her nose was bleeding just like Misty's.

"Let's go to the nurse's office and get you girls cleaned up!" Mrs. Brown said. Taking each girl by the arm, they made their way into the building.

When Russell got home, Tina filled him in on Lindy's escapade.

"Like I said yesterday, I figured the girls might have some adjustment to the new school, but nothing like this!

"What a story!" chuckled Russell. "But I'm kind of proud of Lindy for not backing down!"

"Listen to you! Just because we don't have a son! It's usually Kerry Lee who is the tomboy," said Tina, setting the table for dinner.

"Where is Lindy . . . I want to talk to her about this!" Russell shouted down the stairs. "Lindy, can you come up here, please?"

Lindy and Kerry Lee appeared. The blond princess-like Lindy had a black eye. Russell went over to her, tenderly.

"I heard you had a rough day at school with couple of 'farm girls.'"

"You mean . . . a couple of kicking mules?" remarked Lindy, sadly. "Look at that eye!"

"It's okay . . . Misty, the bully, has two black eyes," laughed Kerry Lee.

"What?" Tina was shocked.

"I figured she had it coming," Lindy explained.

"Looks like you had to defend yourself against a little hell cat. It's not just for the boys," said Russell.

"Where was the teacher on monitor patrol, I ask you?" wondered Tina.

"She came over eventually. We had to go to the office, but I didn't get in trouble. They seemed to already know that Misty and Sue were troublemakers," explained Lindy.

"Maybe you turned out to be a peacemaker in the long run?" Tina smiled.

"I guess so . . . Mrs. Elgin said something like that," said Lindy.

"What a week in the life of you two girls. I promised Kerry Lee we could go back to the Fun Center Saturday to ride bumper cars. Maybe we all need to go to the Fun Center this Saturday and have a good time. What do you say?" Tina suggested.

"Sounds good to me!" agreed Russell.

"Yeah!" agreed Lindy.

"I want to go back," said Kerry Lee.

"Okay . . . then. Let's put another ice pack on that eye, Lindy." Tina walked off with the girls to get the ice pack.

***

A few months went by, and it seemed like the girls were growing up so fast, especially Kerry Lee, a tanned, athletic blond with short boyish hair. Tina drove up to a Gymnastics Plus Building with Kerry Lee. She parked, and they walked inside, Kerry Lee, in her gym clothes.

"We have an appointment with Bruce Jenkins, one of your coaches," explained Tina. The receptionist called him out. In moments, Bruce appeared.

"Oh hello, Mrs. George . . . and this must be Kerry Lee," Bruce smiled.

"Hi," Kerry Lee said shyly.

"Yes. She is currently enrolled in youth soccer, but I wanted her to keep up with her gymnastics lessons. We just moved here from California a few months ago."

"Yes . . . She will be better at soccer if she keeps up with her gymnastics. If you can leave her here with me for about three hours, I can run a good evaluation on her. Let's see." He looked at a paper on a clipboard. "She is nine years old?

"Yes. She just turned nine at the end of December."

"Okay . . . I'll check back with you when you return in a few hours," smiled Bruce.

"That's fine. I can do other shopping and banking, and return about four o'clock," agreed Tina.

"That's just perfect." Kerry Lee went inside with Bruce to begin her evaluation, as Tina drove off to do her errands.

Inside the gym, Kerry Lee was going through a battery of gym exercises and moves on the high bar, rings, horse, plus jumping and tumbling on the mat.

Bruce watched Kerry Lee go through her moves with grace, and exceptional strength and speed. He became more amazed by every moment that passed. He marked points and times off on his paper, and kept the notes as she progressed. Coach Bruce looked up, amazed. Kerry Lee walked over to him, and smiled a girlish grin.

"How did I do?" asked Kerry, wiping her face with a towel.

"Very, very good, Kerry! I'm quite proud of you," the coach replied.

Tina returned to the gym right at 4 p.m.

Coach Bruce walked out with Kerry Lee. She was bright and sharp, and not even tired.

"Do you need something to drink, young lady? Tina said reaching in to a bag, "Here's a small grape juice for you! Why don't sit over there with the other kids from the class and drink it?"

"Thanks, Mom!"

Bruce walked over to Tina with his clipboard. "Mrs. George . . . May I have a word with you over here?"

"Sure . . . I'll be right back, honey," Tina said to Kerry.

"So, what planet did this kid come off of?" He laughed. "I mean she's only nine years old!"

"Yes?"

Tina, your daughter is unusually gifted in gymnastics . . . and probably everything else. I mean she could train for the Olympics, seriously. The sky is the limit. She could choose any field of sports to compete, not just gymnastics . . . If soccer is ever an Olympic sport . . . that too," Coach Bruce explained.

"That's good news . . . I think. Her father will be proud! She's been showing signs of unusual athletic talent ever since she could walk and run . . . even in kindergarten," said Tina.

"I'm not surprised. I'm suggesting that she train in gymnastics twice a week," said Bruce.

"She belongs to the Youth Soccer Association. They play every Saturday," explained Tina.

"I see. Well, get back to me. You should be very proud of your daughter. I'd like to be sure she's getting the best training!"

"Thank you!" Kerry Lee walked over with a straw in her grape juice.

"Hi, honey . . . It's about time to go." The news from Coach Bruce confirmed something Tina already knew in her heart about the athletic talent of little Kerry Lee.

As Tina served dinner that night she told Russell, "The coach up there at the gymnastics place was very enthusiastic about Kerry Lee. He spent three hours evaluating her, and said she had a lot of athletic talent. The 'sky's the limit,' he said."

"Well, Kerry, that's good news. I'm proud of you!" said Russell, sounding like a very proud dad.

"Thanks Dad. It was fun going through all the gymnastic moves up on the bar, and stuff like that," Kerry Lee replied, with one fork in the mashed potatoes.

"I wish I could have been there, hon." Russell smiled.

"Yeah, Dad! My thing is dance and ballet, really . . . but Kerry is the athlete," admitted Lindy, feeling somewhat misplaced with all the attention Kerry Lee was getting.

"He thinks she should be going twice a week to gymnastics training," said Tina, passing on the report.

"Hmm . . . I don't know. She is also involved in youth soccer. We'll have to think it over," Russell pondered.

"That's what I said," agreed Tina.

"I like both . . . I think I could do both," said Kerry Lee.

"But you have to have time for school and homework. We'll have to think about it," Russell replied in "dad" tones. Lindy was at the dinner table still finishing her food.

"Mom, can you meet my best friend, Jenna, tomorrow? She wants me to come over," said Lindy. Tina was busy clearing the dishes.

"Okay, honey. I'll talk to her mom. We'll set it up."

"Oh, okay . . . I want you to meet her mom too. There's a special reason."

"Oh yeah?" asked Tina.

"You'll see when you meet her tomorrow," replied Lindy, with a mysterious smile.

***

The next day, in the late afternoon, Tina headed toward Jenna's house. Lindy went over after school, and Tina was on the way to pick her up. She saw the Irish Court street sign. Tina pulled into the driveway, then went up to the front door, and rang the doorbell.

Eileen Collins opened the door, and greeted Tina with a smile. She was a medium-built blond woman with a soft-spoken voice and gentle manner. Tina immediately noticed that a large Holy Bible was visible on the bookshelf, and a framed needlepoint graced the wall with "God Bless Our Home."

"Oh, hello! You must be Tina, Lindy's mom.

"Yes."

"I think the girls are still playing in Jenna's room. Lindy, your Mom is here!" Eileen called out. "So you just moved up here from California a few months ago?"

"Yes, I'm bracing myself for the winter here. It will be different!"

"Yes, it will be." Girls' voices echoed down the hall then the girls appeared.

"This is Jenna . . . my new best friend!"

"Hello Jenna," Tina replied politely.

"Hello. I'm so glad you moved here. Lindy and I have been having a good time playing at school, and over here at my house." Jenna glanced over at Lindy with a broad smile.

"Mom . . . Eileen has something to tell you." Eileen paused, searching for the right words.

"I heard, sort of round about through Jenna, that you and your husband chased the Zodiac killer in the Bay Area back in 1978. Apparently, it ultimately led to his . . . uh, permanent disappearance?"

"You might say that."

"It's odd that we're making each other's acquaintance," Eileen hesitated, then continued. "I ran into the serial killer, Ted Bundy, years ago when I was a student at Central. One night he tried to get me to accept a ride from him, but I wouldn't. He even followed me to a restaurant, and continued to try to get me to come with him. He was creepy. I knew better. Just by chance two police officers walked into the same restaurant where we were. Once he saw them, he immediately backed off of pressuring me. A woman who was not so keen on her instincts did accept a ride, and she wound up killed. Later on, somebody else gave testimony of that night, and put him behind bars . . . permanently."

"Well that is . . . really a strange coincidence." Tina looked over at Lindy and Jenna, feeling a little surprised.

"Sorry if I spoke out of turn, Mom. I thought she should know."

"It's okay, Lindy. It looks like we both had some angels working overtime on those nights!"

"Your daughter has already been such a blessing to us. I can tell she was raised in a godly home." Eileen smiled.

"Thank you . . . I appreciate that! Yes, we all worked as a family in a very large Christian television network in the Bay area. We had to pray for God to give us extra patience to deal with that crazy lifestyle. And I think he did." Tina smiled.

"Kerry Lee and I were both actresses at times . . . mostly commercials," Lindy said.

"Yes, you were . . . and very good ones too," replied Tina. "Well, Lindy, are you about ready? I should get home and start dinner."

"Okay, mom."

"Thanks for letting Lindy come over! God bless your evening now," said Eileen, standing at the door as they left.

Later, Tina cleaned up after dinner, while Russell worked late at the plant. He had already warned Tina it would be a very late night. She looked troubled, and preoccupied.

"Mom, can Kerry and I go downstairs and play?" asked Lindy.

"Sure, girls. That movie you were looking for is on the table. I found it this morning."

"Thanks, Mom!" The two girls bounced downstairs to the family room.

Tina took off her apron. She moved slowly toward the chair as she recalled the past, remembering scenes such as leaving the church, and looking back, sensing the presence of angels. She recalled seeing the Zodiac as he was leaving the first lover's lane area by the beach, late at night, then pulling behind him as he was parked by the second couple, and then she remembered seeing him at Vista Point, as he dashed back to his car and raced off. Scenes rolled through her mind of the chase on the freeway. Tina looked frustrated reliving the scene when the car pulled out in front of them at the last moment, blocking her view of the Zodiac car. She remembered the minister speaking: "Darkness cannot stand in the presence of light. It must flee. Let God's righteousness be in you, and the enemy will have to go!" Tina remembered the Bible on Eileen's bookshelf, and Eileen saying, "God bless you now!" as they left her home that day. "Oh . . ." She put her face in her hands. "There is some kind of message here." Tina looked around as she walked slowly across the room. She talked softly to herself.

"We're not perfect, but somehow God's righteousness in us defeated the evil enemy in both of *them* . . . driving them back, and into chains."

Tina remembered her girls in Sunday school singing, "Jesus loves me, this I know. For the Bible tells me so. Little ones to him belong... they are weak, but He is strong."

"We are weak . . . but He is strong," said Tina, remembering the lyrics of the song.

The girls heard their Mom from downstairs, and came up to the kitchen.

"Are you okay, Mom?"

"Yes, I'm very okay. Girls, sing 'Jesus loves me' for Mom. They sang softly and tenderly for Tina. "Jesus loves me this I know, for the Bible tells me so. Little ones to Him belong, they are weak, but He is strong . . ."

Tina remembered how many children have sung that song for decades all over the world, all races and countries.

"*We are weak, but He is strong.* Do you get it?" She put her arms around the girls, and gave them a hug. "We are weak . . . but He is strong!" A little tear trickled down her cheek. Tina remembered what the real leading force was in this life, and in all things, even that night in the Zodiac chase.

The next morning, the kids had already left for school. Tina and Russell were at the kitchen table having coffee. Russell put the newspaper down.

"Jere and I are not sure what we're going to do about this potential account we have overseas. It could be a great opportunity. But . . ."

"But what?" wondered Tina.

"Those plant managers over there want us to lie about some things . . . . cover up some things."

"Oh?"

"I just don't want to go there . . . neither does Jere. We are going to probably tell them today." Russell sighed.

"It's for the best . . . I'm sure. More business will come from somewhere else, or they will see a new avenue around it without the lies."

"You are so wise, honey!" replied Russell, smiling at Tina.

"Russell, I'm having an epiphany about something."

"Oh? What is it?"

"Somehow God chose to use us to put an end to the Zodiac killer because . . ."

"Because . . . ?

"He could trust us and because we could channel His light and power to the dark situation and dissolve it. Actually, *He* dissolved it. He does it all the time through people who go as far as to trust Him and rely on Him. Look how people who love God go to the needy, and bring new life and light . . . rebuild communities after earthquakes, feed the hungry…I mean, don't we see it all the time in our everyday lives because we trust God about things . . . our lives, our kids . . . our 'daily bread,' really. Also . . . it was not our 'appointed time.' It was not our time to die . . ."

"We have too much yet to do and accomplish yet in this life," Russell replied back to Tina, softly with understanding.

"You are right. I didn't make the connection at first . . . but you're right."

Russell put his hand on hers. The morning light seemed to flood the scene and shone even farther, right into their hearts.

CHAPTER THIRTEEN

ANGELS APPEAR AGAIN

The First Thanksgiving

Tina put the Thanksgiving turkey in the oven. The kitchen was filled with the warm festive smells of the holiday. Russell, Lindy, and Kerry Lee were already dressed for a hike in the mountains and the snowy hills. "We are going to take a drive up Highway 410 into the mountains. We'll do a little hiking, and pick up some firewood to load in the van. By the time we get back, the turkey should be done," Russell explained to Tina.

"And the table will be set. Don't take longer than about three and a half hours, okay, hon?" asked Tina, taking out the pies.

"Okay. It's close by, about half hour's drive to Whistling' Jack's. Girls, wait until you see that big stuffed moose as you walk in. Are you bringing Puppins?" asked Russell.

"Yeah, let's bring Puppins!" Lindy agreed.

"I'll get him!" said Kerry Lee, starting for the backyard.

Soon, Russell, the kids, and their small dog were loaded into the van. Russell closed the van door, and soon was driving up toward the mountains. Kerry Lee was up front with Russell, and Lindy was behind with the dog in the back of the van. The back was open for the firewood they planned to collect.

The tall evergreens were elegant and beautiful as they lined the highway like tall majestic giants. The skies were blue and the air was nippy. The van sped along the road toward the lodge, and the best firewood areas. For the most part the roads were clear, but in the Northwest at the end of November, winter was nearing, and ice showing up in patches anywhere on the roads was probable. Russell was looking around out the window at the road conditions. Suddenly, trickling in from the unseen realm, a black mist slowly appeared as if out of hell. It followed and enveloped the van. Fire unnaturally leapt up from the ice patches on the road ahead. The Zodiac demon appeared, hidden in the brush of the pine trees, as he looked out at the van approaching on the road about where he expected the accident to happen.

"The roads look good so far," said Russell, brightly. The kids were happy and wide-eyed, enjoying the beautiful wintery forest. Being from California, everything was so new, and the environment was so different and refreshing in their new home area. Lindy held Puppins as they watched the beautiful mountain scenery fly by. "We're almost to Whistling Jack's. Jere and I came up here for lunch one day. I think you girls will like it! The Naches River runs by it too!"

The roads ahead began to show heavier signs of snow and ice, and the deadliest of all: *black ice*. Russell was driving a little too fast for the mountain roads. The speedometer read 55 miles per hour.

Suddenly, the tires started hitting the slippery snow and ice. Just beyond the visible snow patches, the van slid into a dangerous stretch of black ice. Their vehicle began to spin out of control. The van spun around a total of four times, then began to slide over a steep cliff-like ravine. Looking down it was a one thousand-foot plunge, with a raging river far below.

"Oh . . . no! Hold on girls!" Russell cried out.

Kerry Lee screamed and closed her eyes, bracing for the worst.

"We're gonna die!" Lindy cried out.

Unseen to them in the physical realm, large transparent guardian angels suddenly appeared like giant light beams. Numerous shining angelic beings instantly swirled protectively around the van, controlling its direction, and softening the impact of the fall.

The van whirled around and went off the road into a ravine by the river, but was stopped by the trunk of a large tree where it finally rested. Three large angels held the van in their huge strong arms while several others looked on. Then they followed after Russell, Lindy, Kerry Lee, and Puppins, cushioning the blow of their impact, which should have been deadly.

A disheveled-looking Russell soon emerged from the van, and looked around. He looked back inside.

"Is everybody okay? Girls?

"My knee has a little cut on it!" said Kerry Lee, showing her knee.

"Thank God for seatbelts! I have a first-aid kit in the glove box. Let me get it. Lindy, what about you?" Lindy was holding the dog, and looked up with her tasseled blond hair.

"Oh . . . my head! Even my ponytail hurts!" she moaned.

"Let me see. . . Come here," said her dad." Russell looked into her eyes, and held her head in his hands. "How's your neck?"

"Okay, I think," Lindy replied with a little laugh. "Dad, you tore a big hole in your pants!" Russell looked down at his jeans.

"It's okay . . . I think we're doing pretty okay. Let's work on climbing back up the hill, and getting back up onto the road. I think I saw a house back there where we can make a call and get a tow truck out here." They carefully climbed out of the van, and started up toward the road. Unseen to them, the large angels helped propel them safely to the top of the steep hill. Puppins followed behind them, unhurt, only a slightly bent tail.

"Look . . . there!" Russell called out. They walked up to the front door of a large log home. The huge rustic cabin was the home of a big game hunter. Russell rang the doorbell. The man and his wife came to the door.

"Sorry, pardon us. My van took quite a spin on the ice back there. We were in a wreck! Can I please use your phone to call a tow truck?"

The hunter-homeowner, wearing jeans and a plaid flannel shirt, looked Russell and the kids over with a surprised expression. At this point, the family looked a little disheveled, with torn clothes. By now, Kerry already had a big band aid on her knee.

"Sure . . . by all means! Come in!" His wife looked over the children, wondering if they were hurt. Russell and the kids entered the house, as Puppins followed.

"Are you all right, girls?"

"We're a little banged up, but I think we're okay," Lindy replied politely.

"This is our dog, Puppins," said Kerry Lee with a little smile.

"Here's the phone right over here," the man said to Russell.

Inside the huge rustic cabin-style home, there were luxurious surroundings, including furniture from Africa and a plush white carpet on the floor in the main living room. There were artistically stuffed wild animals everywhere, apparently the man's trophies. As they glanced around, they saw a stuffed cougar, a large black bear, and a polar bear which stood about twelve feet high on its hind legs. A skylight above his head gave the polar bear enough room for him to fit in that spot.

"Look at that polar bear!" Kerry Lee said. Puppins followed, as she walked over for a better look. Kerry Lee looked like a midget next to the huge polar bear. Looking up at the twelve foot bear, Puppins squealed and wet the rug. Lindy laughed in spite of herself.

"Oh, no!" Russell walked back into the room just in time to see it.

"Sorry," he frowned. "I did reach the tow-truck people. They are on the way. Thanks so much!" He looked back at the yellow mark on the carpet in front of the lofty polar bear. "Can I pay for the cleaning?" asked Russell.

"Don't worry about it. You've had enough trouble for one day," the hunter laughed. He and his wife showed them to the door so they could get going.

"Let me give you a ride back to your van in my car," the kind hunter offered. "The tow truck should be along soon."

Shortly, Russell and the tow truck crew were on the road surveying the situation, making plans to get the van pulled back up on the road. Kerry Lee and Lindy looked on, wide-eyed.

Nearby, unseen to them, the spirit of the Zodiac hid within a large bushy pine tree. He looked on with large, red, glowing eyes. He seemed very displeased that his evil plan did not succeed. He gave out a miserable whine.

Meanwhile, Tina was in the kitchen back home. The roasted turkey was in the oven almost completely ready to serve. She was setting the table when the phone rang. It was Russell. He had gone back the hunter's home and used the phone.

"Hi Tina . . . Honey, we might be a little late in getting home . . ."

"Why, what's wrong?"

"The van hit some ice and we went off the road. We were in a bad wreck!"

"What?! Tina cried out in shock. Are you okay? How are the girls?"

"We're okay, just a little shaken . . . just a few cuts and bruises. We spun around three or four times and wound up in a ravine. A big tree stopped us from going any farther."

"Thank God!"

"We're waiting for the tow truck to pull us back up on the road. I think the van is drivable. We'll be home in a couple of hours, depending on when the tow truck gets here."

"Well you might have to wait a little longer for the turkey now!" she laughed, teary-eyed. "I'm glad you and the kids are okay . . . That's the main thing! I love you!"

"I love you too," said Russell tenderly. "We'll be home as soon as we can." They said good-bye, and Russell hung up. Tina put the turkey in the oven on "warm," and said a thank-you prayer to God for their safety and protection.

Soon, the skilled tow-truck crew had the van back up on the road. It looked surprisingly unharmed. Russell got in with the kids, and started up the van. It seemed fine, just as Russell had hoped. They drove off toward home, feeling well rescued, to say the least.

The Spirit of the Zodiac, looked on with red glowing eyes from his hideout. He seemed displeased that his evil plan was foiled. The area where he was situated inside the tree began to smolder, and flame. He soon disappeared into an angry wisp of smoke.

Soon, Russell and the kids and dog arrived back home. They drove up to the kitchen entrance with a new sense of joy, and just a great feeling, happy to be alive. They eagerly rushed inside. The smells of Thanksgiving warmly greeted them. Tina was centered on only one thing: that they were all safe.

"Thank God you are all okay!" Tina cried a few happy tears as they embraced each other.

She got a glance of the van through the window of the kitchen door. "Russell, the van doesn't look like it was in a serious wreck like that. It hardly has a scratch on it."

Russell just smiled. "Believe me . . . *it was a serious wreck!*"

"Russell, do you suppose . . .?" Tina was remembering their angel interventions in the past.

Russell smiled that "knowing" smile. He knew what she was thinking!

The turkey was still perfect and the table still looked festive. Their faces shone with a happy glow just to be together again and safe. A happy Puppins wagged his tail, perked up his ears, and and begged for scraps.

"Well, we won't have to go to too much trouble figuring out what we're grateful for this Thanksgiving . . ." said Russell, serving up the turkey.

"I'm so glad you are all safe!" Tina said again, feeling a little emotional. She served up the mashed potatoes, and handed the rest of the food around to each one of the family.

"You should have seen what Puppins did when he saw the gigantic stuffed polar bear inside the big game hunter's house." Tina looked back at Kerry Lee with a curious look.

"He got so scared when he looked up at that bear," Kerry Lee began, "that he went right on the carpet!" Lindy laughed.

Oh, no!" Tina winced in embarrassment.

"Oh, *yes!*" Russell laughed. It was so good just to be together, and safe. They knew it would be a Thanksgiving to remember in a special way forever.

Outside the door, their tall guardian angels just smiled, and then quietly disappeared into light beams that travelled up toward the sky, back home to the heavenlies.

CHAPTER FOURTEEN

A NEW ATHLETE EMERGES

Youth Soccer—Spring Season

After weeks of preparation, it was time for the big Spring Soccer Tournament in Gig Harbor, near Seattle. Tina packed in Kerry Lee with her gear, like all the other soccer moms who were organizing their kids' equipment in cars and vans. Soon, Tina, along with Kerry Lee and some of the other girls from the team were on the road. They were wearing team T-shirts that read "Bobcats." During the long drive, Tina asked the girls, "Do you remember how you got your name?" "Yeah, a little blonde girl shouted, "Chuck wanted to call us the Tigers since the uniforms were orange and black. But you wanted to call us the Bob Kitties!" Kerry Lee chimed in, "He didn't like that at all! Then you said, 'Okay then, *Bobcats!*' and we've been Bobcats ever since!"

As everyone unloaded at the motel, their coach, Chuck, and his wife, Lynne, talked to the girls on the team.

"Everybody, get a good night's sleep! We'll meet for breakfast at 10:30 a.m. The warm up for the game starts at noon, sharp!" Chuck announced to all the teammates. Gig Harbor was a charming seaside town near Seattle, a great setting for the spring tournament. As they ate breakfast, they enjoyed scenes of the town and the bay from the restaurant. Soon it was time to get over to the soccer field. The day of the big tournament they had waited and practiced for since last

November was nearly here. They had just gotten back on the field to practice again that February following winter break.

The team was shaping up well and things looked promising. Chuck was proud of the team of nine-and-ten-year-old players. They'd made big strides in learning how to play the game skillfully. Soon, the Bobcats arrived on the field, and they began to take their places. It was not long before Kerry Lee was in the heat of the game, racking up big points for her team. Kerry Lee ran at great speed straight toward the ball with a brave, no-fear attitude. She was taking body shots on her arm, upper chest and back, racking up points as the happy crowd cheered. Tina watched with amazement. The soccer moms from the Bobcats were rooting enthusiastically. Tina had never seen anything like it. Was this her daughter? When the game was over, Kerry Lee walked off the field toward her mom. Her coach and teammates gathered around her, lifting her up on their shoulders like a hero. Tina rushed over to her daughter.

"Kerry Lee . . . I could hardly believe my eyes! I think I'm going to get you a new T-shirt that reads, 'body shots' on it!" Kerry Lee gave her a big grin.

"Thanks, Mom!"

Back at home the next day, Tina tried to describe the game to Russell.

"I'm not even that much into sports, but what I witnessed on that soccer field was amazing! Russell, honestly you should have been there!" said Tina, who was at a loss for words.

"Did you take pictures?" Russell wondered.

"No . . . but somebody had a video camera. I just never have seen anybody move like that on a soccer field . . . and run up to the ball and take shots all over their body. I think my mouth must have fallen wide open!"

"Now you know why Chuck and the other soccer moms are so fanatical about Kerry Lee not missing a soccer tournament."

"Yeah, I know but working in real estate now, and with these games always on the weekends out of town, I'm losing deals. When we got back, I called my clients. They wrote an offer on a house we were discussing with, another agent—because I wasn't in town!"

"Ouch!"

Yeah . . . that was a very expensive weekend!" groaned Tina.

We'll have to work something out." I'm sure the other soccer moms would be willing to help with rides."

"Please! Could you work on it? You know Chuck and some of the couples even better than I do," Tina implored.

Russell and Chuck managed to coordinate with the other soccer families to make sure that Kerry Lee always had a ride to the weekend games. It was well worth the effort to the coach, Chuck, and other soccer families to be sure Kerry Lee was present and playing at all the games. She continued to grow in strength, speed, and skill in soccer. The whole team excelled in skill way beyond their beginning days on the team.

Week after week, Kerry Lee scored big-time points for the Bobcats in every soccer game with win after win! Russell loved seeing his daughter play like a champion, darting around the field at high speed, doing precision maneuvers, and taking body shots. She and Lindy developed a special drill for the body-shot moves and practiced them during the week at home on the lawn. It was a special drill the two girls developed. Kerry Lee took more body shots and racked up more winning points than anyone had ever seen in Youth Soccer Association history. Now, with such an excellent winning record, the big day would soon come.

"The Bobcats are going to the American Cup in Seattle!" Coach Chuck announced happily.

The American Cup – Seattle – 1994

The day of the tournament practice, Russell and Kerry Lee were up early in the morning. Soon, they headed out in the family car over the Snoqualmie Pass toward Seattle. It was about a three-hour drive. The snow-covered peaks were visible in the distance, as they seemed to fly over the pass, headed toward Seattle. Russell and Kerry Lee smiled at each other with new anticipation. They were so excited to participate in the big statewide tournament, the American Cup!

After arriving, Russell and Kerry Lee got in a lunch and a nap at the motel. Later, they headed out to the soccer field in Seattle. Other teammates from the Bobcats gathered around them with Coach Chuck. It was so great to be together for the event, and to hope for a possible win. If they did win the event, it would be a great honor—the honor of being the number-one youth soccer team in Washington State.

The team had a strong practice session. Chuck worked them hard on the field with a variety of maneuvers. He watched Kerry Lee with the ball.

"Great going! That drill you've been developing with your sister is brilliant!" Her friends and teammates practiced the ball drill with her. Later, the team and their parents had dinner together at a restaurant near the motel.

"I'm very proud of all of you! All I ask is that tonight, every one of you hit the hay early—no late night movies, or anything. We all have to be sharp for the big game tomorrow!" said Coach Chuck.

Russell kept their promise to Chuck, and Kerry Lee headed toward bedtime early.

"Aww, Dad . . . It's only nine o'clock," Kerry whined.

"Remember what your coach said. You'll thank me tomorrow," Russell reminded her. "I want to see you with your jammies on, and your teeth brushed. It's lights out in fifteen minutes!" Soon, they were both in their beds, lights out, trying to sleep.

"Dad, it's hard to sleep when I'm so excited!" Kerry said.

"Try your best, honey . . . Lay there, be still, and you will get sleepy. I promise."

"Okay, Dad."

***

The next day, the team had a good breakfast and a quiet morning. They reported to the playing field at noon. The girls on the team were in good spirits filled with excitement and happy anticipation. Would they win the American Cup? There were eight top teams who had been competing. Now it was between the Bobcats of Yakima, the Sun City Strikers of Seattle, and a few other top teams from around the state.

Kerry Lee walked onto the soccer field that day looking like a true athlete; even though she was all of ten years old, she moved like a champion. The girls on the other team looked her over warily. They'd heard rumors about her already. A group of eight girls eyeballed her, and then backed away, cautiously moving over to their side of the field. Kerry Lee took a few sips out of her water bottle, and handed it back to her dad.

"Dad, can we pray?" Kerry Lee asked, looking up into her dad's eyes.

"Sure, honey!" He knelt down on the grass on one knee while Kerry stood by him. Russell put his hand on hers. They prayed silently with closed eyes. It was a tender moment. In a few minutes, Coach Chuck came up behind them, and gave them an embrace and a warm smile.

"Let's play ball! Are you ready to clobber 'em?"

"Yeah!" Kerry Lee laughed.

The coaches called everyone to order. The team quickly organized, then moved out onto the field. Chuck had Kerry Lee move to the middle of the field where she threw the ball into the center of the game. The team players jumped in, and the ball was soon flying madly. Kerry Lee waited for the chance to work her magic with the ball. They were playing a Seattle team named "The Sun City Strikers," and the name was printed boldly on their T-shirts in red.

Finally, she got her hands on the ball, and kicked it with great strength and careful aim. Another player or two maneuvered the ball. Kerry Lee moved closer to the goal, and when the ball came back to her, she kicked it right past the opposing team member, and into the goal area. The crowd cheered wildly. The ball was thrown back in, and was kicked all around the field until Kerry positioned herself to run full force into the very fast oncoming ball, and took a body shot on her upper arm and shoulder area. The Strikers took the ball back, but the Bobcats got the ball again before very long, and got it once again across the goal line to score more points.

The Bobcats continued to play several rounds of soccer with various top-ranking teams around the state. Russell and Coach Chuck cheered as Kerry Lee continued to play with more dramatic body shots, the ball flying high into the air and across the goal line again and again. The frustration on the face of the goalie from the opposing team told the story. The coaches from the Seattle teams looked on with amazement.

"What planet did this girl come off of?" one of them asked, looking puzzled. A spectator standing close to him agreed.

"I've never seen anything like it!"

After the final round of the day, the gigantic trophy, measuring over four feet tall, was awarded to the Bobcats, as the winners of the American Cup! Coach Chuck proudly held the trophy as Kerry Lee, Russell, and the girls from the team and some of their parents clustered around him, laughing and cheering. The entire crowd cheered and clapped excitedly.

Chuck leaned over to Russell and Kerry and whispered,

"I'm proud of all the girls on the team, but, you had a lot to do with us winning this trophy!"

"Thanks, Coach Chuck . . . I did my best!

"No, it was more than that." He put his hands together as if praying, remembering their prayer. Russell smiled, and walked off into the distance with his daughter, holding her hand tenderly. They had a memorable drive back and a special time together as father and daughter, sharing stories and building memories.

Monday morning, they were back in their regular routine. Russell and Tina were at the kitchen table still having their morning breakfast, conversing about the past weekend. Lindy and Kerry Lee were getting ready to leave for school.

"Have a blessed day at school, girls!" Tina said as she got up to hug them. "And Kerry Lee, I am so proud of you and your team winning the American Cup in Seattle!" Tina gushed with motherly pride. Kerry Lee grinned, and blushed.

"It was fun, Mom! We prayed."

"Yes. I heard about that! Your daddy told me."

"That means your team took the top award in the state of Washington! The article should come out in the paper by tomorrow," said Russell.

"We'll watch for it, honey," promised Tina. The girls took their book bags, and left for school.

"We have some amazing children, you know?" Russell said, feeling a healthy sense of pride.

"Yes, I just wish Yvonne had moved up here with us!" Tina said, looking a little sad.

"Well, she was very big on staying behind and finishing her schooling to be a personal trainer."

"Yes . . . and she's done so well at it, too! You know, I just talked to her the other day! She was bursting with excitement. Yvonne was telling me that she will be helping to open the first of six women's gyms with celebrity owner, Joyce King! She was so happy because she said that Joyce told her she could do personal training and aerobics classes there at the Pleasant Hill location which is right next to Walnut Creek, where she lives. I wish I was there to see it unfold," Tina pined. "But this American Cup thing . . . I'm so proud of our little girl, Kerry Lee."

"I am too. And to think she was such a plain little squirt just a year or two ago!" Russell smiled.

"Do you remember how she climbed up that high, tall open staircase at Jere's house . . . on the side of it like a monkey instead of walking up it? I was so embarrassed! But she was demonstrating to us even as a seven-year-old, what kind of athletic talent she had," said Tina, remembering.

"Yes, Jere brings that episode up to me every once in a while," said Russell, rolling his eyes.

"It was shocking!" Tina laughed. Russell laughed with her as they talked more about Kerry's future in sports.

"Russell . . . I'm concerned because her coaches . . . soccer, gymnastics, and track, are all talking about her being in extra training because she has potential to become an Olympic athlete. How will this affect our lives? I mean, they want her to travel here…compete there . . . train hours for this event and that event."

"That reminds me . . . Her track coach, Brent, has been discussing her track speed scores with me. He wants Kerry Lee to compete in the Junior Olympics in Pullman next month. He says she has the talent to take every first-prize medal and ribbon in the event."

"That's what I mean. Where is all this going?" wondered Tina.

"To a good place . . . I hope. Isn't that what most parents hope for?"

"I . . . guess so."

"When she was born, I held her in the recovery room. I told her she would be my camping buddy and hiking companion, my athletic champion . . . and that she is!" said Russell, fondly remembering.

"Well, you wanted a boy. Kerry Lee is kind of a tomboy! She already gets mistaken for Lindy's little brother all the time!"

"Well, Lindy is such a tall, blond Barbie-doll type . . . long, blond ponytail and everything.

There's only tree and a half years difference between them, but they look so different like 'Mutt and Jeff.' I just love watching them together though. Lindy is so protective, and teaches her little sister everything and loves her so much!" said Tina, remembering fondly.

"I was so amazed and proud that Lindy won the top honor in the Junior Miss America Pageant for our region. We worked together on it so hard, but when they called out her name, my heart almost stopped!" Tina said, remembering fondly.

"When they wanted to move their rooms right next to each other it was kind of a hassle to move everything down the spiral staircase, but I'm so glad we did it!" said Russell.

"I know, you're right about that," Tina agreed. "Kerry loved trying on Lindy's pretty dresses even though they were way too big for her. One day I was down here with the laundry basket, and glanced in her room. Lindy was standing Kerry in front of the big mirror, and putting her Junior Miss Beauty Queen crown on her head. Kerry smiled a big smile. It brought tears to my eyes," Tina said, remembering fondly. "She also bought Kerry Lee her first children's Bible, the 'Adventure Bible,' and spent time reading to her."

"Yes, she was a big influence on Kerry," Russell agreed. "One Sunday, the girls were running late in getting ready for church. I came down here to check on them. Apparently, Kerry was not yet dressed, and wasn't sure she wanted to go to church. Lindy came down on her hard in a tone of voice that must have sounded like John the Baptist! 'Kerry, if you don't change your ways, you are headed straight for *hell!*' You never saw a kid get dressed so fast!" Russell laughed.

"I know . . . We have great kids. We're very lucky!" He smiled. Russell put his hand on Tina's as they sat together at the table for a few moments, but soon it was time to go. He got up and took his coat. "I need to get going . . . I'll see you tonight, honey!"

CHAPTER FIFTEEN

NEW DISCOVERIES

I t was late, getting close to 10 p.m. The clock on the wall revealed the time, as it gently ticked in the quiet of the evening. Tina was up late putting dishes away in the kitchen watching the TV that sat on a cabinet in the far corner of the room. All of a sudden, a new ad came on. It was introducing an upcoming documentary about to air at the top of the hour.

"Coming up . . . *The Greatest Unsolved Mystery of the San Francisco Bay Area: Where is the Zodiac Killer?* Stay tuned for the latest documentary about one of the greatest unsolved mysteries of all time. Where is this phantom killer who terrified the citizens the Bay Area in California for well over two decades? Now, over ten years since he disappeared, our investigative reporter, John Ramiro, will interview reporters, police, witnesses, and forensic scientists to give the most updated evidence on this famous unsolved case."

Tina stopped cold in her tracks. She took off her apron, and stood near the TV to listen carefully. Tina's face was lit only by the light of the television. She looked both very serious and very curious. "Another documentary on the Zodiac? Unbelievable," Tina said, talking to herself again. The announcer continued, mimicking the voice of the Zodiac killer, with dark haunting music in the background:

"This is the Zodiac speaking: I am the murderer of the taxi cab driver over by Washington Street and Maple Street last night. To prove this, I have a blood-stained piece of his shirt. I am the same man. I cannot stop . . . an evil force comes over me, and I cannot stop . . ."

As Tina watched, a male announcer appeared outside a building, as he spoke.

"I am standing outside the *San Francisco Chronicle* building. Since the mid 1960s and up until 1978, writers from the *San Francisco Chronicle*, Don Avery and Herb Caen, received taunting letters from a man called the Zodiac. He often wrote after he did violent murders, and sometimes before, threatening to do murders, if certain conditions and bazaar requests he outlined in great detail, were not met."

The reporter, John Ramiro, read the copy: "This is the Zodiac speaking: I have become very upset with the people of the San Francisco Bay Area. They have not complied with my wishes for them to wear some nice circle with the cross-hairs buttons . . . my Zodiac buttons. I promise to punish them if they do not comply! I will respond by annihilating a full school bus. But now school is out for the summer, so I punished them in another way. I shot a man sitting in a car with a .38. The map coupled with the code will tell you where the bomb is set. You have until next fall to dig it up." The documentary host, John Ramiro, continued the story:

"The code at the bottom of the letter was never broken, and the bomb was never found."

Tina listened with rapt attention. She was sitting in a kitchen chair now, leaning forward.

"With increased technology, DNA samples were taken from the stamps the Zodiac licked to mail his letters to the *San Francisco Chronicle*."

"Although the police attempted to attribute the Zodiac killings, five documented that we know of for sure, to certain Bay-area serial killers already in prison such as the Hillside Killer, and some others . . . all these men were freed of suspicion because their DNA did not match that of the man they called the Zodiac . . . " Ramiro reported.

At this, Tina jumped up, and began to talk to herself. "See there? I told the police in both Vallejo and San Francisco that those men were *not* the Zodiac . . . not any of them! But they would not believe me! I knew because I know what he looks like!" Tina looked nervously at her watch. "Oh where is Russell? I've got to tell him about this!"

John Ramiro continued: "The Zodiac was fascinated by a play, the *Mikado*, which played at the Geary Theater. He sat through it time and time again. He seemed to identify with the character Ko-Ko the Executioner.

"In this Gilbert and Sullivan play, we learn that Ko-Ko was at one time condemned to death for flirting, but reprieved at the last moment and raised to the exalted rank of Lord High Executioner. According to the lyrics of the Gilbert and Sullivan play:

"'And so we let out on a bail, a convict from the county jail, whose head was next, on some pretext, condemned to be mown down off, and made him Headsman, for we said who's next to be decapitated, cannot cut off another's head until he's cut his own off.'"

Time continued on, as Tina took in the facts from the documentary. She was sitting closer to the TV now, hands on her knees, spellbound by this information. The host continued to walk through the story, and reported further known facts.

"Because of some perceived wrong in his own personal life, it seemed that the Zodiac came to identify himself with the character Ko-Ko, the high executioner. This character acts in the play as a combined judge, jury, and executioner. San Francisco detectives started examining programs, studying any possible clue to the killer's identity, and even interviewed people involved in the local production of the *Mikado*. Their efforts to find any answers led them yet into another dead-end street."

"Four years later, in January 1974, the *Chronicle* received another mailing from the Zodiac, once again referring to the *Mikado*. This time it was a song lyric sung by Ko-Ko the High Executioner: 'He plunged himself into the billow wave, and on the echo arose from the suicide grave . . .tit willo . . . tit . . . willo . . . tit willo . . . to his lover . . .'"

At that, Tina suddenly became wide-eyed, and bolted straight up.

"Listen to that! 'The billowy wave . . . the suicide grave'! That's how he died . . . he walked into the ocean! He walked into the ocean because he did not want to be picked up by the police after we saw him stalking couples that night! Tony was right!" Tina continued talking to herself, as she recited the facts.

It was close to 11 p.m. by now when Tina heard a noise at the door. Russell had returned home. Tina was practically breathless as he walked into the room. "Russell . . . you will never guess what I just saw on TV this evening . . . the latest documentary about the Zodiac Killer!"

"Not him again. Did you save me any dinner? Sorry that meeting with Jere and Paul went so late. Where are the girls?" Russell opened the refrigerator, and took a few bites of food.

"It's late. They've been in bed for hours. Honey . . . in this documentary, the Zodiac sent a letter to the *San Francisco Chronicle* in the mid 1970s . . . In '74, he went to see the play the *Mikado* all the time at the Geary Theater. He quoted from it saying, '*He plunged himself into the billowy wave...an echo rose from the suicide grave . . . tit willo . . .tit willo . . . tit . . . willo . . .*'"

"Tit. . . willo . . . tit . . . willo?" asked Russell, raising a curious eyebrow.

"It had something to do with the play. It was a threat to his lover that he might die of a broken heart, and plunge himself into a billowy grave . . . Russell, don't you see? Tony, Yvonne's friend, was right. His grandfather, the detective, was right! After he left us that night, he drove south down the California coast all night to Santa Barbara, parked his car and walked into the ocean, and committed suicide because he could not bear the possibility of being picked up! He mocked the police. He would say to the newspapers, 'You blue meanies could catch me if you weren't so lazy, and would get up off your big fat asses.'"

"*Tina . . . !*"

"*Sorry* . . . that was a quote from the Zodiac. Russell, he *believed* we saw him! We saw what he was doing, fully, and he believed we saw his license plate. We had every chance to see it. Even though we didn't, he *believed* we did. He believed it was all over, and that he was finally discovered . . . He was toast!" emphasized Tina. Russell looked at Tina. He stopped chewing his food.

"Tina, you're right . . . You are absolutely right."

"You see then? I think it was destiny that we helped put an end to the Zodiac killer. We went to that 'angel church' right before the chase . . . and everything!"

"You might be right, Tina, but I'm really tired. Let's call it a night, and talk about it later." Russell gave her a little kiss on the forehead.

"Okay . . ."

"Let's get some rest, honey."

"I've got to call John Ramiro at ABCN tomorrow. He'll talk to me . . . We were TV producers ourselves. The San Francisco Police should be taking another serious look at that clue . . . That's the missing piece of the puzzle!"

"It might be . . . it might be." They turned off the lights, and went upstairs. It was time to call it a night.

The next morning, Tina worked on getting Russell off to work and the kids off to school. She gave a little peck to Russell on the lips . . . and a hug to Lindy and Kerry Lee.

"Have a good day today, girls! Good luck on that math test, Lindy . . ." Tina turned to Russell. "I have a few houses to show, and work to do up at this real estate office this afternoon, but this morning, I have a few calls to make to New York . . . then to San Francisco!"

"Yes, I bet you do! Tell me later how it turns out, Tina." Russell said, planting a kiss on her cheek as he went out the door.

Tina, wearing jeans and sweater, gathered the notes she'd taken from the television documentary, picked up the phone and dialed the number.

"ABCN Television Network. Can I help you?" asked a telephone operator.

"Yes, I'd like to speak to John Ramiro, please."

"Let me connect you to that department."

"Investigative news desk. How can I help you?"

"My name is Tina George . . . and I need to talk to John Ramiro. I saw the documentary he produced on the Zodiac killer last night. I was a television producer myself in California for quite some years, and I will have to say it was very well done."

"How can I help you, ma'am?"

"I need to talk to John Ramiro because . . . I know what happened to him."

"To whom, ma'am?"

"*The Zodiac*, of course. Can you get John Ramiro for me?"

"Let me see if he's in the building," the news desk receptionist responded, now sounding more interested. There was a silence while Tina was on hold.

While waiting, she got out her address book, and looked up another number: "San Francisco Police Department. Here it is." Finally, she heard a familiar voice on the line from the documentary.

"Hello . . . This is John Ramiro, speaking."

"John, this is Tina George. Listen, good job on the documentary on the Zodiac killer. I had to call you because your documentary was the best and most current I have seen to date. But it was still missing important information. My husband, Russell, and I were the ones who chased him in mid-October 1978. He disappeared forever after that night. It's on police record."

At hearing this, Ramiro became very serious. "Did you get a license plate . . . a name?"

"No . . . if I had that, I would have given it to the police many years ago! We saw him stalking couples in three locations. After the third stop, we deterred him from almost gunning down a couple standing alone at Vista point. My husband said, 'That's the Zodiac. Let's get him! I was pregnant with my middle daughter at the time."

"Well, that's pretty bizarre. Weren't you scared?"

"You would have to understand the personality of my husband. He was the bold, maniac driver; I was just the passenger. The object was to get the license plate number, then back off. The Zodiac shot out way ahead of us, going out any way he could through the wrong way to get back on the Novato freeway. The old white car looked like a mix of makes—like an old model Ford Fairlane in front with red stripes on the sides. It was a disguise just like him. It had a big engine designed for the escape!"

Ramiro was intrigued. "Then what happened?"

"We chased him at high speed, way up over 100 miles per hour . . .110 . . .115 or so. We were in a late-model Subaru, but it was no match for the Zodiac escape car. It must have been a military vehicle or something. Just when I might have been close enough to see his license plate, a woman in a car trying to take an exit on the far left of the freeway got in front of me. She blocked my vision, plus we had to slow down just enough to avoid a crash—and then he took the advantage and shot way ahead and escaped! We could not see what exit he took."

"He disappeared on you?"

"Yes, but then we saw an exit for the Highway Patrol, and took that. It was about midnight. An officer was in, and we gave him the full story of what happened at each location, and how we broke into the chase, but lost him. He got on the radio and put out an APB, or All Points Bulletin, and then dropped a surveillance net. He said San Francisco police staff would be calling the next morning."

"Did they?"

"Yes. They called early. I went through the whole story again with Sergeant Tedesco. He said, 'Many people claim or think they saw the Zodiac, but we don't think they did . . . but we are quite sure that's who you saw.' They did not spot the car that night, or the next morning. It was a really different sort of car . . . an old model white Fairlaine with red stripes on the side with bright silver chrome, no less! No, like I said, they did not find the car. He said officers combed the area all night, and found nobody in a car like that. After his encounter with us, we know now he went speeding down the coastal route by the ocean toward Southern California."

"How did you know that?"

"Well, for starters, we had always told the kids not to talk about the Zodiac chase at school with their friends or teachers. We told them, 'Don't say, "My Mommy and Daddy chased the Zodiac."' We were trying to keep the fact quiet that we never did get his license plate. Some ten, almost eleven . . . years later, in high school, my daughter talked to a boy who was the grandson of one of the key detectives on the Zodiac case. The grandfather had passed away, but as a boy, Tony, had followed the inside facts of the case for years until he was a teenager. He told me a lot! He said, 'I'm going to tell you exactly what happened after he got away from you on the freeway that night.'"

Ramiro was tense with anticipation. "Yes . . . *yes?*"

"At the moment we lost him, apparently he took the highway one exit, then drove south down the coastal route toward Santa Barbara. He must have gotten there about dawn, according to Tony. He parked his car there. Then at some point, he made the fatal decision. He walked either from the cliff, or ground level, into the ocean and committed suicide . . . He drowned himself. Tony said that he was found washed up on the shore in the same time frame, like the next day or so, as our chase," Tina explained.

"Something is missing here . . . He was found washed up on the shore?" Ramiro wondered.

"It was the guy the police always thought it was for years, but they couldn't pick him up for a lack of connection with a Zodiac crime . . . or homicide . . . washed up on the shore. Tony said that along with us seeing him stalk couples in three locations, then him nervously leaving the scene at high speed . . . .plus the Zodiac writing the *Chronicle* saying he was going to strike that weekend . . . it would have been enough for them to have picked him up. Obviously, he would have rather faced death thinking he was going to wind up in 'Paradise' with all the people he killed as his slaves over there serving him. That's what he believed."

"That's pretty wild!"

"John, you're forgetting the 'most wild' thing of all: the quote by the Zodiac from the *Mikado* play, remember?"

"Let me see . . . something about the 'billowy wave' . . . The 'suicide grave?'"

"*Yes! That's it*! 'He plunged himself into the billowy wave, and echo arose from the suicide grave . . . tit willo . . . tit willo.'"

Ramiro remembered it well from his own program. "*Of course!*"

"There was over ten years of silence until the high-school kid, Tony, a friend of my daughter's, called me with the information. Leave it to a high-school kid to put it all together. A television network in San Francisco did a documentary, '*The Zodiac . . . Ten Years Later.*' They re-enacted the chase he had with us and depicted us as the last people to see him alive. A couple we'd known since their high school years later became television producers. They were one of the few who knew our story and leaked it out to the network where the husband was employed. But they didn't know yet about him walking into the ocean . . . because we didn't know that yet either."

Ramiro was overwhelmed. "Wow! Have you talked to the San Francisco Police lately?"

"I've tried . . . many times, believe me." Tina talked a little further with the producer of the documentary, as he seemed quite intrigued hearing the "new" evidence from Tina, and then they said good-bye. She gave herself a brief rest, getting some orange juice from the refrigerator. Soon, she was ready to tackle the next call. Tina dialed the familiar number.

"San Francisco Police Department?" Tina soon found herself going through the old familiar story with a new officer. She changed positions on the couch, midway through her old, lengthy Zodiac story.

"We chased him at high speed after seeing him stalk couples in those three locations . . . The chase was initiated from the parking lot at Vista Point onto the Novato freeway . . ." Time went by, as Tina put her feet up on the couch, trying her best to be comfortable.

"Don't you see? He walked into the waves . . . He committed suicide rather than be picked up by the police. He mocked the police for not being able to capture him. I was very disappointed I did not get a call from the police to look at a morgue shot or some-thing . . . I mean, I know exactly what he looks like, and what he was wearing that night." Tina sat up. "Sergeant Tedesco was eagerly waiting to have someone for us to look at. But unfortunately, there was no communication between Santa Barbara authorities and San Francisco police."

"Well, it's been a long time . . . I don't know, ma'am," said the police investigator.

"But somebody could go back and check those old records. Don't you want to solve this case?" asked Tina in a straightforward fashion.

"Why don't you call back and leave a message on the Homicide voice mail."

"Listen, San Francisco Homicide has not called me back in over twenty years. The original group was totally with us, but the new people don't seem to know who I am, nor my husband," explained Tina.

"That's the only suggestion I can think of."

Tina stood up. "Okay . . . let me think about it." She paced around. "I don't know why this is so hard to incorporate into the 'facts bank' over there. I mean, you must have one," stated Tina, as she continued on. "You know, many people in the San Francisco Bay area have spent a lot of years being terrified of this man . . . a notorious killer who has actually been dead since about October 15, or 17, thereabouts, in the year of 1978! The people of the Bay area, particularly women, wonder is it safe to walk here or there? 'Can I really walk out there with my boyfriend or husband and look at the stars . . . or is the Zodiac around the next corner somewhere?' It would be nice to put it to rest, you know?"

I understand, ma'am."

Tina was becoming exasperated. *"No, I don't think you do!* You know what? Good-bye. I don't know why I bother to make any of these calls, truly." Tina hung up. She put her hands over her face in frustration. She almost cried, but resisted. "There is a certain kind of blindness concerning this Zodiac story . . . I'm just tired of fighting it."

Winter . . . The Following Year

The snow was falling in Yakima, a whole new experience for Tina, Russell, and the family. Whenever Californians moved to the Northwest, this was the part they just did not count on at first. Tina looked out the large-view windows in the kitchen. The snowflakes swirled and fell on the pine trees, lawns, and driveway. She knew soon it could equal about two feet of snow.

"I just can't get used to what goes on with winter around here. Some years they say we have no snow . . . but this year . . . look at it coming down in heaps and buckets!"

"You are such a California girl," Russell, an East Coast guy, kidded her. "It's been a long lunch. I'm going back to the office now."

"It's nice that you can come home for lunch some days. I need to pick up the girls from school and take them to gymnastics this afternoon, but look at that driveway. Yikes!"

"The studded tires are coming soon, I promise!" said Russell.

"They had better be. I need them for showing property in real estate too," said Tina.

"I'm proud of you. You're doing very well in real estate these days," said Russell, approvingly.

"How do I even dress for this weather?" Tina mused as she went to dress for the day.

She emerged wearing a turtleneck sweater, large bracelets, and some jeans. She then went to the hall closet and pulled out some high-heeled boots. "Hmm . . . I'm not sure those are right. Well, they have warm fleecy lining. Oh well . . ." She put them on. "The coat . . . it must be 12 degrees out there. *Brrr* . . . These coats look too thin. Here are some gloves . . ."

After more rummaging, Tina pulled out a full-length mink coat. "Here we go! I'm certainly not going to freeze wearing this!"

Once in the car, she nervously slid, not drove . . . down the steep 100-foot driveway, finally stopping at the base. "Phew! It's a good thing nobody was coming! At least this car has front-wheel drive!"

Tina picked up Kerry Lee and Lindy outside the school at the curb, and continued toward the Gymnastic Plus for Kids building near downtown Yakima.

"Mom . . . look at all this snow! Can we go sledding later?" asked Lindy.

"I want to build a snowman!" squealed Kerry Lee.

"It will be dark by the time we get back from gymnastics . . . so maybe tomorrow," said Tina in "mom" tones.

Tina arrived at the mini-strip mall where the gymnastics building was. She slid through the stop sign and pulled in, going left as she continued into the shopping mall. Tina then slid down the hill into the parking lot near the gym, pointed her vehicle toward the building, and then slowly and cautiously pulled up in front. Lindy looked over at her.

"Mom . . . you are white as a sheet!"

"I ought to be! I think I looked into the face of death at least three times before I got here!" Tina gasped. They waded through the snow banks, and finally got inside.

The gym instructor appeared, and Tina pulled him aside. "Listen . . . They can take their class for today, but I am going to cancel these gymnastic lessons until spring, March or so. It's not worth risking my life just to get down here. I'm used to driving . . . not *sliding*, to my destination!"

The other women, who were wearing warm polyester ski coats, marveled then snickered, at Tina's full-length mink coat with jeans and high-heel boots. "I really do need to go to the Ski Outlet and buy some winter snow clothes. I can't put it off any longer!" Tina said to herself.

Soon, they drove back to their home on Apple View Way. Tina pulled up, stopped, and looked up the dreaded snowy driveway. She then spotted a six-foot-long blue toboggan up by a tree remembering that Russell had just picked that up for the girls to play with.

"I don't know, girls. We have groceries to in bring in too. I have an idea. Let's use the blue toboggan up there!" Tina got out, and opened the trunk while the girls scrambled up to get the toboggan at the base of the driveway. They loaded the groceries onto the toboggan, and then pulled it up the hill by the rope to the lower entry door. Soon Tina was putting groceries away in the kitchen.

I don't know if I'll ever get used to the winters up here!" Tina groaned.

"But we like to sled!" said Kerry Lee happily.

"As long as it's in a safe place like the field or Franklin Park . . . *not* in our driveway," Tina reminded them wearily.

"Yeah, Kerry Lee . . . You almost got hit by a car trying that!" said Lindy, sounding like a big sister.

"I didn't see the car at first! I just kept sliding across the street and right over the hill into the field across the street."

"You're lucky you didn't get hit and rolled over flat as a pancake," said Lindy, frowning at her sister.

"Yes, you *were* lucky! Don't ever try that again," said Tina. "By the way, Kerry Lee. When do you start up soccer again?"

"March, sometime."

"Okay . . . That's okay for the local games, but not for traveling over the pass to Seattle.

CHAPTER SIXTEEN

A FEW YEARS LATER

"**M**om, can you do me a favor? I really need to have you drop this video off at the video store for me . . . Can you?" asked Lindy.

"I practically had a nervous breakdown with you and Kerry Lee learning to drive at the same time. I was looking forward to you girls exhibiting a little freedom in that area. 'Mom's Taxi' is getting tired," replied Tina.

"It's a homework issue, Mom. I'm on a roll, and it's due back today," Lindy begged.

"Okay," Tina sighed.

"While you're there, could you pick up that video Kerry Lee wanted to watch this weekend?"

"I expect a little help in the kitchen over this favor . . . the dinner dishes tonight?"

"Okay, Mom!" Lindy agreed.

Shortly, Tina walked into the local video store. She dropped the borrowed video back into the return box. Then began to look for the video her girls had requested.

"Do you carry *The Prince in New York*?" Tina asked the clerk, a young pretty African American girl, a part-time college student.

"Yes . . . it's in the back of the store on the last row," she replied.

Tina made her way to the back of the store and searched for the video. She saw it and picked it up. Then, as her eye glanced down the row, she saw something else: a recent-release video documentary about the Zodiac killer. Tina went bug-eyed when she saw it.

"What?! Who produced this?" Tina looked over the box. She looked even more carefully at the cover. "A gate opening to a path to Vista Point with a view of the Bay . . . Well, they have that much right." Another young female clerk was nearby who overheard Tina. "Look at this on the cover . . . 'He could still be out there . . .' The young clerk looked on. Her eyes were widening at Tina's comment. Tina took the video up front, and began to check out the first one.

"Well, I'd like to see who these people are. I'm going to check their website, and see how much they know. *The Zodiac is dead.* It happened after a high-speed chase in San Francisco in October of 1978. I know because I was there, and my husband was the driver! The real truth came out later."

By now, the two young clerks were wide-eyed.

"Thank you . . . Good evening!" She took the videos in the bag, and left the store. They watched her walk off, looking at each other in amazement.

Before long, Tina was back at home, showing the video box to Russell.

"Vista Point, eh? Somebody knows something." Russell read from the box. "'He could still be out there.' Well, they actually know nothing, then."

"I don't even want to watch this . . . There's too much negative energy connected to the Zodiac. He was so demon possessed." Tina shivered.

Russell looked over the box. "No doubt."

"I'm interested in who produced this. Let's see how the web page comes up." Tina sat down at the computer. She looked over the web page from the video box cover. "Hmm . . . It looks like they're just interested in potential Zodiac sightings from the public. More potential movie material, I suppose," she sighed.

"Just another dead end. You know, Tina, I don't think they want to solve this mystery," Russell stated flatly.

"Russell, don't you see? Because our story was so buried in secrecy by the police at the time it happened, and the last letter written in mid-October of 1978 was buried by the *Chronicle*, with them thinking it was a fake because nobody turned up dead that weekend as the Zodiac had threatened, the primary pieces of this mystery have been missing all these years!"

"Put that with the identity of the mystery man who washed up on the shore in Santa Barbara County the next morning, or thereabouts, never being established, no wonder this case was never solved!" Russell pointed out.

"You're right . . . How could it be?" asked Tina.

"Have you thought about making another round of calls, just to test the waters?"

"I may. Maybe I'll try a little different tactic . . . like calling the San Francisco DA's office, and the *San Francisco Chronicle*," said Tina feeling a new twist in the story developing.

"Now that's a great idea! May be the DA's office would see a different angle, or avenue, to the old police or coroner's office records. The *Chronicle* might want to take it on as a new story. They might have an investigative reporter that would go back and research it. It could become an all new sensation for them." Russell suggested.

"Maybe . . . maybe not." Tina frowned.

"Is my baby doll turning into a cynic?" he playfully embraced her.

"Well, now, hasn't it been me who has been making the calls all these years?" Tina laughed.

"Let me know how it turns out, honey. I'm curious now."

It was the usual morning weekday mayhem at the George home. The kids were eating breakfast, and Tina was packing lunches for Russell and the girls.

"I'm writing a note to myself not to forget to pack my Realtor key and my open-house signs," said Tina, writing in her day planner.

"You are so organized, honey!"

"Kerry Lee, are you and your dad set for the soccer game at Chesterly Park tomorrow?"

"Yep!"

"I'm ready! I may work a little late tonight so I will be sure I can be off tomorrow."

"Russell, you've had trouble being off on Saturday as long as I can remember. I mean back in California, we missed some of our best friends' weddings!"

"Not anymore."

"Lindy, are your clothes laid out for the ballet recital tomorrow?"

"Yes, Mom!"

"Russell, you cover the soccer tournament with Kerry Lee at one o'clock . . . and I'll cover the ballet recital with Lindy at 2 p.m."

"Okay!" Russell picked up his briefcase. "Jere's waiting for me. We have engineers from France touring our plant today. I've got to get going!" He kissed Tina good-bye. Russell gave a brief little peck to each girl.

"Bye, Dad!" said Kerry Lee, with her spoon in her cereal.

"Bye, Dad!" Lindy smiled.

That afternoon Tina left the real estate office where she had spent most of the day. She drove home, and made most of her calls from her new home office. She called a client that she had been in touch with over a particular property.

"I just wanted you to know I'll be doing an open house out at that home you've been interested in out on Fisk Road with one acre. Oh yes . . . yes. It will be after church, say around 2 p.m., until probably four o'clock. Our secretary will be running an ad for it in the Sunday paper. Yes, well I hope I see you out there!"

Suddenly, Tina remembered that she had meant to make calls out to San Francisco before the day was over. She looked over at the note paper with phone numbers written on it, and sighed.

"DA's office . . . *San Francisco Chronicle.* Do I have the stomach for this?" She took a deep breath. "Yes, I do. Here it goes." She dialed the first number.

"San Francisco District Attorney's office . . . administration." She waited for an answer.

A male voice on the phone answered.

"DA's office. Can I help you?"

"Yes, this is Tina George. I was a lifetime resident of the San Francisco Bay area, but I am currently living in Washington State."

"How can I help you, ma'am?" the male admin voice inquired, dryly.

"I'm calling because I have viewed a number of documentaries lately about the Zodiac killer, and it would seem that they still don't know the true facts about what happened to him. I don't think that it ever needed to be an unsolved mystery. My husband and I are the ones who chased him back in mid-October of 1978. The man who was the Zodiac died shortly after that, as a result of the scenario and the chase that night. We believe we have collected the true facts about that episode. Since the beginning, we had worked with the San Francisco Police on the details— but as time went on, nobody in the new work force seemed to listen to us anymore. I could easily get the idea that nobody really cares about whatever happened to the Zodiac killer these days."

"Oh we care . . . we care," insisted the male voice on the phone.

"Well you could have fooled me." Tina replied coolly.

"Have you called San Francisco homicide?"

"Yes. They have not returned a call to me in about ten years, then only one other time about ten years before that!" answered Tina..

Male voice on the phone: "That's my best suggestion."

"I see. Well, I guess this case will not ever be solved," Tina said. "Everything goes around in an unending circle."

"Why do you say that?"

"We know he walked into the ocean and committed suicide after he escaped a high-speed chase with us in mid-October 1978. A private detective source close to the Zodiac case told to us that shortly after his encounter with us, the guy they always thought it was turned up washed up dead on the shore around Santa Barbara somewhere in the same time frame as right after we chased him, even possibly as early as the next morning. An officer from San Francisco Homicide called me back in October 1978, and said to me that there was no known 'homicides' around Santa Barbara county around that time, then hung up. Do you know what's wrong with that picture?"

Male voice on the phone: "What, ma'am?"

"Finding a body under those circumstances is not classified as a homicide . . . it's classified as a *'John Doe.'* This is what a body is classified as when an unidentified body just turns up. Don't you see? It was a *suicide*. Somewhere, there are morgue records or county coroner records, or something . . . A picture should exist somewhere. Do you understand that my husband and I know exactly what he, the Zodiac killer, looks like?"

"Very intriguing. Once again, we cannot handle that here."

"I see," said Tina. "Well, I kind of thought I already knew how this conversation would turn out."

"I'm sorry, ma'am."

"Good-bye," Tina said, hanging up the phone. Tina looked down at the ground. She felt discouraged. She looked at the notes on her piece of paper. "The *San Francisco Chronicle* . . . I wonder how this will turn out." Tina dialed the number.

She got herself comfortable at different angles. She was obviously going to be telling her story to a journalist at the *Chronicle*.

"You are an investigative reporter . . . you employ many journalists. Surely you would be interested in trying to research this story. There are coroner's records that exist somewhere. The *Chronicle* has a history of receiving letters from the Zodiac. They contained real clues as to how he ended up . . . and I just told you how he ended up!"

The editor-reporter seemed annoyed with her. "Lady . . . My newspaper does not have the financial resources to research this story."

"I can't believe you're telling me this," said Tina with tears welling up in her eyes.

She grabbed a tissue from the box on the counter. "I don't think I've ever been emotional like this until now."

"I need to excuse myself to get to a meeting."

"Of course . . . Good-bye." Tina wiped her nose. Suddenly the phone rang with an incoming call.

"Hello . . .?"

"Hi, honey . . ."

"Hi, honey . . ." Tina was crying.

"Tina, what's the matter?"

"Oh, I just did something stupid. I tried calling the San Francisco DA's office with our story about the Zodiac. They didn't care . . .

and then I tried the *San Francisco Chronicle*. Don't you think they would want to do a fresh story—and have somebody do further research on the Santa Barbara Coroner's reports, and just . . . our story in general?"

"You would think so."

"I personally did hundreds of stories for our television station; you know that. I would have wanted to do it! But we're not in that profession any more. I don't have my press pass or anything anymore. Besides, you can't really do a story on yourself. Somebody else has to do it," Tina sniffled.

"You are focusing on this way too much. Just let it go, Tina."

"I guess, I think I'm just having a bad dream, you know? The Zodiac killer . . . 'one of the greatest unsolved mysteries of all time' . . . *Well, no wonder!*"

"You know what you do when you feel bad, but you really want to feel good?"

"What?"

"You buy a pint of that 'chunky chocolate monkey' ice cream, and eat the whole thing by yourself."

Tina laughed a little, remembering.

"I give you permission to do it."

Russell talked to her tenderly for a while. Tina felt better. But she did go out and buy the ice cream anyway!

CHAPTER SEVENTEEN

BATTLING THAT NEW-OLD EVIL

As the family sat in church one Sunday, Steve, the youth pastor, suddenly stepped up to the pulpit midway through the service.

"Thank you, worship band, for that great music! And now, I have a special announcement. I got a call from Robin Smith, the manager of the local youth detention facility, just last week. She said they spent 2.5 million building this facility last fall, but that they didn't have any money to hire a chaplain like the facilities have around Seattle. 'Steve,' she said, 'I trust you. Can you get together a good group of volunteers to lead a youth Bible study or chapel-type service in here? Your group would have to get cleared all together . . . It would take a few weeks. Just pick a time slot. I'd like to see it start happening pretty soon.' Well, I could barely believe my own ears! I have the applications right here." He held up a stack of papers.

As Tina listened, she felt a strong connection.

"Anyone who is interested in going in there with me, be sure to see me right after the service."

Tina was spellbound. She turned to Russell. "I think I'm supposed to volunteer for that."

Russell looked back at her with a smile and a nod. He knew by now when his wife was on to something.

After the service, a crowd gathered to visit and talk in the open area of the front foyer of the church. Steve, still holding the stack of papers, was talking to an interested couple. Tina walked up as he finished.

"Hi, Pastor Steve . . . I would like to fill out one of those applications." She had a new glimmer in her eye.

"Tina . . . you would be great for this! Here you go!" Pastor Steve smiled as Tina looked over the application.

"I was a youth guidance counselor years ago in a facility in California called Teen Hope. It wasn't a lockup, but the kids were in there for the same sort of reasons . . . overcoming drug addictions, violent crimes, prostitution, runaways . . . My big question is going to be, how can we make a difference going in there one hour a week? But I'm willing to try it," said Tina, with a step of faith.

***

Soon Tina was back at home having lunch with the family.

"I think this would be great for you, Tina! You used to do this type of work years ago before we were married. I've heard you talk about it like it was one of the highlights of your life," said Russell.

"Yes, I was a youth guidance counselor for three and a half years. I used to get those nice little green paychecks from the state of California. But this is strictly a volunteer situation."

"Once a week, eh?" Russell asked in curious tones.

"Yes, one hour. What can I do in that length of time?"

"It will possibly get your mind off the . . .uh . . . other thing we were talking about last week."

"You are such a good mom! It's got to rub off on the kids in there!" said Lindy. Tina hugged her, and gave her a little smile.

"Thanks, Lindy. There are a lot of heartbreaks and hurts in those places, and sometimes those hurts turn into crimes," said Tina.

"They have a dark hole in their hearts, and they need a lot of love to shine in on it," said Lindy.

"Yes, they do!" Her girls came over and hugged Tina. She was thinking about what Lindy had just said. "From the mouths of babes" . . . comes wisdom, as they say.

Pastor Steve met with Tina and seven other volunteers on a weekly basis to prepare for the new weekly youth-detention ministry.

***

About two months later, it was time for the orientation at the Benson-Fort County Youth Detention. The building was basically a teen jail. It had razor wire all around the top of the fences, and electric security gates. Finally, one late afternoon on a Friday, the church van with Steve, Tina, and the group of nine people, drove over to youth detention to begin the first leg of their exciting journey. Pastor Steve drove the van into the first gate then they drove inside the "cage." They all got out and looked around for their guide. A security guard met the team and guided them through the second security door. They were then led in to a conference room with a white board. Robin Smith, the manager Pastor Steve had talked about, soon appeared.

Robin, a nice-looking woman in her 40s with long, reddish brown hair wearing a Holly-Hobbie-looking long hippie dress and low Mary Jane high heels, opened the meeting.

"Greetings! I'm Robin Smith, and thank you so much for volunteering to participate in youth chapel here in Benson-Fort County Juvenile Court!" she announced brightly. Robin pulled out a paper. "I understand that Pastor Steve will be organizing you into three groups—two groups for the boys and one for the girls, each with two or three of you. You might want to take turns as to who comes in each week. Your time slot will be Friday night from 7:30 p.m. to 9 p.m." Robin continued her overview.

"You may see youth in here you recognize from your church or neighborhood. Don't be tempted to talk about them or name them. While they are in here, they have anonymity. I see Steve has ordered some softcover youth Bibles for your chapel services. Very good. If you bring Bibles or New Testaments in from other sources, remember they must be softcover. A hardcover book is considered a potential weapon. Thank you all, and may your efforts be greatly blessed! We'll see you in here next Friday night!" The group was dismissed and then prepared to leave.

"Well, Steve . . . this is going to be an adventure!" Tina said with excitement.

"Just pray before you come in here, for the right direction, and try to think of them as ordinary kids." Steve suggested.

"I will," she responded. Tina was struggling to maintain a balance between wanting to help the teens and just exercising practical safety. One side of her was courageous, and the woman side of her was at least reasonably cautious. She continued to wonder how much impact coming in to the youth detention center just once a week could make on these kids.

Meanwhile, the headlines of the local and regional papers highlighted a number of youth crimes in the Northwest, including Yakima: "Teen Held in Vehicular Homicide, gets Juvenile Life; Two Teens on Trial of Attempted Murder of Police Officer; Fourteen-Year-Old Held in Teen Slaying; Teen Holds Woman Hostage Eighteen Hours; Teen Gets Fourteen Years for Killing Sister; Detectives Search for Teen Shooting Suspects; Gunfire Erupts in Busy Park; Teen Gets 111 Years in School Shootings; Youngest Convicted Killer in the State of Washington: Twelve Years Old; One in Six Teens Will Attempt Suicide; Teen Held at $25,000 Bail at Youth Detention . . ."

These headlines would have been enough to scare off anyone from wanting to go in to youth detention to work with teens, but Tina just held the matter inside, pondering it in her heart.

The following week, she was at home with Russell sitting in the living room talking about their adventures in youth detention.

"It sounds exciting, Tina. You are just gutsy enough to make this thing work . . . So is Steve! How many of you are on the team?" Russell asked.

"Around nine of us . . . maybe twelve, when everyone shows up. We want to have more than one person leading each of the three groups." Tina briefly changed the subject. "Talk about gutsy. I'm not sure what to make of Robin Smith, the detention manager," said Tina.

"How so?" asked Russell.

"She is a strong woman of great faith, beautiful long hair, and a beautiful smile. She probably has teenagers at home herself. Robin likes to wear these long hippie dresses with low Mary Jane high heels. She looks so wholesome and beautiful. It just seems so strange for her to be the detention manger in such a place filled with youth representing such dark violence. She's like a walking light beam. It just seems like she holds that place in perfect balance. I think I'm still in awe of watching her in action," admitted Tina.

"So, why should you be surprised?" asked Russell.

Tina gave him a questioning look. Russell clasped her hand tenderly.

"Haven't we been watching the principle of God using people to be light that dissolves darkness? I'm proud of you, Tina. You're going to see it happen again, just in a different way!" Tina smiled. She knew exactly what he is referring to.

Finally, after numerous setbacks as far as a first Friday night starting date, the team finally met at the church and began preparing to go over to the local youth detention facility to do their first program. Soon everyone was loaded into the church van with their Bibles, videos, and other materials. They headed toward the youth facility, feeling a sense of the unknown, yet were excited.

***

As the church van approached the youth detention building, it seemed the natural realm peeled back to reveal the spiritual realm— as the building itself seemed to give the appearance of the body of a large dragon. The dragon watched the approaching van of the ministry workers, and flamed out a stream of fire in burning anger toward the youth workers. As a being from the dark annals of hell, he knew that his very existence in the hearts and souls of these youth was threatened.

Other demonic creatures appeared. They were around thirteen feet in height, and very reptilian-looking in appearance. They had long claws and curled horns like a ram. They hissed and snarled as they saw the team that planned on going in to talk to the youth, whom they considered their captives. One of them was the hideous demon who was the same one who let out a scream beside Russell and Tina's window so many years ago, as the truth about Zodiac story was unveiled in the conversation between Tina, and her daughter's friend, Tony. He was unusually vicious in countenance, and he was aware that Tina was on the scene with her friends to attempt to take territory he perceived belonged to him and the others. He snarled viciously as he looked out upon their arrival.

Tina, Steve, and seven other ministry team members climbed from the van and headed for the first security door. Numerous tall, shining angelic creatures appeared in the spirit, present, but yet unseen. They were fearsome-looking warring angels who bore large swords and shields. The large dragon snarled and sent a long, threatening stream of flame out in their direction. They entered the second door, which appeared to be the mouth of the dragon. Once they entered, the hellish dragon was suddenly weakened and disappeared into only wispy shadows, as a great light began to take over. The fearful demons suddenly fled out of sight at the presence of the great and powerful warring angels.

The electronic doors made their loud *ka-chunk* release sounds, as Tina, Steve, and the team made their way inside, toward the master-control area, where they would be assigned by the staff their prospective classrooms to speak to the youth.

Once inside one of the rooms, the boys in their bright orange "juvy" uniforms filed in. The team shook their hands, one by one, greeting them warmly. Bright praise music was playing on a portable boom box. The group of youth who had just filed in were seated now. Unseen in the shadows, unhappy demons looked on, watching the threatening scene.

"Hello! I'm Pastor Steve . . ."

"I'm Tina . . ."

"I'm Michael . . ."

"I'm Susie . . ."

The youth, mostly teen boys, looked happy, open, and receptive. Pastor Steve continued to lead the session. "We're going to share some thoughts and personal stories with you." He turned to Tina. She smiled and started.

"Our goal is to share with you how you can know God in a personal way . . . just as we do. Did you know that the Creator of the universe, the sun, the moon, and stars, wants to 'hang out' with you?" asked Tina.

"Yes, Tina, that's true! I first found the Lord Jesus Christ as my personal savior at the age of only sixteen, the age of many of you. Once He filled me with His love, His peace, and His strength, I didn't need drugs or bad relationships to fill that void anymore," said Michael pitching in. He looked back over at Tina.

"We all have a God-size void, like a big hole in our hearts... Only God can fill it! "Tina picked up the thought as she walked around, arms and hands animated as she spoke. From the unseen realm, hideous demons watched from the dark corners and sidelines of the room. Unknown to her, she knocked and punched an unseen demon in the face, as she gestured. "No relationship, no person can fill it, no drug, no high. *Only God.*"

"I was only 14 years old," she continued, "when I discovered that I knew *about* God . . . but I didn't *know* Him. There's a big difference. When you invite Him in, He gives you a kind of power connection. It's like a gigantic light, a great power source that will dispel that darkness in your heart. He will keep His promise to help you with your life, so you will never again be alone. Listen to this: 'For I know the plans I have for you, says the Lord, for good, not for evil, and to give you a hope and a future!' This verse is found in the Living Bible at Jeremiah 29:11.

This is what you need to do to have real life, real light, and illumination in your life. I did this at age fourteen. It's by far the greatest thing I have ever done for my own life. I'm kind of like the time traveler coming back here to tell you now, today, that this is the greatest thing you will ever do in *your* life! Receive the light and strength of God into your hearts tonight."

As Tina spoke, angels appeared in the unseen realm, blocking the angry demons with their angelic swords and shields, who held the hearts of many of the youth in the room captive.

After the various team members shared their thoughts and stories from their own lives, they opened up a discussion time for the youth. The time seemed to speed by as eternal questions were answered, and ruptured hearts were mended.

Tina, in closing, said, "People will let you down, but God is faithful and he will *not* let you down." Pastor Steve stepped up front and prepared to close.

"All of you who are ready, let's pray together now. We brought Bibles for you that you can keep, and read further," he said, reaching into a box.

Many of the youth began to pray with the team. They knew they needed to receive Jesus Christ into their hearts and as their personal Savior to achieve the light and power the team spoke of, but it was an all-new idea for most of them. What they did know was that they wanted to know God like the way Tina, Steve, Michael, and Susie talked about. Some knelt down by their tables. As they did, angels in the spirit realm took over, and the room seemed to fill with the light of God. The unhappy, snarling demons had to leave and shrink back into the dark shadows. It was a victorious night!

At the end of the evening, the team gathered back at the master-control area to prepare to leave through the front security electric doors.

"What an amazing evening!" Pastor Steve beamed happily.

"It was for us, as well! The kids were really open. I could just feel the coldness and violence in them melting away," said Sarah from another group held in classroom two.

Bill, on the team from classroom 3, remarked to the facility officer, "I think you're going to begin to see some changed hearts in this place!" He smiled.

As they left and walked out toward the church van, angelic activity appeared once again in the unseen realm. The large bright-shining angels dashed toward the huge, threatening dragon, and drove a powerful spear of light through him. He roared and writhed, trying to rise to a fight, but then he fell, and rolled over dead. As the church van drove off back toward the road, all the angels and demons disappeared, as light filled the darkness, and the landscape and buildings once again looked normal as before.

Tina drove home and pulled up to the front of the entry by the kitchen. She walked into the kitchen about 9:30 p.m. Russell was making a sandwich.

"Hi, honey . . . How did it go?"

"Magnificent . . . amazing! I can't even describe it!"

"Really? That good, huh?" Russell marveled.

"The kids responded really well . . . far better than you would expect." Russell offered her half a sandwich.

"Have a half? I was about ready to make some tea."

"Sure . . . thanks. I don't know, but it seemed like turning on a light in a very dark place. They saw it . . . and felt it . . . and they wanted to leave their violent ways, abuse, and addictions behind," Tina explained, feeling the excitement.

"Wow, that's great, honey! When are you and the team going back in?"

"As soon as possible, or at least in a week . . . I'll have to ask," said Tina.

"Well, I'm proud of you . . . and Steve and everybody."

"Are the kids in bed?"

"Yeah . . . tomorrow Kerry Lee has a soccer tournament, and Lindy has dance lessons," Russell reminded her.

"I almost forgot . . . I've been having a little too much excitement." Tina smiled. "Tomorrow will be another day . . . more real estate work. The next session of youth chapel will roll around quickly at youth detention. I can hardly wait!"

***

Their lives in Yakima continued to enrich and build even more as Russell soon developed a new worldwide business for the corporation. The rest of the family all moved forward, blossoming into new talents. Kerry Lee was developing in sports and music; Lindy continued to develop in academics in school and in dance classes; Tina continued in real estate and studied at the Graduate Real Estate Institute. It just seemed like the "Sold" signs delightfully kept appearing on Tina's listings, and life was in full-forward positive motion. By now, Tina had a new and deeper passion: working with the youth-detention ministry. It seemed that Friday nights just couldn't roll around soon enough for her to go in and see the youth there. There were a significant number of them changing, leaving the old life behind, and reaching out for new directions.

Every week as the church van and the team drove up to the youth jail, it was an exciting new challenge. Before long, Tina often came to call it a "rescue." These youth had to change and put into practice new life pathways by their eighteenth birthday, or it was prison, not just youth detention anymore. The whole picture would then become much more serious. If they failed to get a new direction for their young lives, it could mean prison for life. It was a race for time to help them stop their cycle of re-offending.

Week after week, Tina, Pastor Steve, and the team from the church drove up to the youth detention facility and went in to experience a whole new adventure with the troubled teens. The team had begun wearing jeans, turtleneck sweaters, boots, and black leather jackets. The look was very urban, but it worked well.

When they arrived, it was always the same: a confrontation in the spirit world, a clash between the demonic and the angelic forces over the lives of the youth steeped in such deep darkness. But as they moved toward the door, the transparent, reptilian demon creatures had to peel back, and step aside. The mission was just too important. The light always broke into darkness and the darkness just had to go . . . especially there.

Tina, Russell, and the family always made it a practice to be in church on Sundays. Their church was delighted that the ministry to the youth in detention had been going so well. The juvenile court staff, the police, and the judges couldn't help but notice. One day the senior pastor, John Bennett, happened to be in his office when an interesting phone call came through. He was sitting at his desk in his church study preparing for his Sunday message when the phone call came in from one of the juvenile court judges.

"Hello. Pastor Bennett here."

"Hello, Pastor. This is Judge Conners, Benson-Fort Juvenile Court."

"Well, hello. What can I do for you?" asked Pastor Bennett, seeming a little surprised.

"Pastor Bennett, your group that has been going into the youth-detention facility is doing a remarkable job! I have teen offenders coming before me every day, mostly boys, incarcerated for serious crimes, armed robbery, car theft, vehicular manslaughter, gang shootings—but now they are changing so drastically. The difference in their attitudes from past hearings with me and now is like night and day! They are reading their Bibles; they are repentant of their past; they are getting off drugs; they want to be different . . . and there are *so many of them!"* remarked Conners.

"Well, that certainly is good news!"

"I have one question for you."

"Yes?" replied Pastor Bennett.

"What in the world are they doing down there?" exclaimed Judge Conners.

"Well, they are shining the Light of Jesus Christ in a very dark place!" Pastor Bennett smiled.

It was not long before even the local and regional newspapers began to reflect the new trend: "Teen Crime Rate Falls Sharply" . . . "Gang Violence Seems to Come to a Halt" . . . "No More Youth Homicides Yet This Year" . . .

It was a new experience of applying the same timeless principles over and over again.

"Put God into the equation and anything is possible! His power dissolves all darkness in the human spirit," Pastor Steve would always say.

It was Friday night again and Tina, Pastor Steve, Susie, and Michael were doing a session in the youth-detention facility with about twenty-five boys in a classroom. They obviously looked like gang boys with low-rider haircuts and tattoos on their arms. In the unseen realm in the spirit, hideous demons crouched down around the room and way in the back. They had now been made weak and powerless by the God-charged atmosphere. One demon tried to rise, but fell down again, losing all strength. Tina spoke passionately.

"Who is ready to turn their lives around tonight? He has been waiting all this time for you, but you have to move out first."

"It doesn't matter how far you slipped back into the darkness, you can make it right tonight!" added Pastor Steve. Then Michael stepped forward.

"God is going to give you a whole new destiny, but you have to want to change. You have to *mean it!*

"The Bible says he wants us to be the 'light in the darkness . . . the light of the world.' But first you have to have it for yourself!" said Susie.

Upon hearing this, the demonic creatures attempted to rise and charge. But as Pastor Steve moved his hand in front of them, a flash of light disempowered them again, and they all fell back down.

"God wants to give you a whole new destiny, but first you have to leave your dark deeds behind and go after Him. Who wants that new life tonight?" Hands flew up from almost the whole group. "Great! Let's pray!" The group of boys all bowed their heads. It was the end of another amazing evening in youth detention, and a beginning of a new life for many of them.

Later, Tina was sitting up in bed with Russell. They had been reading, but seemed ready to turn the lights out.

"Tina . . ." Russell gave her a little kiss. I am proud of what you and Pastor Steve are doing in youth detention. It has even been hitting the papers, but we haven't had a 'date night' on Friday night in a long time," Russell reminded her.

"I tell the boys, 'You're my date for Friday night!'" Tina kidded him.

"Exactly . . ."

"We could always go out on Saturday, Russ," Tina, replied with a little dry sarcasm.

"The point is . . . I want to spend some quality time with you." Russell snuggled up to her a little closer. I didn't tell you, but Jere wants me to take a sales trip for the company to Southern California in about a week. I want you to come with me. It'll be our special date. Jere's parents, Rolf and Mary, already said they could take the kids for a few days. What do you say?" asked Russell romantically.

"Mmm . . . That sounds nice. All my real estate sales are closed too. I have no problem leaving town right now!" said Tina.

"It a date then!" He kissed her once again as they ducked under the covers. Tina giggled, feeling like a young bride.

At dawn a few days later, Russell and Tina were driving on the freeway toward the Southern California route to their destination. After many hours on the road, they drove past the Welcome to the City of Santa Barbara sign.

"I know what you're thinking, Tina. I promise you a walk on the beach out there before the week is over." They drove a few miles farther, then entered the driveway of an upscale hotel with palm trees, patios, balconies, and a beautiful pool.

"Here, we are! Let's get our luggage. You did pack a swim-suit, right?"

"Yes, I did pack a swimsuit!" Tina laughed.

The next day, Tina spent the afternoon leisurely relaxing by the hotel garden pool. It became late afternoon. She glanced at her watch.

"Russell should be returning from his sales meetings soon. I wonder if he's left me a message on the hotel phone."

Tina went back to their room, and saw the blinking message light. Russell's message was the on the voicemail: "Hi, honey . . . Be ready for me to pick you up and take you out about 6 p.m. The guys here told me about a really great place for dinner!"

An hour later Russell and Tina were enjoying dinner in a very classy, modern California cuisine restaurant. There was an upbeat, contemporary band playing. After dinner, Russell took Tina by the hand and led her onto the dance floor. They held each other close as they danced to its beat. Rekindling feelings of their early dating days, they lingered on into the night until the band stopped playing and began to pack up.

The next morning, Russell and Tina enjoyed sleeping in at the hotel. Unseen by them, were the headlines in the local papers just outside on the stands which read: "Shark Attack—Sand Pointe Bay."

Tina was awake looking at a map when Russell woke up and stretched.

"I want to take a walk on the beach . . . right here." said Tina, pointing at the map they picked up at a gas station on the way.

"I knew you would remind me," Russell said with a yawn.

"I can tell it's going to be a hot day. Let's swim too!" suggested Tina.

After a very nice lunch at the hotel, Russell and Tina dressed in their beach clothes and drove to the Santa Barbara coastline. They drove their car into a public parking area. Soon, they were walking over to the shore line where the foamy waves lapped up on the sand at the water's edge. They kicked off their sandals as they let the foam and waves come up around their ankles.

"What a beautiful day for a swim and walk on the shore. I wonder why more people are not out here today?" wondered Tina, looking around.

"Yes, I'm surprised more people aren't here too" Russell agreed. They went back to their blanket and bags, then decided to walk into the waves for a swim. Soon they were swimming, laughing, and enjoying the water.

Nearby, the spirit of the Zodiac appeared in a black mist, camouflaged in a large bushy Joshua tree that had been formerly struck by lightning, the deep black-ashened scars still showing. He looked on unhappily as Russell and Tina played in the waves. Then his bony finger appeared over the waves, and a mysterious and mystical black mist appeared over the ocean waves as the water began to whirl around at his command. Sharks suddenly appeared out of thin air under the water and were summoned out of hell to travel toward the area where Tina and Russell were swimming.

In a sudden flash of light, large transparent, shining angels appeared upon the scene, and began a new intervention. As Tina swam on top of the waves, she suddenly felt something in her eye like a grain of sand.

"Russell, something's in my eye! I need to get out for a minute!"

Russell called out over the noise of the ocean. "What? Let me help you!"

Underwater, the sharks moved quickly and swiftly toward Russell and Tina. The Zodiac spirit, smiled and laughed a sinister laugh from the Joshua tree. The sharks prepared to charge Tina. Within split milliseconds, Tina got out of the water. Russell followed, just missing a serious and deadly encounter. The shark heads showed, bobbing on top of the shallow waves, as if to watch their almost-victims walk away freely on the sandy shore. They both walked back to their beach blankets, unaware of the danger that almost befell them. Tina got out a compact with a mirror, and studied her eye carefully.

"I think I got some sand in my eye!" said Tina. The sun reflecting into the compact seemed to give off a bright flash of light. "Oh, that's bright!" Bright, tall transparent angels appeared briefly, then disappeared into the skies once again. "I think I'm okay now." Tina looked at her eye carefully, one more time, in the small compact mirror.

Inside a large Joshua bush nearby but hidden, the now unhappy Zodiac spirit went up unhappily in a cloud of smoke with a whining groan. His dark defeated spirit was then speedily torpedoed back to the smoky, fiery abyss of hell where he would lie in wait for yet another human host who would once again be foolish enough to entertain him.

"Do you smell something burning?" asked Tina, sniffing the air as she dried off.

"No! Let's take that walk now."

Russell put on some denim shorts, while Tina put on a long beach skirt.

They walked arm in arm for a while in silence, as they looked out over the ocean waves in the distance rolling to the shore in front of them in regular rhythms.

"I already know what you're thinking Tina . . . Somewhere along here . . ."

"In mid-October of 1978, the Zodiac killer walked into the ocean, and was silenced forever. Yes, that's what I'm thinking. We don't know a name . . . We don't know an exact time . . . We just know he did it," mused Tina.

They glanced out along the miles of coastline in front of them. The white seagulls flew all around and skimmed the water looking for small fish, as they walked and shared thoughts about the disappearance of the man who was at the center of such great mystery for so many years.

"I can't get over the fact that the San Francisco Police recognized us as prime witnesses," Russell started, "yet the man they always thought it was, washed up on the shore here in this area, in the same time frame, and we did not get a call to look at the body or at least a morgue shot of the body."

"Yes, it seems inconceivable. Did they really want to solve the case or not? Maybe they really didn't . . ."

"Why do you say that?" asked Russell, looking over at her.

"The Zodiac made the entire Bay area police force look really bad. Maybe when they found him, they were just ready to put it all to rest quietly. Although, because I'm sure he believed he had been fully discovered, the police could have been two heartbeats away from solving the whole thing! Here's the other amazing thing . . . How does an old white car with big red stripes on the side—with silver chrome—with a big engine in it, parked on the shore near the dead guy, go unnoticed?" asked Tina.

"That's a very good point."

"You know what else? I'm sure he walked into the ocean with the gun in his left pocket . . . just like where I saw it that night. Leaving it in the car would have identified him . . . *double* identified him," Tina reasoned.

"The biggest mystery really is . . . why the mystery of the Zodiac killer was never solved?" Russell looked out over the waves. "There were just too many floating pieces that were never put together in this case." They walked a little farther. The blue skies reflected on the ocean, and the waves and foam tumbled up on the shore in small little foamy waves.

"You know who really put the pieces of this mystery together?" asked Tina.

Russell looked over at her, waiting for the answer.

"Two teenage kids having lunch together in their high school cafeteria . . .Yvonne and Tony!" Tina smiled. Russell smiled also, remembering. *"Of course!"*

"With all the millions of people in the Bay area, what are the normal odds those two would ever meet?" Tina asked.

"Ah, yes . . . amazing. Well, it was all part of destiny, don't you know?"' laughed Russell. As they walked a little farther down the shoreline, Russell changed the subject. "What a beautiful day . . . I wonder how the Mariners are doing in the big game in Seattle this weekend?"

"Oh, you and your football . . . You're such a football guy!"

"That's baseball Tina . . . *baseball!* How many sand dollars do you think washed up on this shore last tonight . . . Five thousand . . . ten thousand . . . Look at them!"

Tina gave Russell a goofy look. *"Russell . . . can we talk about something really important here?"*

"Oh Tina, I'm just trying to lighten you up!"

As Russell and Tina continued to walk hand in hand on the beach, the waves continued to gently lap up on the shore before them on the smooth sand. They walked, enjoying the small foamy waves, ankle deep, delighting in their surroundings. Tina snuggled her toes in the soothing wet sand.

Suddenly, shining angelic creatures appeared, moving from the sky to the ground behind Russell and Tina, as if following them. They were the same ones who followed Russell and Tina out the back door of the church the night of the Zodiac chase, years prior. Tina stopped suddenly, as she received an instinctive, intuitive feeling. She turned and looked her.

"Who's there? Russell, did you hear something?" She gave the same inquisitive look that she did the night when she sensed the angels were coming out of the side door and down the steps of the church. She paused again for a moment to put her "antennas" out and feel the moment. Tina seemed to feel the angels smile. She felt and sensed their presence.

"Tina, what are you doing? Are you coming?" She finally caught up to Russell. They walked a little farther, as they continued to talk.

"It seems strange, but I feel the presence of angels again. I'm sure they protect and watch over us more than we will ever know!" said Tina, reflectively. She looked out over the ocean as the wind blew gently through her hair. Tina continued, as she spoke her thoughts aloud.

"I think that the man who was the Zodiac was so terrified that he was discovered that night, that it became more appealing to him to walk into the waves and take his life, than to risk that he would be picked up by the police the next morning."

"I think you're right, Tina. What was the quote again from that play, the *Mikado*, he sent in his letter to the *Chronicle*?" asked Russell.

"He plunged himself into the billowy wave, and an echo arose from the suicide grave . . . tit willo . . . tit . . . willo . . ." Tina recited from the Zodiac's own letter. from the Zodiac's own letter. "The police call it the 'Exorcist letter.' Boy, were they wrong about that. It was the 'billowy wave letter'!"

"Wow, what a giveaway . . . the main clue! The missing piece of the puzzle! After that day, he disappeared forever," said Russell, shaking his head.

"He mocked the police, calling them the 'Key Stone Cops,' and the 'fat blue meanies.' It was an unbearable thought to him that he would ever actually be caught and picked up by the police that he mocked and scorned! It was far more appealing to think about dying, and going to 'Paradise,' where in his opinion, he would be served by the people he killed, who would be his slaves forever," Tina remembered. "Some of them were very beautiful women. Did you ever see pictures of them?"

"No, I haven't! Well, it looks like this mystery will never really be completely solved until there's one more piece of unquestionable evidence that appears someday . . . some new piece of evidence that will just come floating along."

As they continued their way down the beach with the small waves splashing up over their feet, it was as if time itself seemed to stand still. The ocean shore was quiet that day with no other people around, and it seemed like it was their own appointed time with that special place.

Meanwhile, yards behind them, close up in the small waves, an object was tumbling to the shore. That object was a 9 mm automatic weapon with an engraving on the metal section on the front. It bore the familiar Zodiac symbol. It had aged, and it was a bit rusty, but was unmistakably the same gun handled by the Zodiac when he was living and active during his crime history. It was the same gun that he had held in his hand so proudly when bragging to the police that they would never capture him.

It came to rest on the sand now, in plain view. Russell and Tina were walking far ahead in the distance, but in order to walk back to their car, they would soon pass that way again. Destiny is a strange and puzzling thing. It appears and presents itself, but we still have to find it, believe in it, and then it can happen and become real. Just as life itself is sometimes truly its own kind of puzzle, we have to discover and put the pieces together to find the perfect fit, and then it all makes sense . . . just like the story of the mysterious phantom-like Zodiac, and the demon who held him captive!

by Katherin B. FitzPatrick
Based on a true story.
For more information go to:
www.whateverhappenedtothezodiackiller.com/ or
www.kathiefitzpatrickauthorsfellowship.com

***

For more information on the real life Kerry Lee in this story
see the book: "Angel Promises . . . Remembering the Youngest
Firefighter," by Katherin B. FitzPatrick: Deep River Books or
Amazon.com

John FitzPatrick, the real life man as depicted by the character, Russell who chased the Zodiac Killer in mid-October 1978, with his wife Kathie, a passenger in the car. Here, John is standing in front of the Golden Gate Bridge, circa 1974. John FitzPatrick was deceased in 2008.

San Fran. Chronicle

Please Rush To Editor

Stamps in this book have
been gummed with a matte
finish adhesive which per-
mits the elimination of the
separation tissues.

This book contains 25—
8¢ stamps —four of this
page and one each on
three additional pages.
Selling price $2.00

I saw + think "The Exorcist"
was the best saterical com-
idy that I have ever seen.

Signed, yours traley :

He plunged him self into
the billowy wave
and an echo arose from
the sucides grave
   tit willo   tit willo
      tit willo

Ps. if I do not see this
note in your paper, I
will do something nasty,
which you know I'm capable of
doing
,   ✝

                    Mc - 37
                    SFPD - 0

324

The "Billowy Wave" letter in which the Zodiac quoted a passage from the Japanese themed play, "The Mikado" . . . "The billowy wave . . . the suicide grave." The police wondered if he would ever commit suicide this way if he was backed into a corner. In mid-October of 1978, at the Vista Point lookout, it would seem that circumstances provided "the corner."

WANTED

SAN FRANCISCO POLICE DEPARTMENT

NO. 90-69   WANTED FOR MURDER   OCTOBER 18, 1969

ORIGINAL DRAWING

AMENDED DRAWING

Supplementing our Bulletin 87-69 of October 13, 1969. Additional information has developed the above amended drawing of murder suspect known as "ZODIAC".

WMA, 35-45 Years, approximately 5'8", Heavy Build, Short Brown Hair, possibly with Red Tint, Wears Glasses. Armed with 9 MM Automatic.

Available for comparison: Slugs, Casings, Latents, Handwriting.

ANY INFORMATION:
Inspectors Armstrong & Toschi
Homicide Detail   THOMAS J. CAHILL
CASE NO. 696314   CHIEF OF POLICE

The famous 1969 "Wanted Poster" of the Zodiac Killer created for the police with the help of an eye witness who survived a Zodiac attack. Although the experiences were years apart, Kathie FitzPatrick says she will have to agree with her co-eyewitness of the Zodiac, "Sharon" of Napa, CA. When asked by the police they thought the drawing looked like him, the answer from both of them was the same: "Kind of . . . but not really."

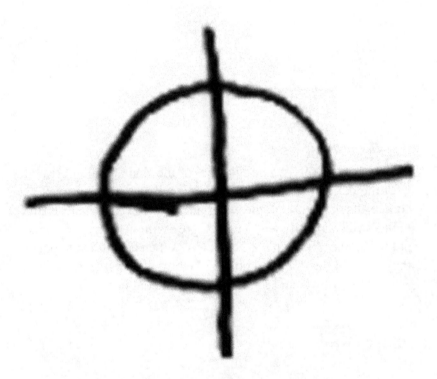

The Zodiac logo, the circle with the cross through it, written by his own hand. This symbol he often left at the scene of his Zodiac crimes.

The FitzPatrick Family

CPSIA information can be obtained
at www.ICGtesting.com
Printed in the USA
BVHW040201140122
626210BV00015B/585

9 781629 525624